Wizard Constable

Wizard Constable

by

Tom Van Natta

Jorac is allergic to magic, but not to action!

CHAVANCH PRESS

Wizard Constable

ISBN 978-0-9831741-0-3

Printed in the United States of America

Published by Chavanch Press, LLC
PO Box 271370
Fort Collins, Colorado 80527

Cover art by Susan Van Camp
http://www.artbysvc.com

Cover design by Ann Harbour
http://www.ahtechservices.com

Book website: http://wizardconstable.com

This book is dedicated to my family for their help and support, and to the authors who have inspired me – Eric Flint, Mercedes Lackey, Louis L'Amour, and many others – who are all cracking good storytellers.

Table of Contents

Chapter 1 - Working for Wizards 1
Chapter 2 - Squadleader 7
Chapter 3 - Constable Work 22
Chapter 4 - Madame Velsop 32
Chapter 5 - To Pigtown 44
Chapter 6 - Swampside, Again 59
Chapter 7 - To The Swamp 68
Chapter 8 - An Unexpected Reunion 80
Chapter 9 - A Night in a Shack 87
Chapter 10 - Following a Guide 98
Chapter 11 - An Odd House 108
Chapter 12 - Sleeping Wizards Lie 114
Chapter 13 - Sphere of Influence 135
Chapter 14 - Meet the Chiefs 148
Chapter 15 - We're Having a Party 155
Chapter 16 - Pergimtor's Reaction 174
Chapter 17 - Jorac is Confused 177
Chapter 18 - An Assignment 190
Chapter 19 - A Journey Planned 197
Chapter 20 - A Journey Begins 204
Chapter 21 - Training Recommences 216
Chapter 22 - A Surprising Side Trip 234
Chapter 23 - Jorac Runs an Errand 243
Chapter 24 - A Quick Wedding 254
Chapter 25 - A Rejoining 264
Chapter 26 - Casualties 271
Chapter 27 - A Glimmer of Dread 288
Chapter 28 - Jorac Awakens Alone 304
Chapter 29 - Heading Home 318
Chapter 30 - Trouble at the Gate 324
Chapter 31 - The Investigation Begins 338
Chapter 32 - A Wizardly Flu? 355
Chapter 33 - A Council (of Sorts) 370
Chapter 34 - Worry and Dancing 383
Chapter 35 - Unwelcome Visitors 396
Chapter 36 - Unwelcoming the Visitors 405
Chapter 37 - Jorac Has a Headache 417
Chapter 38 - A Man in a Bathrobe 429

Maps

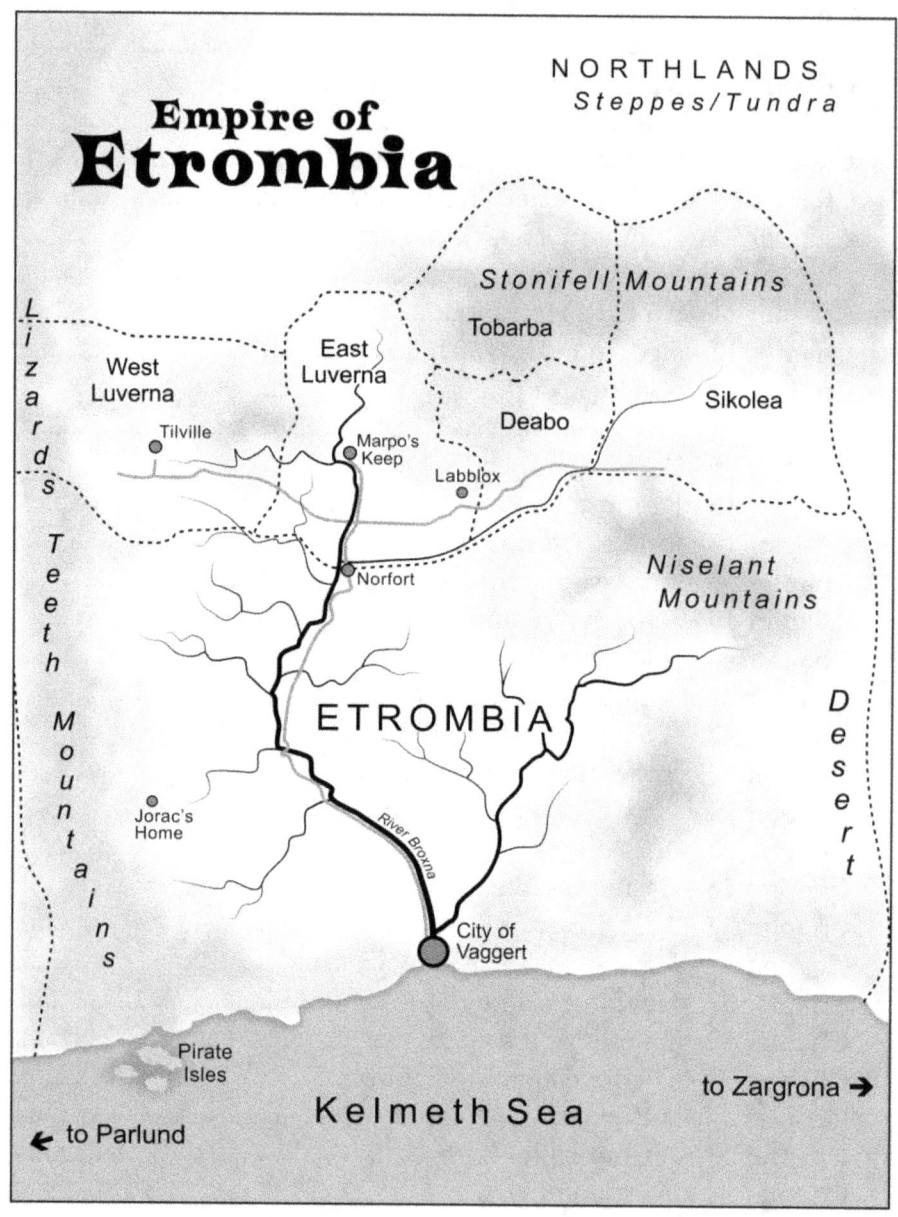

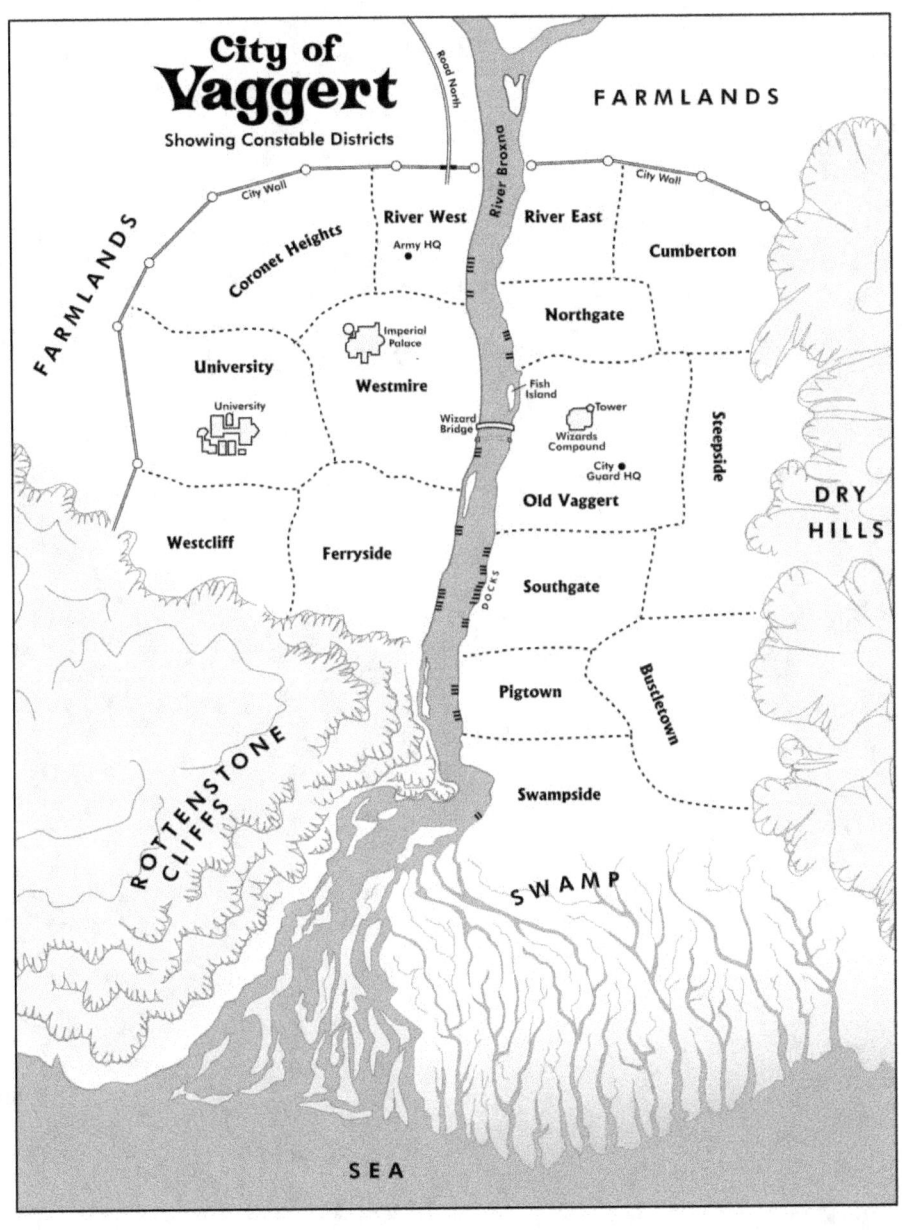

Chapter 1 - Working for Wizards

Jorac hated working for wizards. They were bossy, cryptic, and ungrateful. But now it was his job. He sat in his small office at the base of the Wizard's Tower, doing paperwork like most mornings.

"Kellor, come to the council room." The imperious voice rang in his ear. No "please," no "Mister," "Constable Kellor," or even "Jorac." With a sigh, he finished the column of sums of petty expenses he was working on and, not for the first time, told himself to find another job. When he took this position a few months ago, everyone thought he was being promoted to a life of slothful ease. Hah!

As he climbed the 156 stairs to the council room, he counted them, again. The high-level wizards who worked near the top of the tower merely levitated up the stairs; they were no bother to them, but Jorac had to trudge up and down them – and swore to himself each time. He was still young, not yet thirty, but he had recently spent far too much time cooped up in his office. The wide stairs wound around the outside wall of the tower and weren't very steep, but he was puffing by the time he reached the top.

He waited on the landing at the top for his breathing to calm and then opened the door and entered the council room. The door was warded and wouldn't have opened if the wizards weren't ready, and knocking only annoyed them.

There were seven wizards standing around the large pentagonal room, talking among themselves. They ignored Pergimtor, the head wizard, as he motioned Jorac to approach and then waved his hand so that a map of the city appeared in the air. Jorac, as always when he was around actual magic working, had the strong urge to sneeze. This mild, rare allergy was why he had recently been plucked from the Vaggert City Guard and selected for the thankless position of Wizard Constable.

Jorac stood still for a second until he was sure he wasn't going to sneeze, then approached the High Wizard. Pergimtor was gray-haired, and of late middle age, but was younger and steadier than some of the other rickety council members. He pointed to bottom half of the map. "Magic in this area is disappearing. You go find out why."

"Disappearing, Esteemed High Wizard? How does magic disappear, sir?" Jorac longed to omit the honorifics – he'd grown up in a determinedly democratic household – but wizards were a testy bunch. Best to be safe.

"We don't know. We want you to go there and find out. Smell it out, that's what you do. Now be gone."

Jorac took a deep breath and respectfully placed his palms together. "Esteemed High Wizard, if I am to succeed in obeying your command, which is my fervent desire, I'll need to know more about this. How do you know it's missing, and in this area?" Jorac thought he was laying it on a bit thick, but Pergimtor didn't seem to mind.

In impatient, exasperated tones, Pergimtor said, "Don't they teach you anything? Oh, yes, I forgot, you're a simple." That was wizards' unflattering term for non-wizards.

He continued as if he was talking to a six-year-old. "Magic comes from shaping mana. Mana is everywhere, given off by all living things – even some plants and minerals, at a low level. But you can't go grab it, you have to wait for it to be emitted; then a wizard can gather it and reshape it to his own will. There are a few exceptions – be grateful we keep close watch for death magic. . ." He stopped himself and pointed to the map again. "When we visit this area, there's magic missing. The people and animals there are fine, but they aren't giving off the mana they should be. Go find out why."

Another Council wizard had come up beside him and started speaking. "It's been happening for months. My territory is. . ." but Pergimtor interrupted her.

"Darlora, enough. I have done as I stated."

2

Darlora was a young-looking, shockingly beautiful woman with long, bright red hair. Jorac figured she'd done some magic to her looks, because he remembered meeting her family once while he was a normal city constable, and they were a thin, weak-chinned, pimply bunch. He turned to her and spoke.

"Milady Wizard, can you point out the areas where I should look first?"

She walked up to the map and drew rough circles with her finger. "Southgate, Pigtown, Swampside. Somewhere around there. Go find out! I need..." – at Pergimtor's warning glance she stopped. Pergimtor pointed vaguely toward the door, and Jorac bowed and went out.

Outside on the landing he sat on the exquisitely beautiful padded marble bench and quietly cursed his luck, his job, and his life. He figured Darlora had been about to let slip that the highest-level wizards had carved the city into territories and milked them for magic power like a farmer milks a cow, but he didn't see what that mattered to him. What did matter was that she'd named the three worst areas of the city of Vaggert.

Southgate was bad enough; it was the rundown old docks district, with worn wooden wharves and rough bars filled with sailors and whores. Pigtown was the area of stockyards, chemical shops, tanneries, and slaughterhouses; besides the pigsties, it was named after the smell of the people who worked there, generally from the lowest classes. But Swampside was the worst.

Part of what was now Swampside had been the old Wizards Quarter, destroyed in suppressing Aplath's Rebellion some eighty-odd years before. Wizards loyal to the Emperor had cast a mighty spell to suddenly lower the ground there, flooding the area and destroying all the buildings (along with Aplath and his fellow rebel wizards). Now the area was a sickly swamp; the river and sea seeped in and out with the tides. No one lived there if they didn't have to, but some would rather take their chances with the snakes and giant poison frogs (and worse) than with the city constables or criminal gangs pursuing private feuds. The constables made regular sweeps through Southgate and Pigtown (when they had sufficient manpower), but no one patrolled the deeper parts of Swampside except the monsters.

Jorac wondered how he was going to cope with Pergimtor's frustratingly vague directive: Go investigate the disappearance of something he couldn't see or define from parts of the city he knew next to nothing about. Still, he thought, if someone was illicitly harvesting mana in one of those places, it would have to be some sort of wizard, wouldn't it? A wizard doing magic? With his allergy, that was something Jorac could detect – at least if he got close enough to it. It was a start.

He heaved a deep sigh and made the long trip down the stairs to his office. He put away his paperwork, changed into the plain uniform retained from his earlier, simpler job as ordinary city constable, and grabbed the heavy, ornate badge of office he wore on a wide ribbon around his neck when he was acting as Wizard Constable. It was an ugly thing, made of tarnished silver with a central figure he thought looked like a cow with three glass eyes. Legally, the badge allowed him to command any city constable, and most citizens. In practice, "command" was far too strong a term.

* * *

He got his first break of the day when he found Cerom on duty at the Vaggert City Guard's main office. Jorac had known him for years; they'd been constable trainees together. Cerom understood Jorac's delicate position when it came to asking for help from the city constabulary.

The two old friends greeted each other. "Hi Cee, how you be?"

"Hey, Jay, whadda ya say?"

"Sorry to bother you, but I'm going to need a few of your boys for a quick patrol."

"Where, when, and how many?"

"Southgate and Pigtown, and you tell me."

Cerom frowned. "Damn, they trying to get you killed? Those are rough areas, both of them. We try to stay out of there at night – unless it's important?" Everyone knew the guard was woefully understaffed, and most people liked it that way. The rich hired private guards, and the poor did as best they could without them.

"Daytime is fine, but if you can, I'd like it to be soon. I just need a small squad for one day."

"What are you looking for?" On seeing Jorac's impassive face, he said, "Okay, okay, I know you and those damned wizards. I just need to know what to tell my boys to watch out for."

"All I can tell you is that it's nothing specific, and there are no threats I know of. I just need to make a fast sweep through the area, look around, and follow my nose." Cerom knew about Jorac's magic-sensitive nose, and also knew enough to not mention it.

"Heh. Sure, follow your nose. . . Well, since all you need is protection, four or five men ought to be enough." He thought a moment. "I got a new boy last week, a greenie right off some northern farm, and he should go along too. He needs to see those areas first-hand, and maybe you can give him a little orientation while you're at it. I think he's going to be a keeper. Horxien is his name; they call him Hox. He's still wet behind the ears, but he's about eleven-teen feet tall, and strong, and moves pretty good too."

"Sounds good. . . and do you have someone who grew up there, maybe could guide us around?"

Cerom snorted. "Hmph. Half the recruits we get come from that area. Half we bounce out when they try to lie right through their oath-taking, and half the rest leave when they have to pull some nasty detail, or backslide into their old ways. But I've got a few I can send who probably know their way around. . . I'll juggle things a bit. I'll have them ready after breakfast tomorrow – you buying them lunch?"

Jorac sighed. "I'm buying them lunch. More damned paperwork."

Cerom chuckled and said, "You know, everyone envied you when you got that job. Cushy work, triple the pay, and that badge that lets you give orders to any commoner or soldier. Now I'm not so sure."

Jorac raised his eyes heavenward. "My first week I used the badge to get an army squad to drag a boat out of the mud, to see if the hole in the bottom was caused by a wizard or normal stupidity. They complained, and I had to write a report. They appealed to their Captain, and I had to write a report. The Captain appealed to the Duke, another report. And then another report just for the High Wizard, and finally a separate report explaining where all the special report paper and quills had gone – bloody accountants. When it all settled, the principle was firmly established. I can command any small army squad to do the bidding of the Wizard Constable, and I'll only have to spend three times the effort – and days and days afterwards – writing the reports. Now that's power for you."

And with that he left, to Cerom's amused but sympathetic grin. The city constables had their own problems, but at least writer's cramp wasn't one of them.

Chapter 2 - Squadleader

The next morning, Jorac went back and met the squad he would lead. Cerom had exaggerated only a little when he called young Hox eleven-teen feet tall; Jorac was average height and he doubted if he could reach up and touch the young man's nose. The other four looked more like normal constables – not dumb but not bright, lightly scarred, square-jawed, and determined – except for one balding, long-nosed fellow who resembled a rat. All four wore the same semi-official uniform of gray tunic, wide belt, leather pants, and high boots, with the badge of the City Guard pinned on the shoulder. Jorac was dressed like them but had his Wizard Constable badge. Hox wore the service's largest gray tunic like a tight shirt, and since he hadn't taken his oath yet, didn't rate a badge.

This being a simple patrol, the men were armed merely with standard-issue constables' cudgels, thigh-length clubs they hung on their belts and held with leather loops at the knee. Hox's was outsized, a two-hander for anyone else.

Jorac spoke to them. "I'm thinking it should go easy today. We're just doing a fast reconnaissance. Anybody catches your eye, wants to talk, remember it for later, not today. Anyone tries to hide something, let it slide this time. We need to get Southgate covered this morning, and get out of there before the sailors on leave wake up. We'll check out Pigtown, maybe parts of Swampside in the afternoon, and be back here by dinner."

"What are we looking for?" one of the men asked.

"You're looking out for me, and I'm walking the streets, looking for wizard things, that's all I can say." The men looked a little uneasy at this, but accepted it. "I drew this map – copied it from your maps, really – and here's our route this morning." He put the map on the table. "Does it look okay? Any problems?"

The men looked it over and suggested a couple of minor changes. Jorac said, "Most of you know I was a city constable for a couple of years, but I was assigned to Northgate and the merchants' areas around there. Never had to work in this part of town. So, let me know before I do something stupid, right?" With that, they set off.

They walked; constables were used to it, and Jorac would have had to fill out another expense report if they'd hired a horse and wagon. It wasn't too long before they reached the edge of Southgate, where the main streets were wider and paved with rough cobblestones to withstand the heavy carts that brought cargo up from the ships.

Jorac started off at the back of the squad, but soon decided Hox should bring up the rear, since he could see over all their heads. The rat-faced man – Schrog by name – took the lead. Jorac hadn't worked with him before, nor the other men, but he knew Schrog's reputation as a rough, canny fellow with street smarts.

Schrog kept a quiet running commentary as they went down the streets in rough formation. "Warehouse. . . tavern, whorehouse, tavern, sweet shop, chandlers, whorehouse, rope shop. . ." Schrog seemed to know all about the area, even the places that were closed and showed no sign or placard.

Hox was wide-eyed. At one point he asked, in his broad north-country farmer's accent, "How do you know that place is a tavern and not a bawdy house? Did you used to patrol around here?"

Schrog snickered. "Nay, it's by de smell. Rotten beer, but witou' cheap perfume. Now dis one here" – he pointed to a narrow building set back from the street a bit – "might be a private house or a money changer or sump'n. Dat one over dere is easy, dey buys and sells fish – see de sign?" After that, the whole squad started naming the types of businesses they passed, correcting each other, and generally enjoying themselves more than on a normal patrol. They had the rare luxury of ignoring things like a quickly slamming door or a man who suddenly turned down an alley and started running. They had the streets mostly to themselves; even the stray dogs and cats that frequented the docks district seemed to be sleeping late that morning.

The wizard-spelled district fountain that provided an endless stream of safe, clean, fresh water was the only busy place they passed, as servants and housewives from all over the area filled up jugs and buckets. The people there merely glanced at Jorac and his squad and returned to their tasks, which he thought was a good sign.

Jorac started sneezing a bit as they passed one warehouse yard, where big ugly horses were hauling tall, creaking carts around. Soon, though, the rest of the squad started sneezing from the grain dust blowing from inside, and he decided it was nothing to worry about. That was the one of the problems with his allergy to magic; it wasn't the only thing that could make him start sneezing. But magic made him sneeze every time.

By noon they'd completed their walk down all the main streets in the area, without Jorac detecting any magic being done. Since they'd set a good pace all morning, they were getting hungry. Jorac asked a passerby and was directed to The Flying Pie, a nearby riverside tavern that prided itself on its food, not its drink. He quickly checked it out; the air inside smelled wonderful, like fresh bread and soup made with ingredients that weren't half rotten. He motioned his squad to come in.

Without saying anything, they easily found adjacent places to sit at one of the long tables – the other patrons were glad to give up their seats and not sit next to constables. The whole squad heard Hox's stomach growl as they took their places; he grinned sheepishly. Jorac could see that other diners were mostly having a thick meat stew.

The bored-looking middle-aged barmaid, who was probably the owner's wife, came over to the table and said, "What'll it be?"

Jorac would have to justify the expense with his bosses of course, so he asked, "How much for food for six?"

"Grog, ale, or small beer?" A couple of the squad members said "ale," but Jorac overrode them with "Small beer." To the squad members he said apologetically, "Long afternoon ahead."

"Should be eighteen coppers, but I'll go sixteen for you constables."

"Eighteen, and the boy there gets his fill."

She sized up Hox's height and width, and said with good humor, "No deal. Eighteen and he gets double. Got a boy that age m'self, if not his size."

Jorac smiled back. "Good enough. He can live on short rations until supper."

The food was as good as they hoped, and the group told stories as they ate. Some were tall tales for Hox's "benefit," but they all seemed to like the huge young man and didn't fill his head with too much fiction. Hox also told a story on himself, and Jorac figured being able to laugh at himself like that would take him a long way as a constable.

As they were wiping their bowls clean with the last of their bread, Jorac turned to Schrog, who was sitting on his left, and asked, "Which of the squad do you think knows Pigtown best?"

Schrog looked around at the other three constables, who were teasing Hox again. "I figgers dat'd be me," he said.

"If you want to hide something there, where do you do it?"

"How big? Small, yer pocket'll do de job, anywhere. Who you figger to hide it from?"

"I have no idea, sorry, but let's say it's the size of a small room at least." Jorac had seen some of the magic labs and conjuration rooms at the Wizard's Tower, and it seemed that they used a circle to stand inside to do their strongest magic. He wished the wizards weren't so secretive.

Schrog paused a moment, and his eyes narrowed a little in concentration. His resemblance to a rat was really quite striking, and helped not at all by his short, bristly haircut and receding hairline.

"Well, you bein' Wizard Constable an' all, I figgers you lookin' fer somebody doin' bad magic, or somebody doin' magic but not bowin' right, or stickin' money in de right hand. Nay, I knows you can't say nothin'."

Jorac nodded, appreciating Schrog's understanding.

"De t'ing is, ain't nowhere good hiding in Pigtown. Law says all de smelly jobs gotta go dere. Most folks who works dere have a dam' hard time gettin' de smell gone – stays in your clothes, in your skin, so you don' even notice, but other folks dam' sure notice. Dat's why when de whores get real low, dey ends up in Pigtown. Ain't nothin' lower den a Pigtown whore, nobody who don't live dere can stand 'em – and dat's how come if you wanna insult a slit real bad, you calls 'er a Pigtown whore. So anybody hidin' dere, he start smellin' so bad, he be stuck dere, near enough. Couple months maybe to wear out de smell."

Jorac said thoughtfully, "So if you spent much time in Pigtown, you'd have to hire a wizard to get rid of the traces, wouldn't you?"

Schrog shook his head emphatically. "Nope. Dat won't work, not all de way. I heared about a guy dat hired a wizard to clean him up. Big money lender, doing trade wit' all de pig dealers, wanted to meet wit' a fancy uptown birdie, a real looker she was. Hired himself a top-line wizard to cast special spells, cost a pot full. Ended up not havin' to pay, 'cause even after spells and scrubbin' and all, he still stank some." Schrog grinned sardonically. "So dat's why I say ain't no good hiding in Pigtown. Not if you wants to leave an' say you ain't been dere, or spend a week or more scrubbin' yer butt."

Jorac thought about it for a minute. Schrog obviously had little education, but that certainly didn't mean he was stupid. "Suppose you just worked on the Pigtown outskirts? Would that keep the smell down enough so people couldn't tell where you'd been?"

"Dat might work. Folks who work hereabouts likes to get away from de smell if dey gots de money, dat's why dey mostly lives up at Pigtown Hill. Tain't really Pigtown dere, dey calls it Lower Bustletown if dey're gettin' fancy."

Jorac nodded, thought a moment, and then spoke to the rest of the squad. "We need to figure out a new route. I don't think we need to go all the way into Pigtown this afternoon. We can just hit the areas around the perimeter." This brought general nods and smiles all around.

Jorac started to draw on the table with his finger. "Pigtown just starts south of Southgate, and there's the river on the west. So let's head east around Pigtown, south through the Pigtown Hill area, and then west again. . ." He looked at Schrog. "Where does the south end of Pigtown stop?"

"On de east side, dey keep up de old district wall pretty good, but in de south, not so much. Tain't no real line, dere's a fence some places, sometimes it just kinda fades into Swampside, den de swamp. Hard to build dere, ground is soft, yer house might sink. Don't smell so dam' bad dere, most of de time, but if it rains real hard den it washes down dere from Pigtown and you get a big dam' stink. And dat's when dem big fockin' frogs and such come up outta de swamp, too."

Jorac said, "We'll still need to check it out, I'm afraid."

Schrog sighed. "Figgers. Well, after one day we won't stink too terr'ble bad, we be careful where we steps."

Hox had been listening with interest, and said appreciatively, "You certainly know a lot about lower Pigtown. Did you grow up there?"

Schrog frowned angrily and clenched his teeth. His hand gripped the empty beer mug he was holding so hard his knuckles turned white.

Jorac quickly spoke up, "He's a greenie, Schrog. No one told him."

To Hox, he said, "Once your oath is accepted and you finish your constable training, you get a clean slate. We don't ask questions like that. Ever. Someone wants to tell you, no problem, but we never ask."

Hox realized he'd made a grave mistake. "I'm sorry, Mister Schrog. You've helped me learn this job, and I didn't mean to insult you in the least. Please forgive me." He looked stricken.

Schrog took a deep breath. "Ehh, nevermind. Now ya knows. Tain't everyone so forgivin' as me, so watch yer ass. Now fergit it."

At that exchange, Jorac started getting up and the squad decided it was time to go.

* * *

As they made their way south along the river toward the north side of Pigtown, Jorac noticed that Hox looked troubled. He let the squad get a little ways ahead, fell in alongside Hox, and quietly asked him, "What's wrong? Schrog will forgive and forget, and so should you."

"It's not that. But if no one asks about where you came from and what you've done, how do you know bad people aren't joining up?" His eyebrows were pulled together in worry.

"The wizards have a way of weeding out that type. Tell you what, why don't you come and see me after work this evening and I'll tell you about it, okay?" Cerom wouldn't mind if he preempted the regular orientation speech; this was clearly the time the kid needed the information.

Hox nodded slowly, but still looked a bit doubtful.

"Don't worry, really. There's a pretty careful screening. I'll tell you about it tonight."

After a time they passed a small gaggle of food carts. "Last food before Pigtown" was their cry. Schrog pointed out a vendor hawking spicy bread sticks and said, "Dose be de ones to get if yer goin' to Pigtown. Some o' dem spices stop up your nose a bit."

As they neared Pigtown they could already begin to smell the alchemical plants and perfumeries that marked the start of the area; the truly noxious smells were kept further inside. Glad to avoid the worst of it, they turned east away from the river and began to skirt the area. They got to the base of Pigtown Hill with no problems, and decided to go a few blocks up the hill before turning south. This part of the city was mostly smaller houses and larger rooming houses, with a striking number of laundries and bath houses serving those who worked in Pigtown. This time of day the streets weren't busy, and none of the locals who saw them paid them much attention. They found a few vantage points to look down into Pigtown proper, but things looked calm there.

They kept going south, and the neighborhood ended at a path above a swampy area. There they turned west and began to follow the path back toward south Pigtown and the river. It had taken over an hour to skirt Pigtown proper, but from Schrog's description, they'd be glad they avoided it.

As they came off the hill at the south of Pigtown, the first thing Jorac noticed was the smell. It was noisome, but not as overwhelming as he'd feared. He said, "Hey, the smell isn't so bad, at least this part."

Schrog smiled sardonically. "Eh, we gots a good day. Wind offa de hill dere, not down de river, an' it's dry. Day after a rain, de wind down de river, stink would rightly gag a statue."

To Jorac's surprise, there were many more people walking in the streets or standing around doorways than they'd seen in the better areas. These were a rough lot; almost every man had a few facial scars or a missing ear, and some of the women seemed to go out of their way to look ugly.

And the people were loud; there were many street sellers shouting loud, bragging calls about their wares; some had children yelling for them to better pierce the hubbub. Shouting was one of the things he used to discourage as a city constable, but here it seemed that the rule was the louder, the better. A few people called directly to them as they passed by, a hard mixture of dubious-looking vendors of dubious food; old, toothless whores, and cold-eyed procurers or gambling-house barkers, with a few piteous beggars thrown in.

The first few houses in the area were only a little more run down than those in Southgate, but as they got deeper into the area – call it south Pigtown or north Swampside – he noticed how ramshackle everything was. There were slops (and worse) thrown into the narrow streets, which would be one of the things a constable was supposed to punish in the better areas of town. The buildings – huts, hovels, lean-to's – were made from scraps of wood poorly covered with hide and cloth and crammed together with very little order. More than once they found some shack, or a whole collection of them, where they expected the street to go through.

They passed the large magic-powered water fountain that served this area – the southernmost fountain in the city – and found a thug there guarding it. Perhaps he was charging for access, which was strictly against the law; he started waving people by and scuttled out of the area as the team approached. Jorac thought he'd tell Cerom about this when they got back, but today he wasn't going to say anything.

By unspoken accord, the group tightened into two rows of three, with Schrog in the front and Hox and Jorac in the back. Jorac thought perhaps he should have brought a larger group, or at least had a chance to talk tactics, because from some of the looks they'd gotten, he didn't believe the locals had much respect for their uniform. In a crowded area, a man walked alongside for a few steps, and Schrog slapped at a reaching hand and pulled out his cudgel, and the pickpocket ran off with a yelp.

The rest of the Constables pulled out their clubs when Schrog did. The squad in uniform with cudgels in their hand drew more attention, but people avoided them more, which Jorac thought was all to the good. He decided they should have checked out swords from the armory instead. He was a good swordsman, and equipping the others with the short, chopping swords that Constables occasionally trained with would at least make them look more intimidating.

Jorac noticed Hox had grown saucer-eyed at a "professional lady" lewdly displaying *all* her wares, legs apart, in a crib no wider than Hox's broad shoulders, so Jorac nudged him gently.

"Rough area. Keep an eye out for danger." Hox nodded and resolutely looked away from her and instead at the small, tough-looking pimp loitering nearby, who eyed them with seeming indifference.

They worked their way through the area, following the winding, narrow streets, with Schrog leading, seeming to follow a way he knew. Jorac was content to look out for danger and try to smell for magic – and wished he could avoid most of the things he did smell, human waste mixed with sour mud being at the forefront.

They made a rough circle through the area, finding nothing of note, and by late afternoon they were almost back to the better houses that marked the edge of the area. They were starting to relax a bit, talking about heading back, when a compact middle-aged man with a bare broadsword suddenly stepped into the street ahead of them. He looked like an old prizefighter, badly scarred from years of brawling. Behind him, emerging from an alley, was a group of eight or ten rough-looking men armed with staves, clubs, and axes. They stopped about twenty paces away.

"Gotcha, Schroggie. Dey tol' me you was around. You t'ink I'd forgotten, eh?"

Schrog took a step back, as Jorac and Hox stepped forward from the back row, and the squad tightened into a defensive group and slid over toward the nearest wall. Schrog started to speak, but Jorac overrode him.

"Interfering with Constables in the course of their duty will get you put on the work gang. Or worse. And waving a sword around is against the law, too."

The man with the sword sneered. "Oh, I am so scared. Schroggie knows how we deal with constables, don't he?"

Schrog spoke up. "Kullo, she weren't yours. Nor mine. But she dam' sure weren't yours to sell. Now clear off."

Kullo spat. "Now why don' you jus' make me?"

The street had cleared behind Kullo's group. Jorac took a quick glimpse and found the previously busy street behind him was now empty too. Kullo spoke to him. "You dere, you jus' leave Schrog to me and you boys kin go. Dere's more of us den you, and all you got is jus' dem little sticks."

Jorac knew the cudgels he and the squad carried were no match for the swords and axes of Kullo's group, but constables carried unofficial weapons as well, usually a long knife, and (except for Hox) they were doubtless better trained. But he still didn't like the look of this. They should have brought crossbows or more men. Probably both.

Jorac didn't answer, and the squad just reached for their knives. They would stick together – no one believed Kullo could be reasoned with, and they weren't about to sacrifice one of their own.

After waiting a few seconds for a response, Kullo said "Have it your way. At 'em, boys!" His group started walking forward at an easy pace, spreading out, while Jorac's squad put their backs against the wall and spread out just a little, to give each other fighting room. Jorac looked at the rough but ill-trained attackers, and knew that if he had a sword he might do some real damage – or get himself killed. He had a bit of the old berserker blood in him, and had to fight sometimes to control it. But this time he had other plans.

He didn't reach for his knife when the others did; instead he reached for his badge of office. He waited for the attackers to close in a bit, and almost waited too long, because they suddenly started charging toward the constable squad with a wordless yell. As Hox stepped forward and poked his oversized cudgel at the face of an axe-wielding man, Jorac pushed in all three eyes on the badge. There was a thunderclap, and (just as he had been promised) everyone within ten paces froze in place.

Everyone except Jorac of course. The spell he had triggered still allowed him to move, so he was leaning over with his hands on his knees, trying to recover from a nasty sneezing fit, when the investigating wizard flew in a half-minute later. The wizard was a short, fat, bald one he didn't recognize, but he recognized the attitude all too well.

"What's going on here? Why did you trigger that spell? I was busy with some important reagents and you interrupted me."

Jorac stood up, and as he wiped his running nose on his sleeve he thought, not for the first time, that *wizard* should be a curse word. This wizard seemed to be rather angry, and it was never a good idea to anger wizards, for they had short tempers and long memories.

"Sir Wizard, I was sent here by High Wizard Pergimtor" – *drop the name first*, thought Jorac – "to investigate certain matters. When my squad was attacked and almost overrun, I did as the Wizard Council bid me and pressed the eyes on the badge of office, to summon help." Mentioning both the High Wizard and the Council was a clever bit, Jorac thought. It seemed to cool off the wizard a bit; they were very conscious of rank.

"Hummpf. Well, that as may be, but I'll expect to read the report on this, tonight. Now, which of these ruffians are yours?"

Patience, patience, Jorac thought. *Just because six of us are wearing constable tunics. . .*

Jorac pointed out his squad, and the wizard quickly unfroze them; Jorac backed off and managed to only sneeze once more. He could pass off his initial sneezing attack as part of the wizard-summoning spell, if he was asked, but he wanted to keep his allergy a private matter, as best he could.

The squad regained motion slowly, and started stretching their muscles. Jorac cautioned them to wait quietly but thought he needn't have; even the thickest constable knew to keep small and quiet around wizards.

"Is that all?" the wizard asked, obviously impatient to be away. "The others will be released when the spell wears off in an hour or so; you can take care of them."

"Sir Wizard, these other men will need to be transported to the gaol. Look, this one is swinging an axe; the spell stopped him just in time."

"And you expect me to lug them? Already I have to recharge the spell you used. Do you know how hard it is to link that spell to that amulet and the user?"

Jorac tried to look humble and sincere. "It's deeply appreciated, Sir Wizard. As you said, I'll be writing a report for you and the High Wizard on this. May I know your name, please?"

"Hummpf. I'm Ruejeo. Blasted simples. Very well, wait here." The wizard disappeared with a pop.

One of the men said, "Damn! I could hear and see and smell and all, but I couldn't move. Something wouldn't let me fall over either, but, damn. Damn!" He shook his head violently, as if to clear it. "I'm dodging from that axe coming toward me, and we both stop moving. Look at him!"

Before Jorac could do any more than look, the wizard popped back, carrying a long, rolled-up purple carpet. He eyed the dirty street distastefully and motioned everyone back, then mumbled a few words over the carpet, waving his hand in an intricate gesture. The carpet unrolled and hovered a bare thumb's width off the ground, not even touching it at the edges.

"Put them on this and I'll cart them, this time. Next time take a wagon with you."

Jorac smiled to himself about the impracticality of the wizard's suggestion, and turned to the squad. "You heard the Honorable Wizard. Let's move them to the carpet." Jorac made a finger-to-lips motion to the squad as he said this – he didn't want any loose words to anger the wizard when things were going well.

Silently, the squad shifted Kullo and his band of cutthroats to the carpet. They found they could wrench the weapons from the frozen men's hands, with some difficulty, but not change their positions, so they ended up tipping them over and carrying them to the carpet by their arms and legs. They discovered that men frozen in attack postures don't stack very well; when they were done, Kullo and his men filled most of the carpet and made an awkward load. They put the confiscated weapons on the carpet too, in between the stacked men.

As they finished, the wizard pointed to the carpet and said impatiently, "Well, hop aboard. Quickly now! I don't have all day."

Jorac's squad started mumbling skeptically, and he felt the same way. "Sir Wizard, it seems" ... *dangerous, foolhardy, frightening, unsafe* ... "as if we could unbalance ourselves in flight and possibly tip over."

Scornfully, the wizard said, "Just hang on to each other. I'm not a novice; I'll move the nearby air with the carpet, and as long as you don't jump off you'll be fine."

The squad member behind Schrog said, "The weight won't be too much?"

Jorac glared at him, but the wizard snapped, "I can lift twice this weight; I'm not a snot-nosed apprentice you know. But I'm not going to unload them for you! I've got reagents working, dammit! Hurry up!"

Jorac turned to his squad and said, "If we want to finish with these bastards, we've got to do it. Get on the carpet and kneel down where you can. We can reach around these bodies and link arms."

Reluctantly the squad did as Jorac said, and everyone hung on to each other tightly.

Blessedly, the flight back to Vaggert City Guard headquarters took only a few minutes. There would probably have been a grand view, but the one time Jorac peeked, he saw everyone else's eyes closed too, and the ground rushing by dizzily.

When they landed just outside Cerom's office, Jorac sent Schrog to find helpers, and by the time they had the carpet unloaded, there were a number of constables helping, and commenting. Cerom even came out from behind his desk and peered at the frozen men. The minute the carpet was emptied, Ruejeo rolled it up and disappeared.

Cerom smiled broadly at Jorac and his squad. "Well, well, well. Damn fine work – you got Kullo, and I guess most of his gang – stinking slavers! We've been looking for these bastards for quite a while now. How did you manage it?"

Jorac answered with a sigh, "Schrog can tell you all about it. I owe these men a drink or two, but that'll have to wait. Right now I've got to go write a report."

Chapter 3 - Constable Work

While he was working on the report, Ruejeo appeared in his office and rudely demanded the Wizard Constable badge of office, disappearing as soon as Jorac handed it over. As he was finishing the last part of the report, listing the day's expenses, the badge magically reappeared in the circle on the floor near his desk, presumably recharged, and that set off another sneezing fit. He went back and added some handkerchiefs to the expenses; he'd buy them tomorrow. *Wizards!* By now it was a well-worn curse word, in his mind at least.

He'd finished his report – it was short on details except for Ruejeo's part, for he hadn't found anything magical – and was putting his papers away when Hox came to his office, guided by Schrog.

Schrog said, "Ya wanted ta see de kid?"

"He was just wondering about the screening process for constables, and I told him I'd explain. Let's go down the street and I'll buy you both a beer."

Jorac had found a nearby tavern that served only non-wizards, a restriction that made it rather popular. Even here near the Wizard's Tower, ordinary people tried to avoid wizards when possible, especially wizards who'd been drinking. It didn't mix well with the subtle hand-passes and complex incantations needed for spellcasting. If the caster (and those around him) were lucky, a missed pass or mispronounced word would merely cause the spell to fail. But a persistent rumor was that the lifelike statues in front of the Wizard's Tower, "Wizard and Apprentices," were actually real people turned to stone by the mistake of a tipsy spellcaster, despite the prominent plaques with the stonecarver's name.

Since it was early evening, the tavern wasn't yet very crowded. Jorac ordered a pot of ale and three mugs, and sat down in a comfortable corner with Schrog and Hox.

To Schrog he said, "Hox was wondering how the Constables can offer a chance to start over, without having them overrun with crooks." He turned to Hox and continued, "I can see how that might worry you, but it's really no problem. You aren't really supposed to go on patrol until all this is explained to you, but Cerom thought sending you with us today was a good chance for you to see the city."

Hox nodded, "Yes, he told me my training was out of order because of your patrol."

"Here's how it works. When you're ready to give your final oath, you meet privately with the Commander and tell him everything you've done that's bad, or hurtful, or dishonest. There's a wizard there when you do, and he can tell if you're lying – it takes a real good wizard for that, but it's worth it. Some say the wizard can force you to speak the truth; I don't know about that, but I know if you don't talk, out you go. If you've done some things, but you won't be doing them anymore, and you mean it, you can get in." He smiled sardonically. "We lose quite a few during the week they take the oaths."

"Ooh." Jorac watched Hox thinking through the ramifications of that.

He went on. "They ask pretty good questions, and the last question they ask is if you've told them everything."

"Oooooooh." Hox nodded slowly. "That makes sense. Now I see what you meant." He paused, then looked young and curious again. "So I can talk about it if I want?"

"Sure, it's not a problem. Personally, I never minded telling folks why I joined up, but it's all up to you. Lurro – he had Cerom's job back when I started – had me tell my story a few times, if he thought it could help someone."

Schrog poured himself another mug of ale and said to Hox, "Yer a good kid, I figger. If'n you don' mind, how come you wants to join wit' us? Tain't de pay, dat's fer sure – or if it is de pay, you best t'ink again. It ain't like back home. Lots of folk come to de city, den decide it's too dam' expensive an' go back to de farm."

"He wouldn't ask that once you're a constable," Jorac put in.

"Dat's right. I just wanna make sure you knows de job is mostly jus' walkin' around and listenin' to folks bitch and moan – and not much you can do 'bout it, most times."

Hox considered. "Oh, I don't know... The pay seems alright to me, and it's steady work, and a constable gets respect." Hox spread his fingers and looked into the middle distance. "My folks, they have a farm. Not so big a farm, and I've got three brothers. They're about your size, but I'm a little bigger."

Jorac smiled. "A little."

Hox grinned back at him. "Okay, a lot. I've only ever seen one person as tall as me, at a carnival show at the fair. Standing around having folks gawk at me didn't seem like it was much of a living. Malver – he's my older brother – he found himself a nice fat girl from the next village over, and he's firstborn, so he's getting the farm. It's not big enough to split between us."

He stared into his mug of ale for a few moments and then went on. "With Ma and Pa and my brothers, well. . . there wasn't any food to spare, ever. I tried to do some odd jobs for the neighbors, to pick up some extra work, but there wasn't much around. So I decided to come here to the city. Everyone's heard about the way the wizards make the weather perfect, no matter the time of year, and magic fountains with good free water pouring out all the time."

Schrog interrupted, "Dey didn't tell ya about de extra taxes here, I bet. Dat's why dey still got dat big city wall, helps wit' de smuggling. Never mind, go on."

"I just walked up to the gate, and when I asked the guard if there was work, he looked at me and said I should be a constable, so here I am."

Jorac shook his head in amazement. "You're lucky. Twice lucky. First, most people don't think to ask the guards, so they get steered to some bad area or fall in with a bad crowd. And second, Cerom had a open slot. Usually there's a waiting list, even with the low salary. The Emperor pays for the City Guard, but it's kind of low on his list of things to pay for."

Schrog nodded. "Aye. De spotters at de gate prolly spotted you as a hayseed, but dey likes to work in de shadows so dey leaves you alone. You, de folks notice. Fer a constable, dat be good."

"Spotters? For what?"

Jorac explained. "They start by sizing you up, and seeing what they can steal from you and how. First there's the basic sneak thief, cutpurse, pickpocket. Then gamblers, all crooked. Pimps: are you a potential client or someone they can add to their stable? Worshipers of some god or another – sometimes real, sometimes made up. Barkers for the second and third-rate theaters and shows..." He stopped; he'd made the point. "Anyway, a few of the spotters out by the gates are working for outfits that aren't crooked, but not many."

Schrog's tone was cynical. "Not hardly any. Maybe some o' dem priestly folks be okay. De rest, mostly scum. What he said, an' worse." He took another swallow, and stared into his mug.

Hox asked Jorac, "So, why did you join up? Uh, if you don't mind telling, like you said."

Schrog made a sound that was almost a growl, but Jorac made a small "it's okay" gesture. "Like I said, I don't mind, but it's a long story. Sure you want to hear all that?"

Hox nodded vigorously, and Schrog grinned and said, "Sure. We gots all night an' dere's plenty of ale." Schrog drank up and signaled the owner for another pot of ale, which Jorac paid for. Jorac was a bit amused that Schrog had drunk more than half the last pot himself, though he was the smallest of the three.

After they'd refilled everyone's mug, Jorac took a swallow and spoke slowly. "Just like you, Hox, I came off a farm. We raised sheep in the hills, way over northwest of here, up against the Lizard's Teeth mountains. My father is technically a nobleman, a Baronet, but they say the title was just bought, back when, to make my great-grandma happy. Really my dad is just a farmer.

"It was a big farm; we'd grow crops in the valleys and graze the sheep in the hills. But I never had the feel for the sheep like my father and brothers did, so I talked my father into letting me work with the drovers and stock sellers. That got me off the farm, and down to the villages, and even to the big town at the base of the hills.

"So, on a trip to sell our sheep – I was eighteen then – I met a wonderful girl, the daughter of some livestock merchants in the town. I was down there a week, and I was supposed to come back with the drovers. I did, but she and her brothers came with me. They wanted to see if I was telling the truth about the farm, and I just wanted her with me." Jorac's voice tightened a little at the memory, though he'd been trying to remember only what he did, not what he felt.

"Anyway, at the end of the next summer, we'd been married for a year and we had a little girl, six months old. I was coming back down from my folks' place with the last herd of the season, and her brother met me at the edge of town. . ."

Jorac made his voice as flat as he could, drying any emotion from it. "My wife and daughter had died in a house fire. One of her brothers had been burned, but would live. So. . ."

He shook his head to try to clear the memories, and took a deep breath. "So I took off. I grabbed my camping-out gear and headed west from our farm. You can get through the high mountain passes there a few weeks every summer and I knew the trails. In about a month I ended up in Rabakht. All I had with me was a beat-up pack, a pair of swords, and a bad attitude."

Schrog said, "Hmmm. I hear dey be a rough bunch over dat way. Don' see dem much around here." He turned to Hox and said, "You sees a little guy, black hair, big beard, white robe, looks like he's been in the sun too long, dat be dem. We constables talk to dem nice. Dey don' start no trouble, but dey finish de trouble if someone starts it."

Jorac nodded. "That's a good way of putting it. They're a handful. The tribe I first met with, they didn't think much of me at first, because I got there with my face shaved, and they never cut their beards if they can help it. I had to break a few arms to convince them that I wasn't – well there's no nice way of saying it, a male whore."

Schrog asked cynically, "And how many of dem you have to kill before dey believed you?"

"Actually, none. But I had to break some arms. One of them, I had to break two arms. He came back after I broke the first one; I guess he still didn't believe me."

Schrog chuckled at the description, and poured more ale for everyone.

Jorac paused a moment, thinking back. "You see, I really didn't care much at that point. I just wanted to fight something, anything. I'd grown up with two older brothers who liked to beat up on little Jo-Jo, and when I was a teenager my father brought in a renowned fighting master to teach us. I was the right age to learn I guess; the fighting master said I was getting pretty good. So fighting was one thing I knew how to do. . ." He waved a hand negligently. "Anyway, after I whipped a bunch of them, one after another, they decided I was okay, and finally they made me their war chief."

He didn't add that the tribesmen had started to call him *Shiar,* the name of their war god. He could never tell if it was just a nickname or they thought he was a reincarnation because of the fierce berserk frenzy he sometimes found himself in while fighting.

He went on. "So I led them when we went back to fighting the tribe across the valley. They'd been fighting each other for generations; I don't think anyone knew why anymore. I could barely tell them apart, and didn't care much, but I got to hit someone."

He paused to take a drink and look at his audience. Schrog had the knowing, accepting look of a veteran; Hox was a bit wide-eyed.

"Anyhow," Jorac went on, keeping it short, "I trained them. We almost lost the first fight, but we got better. I taught them tactics and teamwork and such, like I'd been learning from the fighting master and tutors. I led them in battle for two years, till we finally won big, and overran the other tribe's village. . ." – his voice turned bitter – "and then my tribe burned it down and slaughtered them all."

"When I saw that, I decided I was in the wrong business, so I headed back home. My own dad didn't even recognize me at first with the beard and all. I stayed there for a few months, then decided I better do something with my life. Pretty soon I found a job as a guard on a spice trader's wagon. Didn't pay much, but I got to stop worrying if I was making things better or worse. I don't say I slept better – guard work isn't for heavy sleepers – but after a while the bad dreams stopped."

He went on; the telling was easier now. "After my first season with him, the trader got a few more wagons and added a couple more guards for me to supervise. We never lost any shipments, and he did pretty well. After a few years, he was ready to retire here in Vaggert, so he paid me off, and gave me a bonus and a reference. I had guard experience, so I started working as a constable. And then after a few years, they asked me to be the one and only Wizard Constable – and the rest you know." He smiled wryly and pretended to wipe his brow. "The end of a long, long story."

Hox said, "Wow, you've done a lot!" Schrog nodded wisely and was quiet, but Hox went on. "I think I understand what constables do, but what does a Wizard Constable do?"

Jorac made a face. "To tell you the truth, I don't have any real idea of what they want from me. And I don't think they do either. My predecessor was a low-ranked wizard who apparently spent most of his time settling squabbles among the apprentices and other low-ranked wizards. When he quit they said they wanted someone else, with a constable background if possible. So I got the job. It came with a fancy charter, but it doesn't say much, so I make it up as I go along. The pay is good, at least. . ."

The three sat in a companionable silence for a bit, looking around at the other patrons. The tavern was starting to fill up, and the owner escorted customers to tables as they entered.

A pair of men entered who drew everyone's attention. One was dressed in workman's clothes, but the other wore a long, flowing gray cloak with some colored piping at the bottom, meaning he was almost certainly a wizard. The tavern owner came from around the bar and stood in front of the pair.

"Sorry, full up."

The wizard spoke "Don't be daft. There's plenty of room available; bring me two mugs of ale." He tried to go past the owner, who stepped in front of him again.

"I said we're full. Those places are reserved. You'll be taking your custom elsewhere."

The wizard stopped, flaring his nostrils and raising his eyebrows. The man with him looked concerned, and made a little gesture that looked as if he wanted to grab the wizard's arm, but changed his mind. He said, "Never mind, Master Banloz. Lots of places we can talk."

The wizard's brow narrowed, and in a slow, measured tones he said, "We'll sit here. Ale."

The owner didn't move, and Jorac saw the wizard shake his hands free from his sleeves.

Jorac motioned to Hox and Schrog to stay put, and walked over. "Greetings, sir wizard. I'm Wizard Constable Kellor. There's not a problem here, is there?"

The wizard's companion said, "Wizard Constable?"

In an airy manner, Jorac said, "Oh, I report to the Wizard Council. Troubleshooting and such. Not a wizard myself, of course." That was for the owner's benefit. "But I understand wizardry, and wizards." He looked pointedly at Banloz.

The wizard's manner changed immediately. "Greetings, Honorable Kellor." Turning to the tavern owner, he nodded and said, "If the tables are reserved, we would certainly not want to intrude. Good day to you." And he marched out of the room, leaving his puzzled companion to belatedly follow.

Jorac returned to his table and sat down, motioning Hox and Schrog to wait. The tavern owner came over with his thanks and a fresh pot of ale, refusing any payment.

"Glad to help," Jorac said. "I knew you could handle it, but no need to call in your favors. Nothing happened, after all."

The owner said, "As you say, nothing happened – thanks to you. I appreciate it." He went to serve other customers.

Jorac asked Hox, "Did you see the wizard? What did you see from over here?"

"Well, the wizard just stood there, talking to the tavern keeper. He acted kind of uppity, I guess."

Schrog said, rather thickly, "He also shook his hands free, so as he could start doin' wizard stuff. Dat's why Jorac moved in. Here's advice fer ya: If'n ya see a fockin' wizard, steer clear."

Hox was surprised. "I thought people would like them? This is such a nice place to live."

Schrog waved his hands dramatically. "Suppose ya bumps a wizard in de street. So ya says yer sorry, and ya means it, and goes on yer way. Den ya comes down wit' dis bad itch, or yer clothes falls apart, or sump'n. Now, de wizards in de town all gots dis code, dey ain't supposed to do shit like dat, but how you gonna prove it, and who's gonna stop 'em? Dey all says dey works for de emperor, dey bow down on his birthday and all, but we ain't de emperor, okay?"

Hox looked at Jorac questioningly. Jorac nodded. "I've heard tales. Know why the owner doesn't serve wizards in this place? His hair all fell out after he had a dispute about a bill with a wizard apprentice. It all grew back, too, which means it wasn't a natural thing."

Hox was concerned now. "But then won't the wizards get mad if they don't get served here?"

Jorac said, "Well, he raised a stink, and so now he's kind of under the protection of some better wizards. Wizards are rude and like to push people around, but it seems like that's just their nature. Most of them aren't vindictive, and even try to be fair. The problem is that you never know, so you should just steer clear."

Hox was still a little mystified. "So who runs this city? The emperor, or the wizards?"

Jorac grinned and said "Um, 'yes and no' would be the answer. It depends on who you ask, and what part of town you're talking about. The emperor collects the taxes and pays for the Wizard Council, but everyone else has to work – including wizards. The merchants up around Northgate and Coronet Heights are mostly nobles and have most of the money, so if you ask them, they'll say they run the city too."

Schrog said importantly, "Some parts o' de city ain't none o' dem runnin' it, like we seen today. Swampside ain't de only place like dat, but most o' de udder places hides it better." Jorac could finally tell that the six or seven mugs of ale Schrog had drunk were affecting him; he was almost slurring. Jorac was going to have to ask Hox to see him home.

Jorac said, "Still, it's not bad here in Vaggert. I've seen a lot of places, and here I am." He raised his mug in a mock toast. "Beats raising sheep."

Chapter 4 - Madame Velsop

The next two days were Starday and Sunday, the busiest days for the City Guard. Those who worshiped the Father rested on Starday and partied on Sunday, while the followers of the Mother did the opposite. It made for a busy two days for the constables, since a good many people just partied both days and left the worshiping to others. Because Cerom wouldn't have anyone to spare to escort him, Jorac continued his investigations by the simple expedient of sitting on a stool in Cerom's office, helping Cerom with small tasks and talking to everyone who came in, constable, citizen, and criminal alike. He even managed to get one of Kullo's men to open up a bit, but it was mostly bragging and threats. In two days of listening, Jorac heard nothing that might suggest unauthorized magic was being practiced. The only positive things he accomplished were to buy some fancy handkerchiefs and organize a thank-you dinner for his squad the following week.

Finally, thinking it over Sunday evening, Jorac decided he was going at it all wrong. He'd only been talking to non-wizards, and they just saw the situation from the outside, the same way he did. He decided what he needed was more insight into wizardly processes, which unfortunately meant he probably needed to talk to a wizard. But, he realized, it didn't have to be a full-fledged, gold-star, Council-level wizard. . .

The first thing the next morning he went back to his old patrol area, a middle-class shopkeepers' district, and visited the small shop of Madame Velosp, Fortuneteller (Licensed). He'd been responsible for the "licensed" part. Dorrimella Velosp was her real name, and she'd been a plain, frumpy, middle-aged widow who'd started to pick up some extra cash playing a wildly dressed, flamboyant fortuneteller on market days. She'd been as surprised as anyone when a remarkable number of her predictions had come true. Her gift worked as long as the answer was known but hidden. She couldn't tell you who was going to win a horse race, but she could help you find your lost ring, or tell you if your wife was carrying a boy or girl – and if it was yours or not.

Jorac had found her not long before he'd left to become the Wizard Constable. His allergy had shown she was doing real magic, and since he knew she was harmless, he'd arranged for her to apply for the correct licenses and get some basic training in wizard practice before she got into trouble.

He went through the cozy waiting room, gently tapped on the inner door, and heard a deep, sonorous "Enter."

As he walked in, she started to speak in a somber tone. "What questions would you have Madame Velosp ask the spirits... Oh, Jorac!" She waited until he closed the door to continue. Her voice returned to its normal high, cheerful timbre. "Good to see you! I heard you got a new job, working for wizards, right?"

Jorac grinned and nodded. "Hi Dorrie. Business treating you good?

"Heh. Just between you and me, the money lenders are mad at me. I'm paying them off too quick, the greedy so-and-so's." She tipped her head quizzically. "But I divine that you didn't drop in to ask me that. What's up?"

"Well, like you say, I have this new job, and they've given me an assignment where I need to know something about how magic actually works. My bosses are senior wizards, and it won't help to ask them to explain it. They get impatient and think you know it already, or they treat you like a child and over-simplify." She nodded knowingly and he went on. "Dorrie, I hate to speak ill of your new guild, but I don't trust those senior wizards to tell me everything. They seem a little, uh, self-centered."

Dorrie laughed. "Ah, you're right about that! As you say, I wouldn't be speaking ill of my new guild, but if *you* wanted to, you might find me nodding!"

"I figure you just got some basic first-year training, so you may be able to explain some things to me at my level."

"Sure, I'll try." She pointed toward the door. "Flip over that sign so we won't be disturbed."

Jorac stepped outside the door to the waiting room and flipped the sign from "Available" to "Communing with the Spirits," then came back in and sat down. "For starters," he said, "when you gather up your mana to do some magic, where does it come from?"

"Hmmm, can't say I know. The smug old fellow they had work with me said I wasn't powerful enough to worry about such things. He said I had enough for what I was doing, and was too old to learn more. So I can't tell you much about that."

Jorac sighed. "That's all right. What I really want to know is if it's possible to detect magic – mana – as its very smallest component, particle, whatever it is. Just watch where it might go, like watching dust blow in the wind."

"Well, they did teach me that much. Said it was the first thing any apprentice learns. Draw those curtains and I'll show you."

When they'd darkened the room, she closed her eyes in concentration and moved her right hand in a small turning gesture. A little puff of sparkling particles came a short distance off her fingertips, only to be pulled back a second later. The particles might have been blue or green, and they might have given off light or reflected it. It was impressive in a small way, without being showy. Jorac could see how someone with Dorrie's – or Madame Velsop's – theatrical talent could use that effect to great advantage.

Of course, he started to sneeze.

"Oh dear, I forgot. I wanted to show off my new trick so badly, for someone I didn't have to play the Madame for. Sorry about that."

"*Achoo!* No problem, Dorrie. Glad to" – he held up a finger – "*Achoo!* see it. What do they call that?"

"Dunno, they just called it 'Exercise Number Three.' It wows the marks, it does. Worth every penny of those guild dues. That and the sign on the door."

Jorac pulled out his new fine muslin handkerchief and blew his nose. "What happens if you don't pull those things – the particles – back to you?"

"The wizard called them manites. Don't know. Want me to try?"

"Uh, sure, but let me get into the back room first, okay? The farther away I can get the better, but I think I need to see this."

Jorac held his breath, and at his signal, she again made the gesture and produced the manites, and this time they hung there in the air. Jorac could barely see them, so he got closer. As he approached they seemed to break up into smaller particles, and smaller still. Still holding his breath, he put his face up near them and tried to watch as they disappeared. He wasn't sure if they spread out at random as they divided, or if there was some order or direction to it. He hurried back to the back room before he ran out of breath, and started breathing again.

When he was breathing normally again, he returned to the front room and asked Dorrie what she saw and felt.

"Felt? Not much; it doesn't takes much out of you, not like a Reading, and I do four or five of those a day. What I saw was the manites breaking up, spreading out, splitting up, down to as small as I can see. At the end they might have moved a little, but I'm not sure."

"Moved a little?"

"Kind of sideways, maybe. Like over that way. . ." She pointed across the room.

Jorac thought for a few seconds. "You're busy all day, I take it?"

"They're probably lining up outside right now. You were lucky to catch me when I just opened."

"Then I won't take any more of your time. Thanks, Dorrie. This is all guild stuff; keep it under your hat, right?"

"Mum's the word. We wizards are a secretive bunch." She grinned.

"You've got it. Keep in touch, okay? I have an office in the base of the Wizard's Tower now."

"I pay my guild dues there. I'll stop by sometime."

When he opened the door, he found Madame Velosp had two ladies waiting outside, their heads bowed together talking quietly. As he let himself out, he prominently fingered his badge of office and said gravely, "Your assistance in this matter is greatly appreciated, Madame. It is a great gift you share."

Dorrie winked at him as she ushered in her two clients and closed the door.

* * *

Deep in thought, Jorac walked slowly back to his office and wrote a note asking to talk to Pergimtor or Darlora. He walked to the front of the building and dropped it in the message bin, where he was, as always, fascinated to watch the paper disappear before his eyes.

When he got back to his office, there was already a note on his floor saying his audience was granted, immediately. He climbed the 156 stairs (not forgetting to curse the tower designer) and entered the chamber. Pergimtor and Darlora were there, but no others. Pergimtor wore the same loose robe as he'd worn before, but Darlora wore a tighter, thinner robe that did little to conceal her figure. Jorac kept his expression strictly neutral as he noted her perfect face and body.

She said, "Well, Constable, what have you found?" For a wizard, this was polite.

Jorac bowed slightly. "High Wizard, Lady Wizard, I have found no one using magic out of the ordinary. But I can only sense magic being used, and this is not what you've bid me look for. So I've come to ask: can the generating of magic that you described for me be observed?"

Darlora frowned. "Everyone – everything – that I've examined has been completely normal. When I look at them one at a time, everything's fine, but there's something wrong with the area. Not enough mana is being generated."

Jorac asked, in his most respectful tone, "Do you think someone else is gathering the mana?"

Scornfully, Pergimtor said, "Of course that was the first thing we looked for. Wizards can shield their store of mana, but it will leave signs. There are no such signs in these areas, even a distance down into the swamp."

Jorac asked, "What about an automatic collector? Something that would work by itself, like this badge of office?" He held up the heavy badge, glad he'd thought to send the Council a thank-you note when it recently helped save his life. "Could something like this be absorbing the mana you expect?"

"No," Pergimtor said, "it takes a living thing, usually a wizard, to collect the mana. That amulet you wear has a spell put in it, but like any spell it will fade in time if not powered or renewed. That's why it's keyed to the wearer, so his mana will go toward keeping it working. It's really quite a clever spell; my Master developed it for the Emperor's Guard during the war."

Jorac nodded understanding and thought a moment. "Your pardon, High Wizard, but were you not in the war also? Part of the investigation area used to be the old Wizards Quarter, and I wondered if there might be something left from that time that has awoken, so to speak."

Pergimtor shook his head. "I don't think anyone who fought in the war could still be alive. I was apprenticed to Prexilo, one of the Council members from that time. I heard all his stories, many times, of how they shook the buildings to pieces and then sank the ground so it would flood, to deal with Mad Aplath's fireball and firetrap spells. Then they cleared the area with troops backed with wizards. Any of Aplath's circle who surrendered just had their wizardry burnt out of them, but the rest were killed. All of them were accounted for, dead or alive. I don't think you have to worry about survivors in that area."

Pergimtor's speaking had slowed as he reflected; Jorac was a bit surprised to find that he lost some of his haughty manner as he spoke.

Jorac said, very carefully, "Sir, I've heard stories of the creatures that survive in the swamp that's there now. Is it theoretically possible that some renegade wizard, not identified as close to Aplath, could likewise have managed to survive there all these years? I've been told that wizards are very long-lived."

Jorac thought he detected, for the first time, a human emotion from the High Wizard – regret. "No, it's not possible. With enough effort we can change our looks, but we still age inside. I think every elderly wizard turns to anti-aging research in his later years, but as yet none have made any breakthroughs."

"Ah. Thank you." *Surprising he'd tell me that*, Jorac thought. "I had one other question, then. If mana in the area was given off but not immediately gathered by a wizard, what would happen? Would the mana dissipate, fade away, or flow to another area, or what?"

Darlora spoke. "It would break up into very small parts, called manites. They're hard to gather, and spread out in all directions. Some are gathered by those of us with Power, some are reabsorbed even by simp-, by those of you without magic. Watching this happen is one of the earliest apprentice lessons."

Jorac thought this didn't really answer what he'd asked, but was interesting. He said, "Could something have disturbed that process, in this area?"

He got his second surprise of the day when dealing with wizards. Normally cocksure, they looked at each other in doubt. Seeing his opening, Jorac pressed ahead.

"You say watching the process happen is an apprentice task. Could such an apprentice be assigned to me, to work on this investigation?" Jorac didn't want to deal with high-level wizards any more than he had to. An apprentice, one who would take his orders and help him figure out the details of magic, would be just what he needed.

After a pause, Pergimtor spoke. "Hmmm. We shall consider this. Darlora, shield him, while I. . ."

With a whooshing sound, Jorac suddenly found himself standing back in his office, in the circle on the floor where messages sometimes appeared. The shielding even worked; he had no urge to sneeze. *If my employers were always so considerate,* Jorac thought, *I might have come up with a different silent swear word than "Wizards."*

* * *

The apprentice showed up in his office late that afternoon. He was a tall, beanpole-thin lad of about fourteen or fifteen, and greeted Jorac in a shy voice, "Honorable Constable Kellor, I have been assigned to your service. I am called Veseen." His voice was still breaking, and his face was starting to break out – an awkward age.

Jorac was a little distracted, almost ready to leave for the day. He looked at the boy. "Veseen, tell me about yourself."

The boy seemed almost frightened by the question. "Me? I'm just an apprentice. To Master Kirchward who has been assigned to duty in the Emperor's Guard this month. Uh, if you please, Honorable Constable Kellor." His accent said that he came from an educated family at least, perhaps a noble one.

"What did they tell you about this assignment?"

Veseen looked at his shoes and hunched his shoulders. "Sorry, sir Wizard Constable, they told me nothing. I had to ask our chambermaid where to find your office. I apologize for not learning more."

"No problem. Do you know how to do Exercise Number Three? No *don't!*" – he said this last as the boy's right hand started forward.

Jorac glanced at the boy, then looked closer. He seemed to be very worried, almost frightened.

Jorac leaned forward at his desk, and lowered his voice. "Veseen, no harm will come to you. Sorry for yelling at you just then, but whenever I'm near magic being cast, I start to sneeze. It's very annoying sometimes, as you might imagine. It's also useful sometimes, though, so I tell almost no one."

"Yes, sir. I'm sorry. I thought you wanted to test me."

"Not your fault. And call me Jorac."

"Jorac, sir Constable?"

"Jorac. I've been answering to it all my life, and it's a lot shorter than what you've been calling me."

"Yes, sir. Jorac."

"Better. Now, can you shield me from magic effects – simple ones, I mean?

Veseen sounded a little hopeful for the first time. "Yes, sir. We've been learning that all year."

"Can you shield me while you're doing Exercise Number Three?"

Again the boy's voice shrank. "I don't know, sir. I don't think so, sir."

Jorac suppressed a sigh. "You don't have to call me sir all the time, either. Let's give it a try. Put a shield around me, or at least between me and you, and let's see what happens."

"Yes, sir, I mean Jorac."

At the look on the boy's face, Jorac said, "If you fail to shield me, I'll sneeze, but I won't be angry. Just give it a try."

A small grateful smile appeared on the apprentice's face. "Yes, si – Yes, Jorac."

He extended his fingers and concentrated. At first nothing happened, and then the colored particles appeared. Veseen was better at it than Dorrie; the particles flew a handspan off the tips of his fingers and stayed visible about a second before receding back into his fingers.

Jorac held his breath, and for a moment thought the shielding had worked, but then he felt the familiar tickle in his nose. He sneezed five times, while the apprentice stood there looking mortified and frightened. Veseen slowly calmed as Jorac didn't fly into a tantrum, merely sneezed and busied himself finding a handkerchief and blowing his nose.

"S'okay," Jorac said, sniffling. "We can try again later. I have to run some errands now." He began gathering his things. "What are you doing this evening?"

"Sir?" Veseen said, looking puzzled.

"There's a dinner for some constables who helped me out last week on some Wizard business. It's at a nice tavern, good food, good cakes and pies. Want to come?" At Veseen's initial silence, Jorac added, "Speak your mind."

"Well, I'm expected to have dinner in the apprentice hall this night. As usual." By the resigned tone of the last two words, it was obvious he was hoping Jorac could find a way to get him out of it.

Jorac smiled; he remembered being that age. "And who do I need to talk to?"

Veseen smiled back hopefully. "Master Radyry expects me back in the apprentice dormitory by dinnertime."

"I obviously need your talent tonight. Hmmm, what talent is that. . .?"

"I'm very good at lighting candles, sir, from halfway across the room. I'm sometimes known for that."

"Ah, just the thing for those high sconces. No one else will do. Lead the way to Master Radyry."

* * *

The dinner, with the five constables from the previous week along with their boss Cerom, Jorac, and the young apprentice wizard, was a great success. Jorac told them he'd explained on his expense report that this was a "debriefing" meeting, so he wanted to hear some stories!

So the stories had flowed with the wine and ale, some mostly true, some not, but they all were cheerful stories this night. Jorac had specified that this was a stag affair; he could stretch his expense reports to cover dinner for people he worked with, but not wives, girlfriends, or partners of convenience (or commerce). So if some of the stories told by the older constables were a little on the risqué side – well, they were all men there this night and no one got offended, even if Veseen and Hox's eyes got a little big at some of the tales. It was a rare celebratory night off for the constables, and they made the most of it.

* * *

When Jorac got to the office a bit late the next morning, Veseen was there, looking bored. He brightened as Jorac came in.

"Thank you for inviting me to the dinner last night, sir. I mean Jorac."

"Glad to have you, Veseen. Hope you didn't mind us leaving early, but I promised Master Radyry I'd have you back by midnight. I wanted you to see the sort of men we'll be working with. Schrog and Hox will be here later. I told them to sleep in and get here when they wanted."

"I asked Master Radyry about shielding you while doing magic. He said it was probably not possible, because of the way shielding works. I can shield you, or show the manites, but not both at the same time." Again his manner was past apologetic, almost cringing.

"Hmmm, I was afraid of that. That's okay."

Veseen looked relieved, as if he'd avoided a punishment.

"Can I ask you a question? You don't have to answer it if you don't want."

"Sir?"

"Every other wizard I've met around here is pushy and egotistical, and worse, and you're – well, not. Why do they act like that?"

Veseen sighed a little. "I don't mind explaining. The higher-level wizards all summon creatures from the nether planes – imps, sprites, even demons sometimes. They tell us you have to have perfect confidence when you're dealing with those beings. So they try to teach us to act with confidence."

Jorac thought that explained a lot, but not everything. "Seems to me they sometimes confuse confidence with being rude and overbearing," he said, almost to himself, "but then again I'm not a wizard."

Veseen smiled a little. He also looked a little apprehensive. "If you say so, sir." His glance toward the ceiling made Jorac think of their conversation being overheard. Jorac didn't much care what the wizards thought of him, but he didn't want to get his young charge in trouble.

"Okay, thanks, I've been wondering, that's all. Not important." He walked briskly over to his desk. "There are a still a few things we can do this morning. . ."

Chapter 5 - To Pigtown

It was more than halfway to lunchtime when Schrog and Hox got to Jorac's office. They didn't exactly stagger in, but they weren't moving with a spring in their step. Schrog looked the worse for wear, but Hox looked fairly normal.

Jorac was careful to keep his voice quiet and level. "Hi guys. How's it going?"

Schrog said, "I be alright. De little guy here" – he pointed up at Hox – "got us up too frickin' early." He flopped down on the nearest stool and held his head in his hands, staring at the floor.

"Veseen, would you please pour us a drink of water?" Jorac had arranged for a pitcher to be ready, expecting them to be a bit hung over.

Hox said defensively, "The sun had been up for hours."

Without moving his head, Schrog said. "And how long ya been in de bed?"

"I don't know, two or three hours at least. At home we used to get up at first light, but sometimes we'd sleep in until sunup. I can't sleep in the daytime."

"Frickin' youngsters."

Jorac shared a rueful smile with Hox, and shook his head at Schrog. Schrog only lifted his head when Veseen handed them each a cup of water, and leaned sideways against the wall as Jorac spoke.

"Today we go back to Southgate, just the four of us. There are some little magic experiments we need to run. Veseen will handle the magic part, but I'll need your eyes too. I want you to watch what he's doing." The young apprentice got up and pulled the curtains. "He's going to make some tiny magic lights, and they'll break up into little pieces. We need to watch them at the very end, just before they disappear, and see which way they go. It's kind of subtle, so watch closely." He moved toward the door. "You guys go on. I've got to run home; I'll be back in a few minutes."

He and Veseen had done the experiment a couple of times already that morning. They'd watched the manites zoom upward at the end, toward the upper floors of the Wizard's Tower, just before they disappeared from view. The general direction they went was fairly clear once you got used to seeing them.

He walked quickly down the street to the small suite of rooms he rented above a nearby shop and got some clean handkerchiefs, then walked quickly back. He hoped Hox and Schrog hadn't noticed he left just when Veseen was about to do magic. Of course if he kept evading it like that all afternoon they'd probably notice, but figure it was Wizard Business and keep their mouth shut, which was almost as good.

When he got back they were discussing what they saw. Hox had clearly seen the manites turn upwards. Schrog said he wasn't sure, but looking at Schrog's bloodshot eyes, Jorac thought he knew why. He hoped Schrog could handle what he had in mind for the day; he liked the rough constable's street-sense.

"If you're ready, we're going down to Southgate and try this again," he told them. "Maybe get a little of that good soup while we're there."

Hox and Veseen jumped up, but Schrog said "Gimme a min." The older man struggled to his feet, drank another cup of water, and asked the way to the jakes. He looked only a little better when he got back. "I be ready. Hox, you lead off. Keep an eye out like we been talkin' about."

They got on the river road easily enough, and headed south. Hox cheerfully talked to Veseen, telling what he'd learned about the area, while Schrog hung back with Jorac, muttering foul curses about the energy of youth. Hox obviously remembered the good food fondly and set a brisk pace, and the lanky apprentice easily kept up; they started outpacing Jorac and Schrog.

With the young men out of easy earshot, Schrog's foul language about their springy energy grew more vile and more humorous. The more Jorac laughed, the more fetid the maledictions became, so that Jorac finally stopped to lean against a wall as he laughed, and had to call ahead to Hox to slow down.

"Ah, hadn't heard that one before. At least with that family member."

Hox returned with Veseen and looked expectantly at Jorac.

Still grinning, Jorac explained. "Schrog was just discussing how fast you were walking. And he was thinking that being young is a good thing, if the youthful energy isn't wasted. And thinking that energy must run in families, or something about families anyway."

Hox looked confused, at Schrog, Jorac, and Veseen in turn. Veseen was smirking, so Jorac said to him, "Go ahead, explain it."

"Constable Schrog is hung over and cursing his headache, and us in particular. And Constable Kellor is laughing at him a little. He wants us to slow down."

"Oh, okay." Hox didn't parse the part about families, which was just as well.

They set off at a slower pace, and reached The Flying Pie, the tavern they'd enjoyed before, a bit after noon. It smelled as good as ever, and when the server bustled over, Jorac said, "Can we get a private room? – with stew for six? There's four of us this time." He grinned, and pointed at Hox and Veseen on either side of him with two fingers each.

"Ah, good to see you back again. Feeding the hungry is what we like. The room is extra, and we'll need it cleared in a couple of hours. Call it thirty for the lot, and we'll try to fill up that man-mountain this time."

The room was small and fancy, probably rented out for business meetings. A pitcher of small beer and a large pot of their famous stew was brought in. Schrog managed a bowlful,

Jorac had seconds, and Hox and Veseen finished off the rest. After lunch, Jorac tried to explain what they were doing there.

After lunch, Jorac started them on their afternoon's task. "We have Veseen here so he can make those little magic lights, and you get to watch them and see what direction they go. You probably can't really see the exact direction, because the distance is very short; you'll just have to rely on your impressions. Anyway, we'll start here, find the direction, then go that direction and try it again. I'm going to pull down the shades, and you do the test while I go settle up for the food. Be right back. . ."

When he returned, the three were looking out the window, figuring out how the building was situated. Schrog, who knew the area best, said "I figures it be south, or near enough. Hope de wind ain't so bad. Pigtown, we's headin' fer."

Veseen said, "I've heard about Pigtown. Is the smell there as bad as they say?"

Schrog nodded. "If yer lucky, you don't find out. It be bad, 'specially farder in. Ain't nobody goes dere for fun. Kin get rough, too."

They walked south until they could start to smell the noxious area, and tried the test again. It was worthless to try to watch the small manites divide in full sunlight, so they found an apothecary that advertised "Wizard Supplies" and with the help of Jorac's badge of office, begged use of the back room for a few minutes.

Schrog spoke when they were back on the street. "South again. Pigtown, 'less you wants to skirt it again."

Jorac said, "Well, I wouldn't want to go back into Swampside today, not without more of us. Close thing, that was." He thought a moment, then brightened. "How about the same path we took last time, but we stop before heading down into Swampside?"

"Aye, I be hopin' you says that. Maybe wanna go up a few streets, the wind ain't so good today."

The group headed up the hill, and through the same laundry-rich, working-class neighborhood they'd visited the week before. It was all new to Veseen, so Schrog kept up a running commentary; he was obviously feeling better. When they found a dark alley between two buildings, Jorac kept watch from afar as they did another test.

The three reported that this time the manites went north, back toward the city, and a little away from the river. If Jorac remembered his map correctly, the Wizard's Tower was that direction, and he thought back to the day he was given the assignment and Darlora let slip the words "my territory."

"I think we're too high on the hill, boys. I'm not happy about it either, but it's Pigtown for us. Schrog, lead the way. Let's find the first dark area we can inside Pigtown proper." Schrog made a face, and Jorac said, "We could come back at night instead, but I think that would be worse."

Schrog sighed noisily. "Aye, you be right. Alright, if it gots to be done, we'll do it. Everybody, you takes a deep breath. It's de last one you gets. Dis way."

Veseen spoke up. "Uh, sir, can we change our clothes first? I noticed some of the laundries we passed were advertising used clothing."

The other three stopped and stared at the young apprentice for a second – he looked down at his feet and said "Sorry, sir."

Jorac said, "No, it's a damned good idea! Veseen, you speak up whenever you have a mind to. Schrog, I'm putting you in charge. Find us a way of keeping our clothes safe and get some clothes we can wear down there. Nothing fancy, mind you; something we can discard afterwards."

Schrog said, "Damn, I shoudda t'ought of dat. Ain't been here in a whiles. De laundries be dat way, down de hill. Get us some boot covers too, 'cause we didn't bring extra shoes."

They got to the area where the laundries were, just above Pigtown. Schrog ducked down an alley behind the first large laundry they came to, and came back shaking his head. "Ain't trusting this one. Too dirty back there." He checked out a couple more, and finally approved of one that had a sign out front saying "Widow Marpan's Laundry – Clean Clothes!"

Widow Marpan proved to be a short, plump, cheerful woman who was always tucking unruly hair beneath her bonnet. She and her young girl assistant were happy to help the group find suitable clothes from the second-hand stock she kept for sale – especially when Jorac pulled out his purse full of coppers. They had no problem finding cheap clothing for Jorac, Schrog, and Veseen, but Hox was another matter. He finally ended up in a shirt that Jorac believed had originally been a very fat lady's dress, and they had to wait a few minutes while some oversized boot covers were sewn for him. He kept his own trousers, there being nothing even close in size, but found some fabric to wrap around his legs. They put their clean clothes into a drawstring bag that Veseen slung over his shoulder; the laundry-woman offered to keep them but Schrog vetoed that with a short shake of his head.

When Schrog finally approved of their preparations, they stepped outside. He gave them some pointers about the area, and added a warning. "We ain't wearin' constable badges no more, and Pigtown kin get rough. So we gots to look like what dey used to seein'. Hox, you act extra dumb, okay? But if I tell you to hit someone, don' ask no questions first, just do it." Hox dropped his face into a slack-jawed countenance, and said "Duh, okay, boss." Jorac couldn't help but grin; Hox had obviously learned that playing dumb was sometimes a good tactic for someone his size.

Schrog nodded, and tapped Veseen. "Kid, you carry dat bundle and stick right next to me. You be de kid brudder I gots to watch over. Jorac be de guy wit' a proposition, jus needs a place to talk, and I'm de local." He turned to Jorac. "You de guy wit' de money, dem two work for me, so you talk to me, not dem. Dey don' talk, not unless dey have to."

In the most posh accent he could manage, Jorac said, "Would you like me to emulate a member of the noble classes?"

Schrog raised his eyebrows, then nodded. "Dat works. Good idear, in fact. Keep 'em from lookin' at de rest of us so much."

Both Hox and Veseen looked concerned, and Jorac wasn't sure he didn't look the same. "Aw, no worries," Schrog said. "We jus' go in, find a place to do dat little trick, and get out. Jorac still gots dat fancy badge under his shirt, right? Don' wanna to use it if we don' have to, dat wizard sure looked pissed off last time. I don' like being around pissed off wizards. So we does it my way, alright? But we gots de backup, so we be fine."

The trip down the hill wasn't bad, but the smell crept up on them as they neared the area. Then the wind shifted and they got it full force – a loathsome symphony of dead and decaying animals, offal, and acrid chemicals at the forefront, with other unidentified but vile-smelling things hidden underneath, some that burned the nose, some almost sweet. Jorac's first response was a strong gag reflex, but he was able to master it, and after a time it began to subside. *I guess the human nose can get used to anything,* he thought, *even this, but wow! They weren't lying.*

The roads were all filthy, stinking mud, and though a few businesses put down wooden boards for their customers to walk on, those weren't much cleaner than the street. The squad dodged aside as a horse pulling a wagon came up the street, and Veseen got splattered with some foul-smelling mud flung up by the wagon wheel.

They passed a slaughterhouse and some sort of small shop that burned something awful before Schrog led them up some stairs and knocked on the door. Schrog motioned the others to back off as a small panel opened and a face appeared. Jorac was standing with his back to the door, watching the street, and couldn't see the face.

"Whachoo want?"

Jorac turned to Schrog and said in his upper-crust accent, "Are you sure that this establishment can provide us the privacy we need?"

Schrog nodded to Jorac, then said to the man at the door, "Needs a room. Quiet like. Short time." Schrog's accent was even thicker, if that was possible.

"Hot running water?"

"Naw, no beds. Just talk."

"Lemme see." The panel slammed shut.

Veseen said quietly, "What is this place?"

Schrog grinned. "Best you don't ask that. De hot runnin' water, dat's a code for if we wants whores in de room." The young apprentice flushed bright red at this, and craned his neck to look at the building again.

"Anudder t'ing, place like this, dey prolly listen to every word in dese rooms, okay? We knows what we's doing, no need for talk. Jorac, get four coppers out, okay?"

The panel in the door opened again, and the face appeared. Jorac got a good look this time; it was a remarkably ugly face, battered and scarred. "Seven coppers. Half hour."

"Four fer an hour be double price. 'Tain't stupid. Inna hurry, so we go four. Udderwise we walks."

The man at the door grunted and slammed shut the panel, then opened the door. "Let's see."

He spoke to Jorac "Give 'em two, show 'em two more."

Jorac did as he was asked, looking very dubiously at the doorman. The doorman moved aside and pointed to the dial on the water-clock at the end of the entryway. A place like this probably rented most of the rooms by the hour.

They all followed the doorman to a nearby parlor with a rickety table and some mismatched chairs. The room was dark behind tattered, yellowed curtains, and reeked of just-applied cheap perfume. Hox brushed by a curtain, dislodging a cascade of dust, and started to sneeze. When the doorman left and the door was closed, Schrog looked around the room and silently pointed people to where they should stand, Jorac assumed to block spy-holes. He silently obeyed when Schrog waved him to stand by the door.

Jorac said, "It's a bit rustic, but I believe this place will do admirably." He turned and nodded to Veseen.

Returning his nod, Veseen did Exercise Number Three again, and they watched the manites dissolve. Jorac held is breath as best he could, but was sneezing lustily by the time the particles were gone. The other three nodded to Jorac forcefully to signal they'd determined the direction – and with all the dust in the room, Hox and Veseen joined him in sneezing. Without speaking, they left the room and headed toward the front door.

"Hey, you don' like de room?" the doorman said. "Whatsa matter?"

"Back in ten minutes," Schrog told him, and motioned Jorac to pay him. "You lets us in when we comes back with de udder guy, or I have Muscles here bust it down."

The doorman took the money, looked warily up at Hox, and nodded. "You gots most of your hour. Whats you do's is up to youse." The last had the singsong cadence of a well-worn phrase; Jorac thought it was probably the place's motto.

As they headed back out of Pigtown the way they'd come, Schrog said, "South again. Same as before."

Hox asked, "Why did you tell him we'd be back?"

"Dat way dey don' follow us now. Maybe dey watch, see if we worth robbin' when we get back. Not now."

Again, Jorac was glad to have Schrog with them. That was a subtlety he wouldn't have thought of.

A five-minute walk led them back to the edge of the area, and in another few minutes they were back up the hill.

"So now what?" Schrog spoke for everyone.

Jorac answered, "Now we need to plan again. Swampside is no picnic. Even the so-called civilized end we visited."

"I was t'inkin'," Schrog said. "I figgers we maybe wanna talk to de chiefs dere. Dey remembers us right now, prolly treat us okay dis week."

Jorac was surprised. "Nobody out for revenge? Nobody who'll try to show us they're in charge?"

"We took down a top guy dere in just a couple minutes, didn't break a sweat. Dey remembers us, ain't ready to push us yet. Still figgerin' out if we takin' over or what."

"I don't think we're ready to do that," Jorac said wryly. "We need a cover story, but one that won't challenge whoever wants to run the place."

"Maybe we just after de slavers, huh?" Schrog spoke with an unexpected intensity.

Veseen said, "I thought enslavement was illegal? Why don't we stop it?" He had no idea how naive he sounded.

Jorac spoke when Schrog didn't. "Emperor Benneso has outlawed it here. But a few day's sail down the coast is all you need. You've heard of the pirate isles, right? Once you're past our border, our laws don't hold. There's lots of money to be made selling slaves if there's a boat captain who'll haul them, and someone like the late, unlamented Kullo who'll kidnap the weak."

"Late?" Hox sounded surprised.

"Cerom told me he was executed this morning. He'd had too many chances already. The rest of his crew will spend five or six years on the road gang; maybe one or two will turn around. Maybe."

Schrog nodded approvingly. "Heh, good! Rotten sum'bitch deserved it! Good for us too. Dat way we goes to Swampside, tells dem about it, pushes on de other bastards like Kullo, maybe den we don' get jumped."

"I don't mind telling them that – as far as I know, Swampside is barely part of the city anyway – but let's clear it with Cerom first." He looked at the lengthening afternoon shadows. "Let's head back. I think we've done enough for today – and we need to plan our next Swampside trip a little better. It was a little too close for comfort last time."

Schrog and Hox nodded vigorously at the last statement. Veseen had only heard the stories at the celebratory dinner, but they were enough; he nodded too.

* * *

When they got back to the Widow Marpan's laundry, the door was open, and they found four older teen-aged boys inside. One was talking to the proprietor in annoyed tones. Jorac and his group walked in and listened.

"You've ruined this doublet – completely ruined it. The colors are almost gone, yet you can still see that stain." The tallest of the four was speaking. A smaller boy was standing next to him, while the other two, looking rather ill and tired, were slouching near a wall.

The young man had an upper-class accent and rather fine clothes, now wrinkled and dirty. All four had thin swords at their side, which was a privilege of the nobility, so Jorac guessed that they were young rakes returning from a bit of "sport" at the bawdy houses in the district.

"Now look here, young sir. I cannot remove all stains, I told you that. I asked you if you wanted me to try to boil it, and you said yes. If you don't know that you might have to re-dye it, then you don't know much about cloth. The dyers are just down the hill if you want to do that."

The young man didn't take this well. "Listen here, bitch. You ruined it. You pay for it. It cost me three gold."

"Young sir, you owe me twelve coppers for cleaning it."

The young man drew his sword and held it down by his side. The smaller boy next to him said, "Easy, Zarl. Remember what Pa said."

"I remember, little brother, but this bitch ruined it, and now she's going to pay." He raised the sword threateningly, while the widow backed up fearfully.

Jorac looked at his team and motioned toward the two young men up against the wall. He walked up behind the younger brother and swiftly drew the kid's sword from its sheath. Then he took a step to the side and said to Zarl, "I'm a Constable, and I think you need to put that sword down."

Zarl spun to face Jorac with surprise. When he saw Jorac's beat-up civilian clothes and the way Jorac held the sword pointed at the floor, he smiled a cruel smile. "Parf, you witness this. This lying ruffian drew on me." He slowly raised his sword, and turned his body to the side, in a way that showed he'd had some fencing lessons.

Suddenly he lunged forward and tried to skewer Jorac, but Jorac beat his sword aside and tried a simple riposte. Zarl repelled it with a textbook move, a little slowly. Jorac knew he'd have little trouble winning this fight, but he could feel the red fog coming from deep in his brain, the primal desire to simply cut down this *enemy*, using all his considerable skill. His more reasoned side told him that carving up this young fool would bring him more problems than it would solve – though his restraint was a close thing, closer than he liked.

He took a step back and glanced around the room. Hox had the other two young men under control, with one hand on the collar of each. Schrog was positioned to the side, standing on the balls of his feet, ready to move in any direction, watching Parf. Veseen moved to a position in front of Widow Marpan, looking more determined than scared.

Jorac said, "Not in here," and slowly backed up toward the doorway, feeling behind him with his off-hand and feet, never taking his eyes off Zarl.

"Wherever you want, fool." Zarl kept twitching his sword in little movements meant to intimidate. Jorac backed out the doorway and into the street. Zarl followed, keeping his right foot in front at all times, ready to lunge.

When Zarl was entering the doorway, Jorac struck. He tapped the young man's sword with his own sword, and jumped to the side. Zarl's sword hit the doorway as he tried a side cut, and Jorac trapped the sword with his; then with his other hand drew his cudgel, and whacked him smartly across the temple.

Zarl fell to his hands and knees, dropping his sword. Jorac grabbed it and took a few steps back into the street. He hung his cudgel on its loop and pulled his Wizard Constable badge out from under his shirt, then walked back toward the door, carrying a sword in each hand. Zarl was sprawled across the threshold, blocking the way.

"Get up, idiot."

The look on the young rake's face was a mixture of pain, fear and anger. He rolled over, got to his feet unsteadily, and staggered back inside. Jorac followed him and glanced around. No one had moved, except that Schrog had his cudgel out and his arm was holding an unresisting Parf.

"What's your name? Don't bother to lie, Zarl."

Zarl mumbled, "Dukette Zarlan Leganwei." He wasn't very good at hiding his anger, but at least was wise enough not to do anything that looked aggressive. His title made him the heir to the Leganwei family; Jorac had heard of them but knew no details. Jorac said, "You just attacked a Constable with a sword. Thus you attacked the Emperor's representative with a weapon. Do you know what that means?"

Parf gasped, "That's treason!" Even the arrogant Zarl turned white, and the two boys Hox was holding looked thoroughly alarmed. Jorac knew that "treason" was overstating the offense; he just wanted to scare the young men, not cause a major political incident. But he was also highly offended.

He glared at Zarl. "Now here's what's going to happen. You'll pay the lady what you owe her, and then you'll go to your father and tell him what you've done. The law says treason always involves the whole family. If I decide to report this, they'll need to decide if they'll disown you or face the Emperor's justice as a family. I know which one I'd do."

Zarl fumbled a couple of silver pieces out of his pocket and dropped them on the table. He was stumbling and ashen-faced.

Parf said, in a obsequious manner, "You said, 'if you decide,' sir Constable?"

Jorac answered him sternly. "After your father talks to me, I'll decide. Don't let your brother convince you to hide this. If I don't hear from your father inside a week, I'll file a report and include the fact that your family had a chance to talk to me first. Now, drop your scabbards and get out of here." He emphasized the last by pointing the swords he was holding at both of the brothers.

Parf quickly unbelted his scabbard and let if fall; Zarl was a bit slower and more reluctant but complied without speaking, as did the other two. The quartet of teenagers left as fast as they could, and Jorac watched as they walked quickly up the street.

"Bless you, sir. Those young scamps be trouble." The widow was flustered, but quickly recovered. "Now, what can I do for you? You've gotten those clothes a mite dirty, I see."

They managed to trade the old clothes (and the widow's gratitude) for a short bath with clean, hot water, and donned their own clothes. Jorac wasn't sure the stench had all been washed off, but it was much better.

While they were dressing, Schrog explained things to Hox and Veseen. "Bet you was wondering what he were doing dere, right? See, he coudda jus' let the air out of dat young idjit, but he was t'inkin' ahead. No stink raised dis way, dey walk on home. Now dat Duke he'll come and apologize, an' prolly offer a bribe to keep quiet. You heared the rule on bribes?"

Hox replied, "Sure – we never ask for money, but we'll take bribes, and turn the money over to Cerom. Uh, it seems a little unusual."

Jorac explained. "Simple, the Royal Constabulary needs the money. Anyone holds out, they get in big trouble with their mates, and maybe kicked out; sometimes they get a Wizard to ask about it, too, so you can't keep it secret. So constables cheerfully take all bribes – and let the bribers know where the money is going and that they didn't really buy anything."

Schrog added, "But Cerom's good dat way, puts a little sump'n extra into yer pay, kinda like a commission. Most folks learn bribin' don' do no good, but dere's always somebody tryin' to pay us to look aside. So we lets 'em pay – but we don' look aside."

Hox said, carefully, "Well, it seems like a strange way to run things."

Schrog laughed. "Dam' if you ain't right. A week on the fockin' job, and he's complainin' already. Dam' if he won' fit right in!"

Chapter 6 - Swampside, Again

Two days later, Jorac was in his office doodling on paper while thinking of schemes to keep them safe in Swampside. The deep swamp was notoriously dangerous, but they'd met Kullo's gang in what was considered the safer, populated part. Of course he had his badge if there was serious trouble again, but that entailed its own costs. Clearly, the quicker they could do their job and get out, the better, but his damned sneezing made every manite test a big production. He put his ideas aside when Dorrie, Madame Velosp, came to his door.

"So this is where you work now. Quite a step up from walking a beat. I like it."

"Hi Dorrie. Good of you to stop by. What's happening?"

"Just paying my guild dues. I have to pay them in person each month for the first year. Not that I mind; I could use a break from the marks – I mean my loyal customers. They're nice folks, mostly, but they have to tell you the whole story, usually two or three times, before they get to the questions they pay me for. Wears on a body, it does."

"Hmmm." Jorac looked at her for a long moment. "I don't want to pry, but how much do you charge for one of your sessions?"

"Oh, I try to get thirty coppers now. Mostly I let them bargain me down to twenty-five, or sometimes two silvers, if they're good customers." The usual rate was twelve coppers to a silver coin, but it varied, because silver coins were sometimes more than half lead. Copper and gold coins were much easier for a wizard to check for purity, since silver somehow reflected magic.

"So, a gold every four days, or thereabouts? That's a fine proposition." Calling it a proposition was market performer talk; no one had a job or an act, one had a proposition. At five customers a day, she was making about five hundred coppers – one gold piece – every four days.

"Aye. I was only charging four or five coppers when I worked the market, and not always getting that."

"How would you like to do some work for me for a few days? Paying work, mind you." He added the last at her doubtful expression.

"Well, maybe. What do you have in mind?"

"I'm putting together a field team to help with an investigation, and I need someone else with wizard powers to go with us."

She looked dubious. "You know I'm not really much of a wizard, I'm more of a show-woman. That what you need?"

"What I need is someone who can do that trick with the manites, so we can follow them. I think you'd be perfect. You're easy to get along with and you can think on your feet; I've seen you. I've got a young apprentice now who can shield me when you're doing the magic so I won't sneeze all the damned time." He smiled wryly. "Only one trouble. We're going to go do it in Swampside."

She made a disgusted face, and he said, "I think I can make it worth your while, though. If you'll wait a minute, I'll see what they'll pay."

He scribbled a quick note asking if he could hire a Guild Member (Level 1) for a few days to help with the investigation, and at what rates. He showed Dorrie the message, and how it disappeared when he dropped it in the message box at the front of the building. She liked watching it too, and remembered something from her training about how it worked.

They wandered back to Jorac's office and chatted for a few minutes before an answer popped into the magic circle on the floor. He quickly read it and handed it to Dorrie while he finished sneezing. The bottom of the note said, "Approved, 5g/day max. Perg."

"My!" she said when she read it. "For five gold a day, I'd – well let's just say a trip to Swampside isn't the last thing on the list. Who else is going?"

"Well, there's Constable Schrog – he's good, really knows his way around – and Trainee Constable Hox, and Wizard Apprentice Veseen. And you and I make five."

"Five to take on Swampside? With an old lady like me, and a kid?"

"Just to trace the magic. You remember, when you did Exercise Number Three, how the manites all went in one direction at the end? We just need to do that again in Swampside, to see what direction they're heading. If we run into any problem, this badge will summon a Council-level wizard and we'll be whisked out of there."

"Sounds easy. Which means there's something we're missing. But what I want to know is why all this rigmarole anyway?"

Jorac realized he'd have to explain; she wasn't stupid. He made sure she knew this was a guild secret, and then said, "Veseen and I have done Exercise Number Three over and over. If we do it here in my office, just before the manites disappear they start to go up toward the Wizard's Tower." He waved his hand to point upward. "We've tried it all around the city now, wherever we could go without constables for escort, and the manites always go toward the Wizard's Tower. But in the areas south along the river something's wrong. We did the exercise in Southgate and Pigtown and the manites headed south. So, next we need to go to North Swampside and try it again. Quick trip – we'll scout a bit, stop and test where the manites are headed, and come straight back."

"Hmmm. . ." She thought a bit. "You say here in town they head for the Wizard's Tower? Why is that?"

He turned to look at her directly, and lowered his voice. "Dorrie, don't go there, okay? Some sort of secret, only get us into trouble. Maybe strong wizards can pull mana from a distance, but I wouldn't venture a guess if that was true, or why. I keep out of things like that."

She pursed her lips judiciously. "I see what you mean. I'll just take it as a given, then, at the same time we take the gold they're giving."

"That's the spirit. Can you meet me here tomorrow morning, early? You and I and Veseen will go down to the City Guard office and pick up the two constables, then head out to Swampside."

"Sure, I can do that. How long will we be out, do you think?"

"Just a day or two, unless we run into some complication."

"And what should I wear?"

He thought a moment. "I don't think we could be inconspicuous even if we wanted to, but we can at least try to look plausible. Maybe you could be an important person and the rest of us could be escorting you. You wouldn't want to wear good clothes to Swampside, but can you wear something old that used to look sharp?"

"Sure. Madame Velosp is good at looking like an important person. Anything else?"

"Does that pie-seller still set up shop on your street in the morning?"

"Yes – I remember how you like her breakfast pies. Want me to bring you one?"

He handed her some coppers, and said, "Better make it seven or eight."

"Eight? For only five of us?"

"You haven't met Hox yet; he's nineteen years old and about eleven-teen feet tall. And Veseen is fourteen."

She nodded. "Growing boys. I remember my nephews at that age. I'll see what I can do. Oh, one more thing. I promised Ginelda I'd tell you that her daughter is coming back from boarding school next week."

"Dorrie. . ."

"Don't give me that look. I know what you're going to say, that you're not ready to think about that sort of thing yet, even though it's been five years since your wife died. I told Ginelda what I'd do, and I've done it. See you tomorrow." She walked out the office door and disappeared down the hall.

* * *

"Dammit, man, I told you I'd pay extra to take us to Swampside, not Bustletown. Go down the hill!" Jorac wasn't easily upset, but he hated people not doing what they'd agreed to.

"No matter. Not going there, constable or not. Heard too many stories last night. My carriage is worth a lot. My life is worth even more."

Schrog elbowed Hox, and whispered something to him. Hox unfolded himself from the carriage and stood beside it; the driver was sitting on top, but Hox could almost look him in the eye. "Little man," he said, "do you think you could stop us from taking your carriage down there?" Schrog had probably been teaching Hox how to be menacing; he did a credible job because of his sheer size, but his delivery could use a bit of work. Jorac and Schrog also got out, leaving Veseen and Dorrie in the carriage.

The driver sputtered "But... you're constables! You can't threaten me!?" The last word came out almost as a yelp.

Jorac thought he'd better intervene before he had to spend a solid week writing reports, so he stepped in front of Hox and spoke. "We are Constables, and we can commandeer this carriage if need be. But it shouldn't come to that. Just drive down there, and turn around at the wall, and we'll pay you. You don't even have to go inside, and we'll make sure you start back up the hill before we go."

From the other side of the carriage, Schrog added, "Best listen to de man." The words were mild, but the tone was so ominous that the man whipped his head around, left to right, obviously cornered.

"All right, dammit. Get in. If anything gets broken I'll have your job, see if I won't. I know a few people, important people. They don't think much of constables throwing their weight around."

His passengers got in, and the driver turned his team of horses and headed, rather slowly, down the hill. As they neared the log wall that marked the Swampside boundary with Bustletown, he started making whimpering noises, though there was no one around to be frightened of. "Get out, please. I've got a family!" Apparently the stories he'd heard about the area were too much for him; when they were still about twenty paces short of the opening in the wall where the road went through, he swung the carriage off to the side and pulled to a stop. "Please!"

Jorac told Hox, "Go quiet him down. Get him to pull over by the wall. Tell him two minutes is all we need and then he can go back, with us or without us." Hox climbed out of the carriage and spoke briefly to the driver. Then he walked to the front of the horses, led the carriage over to the wall, and stood with them there, keeping them calm. He was obviously used to dealing with horses, unlike most city folk.

With Schrog's help, Jorac quickly closed the curtains in the carriage, then motioned for Dorrie to produce the manites and Veseen to shield him while she did so. Her stream of colored lights only shot out a short distance from her fingertips, but it was enough. And Jorac was pleased not to sneeze, so he could really examine them this time. The four of them carefully watched as the particles faded. From where they were, the city of Vaggert (and the Wizard's Tower) were roughly north, but the dissolving manites still headed south. So they'd have to keep going, into Swampside proper.

They got out, and Jorac spoke to the driver one last time. "You've done what you said, and here's your pay. Now, if you start telling people about coming down this hill, I'll have to start writing reports, and I hate writing reports. The only one I know who likes reports is my boss – and the tax man. The tax man loves reports. But if I start writing one report, I might as well write more. So I don't think we need any of that, do we?"

The driver clutched the small leather bag full of copper coins that Jorac handed him and said darkly, "I make it back up that hill, I ain't sayin' nothin'! You'll never hear from me again!" As he drove away, a little of his spirit returned, because he yelled back, "And I hope I never hear from you either!" He whipped the horses to a near gallop and was quickly gone.

The team organized into a defensive formation, with Schrog and Jorac in front, Dorrie and Veseen in the middle, and Hox in the rear, and then marched south through the opening in the wall. Most of the old district walls from the past century had been torn down, but this one was still in good repair, as Bustletown probably wanted to keep themselves segregated from Swampside. This was the same Swampside entrance Jorac and his squad of constables had taken before, but this time people pointed and murmured as they passed, and mostly got out of their way. Jorac decided it was partly because Dorrie was dressed in shabby finery, carrying a tall walking stick and wearing a heavy lace veil; the group appeared to be escorting her through the area. It was also partly because Schrog and Jorac had belted on short, wide swords as well as their cudgels. But probably it was because people remembered them. Still, they maintained a tight formation and kept their eyes open.

Jorac was looking up the main street when Schrog quietly said, "Got one, follow me." and steered the group down a side alley. He stopped at a stall selling stoneware mugs and bric-a-brac and stared at the stall keeper without speaking. The keeper was a small man, rusty-haired and bronze-skinned, and would have been handsome but for a wide scar across his cheek and chin.

Finally the stall keeper said, "Schrog. What are you doing here?"

"Helpin' you out, Mister. . ."

"Raah."

"Right, I remembers now. T'ought it was sump'n different, somehow. Didja know Kullo got strung up?"

"I'd heard. Means nothing to me."

"Right. You, me, we nebber friends, but we done business a time or two, and done it square. Dat right?"

Mister Raah – Jorac wondered how long he'd had that name – nodded slowly.

"So here's de square deal. Slavers is out, from now on. Brings constables to de swamp. Bad for business."

"Still means nothing to me."

"Constables might look back dere. Might find sump'n somebody else says is deirs." At Raah's hard look he added, "Not me, mind ya, nor my pals here, we got other t'ings to do. But de word come down, find de fockin' slavers, stamp on em, hard. Talk of sendin' whole army troop, or maybe just a squad wit' torches. You like dat?"

Raah just stood there with an uncomfortable look on his face.

"I figgers dey gives it a month. See who takes over for Kullo, stomp him down, not too careful-like. Den do it again when de next guy takes his place. Dis place look different den. Maybe some folks t'ink it's better all burnt down."

Raah paused to consider this. His face was a study in listening to bad news. He frowned at Schrog. "Why are you telling me this?"

"Everybody's got an angle, right? Maybe keepin' t'ings here as dey are makes my life a little easier, okay? Don' make me much difference, I don' live here. You gonna pass de word on dis?"

Raah nodded, still unhappy.

"Means you gots to stomp on 'em yourselves, right? Some bunch of punks prolly t'ink dey de next Kullo, all rich and wit' de wimmen. Boats still come for a while, lookin' for slaves. But you saw de wizards come and haul off Kullo. Maybe dey not so careful who dey take next time."

"All right. Is that all?"

"Dat's all. Oh, except we be here friendly-like. Ain't lookin' under counters, or under de false bottom of dat trunk dere. We just passin' by, de five of us. Heading deep swamp-side, some different business. Wanna pass de word on dat?"

Raah looked positively alarmed at the mention of the false bottom, but relaxed as the rest of Schrog's words sunk in.

"I can do that," he said, then turned and cupped his hands and yelled toward the street, "Runner!"

Three dirty young barefoot boys that Jorac mentally described as "guttersnipes" raced up the side street. When one of them touched the edge of the stall first the other two looked dejected, but hung around. The race winner said, "You gots a job, boss?"

"Need all three of you. Run and tell the Madame and Jimsley and Skowers that this group should be left alone, okay? There's five of them, with the giant. Tell them I say so, I'll explain tonight. And then spread out and tell anyone else you meet to leave them be. A half-copper now, and one more at sundown. Mind you, I'll ask them what time they heard from you. I'm paying for a runner, not a layabout." He handed them a small coin each. "Now go!"

The boys scampered back up the alley, and Jorac and his group all nodded politely to Raah and followed at a slower pace.

When they were back on the main street, Jorac said quietly, "That went well."

"I t'ink so" was Schrog's satisfied reply.

Chapter 7 - To The Swamp

They walked on through Swampside with no further incidents. In, fact people melted before them on the street, and even the hawkers quieted their cries as they passed; Raah's word obviously carried weight here. After about half an hour they reached the edge of town, where a final clearing marked the start of the riverside trail that led south to "deep" Swampside.

Since there was no one else in sight, they stopped there to adjust their small day-packs and their clothing. The men changed into high boots and stuffed their pants into them, and Dorrie removed her veil and fancy skirt to reveal some practical pants underneath. Having been warned about biting insects, all wore long sleeves – for Hox, long sleeves came down to only past his elbow, but he was used to that. It was nearing midday, so Jorac suggested they eat their lunch, some barely edible sandwiches they'd bought from a street vendor, washed down by water from the flasks everyone carried.

As they were finishing up, Jorac spoke to the group. "I was hoping we could avoid this, but we're going to have to go at least a little way into the actual swamp. I did a little reading about it, but I didn't find out much that would help us. Mostly they said it's dangerous, and you should have a guide, and you shouldn't touch anything you don't have to. So all I can tell you is, keep alert and don't touch anything you don't have to. We'll stop at the first place we can and do our test." And with that, they set off again.

The road began as wide, solid ground, but it soon narrowed to a winding trail, squishy in spots, that went around hummocks and through patches of sedges, some taller than even Hox. As before, Hox was at the rear and Schrog took the lead. The pace he set was slower than Jorac expected, and Schrog developed an odd head-bobbing pattern that confused him until he realized Schrog was scanning the swamp around them and the ground ahead, almost before every step.

This part of the trail showed frequent use, with matted vegetation or bare ground on the path itself, and nearby plants cut or trampled back from the margins. Sometimes small paths branched off to the side; Jorac wondered if they were game trails or led to some swamp-dweller's house, but decided to wait rather than interrupt Schrog's concentration with questions.

It was a beautiful sunny day, but it was beginning to be humid and quite warm. Jorac had been told that the wizard spell that gave Vaggert perfect weather gradually faded beyond the city's borders. He found his clothes beginning to stick to him, and there was a rich, swampy background smell of decaying vegetation. Some annoying gnats buzzed around them, but there was no other wildlife to be seen.

After Jorac idly complained about the gnats, Veseen said "Hold up, please. Last week I learned a warding spell that might work here."

He pulled some spell component out of a small pouch he carried, and explained, "I've gotten to the point I don't need the components for a few spells, but this one is still new to me. This is powdered fly wings; it should work for this."

He had everyone stand well back from him, then concentrated and slowly, carefully cast a spell. When he motioned the group back to him, Jorac saw that a small circle around the apprentice was clear of insects. Other people could enjoy it too – but only if they stood right next to him.

"I'm sorry," Veseen said dejectedly. "I wasn't trying to be selfish, but I don't think I helped anyone else with that. I was hoping I could make the circle bigger."

"No matter," Jorac said, "it was worth a try." He'd still rather work with the self-effacing youngster than any number of more powerful wizards. They all shrugged and walked on – at least when they were walking it took a little while for the bugs to find them.

It would have been a pleasant stroll except for the gnats, the squishy path, the increasingly powerful smell of decaying vegetation, and Schrog's obvious concern. At the first dry wide spot outside of town, a lumpy raised area with wide-based trees all around, Jorac called a halt so they could do a manite test.

To provide darkness, Jorac had checked a small tent out of the City Guard's supply depot and asked Hox to carry it. When they unfolded it, it proved to be a floppy canvas box tent, now very worn. To assemble it, they'd have had to find and cut poles to tie it up to, which seemed like too much trouble, so they merely used it as a big canvas wrap. Hox was too tall to fit inside, so stood guard. The other four got inside, using Dorrie's walking stick to hold up the middle, and managed to get it fairly dark. After a little while for their eyes to accustom, Dorrie did the honors again while Veseen shielded Jorac, and they marked the direction on the ground with a stick.

The inside four were happy to emerge from the canvas – it had been stifling inside – and the group talked while they folded it up and stowed it. Their mark on the ground definitely didn't point back the way they'd come, but it was hard to tell exactly what direction it did point. They squinted up at the sun and tried to figure it out. Veseen apologetically explained that a competent wizard could have told the exact direction, but he hadn't learned that skill yet. They finally decided the direction was still south, or perhaps southeast, further into the swamp but somewhat away from the river – crosswise to the trail at this point.

They stood and gazed at the thick, marshy vegetation in that direction. Everyone looked reluctant to go on, and Jorac felt the same way.

"Well, that's it, unless we can get a guide. Schrog, if we go back to Swampside, can we hire a guide?"

"Yeah, dere might be somebody in town. Take a while to find 'em, maybe dey could be trusted, maybe not." He looked down and kicked the ground a little. "But dere used to be somebody lived out dis way who could help. We can go see if dey're still dere."

"Who is it?" Dorrie asked him curiously. Jorac had warned her about asking "pre-Constable" questions, but this didn't exactly qualify, and Jorac wanted to know too, so he didn't intervene.

Schrog looked around, then up at the trees, and said, "Ummm. Err, 'twere somebody I knowed, before-like."

Jorac didn't like to see Schrog uncomfortable like this, but he needed to know. "Schrog, none of us has asked questions about your past, and we aren't going to. But it's pretty obvious you know this area and you still know some folks in Swampside. You're our expert: we need to know if we should go on, go back to Swampside and try to get a decent guide, or head back to Vaggert and get a whole squad to help us. You've been a constable for what, eight years now?"

Schrog nodded, tight-lipped, and said nothing.

"Do you think someone living deep in the swamp is still here eight years later – and would help us?"

Schrog spoke slowly, reluctantly, picking his words carefully. "Umm. I kept my ears open. Dat's all. I nebber worked down dis way as a constable, made sure o' dat, but I knows a guy who knows a guy, dat kind of t'ing. I used to know dis lady who worked de swamp out hereabouts. Last I heared, maybe six months back, she still dere."

Jorac smiled at him encouragingly; Schrog seemed to be emotionally touchy about this whole topic.

Veseen asked, "What can people do out here for a living? It seems very – uh, harsh."

Schrog's voice picked up, happier now not to be talking about himself. "Mostly de huntin' fer sump'n or anudder. Big damn cow-like t'ing wit' fat horns live out dere, good meat, good money fer de horns. Dere de big frogs, size of yer head, and de giant frogs, swallow yer head in one bite. Meat on dem no good, taste swampy, but keep you alive, and de frogskin worth some coin, de bigger de better. Big cats hunt dem frogs too. One guy used to hunt de cats but I t'ink de cats, dey got him.

"Den dere's some folks hunt fer plants, gots to be careful 'cause dey gots all kinds of spikes or poison, and some o' dem vine-traps or honeyplants will eat folks, but if you knows what's what you can make good coin dere. Plants don't move, mostly, 'cept for a few, so takes more smarts but less. . ." – he tailed off.

Dorrie suggested, "Agility?"

"Right, less agility. Good fer de older folks, or cripples, who don' wanna live in de town. Den, some folks hunt de lizards and snakes, or de little colored frogs. Poisonous, most of 'em, don' even want to touch 'em. Sells 'em to de places up in Pigtown, I hear dey goes into dyes or wizard stuff.

"An den dere's de idjits who go huntin' for stuff in de old city ruins. Dangerous place, dem ruins. A few walls and buildin's still standin' dere, but mostly just rubble under de water. But every couple years, somebody comes in with a bit of jewelry or a fancy glass bottle that ain't broke, keeps 'em in drink for a month. 'Twas wizards lived dere, so some fancy stuff laying around. Every kid in Swampside has a go at dat, first chance dey get, and mostly dey come back all cut up on de rubble, maybe sick wit' de cuts goin' bad. Some don' come back at all."

Jorac asked gently, "So what does the lady you know out here do?"

Schrog took a deep breath. "She works de plants. And she does a bit o' healin', cuts and bruises, potions fer bellyaches and fevers. She must be seventy or eighty now, dam' old fer Swampside." He looked like he was going to say more, but stopped.

Dorrie had been listening to all this with interest, and asked "How does a woman out here keep safe? I know the kind of men who'd come to this area, and they aren't the type to just leave someone be, am I right?"

"Aye, you gots the right of it. Dere's a gang or two, but lots of loners too. Anybody hurts de healer lady, dey gots big problems wit' everybody. But still dere be some idjits, so anybody live out here, dey sets up traps, fer de animals or de men, and sleeps light. You finds a shack or sump'n out here, you waits till de owner gives de okay before gettin' too close, or maybe he just finds yer body."

They were interrupted by a call from up the path. "I'm coming through. Stevens."

Schrog called back, "Stevens" and said more quietly, "Means even-Stevens, he won't mess wit' us if we don' mess wit him. If it's just de one guy, just let him by," and he motioned the group to the side of the clearing. A small thin man with a scarf covering his head cautiously approached, carrying a crossbow in his hand, though pointed at the ground. He scuttled across the clearing and up the path toward town, keeping as far away from Jorac's group as he could. As he disappeared up the path they could see he had a small overstuffed pack on his back. Schrog had drawn his sword but kept it down at his side; he sheathed it when the man had passed.

Hox wondered aloud, "What did he hunt?"

Schrog answered confidently, "Poisonous, whatever 'twere. See dat pack? Stuffed fat with dried grass, anudder bag inside. Prolly snakes or sump'n nasty."

After a moment, Jorac looked at him and said gently, "So, would you recommend we try to find the healer lady instead of going back to town?"

"Well, she used to live down de way we's goin'. It was left, right, left, right, right – dose be de turns you take at de forks. 'Tain't too far, maybe a half hour in. Wanna try it?"

Jorac looked at his group – no one objected – so he shrugged and said, "Looks like we're willing. As long as we get back while there's still good light, okay?"

"Yeah, spooky out here in de dark. Don' touch nuttin', got it? In de wet spots, jus' be real careful, and ya take quick little steps. Follow me close-like, maybe two-t'ree steps back."

With that they set off down the path, trying to follow Schrog's lead and be careful at the same time. Travel became increasingly difficult as they turned off the main path and onto less-used side trails. Still, the path was fairly distinct, once they got used to seeing it amid the vegetation.

The first two turns they were to take were fairly clear, but at the third fork the path forked into three, not two, and both of the two left forks seemed equally traveled. After they'd looked around a bit and found no clues, Jorac said to Schrog, "Maybe you can scout ahead? We should do the manite test again anyway; I'm pretty sure we've already lost our bearings."

"Yeah, okay. Don' touch nuttin', don' go nowhere. You'se could sit under dat tree dere, dat's safe grass. Somebody comes by, do Stevens wit' 'em, let 'em by, but don' trust 'em – take yer sword out, right? Back in a few minutes." He took the left-most trail, and was quickly out of sight.

The rest moved under the big spreading tree and got out the tent to perform another manite test. This time only Dorrie, Veseen, and Jorac were inside the canvas, so Hox helped by holding up the fourth corner from outside. The roof flopped a bit, but after a few tries, the inside three agreed on a direction and marked it on the ground with a stick.

When they emerged into the daylight, blinking, they started to discuss what direction the line was. "It's a good thing we tested again," Dorrie said, "I would have sworn our direction was over there." She pointed off to her side.

"Yeah," Jorac said, "lots of turns and no landmarks. That's why we could really use a guide who knows this area." He picked up a corner of the tent. "Let's see if we can get this stupid thing folded tighter this time."

Hox started straightening the canvas, finally lifting it above his head, when his hand struck the tree limb overhead. He dropped the canvas and said "Ow!" He brought his arm down and looked at the underside of his forearm. Clinging there was a small, bright orange and green frog, not much bigger than Jorac's thumb tip. Hox vigorously shook his arm, then flung it out to the side, which finally made the frog fly off into the bushes.

"That thing hurt!"

"Let me look at it," Dorrie said. "Hmmm, I can see the mark it made. Jorac, give me your handkerchief."

Jorac complied, saying "Blot, not wipe, right?"

Dorrie nodded, folded the handkerchief into a pad, and blotted the spot on Hox's arm a few times. When she was done, she looked at the handkerchief with distaste, then folded it in on itself and offered it to Jorac, who shook his head.

"I think that one can stay here – leave it under that bush. Let's get the canvas folded up and get ready to go. Hox, you just sit there."

They did as Jorac said, and then they all sat under the tree and waited.

Veseen was obviously worried, and couldn't sit still. He asked, "Should we yell for Mr. Schrog?" and was disappointed in the negative answer. Waiting was obviously hard on the boy – well, it was hard on all of them, but he showed it more.

Schrog returned a couple of minutes later; by that time Veseen was almost running in circles in the clearing, and there was a raised red welt on Hox's arm.

"I gots it figgered – hey, what happened?"

Jorac explained about the frog, and what they'd done.

"You done okay. Lemme see dat arm. Hurt much?"

Hox said, "Kind of like fire. Tingles, too."

"Put dat hand on de back o' yer neck. Keep it dere – keeps de arm up, keeps de blood out. Let's go – I knows de way now. If de lady still dere, she can help wit' dat arm."

As they fell into marching order, Veseen asked, "Will he be okay, Mister Schrog?"

"Orange ones is bad," was all he said before heading down the middle path.

* * *

Jorac noticed that Schrog set a faster pace this time; either he was confident in this part of the path or worried about Hox. They took two more right forks, and in another ten minutes or so came to a waist-high fence, woven out of some sort of cane or thick grass. There was a wooden gate in the fence, and a simple sign with the word "Madouve" and below it, a large "X" with a closed top. Down the lane beyond the gate was a small weather-beaten house perched on stilts a few feet above the swamp. Beside it was an even more ramshackle small outbuilding, also on stilts.

Schrog stopped, pointed toward the house, and said to Jorac, "You de leader, you call."

Jorac shouted out, "Hello! Anyone home?"

A lumpish figure came from behind the house, covered in loose, ill-fitting fabric. On her head (Jorac assumed it was female, but he couldn't really tell) was a large hat with a veil all around that seemed attached to the oversized tent-like garment she was wearing. Jorac supposed it kept out insects, which could be quite useful.

"Whatchoo got?" The voice was old and cracked.

Schrog shouted back, "Got coin, guy with frog trouble. Orange one."

"How many of you?"

"Two city guys, me, an ol' lady, and a boy." In a quieter tone he added, "Sorry kid, ma'am. Wanna seem harmless."

"Come in, just de hurt one. Move slow. Keep on de path." She moved around to the front of the house and picked up a crossbow there. She held it down in front of her, not threatening but ready for trouble.

Schrog called out "First guy comin'," and opened the gate. Hox's arm had a large ugly red and purple lump now, like a third of an apple just below the skin, and his normal beefy facial color was looking gray.

They watched as Hox stumbled up the lane, and at the healer's direction, sat down on a small bench outside the house. He sat down hard, and the bench promptly slid to one side and collapsed, dropping him to the ground with a sound of pain they heard from the gate, forty or fifty paces away. The healer walked over behind him and looked at the arm, then yelled out, "De lady and de kid next. Den the townie with de coin. You, swampie, last. Wait till dey get here."

Jorac followed Dorrie and Veseen up the path, and at her gesture sat on the ground next to Hox – but not before he jingled his bag of coins. His close-up look at the healer didn't reveal much. Her veil was too thick to see through, and her crossbow was a double one; it had two shots, and the bolts had some shiny paste smeared on the metal tips.

He looked more carefully at the crossbow. It was an unusual design, with a top and a bottom bow, and grooves for bolts above and below. It looked vaguely like two children's hunting crossbows grafted together, and was probably no heavier than a single-shot military model, but of course less powerful. The power wouldn't matter much if you could hit what you aimed at, assuming your target wasn't armored. What an old healer lady was doing with it was anyone's guess.

Jorac didn't like sitting on the ground. He was glad he'd practiced throwing the dagger on his belt from a sitting as well as standing position. He didn't think there was any real danger here, but he kept looking around to make sure no one else was around, sneaking up on them. If the old lady started aiming that crossbow at one of his people, he wasn't going to let her shoot without a fight. But he'd much rather work with her; Hox needed help.

To Dorrie and Veseen, she said, "You two sit dere too. Ordinarily I'd offer you a bench, but you can see what happened." Her voice was nasal and cracked, and her accent, though less pronounced, was similar to Schrog's – Jorac was starting to identify it as a Swampside accent.

When Schrog started up the path, she backed away from them to watch him and Veseen whispered, "Why is she doing this – and why are we letting her?"

Dorrie spoke out loud. "Think, boy. There's five of us, one of her – she's just being careful. Surprised she didn't make most of us wait down there. Anyway, we need her help. Look at Hox."

Hox had put is hand behind his neck again and was obviously in pain. His eyes were closed and even though he was seated, he was swaying back and forth, his breathing deep and forced. Jorac guessed he wanted to moan in pain but was too proud.

When Schrog arrived, the healer pointed to the ground and said, "Sit. Speak about de frog."

Jorac spoke up. "It was orange, about this big" – he showed by holding his fingers apart – "and had little jagged green stripes down its back."

"Green stripes, you sure?"

"It was right in front of my face. Four green stripes."

She nodded. "Wait here." As she moved sideways to go toward the house, Schrog stirred a bit on the ground and she whipped around and started to raise the crossbow. "Stay still, dammit!"

Very slowly, Schrog put his palms on the ground and shifted himself around. "Just sittin'. Ain't goin' nowheres."

She nodded. "Best not."

She disappeared inside, and Jorac immediately noticed a rustle at the reed window blind – the first thing she'd done was to check to see if anyone moved. Smart. A couple of minutes and a few checks at the window later, she came out with a wet piece of cloth and a small earthenware bottle. She was still carrying the crossbow in her other hand and still wearing the hat and veil. Jorac wondered what she looked like and why she stayed covered that way; it must have been uncomfortable and hard to see through.

She wiped the cloth on Hox's arm, and handed the bottle to Dorrie and said, "Feed dat to him. Shake it up first. 'Tis a double dose, about right for his size." She backed up, put her back against the house, and watched them, crossbow still in hand.

Dorrie, stood up slowly, shook the bottle, twisted off the stopper, and helped Hox drink it. He grimaced and said *"Bleagh!* Water." She reached behind him, found his waterskin, and opened it for him. His injured arm stayed up, and he used his other hand to take a drink of water and rinse his mouth.

"What is that stuff?" Hox looked at the bottle. "Tastes foul. Will it help?"

The healer answered him. "It be what keeps you alive. Lucky you came here straight-aways. Caught it early, you be sick now, better tomorrow. Arm good in a couple days." She went over and sat on her steps, where she could see all of them, resting the crossbow on her knee.

"Dizzy." Hox pulled up his knees and put his head between them.

Slowly, mindful of the crossbow, Jorac reached for his bag of coins. "Thank you for helping him. What do we owe you? And what should we call you? Are you called Madouve?"

"You not be swampies, or you ask de price first. We'll talk about dat later. What I want to know. . ." – she ripped off her hat and veil, and her voice changed to that of a much younger woman – ". . . is what the hell happened to my mother. Schrog, you bastard, you better start talking."

Chapter 8 - An Unexpected Reunion

The crossbow was now pointed directly at Schrog, and the old healer lady was revealed to be a young, very attractive woman with short, dark hair. Her eyes glinted, and her mouth pursed in anger – it looked to Jorac as if she was struggling to control herself. It took just a second for him to get over his surprise, then he causally reached down and put his hand on his dagger – just in case.

Schrog said nothing at first, his face amazed. With his voice almost breaking, he said, "Kimie, you're alive!"

"Fockin' right I'm alive. No thanks to you. One day I'm keeping house with my mum, and the next I'm carried into the swamp in a sack and left with a half-crazy old lady. And told not to ask any questions, nor go back, ever. What happened!" She lifted the crossbow and sighted it straight at Schrog, who looked back without blinking.

He drew his knees up and put his arms around them. In a tight, choked voice he said, "Kimie, I may deserve killin', but not for your ma. Was de first decent t'ing I done. Gimme a min here."

"It's Kimma. I ain't a little girl any more." Without the old-lady voice, she pronounced her words a little better, but still had the accent. The crossbow didn't waver at all; it was still pointed at Schrog's face.

Schrog nodded and wiped his tearing eyes with his sleeve, looked at the ground in front of him, and continued in a firmer tone. "Dis is all eight years ago. Kullo had been talkin' about a big score, I didn't know from where. Den your ma came to me, middle o' de night. She was hurt bad. Said she just killed Fergram, remember him? Short guy, liked his drink. He'd got drunk and let it slip dat Kullo's new big score was sellin' girls – not pimpin' em, dat be too easy to trace, but sell em as slaves, put em on a boat and gone. Young girls ten, twelve years old. Had him a buyer and all. You was gonna be one of dem. Anyway, Fergram talked too much, and yer ma sticks him with a knife. Didn't kills him quick enough, 'cause he stuck her too. She comes to me, says to get you outta dere. So I did."

He looked up at her "Kimma, she had a big knife hole in her belly. Blood and shit comin' out of it. You know what dat mean. Best wizard in de city might save her, but prolly not. She say to save you, don' worry about her. So, I did what she said."

He raised his hands helplessly. "I t'ink, where I'm gonna hide a li'l girl? I remember Miz Madouve, she owed me – helped her out of a couple o' jams, stopped a guy from robbin' her one time. So I puts you in dat sack, and runs out here, in de dark. No moon dat night. Got lost. Found her place in de mornin'. Had to leave you wit' her.

"Time I got back to de place, your ma was dead, and a bunch of shit started happenin'. . ." He stopped and shook his head. "Anyways, dat's what happened to yer ma."

Kimma had lowered the crossbow by this point, but it was still held at the ready. "Kullo wouldn't do that to me . . . would he? He was nice to me, and him and my ma were. . ."

"Lovers? Friends? Not Kullo. Kimma, your ma and my ma, dey be whores. Whores ain't got no friends 'cept each other. Dat's why dem two so tight. My ma be older, but dey be like sisters. Kullo, he may be a good customer, friendly, but not no friend."

Kimma thought about this for a little while. "I wondered if it was you carrying me in that sack. I was so scared! You never said a word, all night. Miz Madouve wouldn't ever tell me, neither. Said whoever took me wanted me alive and safe, dat's all she'd say."

"I figgered it best dat way. Dey finds you, den you cain't tell no one."

"So what happened to your ma? She still there?"

Schrog shook his head slightly. "Remember I said a bunch of shit went down? Dat was part of it. My ma, she was gettin' to where she did mostly cookin' and not workin' de customers much. Dey finds Fergram dead, and yer ma leave a blood trail to our place and down to de kitchen. Dat's where dey find her, dead.

"So they rousts my ma, and she don' know nuttin', but dey figures she does. Dey takin' her into de swamp, where dey can get rough wit' her, and I'm comin' back, and I sees dem first. . ." He paused a moment. "Dere was just de two of dem."

A long silence here let the listeners fill in what Schrog left unsaid. He must have gotten part of this story from one of them, and they must have not returned.

Finally Kimma said, "So then what happened? Where's your ma?"

Schrog spoke slowly. "If you go way, way past dem sunken city ruins, up past dat broke-down hill an' down de other side, you kin work your way up to de hills above de city. Hill dere be steep, broken, but you kin make it. Took us t'ree days. Eatin' dat nasty giant frog meat, got sick from de water, but we made it. Dat way, dey t'ink she just disappeared. She gots a cookin' job at some noble's house now, doin' good. I sees her maybe t'ree-four times a year, but gots to keep it quiet. . . Maybe not hafta keep so quiet no more." He looked at Jorac, who nodded.

Jorac decided he had something to add at this point. "Kullo was executed last week. The charge was slavery, escape, and murder. Repeat offender."

Schrog continued, "You know I'm a constable now? Passed de test and all."

Jorac added, "Got a good reputation. Fair man, square man. Good worker."

Schrog smiled and continued. "Got a wife too. Two stepkids, one o' my own." This was something Jorac didn't know; like most constables, Schrog didn't talk about his home life much at work.

Schrog went on. "Miz Madouve, she supposed to get you a city place. Gave her most o' my coin, a fair pile. Kept lookin' fer you in de city; one o' de reasons I took de constable job was so's I could look around. Never found you, after a while I give up; I told her to make sure you was hard ta find, and I figgered she did it. Kept an ear out for Miz Madouve's doin's, kept hearing she still livin' alone in de swamp, but o' course I nebber came myself to check with Kullo around. So what happen' wit' her?"

Kimma smiled a tight smile. "I guess I'm Miz Madouve now. She taught me how to pick the plants, and mix up the potions and when to use what – got a garden right here with some of the plants I need. And she taught me how to get by with the swamp folks. I have a couple of outfits that make me look like an old lady, and with my hair short like it is, and some face painting, I passed – she said I was her sister, come to visit. There's this one kind of tree sap dries clear and shrinks up; she'd paint lines on my face and I'd look like a wrinkled old prune. That's how she taught me the swamp; I used to go out with her every few days, and once in a while on my own.

"But she always made me hide in the house whenever someone came around here – I don't think very many folks ever knew there were two of us lived here. I used to whine to her about that. Then one time I seen two men come up, grab her, throw her down, start to rip off her clothes – and she an old lady, and ugly. I used to complain about how heavy that double crossbow was, too. Stopped complaining after that. Needed two shots, had 'em." She nodded once, with grim satisfaction.

"But she disappeared a few months back. She was getting kind of foggy in the head, went out one day and didn't come back." Kimma choked up a little, then pushed on with her story.

"So I worked on the voice" – her voice temporarily went back to the cracked old-lady intonation – "and I puts on dat fly-proof hat she wore, and now I'm de healer-lady." She walked over and put the crossbow in a rack against the side of the house. "I tried looking for her, looked around all her usual places, for days and days. She was a tough old bird, but the swamp takes more than it gives."

Schrog nodded emphatically. "True dat. Dese folks never heard dat before, but all swampies know it. Most of dem swampies says dey wanna get out, but wait to do it rich. Lots don' make it out, and damn few rich."

Kimma said, "So, Schrog, what are you doing out here, with dese folks? Seems a pretty odd bunch. . ." She stopped herself. "Oh, first we best get the big guy in the shack there, otherwise you gots to carry him. That potion kind of puts you to sleep."

They roused the groggy Hox and led him to the outbuilding and up the steps, which creaked a bit but held his weight. Inside, it was a single room furnished like a small dormitory, or perhaps hospital ward. There was a small fireplace at the end, and four beds – raised platforms with pallets on them – plus a couple of stools and a chair. The small windows were shuttered, so it was dim inside, probably all the better for resting.

Kimma found a pillow for Hox and put him on two pallets near a wall. He curled up on his side, and she covered him with a blanket.

Then she invited everyone to have a seat, and took off her muddy, bulky outerwear and hung it on a nail. Underneath she was wearing a simple shirt and pants that showed she had a good figure, not the lumpy thing she showed her clients. She casually picked up the crossbow and put it on the bed next to her, not aimed at anyone this time.

"Okay, now. What are two constables, a giant, a lady (how dare you call her an old lady, Schrog) and a teenager doing here in the swamp?"

Everyone looked at Jorac. "Well, it's a little expedition I put together on behalf of my bosses. . ." He went on to explain that, as Wizard Constable, he'd been sent to trace where mana was going here in the south part of town. He mentioned the manite test, which was the reason they'd brought wizards along, and summarized what the squad had done on its two expeditions. Veseen and Dorrie hadn't heard about how Kullo and his gang had been captured, and Schrog hadn't been told exactly what they were looking for, so they all had questions. The only thing Jorac kept to himself was his allergy to magic; Veseen and Dorrie knew, and he figured the canny Schrog might have guessed it, but he wasn't going to say anything.

He found himself talking mainly to Kimma. He liked looking at her, and appreciated her little smiles and nods. He liked her attitude too – she obviously had no idea how good looking she was, mainly because she had no one to tell her; in the city she'd have had suitors chasing her every day. *Easy, boy, easy. Listen to that Swampside accent, remember where she came from.*

"... Anyway," he finished up, "Schrog said he knew someone out here who could maybe guide us. He went ahead to scout a path, and while he was gone, Hox hit that tree branch and the frog jumped on him. Ten or fifteen minutes later, we were at your gate."

Kimma nodded understanding. After a moment she said, "Wanna try that manite test again now? I'd like to see it."

"Sure," Jorac said. "Good idea." He looked at Veseen as he said, "Dorrie, you ready?"

They both nodded, and Dorrie waved her hands in the now-familiar Exercise Number Three.

Kimma said "Ooooh, pretty!" For some reason that made everyone laugh, and they had to do it a few more times, amid general laughter, to establish a direction. They laid out a piece of string on the floor to mark it, and looked at Kimma expectantly.

"Swamp directions ain't like city directions," she said. "You can be fifty paces from someplace, take you an hour to get dere – get there safe at least, down de dry path. But anyways, I think that points over toward the ruins, maybe just off to the side."

Jorac thought a moment. "When Hox gets better, can you guide us there? We'd be happy to pay you whatever the going rate is for that."

"Yeah, I can take you there, or anyways Miz Madouve can. Shouldn't take more'n half a day if we don't dawdle. Gots me wondering too. We may have to do that test a few more times along the way, though."

She got up and peeked out the window. "Sun be starting down. You wanna try and carry the giant outta here? Or sleep here? You can stay till he wakes up. I got the blankets, but I'm short on food right now. 'Less you like frog – gots plenty of jerked frog, saves that for emergencies. Supposed to be getting some good grub carried here, tomorrow or next day. Gots plenty o' swamp cabbage, a bit of flour, not much else. Could go hunting, maybe, if you're up to it."

Dorrie said mildly, "I have a dozen breakfast pies in my pack – eggs, sausage, and cheese." When they looked at her quizzically, she added, "Jorac asked me to bring some for our breakfast, and I got a few extras, but then everyone else had already eaten this morning, so I just packed them – I figured we'd get hungry later."

Jorac beamed at her. "Dorrie, I always said you were smart!"

They all agreed they should gratefully accept Kimma's offer to stay until Hox recovered. Kimma gathered her crossbow and baggy over-clothes and invited Dorrie into her house with her to help cook. They returned with warmed-up breakfast pies and some bowls of vegetables, which smelled quite good – Schrog had told them that swamp cabbage was a delicacy, despite the unattractive name, and had to be eaten fresh. This time Kimma left the crossbow behind. She invited Dorrie to sleep in the house with her, while the men would stay in the shack and keep an eye on Hox.

Chapter 9 - A Night in a Shack

Jorac hadn't slept on a bed so lumpy in quite some time, and he awoke in the middle of the night several times, tossing and turning. He must have dozed at last, because there was some light leaking through the window shutters when he stirred again. He went outside and used the tiny outhouse (it reminded him of the one his family had when he was growing up). Here there weren't corn cobs or wads of grass, but a papery, fuzzy leaf of some sort in a small pile near the seat; it proved not as comfortable as the cotton wool used by the rich houses, but better than most alternatives.

When the Dorrie and Kimma came out of the house, the men were up and dressed for the day, and Veseen and Schrog were preparing a list of needed supplies. The squad hadn't been planning more than a day trip deep into the swamp, so they had only the one tent and little food. Hox was still sleeping, and would be another day recovering. The young giant still needed a bit of tending, and would doubtless need some food when he awoke; the pair of day-old breakfast pies they'd saved him wouldn't last him long.

It took only a few minutes for everyone to agree that Schrog and Veseen would go into town for supplies, and Dorrie and Jorac would stay here with Hox. Jorac gave Schrog some money; he'd brought quite a lot, and was mentally composing his expense report. "T'ings go right, we prolly be back by lunch time," Schrog said. "Anyti'ng else you needs?"

Jorac thought a moment. "Yeah, I'd better let our bosses know where we are." He smiled wryly. "Not that the wizards would come looking for me in time to help, but I can probably avoid a lecture if I tell them." He scrawled a brief note on the paper he'd brought and handed it to Schrog. "Can you get one of those Swampside runner boys to take it to a constable? Cerom will know where we are, and he can get word to the Wizard Council for me."

Veseen said "Master Radyry" to Jorac in a quiet voice.

Jorac nodded. "And I need to get word to Master Radyry too. I warned him Veseen might be in late last night, but we're past that already. Here, let me write another note." Jorac forced himself to take his time and wrote a flowery, respectful note to the wizard master explaining that Veseen was safe and would be needed further, stressing how valuable the boy had been on the trip. He could have written less, but it was all true, and Veseen's school marks might benefit.

After Schrog and Veseen set off, Jorac followed the women into the shack, where Kimma checked on Hox. She left a water skin near him and whispered, "He's okay," then motioned them outside so they wouldn't disturb him.

When they got outside, she said, "No fever, arm looks good. Nearly normal color, no swelling."

"When do you think he'll wake up?" Dorrie asked.

"Maybe this morning, maybe afternoon. Hard to tell. That potion mostly makes 'em sleep about one day."

"You know," Jorac said, "we haven't paid you for that potion yet. How much do we owe you?"

"Eh. Well, I tells people anywheres from fifty coppers, up to a couple hundred, depending on how well I likes em. With Schrog here. . . aw, I don't know. Call it a hundred."

Jorac knew he had barely a hundred coppers, and wanted to keep them. He reached in his pocket, opened his pouch, and pulled out a gold coin.

"Sorry, I can't pay a hundred coppers; you'll have to take this instead," he said as he handed her the gold. It was worth about five times her asking price.

"What the hell you tryin' to pull? I gave you my price." She looked as if she was going to throw it back at him.

Jorac put his hands up in a don't-blame-me manner. "Hey, I'm on expenses. I'll turn in a report and collect it back from my bosses. And remember, Hox is so big you had to give him a double dose of potion. Not to mention that you knew what potion to use for his problem and how to use it, and you're sheltering not only the patient, but four other people who came with him! I'm not sure what I gave you is even enough."

"Aw, 'twern't nothin'. Okay, I'll keep it."

Jorac said, "It's perfectly fair, even at your reasonable rates. Actually, what you've done for us is worth a lot more than that. When I get back to the city, I'm going to apply for a reward for you."

"Reward? What for?"

"You saved the life of a constable on duty. One working for the Wizard Constable, so that counts extra, and I know how to do the paperwork. We'll get you compensated."

"Aw, de orange and green frog just make ya sick for a while; it ain't like it was the orange and purple. He'd have lived."

Dorrie stepped in. "Young lady, don't low-rate yourself. You saw what Hox needed and you did it, even after you saw Schrog, and before you heard his tale. And where else were we going to get help for him? You saved his life, and he was on duty, so you get a reward from the constables, or the wizards, or maybe even both. Got to know how to play the game, make them think it's their idea. Me and Jorac can work on that. And don't forget to add on your fees when you guide us; we'll need to make sure that gets paid too." She smiled. "Of course, you've got to come into town to get it."

Kimma thought for a long moment. "Well, thanks," she said quietly. "I guess I can use the money."

Jorac had the impression she was thinking of the future for the first time in a while. He knew what that was like; he remembered the night at his father's house when he realized he had to find something better to do with his life. The next day he'd shaved the beard he'd grown with the tribesmen, and set out finding the job as a guard that eventually led him here.

Dorrie said, "If you're going to make money in your business, here's some advice. You need a special price for nobles and wizards. Five times as high."

Jorac grinned. "And I just paid it, because I'm working for the damned wizards now – begging your pardon, Madame Velosp."

Kimma was confused by the remark, so Jorac and Dorrie explained how Dorrie was able to parlay her limited magical ability, along with her theatrical skill, into a good living.

In return, Kimma explained some of the economics of her business, such as it was. Miz Madouve had a good reputation as a healer, more reliable than most. A few other healers came and went in the swamp, sometimes eking out a living for a few years while waiting for some problem in the city to quiet down. Miz Madouve's clients weren't numerous and couldn't afford high prices, so she often ended up bartering her services for food and supplies. "Sometimes I get two or three folks in a day," she said, "but I go lots of days when I don't see nobody."

Jorac asked conversationally, "So, what do you do on days like that?"

"I put on de outfit, an' Miz Madouve usually goes out swamp-crawlin'. Stuff to hunt out dere."

"Ur, um, like those soft leaves in the privy? I've never seen the like."

"Yeah, stuff like that. Maybe find some stuff I can trade. I should go out again soon, too."

"Mind if I go with you? I want to collect some more of those leaves. I imagine we used a week's supply for you, and if we're camping I'd like some more."

Dorrie volunteered, "I'll sit with Hox. I don't mind." She looked at the shack, not at Kimma.

Kimma looked at Jorac and Dorrie, obviously weighing the offer. Jorac didn't blame her for the caution; despite their constable uniforms and knowing Schrog, she'd only met them yesterday.

Finally she said, "Yeah, alright." Then her voice changed. "But out dere, I'm Miz Madouve, got it? And don't do nothin' stupid."

"I'll obey your every command. I don't want to end up like Hox." *Or with a crossbow bolt in me*, he thought, *and I know she'd do it*. Somehow, that thought more pleased than worried him; competence was something he highly approved of.

Jorac went to grab a few things from his pack and waited in the yard. When Kimma came out, she was wearing the bulky dress that disguised her figure and the thick veiled hat that hid her face. And she was carrying the double crossbow.

"You lead," she said in her old-lady voice.

Jorac went down the path, and closed the gate behind them. She turned the sign upside down when she left.

"Means I'm not dere. Anyone tries anything, dey knows de traps might get 'em. Won' set de yard traps, wit' you folks dere. Yer Dorrie, she already knows to stay out of de house."

Jorac thought it was an interesting way of handling security, as good as many others he'd seen, so he said nothing. Instead he questioned her about the plants along the path. He asked about a low bushy one with a tall thin stalk rising from its center.

The old lady voice answered him. "Dat's snakeplant. Don't do nothin' for snakebite, just kinda peels like snakeskin sometimes. Ain't good for much."

"What about that one?"

"Pop bush. Seed pods go pop after it rains. De swamp mices eat it sometimes. Not good for much either."

Jorac was fascinated, and asked about a few others that caught his eye. She explained that most of the flashy ones he was asking about didn't have much use (except for one that was poisonous). Most of the useful ones were small and blended in well with the swamp.

They went down a succession of paths, with Jorac in front, turning where he was told. Some of the "paths" were a surprise to him, for they included climbing around the base of gnarled trees on spreading tree roots, above an area of standing water. He had to hold on to the tree trunk with both hands, but she managed it easily, and they got back to slightly higher ground.

Finally they went up a thin path and came to a small rocky area ending in a dead-end hillock a little higher than most of the swamp. A few tall, broad-crowned trees grew here, unlike the broad-based ones in the lower areas.

She pointed at the trees. "Dere be your leaves. Just gotta go get 'em."

"Climb the tree there, you mean? I can do that." The limbs were fairly close and looked sturdy enough.

"Yep. You should try to get de new leaves up near de top."

It took only a few minutes for Jorac to climb up the tree and fill the small bag he'd brought. They'd have plenty to replace Kimma's stock, and for the rest of the journey. He looked down and saw that she'd turned her back to the path and removed her veiled hat. It had to be hot for her, and they were in a place where they could see people coming from quite a distance so she could do without the camouflage.

As he climbed down he said, "What's this tree called, anyway?"

"I never heared it had a name." She lowered her voice and switched from the harsh old-lady voice she'd been using. "Miz Madouve never told me about this tree. I found it myself."

"Well, you get to name it then. The soft-wipe tree?"

"Hee. No, I don't think so."

"The Butt-velvet tree? Balm of Behinds?"

Now she outright giggled. "Eh, you're good with the jokes. I don't know any jokes. Not many jokesters out in the swamp."

"You don't know any jokes?"

"Well, one."

"Let's hear it."

"It's dumb. . ."

"That's okay."

"All right. What's the difference between an apple pie and a cow pie?"

"Um, I don't know."

"Well, I'm never sending *you* to the bakery!"

Jorac laughed, and she did too – she didn't sound much like Miz Madouve when she laughed. It wasn't very funny, but she told it well. "Yep, that's dumb," he said with a smile. "You should learn more jokes." What he really thought was that she should laugh more, but he couldn't say that to her.

"Well, maybe. Never thought about it much."

"Oh yes," he said rather bitterly. "I know the feeling. Too busy with today's troubles."

She turned and looked at him. "How do you know about that?" Her voice was her own, pitched low and intent.

Jorac sighed. She deserved an explanation, but not the usual tale he told young men who'd just been dumped by their sweetheart. "My wife and daughter died in a fire. Seven years ago. For a few years after that, I don't think I was very good company."

She looked at him with surprise. "At least it's better knowing, I guess. I always wondered about my ma."

"I'm not sure about that. I saw. . . I saw the cradle, the one I carved, or what was left of it after it burned. Maybe I shouldn't have gone in there, but I had to know." Jorac's voice grew husky, and tears welled in his eyes a little. He'd never talked about this before, but somehow he felt she'd understand.

Her eyes went wide, her face very solemn. "Oh. Maybe not better. Different, anyway."

"I'd go that far. But after a few years raising hell, I went back home, took a wagon guard job, finally ended up a constable."

"You like it?"

He thought for a bit. "I guess so. It's kind of like what you do; I get to help people now, at least sometimes."

She stood there for a little while. Jorac couldn't read her face, but it looked like she was considering something. He decided it was a good face, not just a beautiful one, but one with character too.

Finally she said quietly, "Good to hear."

Nice face, but watch yourself. Jorac found his mind going down a little-remembered path, one of interest in a young lady without a small part of his mind constantly worrying about her safety. *At least this girl can take care of herself.*

She put back on her veiled hat, and pitched her voice back into the old-lady tone. "Eh, we should be goin'. Schrog be back soon."

* * *

When they got back, all was as they left it, but it quickly changed. Within a few minutes, Schrog and Veseen returned, and when they took their packs into the shack, they found Dorrie talking to a just-awakened Hox.

Jorac asked, "How you feeling?"

"Like I slept too long, that's all. My arm doesn't hurt much now. Need a drink, need to go to the necessary." Dorrie handed him the waterskin, and Jorac and Schrog helped him to his feet. After a few moments to steady himself, he walked out to the jakes. Jorac walked with him, just in case.

Kimma came out of her house to watch Hox walk back to the shack. "Still feeling a bit dizzy, are you?"

"Yes ma'am. Thanks for that potion."

"Glad to help. Let me see that arm... yeah, looking good. Well, eat a bit, rest, get a good meal tonight, and tomorrow you'll be good as ever."

Hox nodded groggily and went back inside. He sat carefully on the sturdiest-looking bed and found it held his weight, and Dorrie showed him the cold and soggy breakfast pies, now over a day old, which he ate happily. Jorac figured with him eating like that, he was going to be fine.

* * *

Schrog had bought mostly food that would keep for a few days – salted meat, eggs, a pot of pickled vegetables, waybread – and also some fresh fowl and fruit for this evening. They spent the afternoon discussing the swamp, repacking, and resting. Jorac and Schrog found some tools and roughly repaired the bench that Hox had broken so that it was as good as before, which wasn't saying much.

That night, Kimma invited them into her house, which was smaller but more comfortable than the shack they'd slept in. Jorac was surprised at how clean and nicely decorated it was, out here in the middle of the swamp; inside it looked like a home, not a shack. Kimma and Dorrie cooked again; Jorac and Schrog had offered to help but were turned down with amused grins.

The dinner was good, and they talked mainly about cooking and food; it was a friendly topic, one everyone could join in. Kimma admitted she wasn't much of a cook. She'd never paid attention when she was a young girl living in the city, and though Miz Madouve was a good cook and taught her some things, they only had what the occasional trader brought them and the limited larder of the swamp to work with.

Schrog talked about his mother's job, cooking for a big house. "Kimma, if you want, my ma can teach ya' cookin'. Good cookin', I mean. She got some sauces fit fer de emperor."

Kimma looked at him with interest, and Dorrie added, "Yeah, that's something you need to think about – getting some training and finding a position. Do you really want to spend your life out here in the swamp, hiding from everyone? Some folks want to be alone, but you don't really strike me as that kind of person. And a woman alone, well you already saw what happened to the old Miz Madouve."

"I used to think about that all the time. Not so much recently. Been too busy keeping Miz Madouve from doing something foolish. Why, you got some idea?"

"Nothing specific yet, but I'll think on it. I know some people at the market in town, and I can ask them." She paused a moment. "When I'm working with my customers, I'm. . ." – she dropped her voice a half-octave and added a slightly spooky overtone – "Madame Velosp, at your service. What would you have me ask the spirits on your behalf?" Her voice returned to normal as she continued, "Can you do any different accents? Might help me figure out what kind of job we can find you."

Kimma looked demure and said, "My mother always asked me to speak with the utmost accuracy, good diction, and correct grammar." She said it in a cultured, upper-class accent.

Everyone stared at her as she continued. "My mother was quite forceful on the subject. She asked me to listen to the manner of speaking in certain of the card rooms. She had me assigned to serve drinks and wait quietly in the corner, when the right sort of people were there. Also, she had one or two of her gentlemen friends converse directly with me, and asked me to observe their particular linguistic practices, and emulate them when the occasion suited."

Jorac was floored. Speaking like that, she'd be accepted in any of the finer places in the city. Better than he would, to be truthful – he was still working on losing the last of his farm-boy accent and improving his vocabulary. People's manner of speaking was important in the city, and it had taken him a while to figure this out.

Then her usual accent returned. "But I figure talking that way 'round here ain't no good. Draws attention."

Jorac's open admiration must have showed, because she looked at him, blinked twice, and looked away, a little embarrassed.

Dorrie said, "Girl, you've got a real talent there. I *know* we can find you a place in the city."

"Well, maybe," Kimma said doubtfully. "But Miz Madouve ain't ready to go traipsin' off yet. Got too many good customers here, and they depend on me. Who'd do the healin' if I left 'em?"

"Didn't you say there were a few other healers?"

"Well, yes, but they come and go. Sometimes they go back to the city, sometimes they make a bad mistake and the swamp gets 'em. Miz Madouve was – is – the only steady one."

"Oh, I understand," Dorrie said. "Well, we can think about it. We'll talk later." And then the conversation drifted off to other subjects.

That night, trying to get to sleep on his lumpy pallet in the shack, Jorac thought about the possibility that Kimma might be willing to leave the swamp. Dorrie was right: with the girl's amazing facility with language, she could do very well in the city. . . He sternly put that intriguing idea aside and thought about tomorrow. Now with Hox essentially recovered and "Miz Madouve" to guide them, they could go on and follow where the disappearing manites led, at least for another day or two. If nothing was resolved by that time. . . well, he'd just have to decide what to do then.

Chapter 10 - Following a Guide

Early the next morning the group grabbed a quick breakfast and loaded up for their journey toward the ruins, following Kimma and Schrog's suggestions about what to bring. Schrog's sword was left behind in favor of a large knife he buckled on his thigh. Hox was given Schrog's regular-sized cudgel, but Dorrie's walking stick was kept, as was Jorac's sword. "One of each" seemed to be the plan.

Finally, they were ready to move out. Kimma donned her bulky clothing and concealing hat, and became Miz Madouve, complete with the old-lady voice. "Best I talks dis way all de time out dere. Sound travels sometimes."

She had them all go down the path a short distance from her house, and then went back. "A little sump'n to welcome de folks who shouldn't be dere." She went into the house for a minute, then picked up her crossbow on her way back. As she came down the path, she moved a few stones that marked the path's edges – now it led the other way around a large rock, where Jorac figured there was a trap of some sort. Rough place, this was.

She turned the sign at her gate upside down, and said, "All set. Schrog, you lead off, I'll trail."

Hox said, "I'm always in the back, because I can see over everyone."

"And I can hide behind you, and I gots dis" – she patted the crossbow. "Go on. Stop at de forks if ya wanna talk it over. To start we wants left, sharp right, straight."

As Jorac and his city-dwellers learned, the swamp had three distinct types of land. First was waterlogged bogs or weed-choked ponds; you could see best in this type of area, but the only way to cross them was to wade or swim, and the water was brackish and cold, so these were avoided. Then there was a sort of watery forest with big droopy trees standing in shallow water, interspersed with occasional drier islands of thick, thorny underbrush.   You could cross these areas by walking on the slippery, spreading tree roots; often some swampie had left a log or a rock in a strategic place allowing easier passage. The easiest to cross, but hardest to see across, were the drier areas with raised hummocks of grasses and tall sedges. The three types were intermixed, so within a couple of minutes, Jorac found himself helping Dorrie cross a small pond on a fallen tree, making good time across a grassy area, then following the group stepping gingerly across a succession of tree roots, carefully holding on to the tree branches and trying not to get their feet wet.

More than once someone's feet slipped, but they were moving slowly and were both lucky and careful, so no one fell completely in the water. The water here was full of muck, algae, and tiny insects.   Yesterday, preparing for this trip, they'd learned you had to both filter and boil the water if you wanted it to be safe to drink – and even then, it never tasted very good.

They'd been working their zigzag way across the swamp for about an hour when they first started seeing the occasional standing wall, in the distance, never close to the path. It was another half-hour before they could get close enough to the half-sunken city to see some of the ruined buildings. They certainly weren't the first visitors here: starting at the outskirts, bricks and stone from the nearby buildings had been used to make rough paths that led into the city. This made travel easier, and as soon as they came to a more-intact old building that gave them enough darkness, Jorac called a halt and they once again checked the direction the manites went. Almost straight ahead; slightly to the right.

Miz Madouve's voice came from behind the veiled hat. "Damned luck. Of course, dat's de only kind I got."

"What do you mean?" Jorac asked.

"We comes in at de top of de city, and now we aimin' at de bottom. I could'a picked a different path, we'd be dere now."

"Or it might be somewhere in the middle of this area?" Dorrie suggested, ever the practical one.

"Maybe, but not with my luck." She pointed ahead. "Anyways, we can go mostly straight now. Easier to find a path t'rough dese ruins, but gots to watch out all the same – dere be some gangs dat like to work dis area, diggin' up de old wizard-stuff. And stay out of de water, nasty stuff hereabouts."

They worked their way slowly, carefully through the ruined city, climbing over piles of rubble and traversing roofs and the upper levels of roofless buildings to avoid the oily, stagnant water that came up to about the tops of the buildings' door frames. It had been over eighty years since Aplath's Rebellion had been crushed here, but much was still surprisingly intact. A number of brick and stone buildings had apparently collapsed when the streets were suddenly lowered and the water rushed in, but some sturdy buildings were still standing, their timbers covered with moss. There were no trees here, although low, waxy-leaved shrubs grew everywhere in the rubble; Miz Madouve said not to touch them, they were mildly poisonous. The air smelled dank and mildewed, with a strange, unnatural undertone.

As they got further into the city, Jorac noted more signs of human passage – an occasional symbol scratched on a still-standing wall, or a cut log placed to let them cross a flooded street. As in the swamp, Kimma seemed to know exactly where they were going, directing them along a mostly invisible path. They'd just been climbing over the unsteady roof of a partly collapsed brick building when they heard the ring of a metal tool hitting stone, off to the side of their route. Schrog and Jorac both immediately held up their hands, meaning "stop and be quiet." They heard it again; it was coming from a clump of somewhat more intact buildings ahead.

They huddled together for a quiet conference. Jorac asked, "Should we try to go around? Or talk to them?"

Schrog shrugged. "Might help us to ask 'em about dis area – maybe dey knows what's off in de direction we goin'. Six of us, prolly pretty safe."

Miz Madouve nodded agreement. "I be de healer-lady, so I best does de talkin'. I won' call out till we gets close, don' wanna scare 'em."

Schrog hesitated, then nodded. "I backs you up. I should carry dat crossbow." She agreed and handed it to him.

He examined it with some curiosity. "Ain't dis too light to do de job? Not much range."

"Don' need much range here in de swamp. De second shot more den worth it."

"If'n you say so. . ." he said dubiously.

Jorac said to her, "I'll be on your other side. Behind us, Hox, then Dorrie. Veseen, you bring up the rear. Look around all the time, never mind what they're doing up front, and call out if you see anything moving, anything at all. Oh, one more thing." He looked at Miz Madouve. "Maybe you need to hobble a little bit more – or was the old lady that spry?"

Jorac got a very quiet "I was planning on it, thanks" in a small, girlish voice. Then she continued, a little louder, in the cracked, old-lady voice. "She used ta hold onto my arm an' say 'Oh, my aching legs' – 'cept when she'd spot some sweet berries or sump'n, den she'd leggo my arm 'n beat me to 'em."

Jorac said, "Quite a character." Even he wasn't sure if he meant the old lady or this new hybrid.

Dorrie said, "If you want to learn how being old and tired looks, just watch me. I don't have to act." Everyone smiled at this, but she had a point. A two-hour walk like this, across rough terrain, was hard on everyone.

They started toward the hammering noises, with Miz Madouve acting properly rickety and holding Jorac's right arm, and Schrog a little off to her other side with the crossbow in his right hand.

"Yo!" Miz Madouve's old-lady voice wasn't loud enough, so Schrog yelled, "Hey, swampie!"

That got their attention, and a couple of men climbed up out of a ruined house and onto a flat roof next door. They were dripping wet, and a third man appeared and handed them cloaks to cover themselves. The weather was mild and sunny, but the swamp water was frigid; Jorac wondered how they could stand it.

"What do you want?" the third man yelled back.

"Miz Madouve wants to talk. Stevens," Schrog yelled.

After a brief conference, the third man yelled back, "Come on in." They could see that one of the others said something to him, and he added, "Stevens!"

Jorac's group worked their way toward the three men. When they got about halfway there, Veseen said quietly, urgently, "Pssst. I saw something move, in the building next to them. That tall one, I saw something on the roof."

Jorac said, "Got it. Good work. I'll watch that place; you keep looking around."

As they approached, they could see that a long, narrow, flat-bottomed boat had been towed up to the flat-roofed building, filled with tools and supplies. When they got near the men, they saw that the two who'd been in the water were covered up to their neck with some sort of heavy grease, and looked like brothers. They shivered a little despite the cloaks. The one who'd brought them the cloaks was older but taller, stronger, and better dressed; he spoke first.

"You are Miz Madouve, I take it?"

Before she could respond, one of the workers spoke up. "O' course she be Miz Madouve. Good ta see ya again."

"Hatlo, Hario, you look. . . wet."

"Aye, ma'am. Basements hereabouts have some good loot sometimes, but it don' come ta you."

The dry man started to speak to them, but Schrog interrupted. "Now dat you seen we's wit' Miz Madouve, why doncha get yer guy down from dat roof? Makes me nervous-like." He'd been carrying the crossbow hanging down a little behind him, and now he just turned his elbow and shoulder to move it forward a little, showing them the crossbow without raising it.

The larger man looked surprised, but Hario just looked disgusted. "Told ya, Gleben. Cain't sneak up on swampies."

Gleben turned and yelled, "Toop, come on down. We got visitors."

Hatlo yelled, "Miz Madouve's here. It be safe," and in a quieter voice told Gleben, "You gots to let him know dat."

Toop cautiously put his head around the corner of the building, then slung his crossbow across his back and started to gingerly climb down a wobbly staircase.

While they stood waiting for him, Miz Madouve looked at Hatlo and Hario and said, "How's yer ma doin'?"

Hatlo said, "She gets ou--, I mean, she comes back from her visit to her uncle next month."

Hario added, "Dat visit, up in de dry country, do her good."

Even Jorac could read between the lines; their mother wouldn't be the first to need a jail term to stop drinking.

"Dat's good," Miz Madouve said. "You'ns come on by when she's back, right? Couple of potions I want her to teach me." The two brothers nodded.

When Toop joined them, Hatlo looked around at Jorac's team and said to the healer, "Not dat we ain't glad to see you, but whatcha doin' out here? Not de usual type of folks dat come out here, right? Somebody need healin'?"

She said, "Everybody's gotta bring in de coin sometimes, right? I'm doin' some guide work. What kinda angle you workin'?"

Hatlo said, "Gleben here t'inks he gots a lead on some fancy jewelry in a basement hereabouts."

Gleben added importantly, "I obtained a book, with an old map in it, that showed some of the businesses that used to be in this area. I believe this is the street that had a magic shop specializing in lockets, amulets, and charms. The end of Aplath's Rebellion was both unexpected and quite sudden, and from what I've read, most people seemed to think themselves lucky just to escape with their lives. Therefore, I deduced that there should be some abandoned merchandise still salvageable, and of course items that old are rare, and quite valuable."

"Hmmm. Interestin', good luck to ya," said Miz Madouve. "We jus' needs a little favor. You know anyt'ing unusual over dat way?" She pointed off toward the last direction they'd watched the manites go.

Hario and Hatlo looked at each other doubtfully. Toop looked at the two with a raised eyebrow, then said, "We gotta tell her. She's de healer. Always need favor from a healer."

Hatlo said, "Yeah, but. . . Okay, you tell her. Don't sound right if I tells it."

Toop said, "Don't sound right no matter who tells it. But I'll try. . . Lesee, over dat way, maybe twelve or fifteen blocks, is a yellow house. It's made all o' yellow brick, only one dat's two stories, wit' a big roof someone added, looks newer. Sits up on a little rise, not so wet dere. I first heared de story maybe ten years back, from an old swampie who's dead now. Said him and two other guys found dis yellow house, door sealed shut, and when one of 'em climbed in de window, he disappeared. Heared a scream, dat was all. So de other guy chases in after him, and he disappears too. First guy, never seen no more. Found de second guy later, crawlin' out of a pond, said he was suddenly way high in de air over de swamp. Twice lucky – he hit a pond, not a tree or sump'n, and he could swim a little.

"After a couple days, dey go back to look at de house again – tossed a rock in de window, heard it hit de floor. Tossed a rat in de window, listened real close. It didn't hit de floor, but dey heard sump'n crash tru' de trees a ways away. After dat, dey don' never go near dat area agin. No tellin' what other weird stuff happen 'round dere. I was dere once, tossed a frog in de downstairs window. Same t'ing, it never hit de floor inside. You can see inside, looks empty, just a little dirty."

The two brothers nodded wisely, and Hatlo said, "All us ruin runners know about dat house. Sometimes a new guy shows up, wanna be chief. He be a good guy, we let him know ain't no chiefs out here, we do pairs and partners and such. He make trouble, be a bully, well, first t'ing he try is make us tell him about our new finds. So we tells him about dis great find, in dis yellow house. And de problem goes away."

Gleben listened, fascinated, and a little worried. "Am I a chief, then, in your way of thinking?"

Hario smiled and said, "Naw, don' worry, you a boss, ain't no chief. So long as you pays us, you be de boss and we does what you say, unless we quit. Chief, he try to tell us what to do, no pay, no quittin'. Besides, you pays coppers, plus de ten percent of what we finds."

"Ten percent each," said Hatlo.

"Each," said Toop.

"Yes, ten percent for each of you – but first we pay the expenses, your food and wages, then we split up the rest. And why are we repeating this? I don't mind clarifying it, I'm just curious."

"Dat way de healer-lady hears it. T'ings go bad, she heared it, maybe get t'ings straight."

Gleben nodded, satisfied. "Ah, I see. A trusted intermediary. There is a long and hallowed tradition. . . well, some other time. I suppose I'm more a scholar than a treasure hunter. I suppose we should return to our questing."

When Gleben had first started speaking about their treasure hunt, Jorac had thought of Dorrie's ability to find hidden things. While Gleben's crew prepared to get back to work, Jorac pulled her aside and said quietly, "Think you could find that jewelry?"

"Good chance."

"Maybe pay off that favor right now, so Kimma doesn't owe them?"

She looked at him with a twinkle. "Yeah, I like her too. Let's do it."

They rejoined the others, and in her deeper voice, Dorrie said to Gleben, "Madame Velosp has a question for you. Can you accurately describe the jewelry you are searching for? Have you seen identical ones, or ones very similar?"

Gleben asked, "Who is Madame Velosp?"

Dorrie said, "You are speaking to her, sir. You might find it. . . profitable. . . to answer the question."

Jorac said, "Madame Velosp is a licensed wizard, and a specialist in finding items lost."

With a what-the-hell gesture, Gleben said. "A couple of types I know about. Sometimes it's a little bottle – usually silver, or blue glass, with a little ribbon around the neck, or sometimes a little silver chain instead. Maybe three fingers high, half that across, plus a stopper of the same material, sometimes plain, sometimes fancy. Or it could be a green or black locket – perfectly round, with a little hinge that opens up to let you store something inside. Will that do?"

"Admirably." She nodded at Veseen to shield Jorac, closed her eyes and concentrated. In about three minutes she started slowly turning around, her eyes still closed, then opened them. She pointed down the street.

"On this street, perhaps half a hundred paces away, there are two ruined houses, both made from the same dark red brick, that started out as copies of the other. In the street in between them, there is an underground cellar between the two houses, now flooded. You should dig there."

The men stared at her, unsure of what to make of her pronouncement.

Jorac spoke up. "Madame Velosp does not wish Miz Madouve to owe any favors on her behalf. If the items you seek are there, will you consider the debt discharged?"

Gleben raised his eyebrows and said slowly, "I suppose so. Are there more than just one or two?"

Dorrie said, in chilly tones, "There are. You need not doubt Madame Velosp," and turned away.

Jorac motioned to his group, and they prepared to go. Miz Madouve's voice came from under her veil. "We be headin' out den. Thank'ee for your help. Maybe we sees you on our way back."

The treasure hunters were deep in a discussion about whether to try looking where Dorrie suggested or continue under the current house, and just waved as they departed.

Chapter 11 - An Odd House

Jorac's team moved on for a few blocks, until they found a sheltered attic where they could do another manite test and talk about where they were going. Their test showed the manites still disappeared in the same direction – according to the ruin runners, the direction of the yellow house. Maybe the manites moved a little faster now, or started moving a little earlier before they dissolved, but it was hard to tell for sure.

"What do you make of that tale?" Jorac asked. "Assuming their story is true, a house with properties like that has to be wizard-powered, doesn't it?"

"Gotta be," said Schrog.

Veseen said, "I think I know what might be protecting that window; I learned about it in school. It's called a Rematerialization spell. It causes the target to dematerialize in one place and reappear somewhere else. It's a simple spell, but it only works on things that are very light, or are alive, and it takes a lot of energy. Especially if the target reappears far away."

"Hmmm," Jorac said. That was probably the spell the Council-level wizards used at the tower; if that kind of energy-hungry magic was running automatically here in the swamp, his bosses would certainly like to know about it. "I think we need to go check out the yellow house and see if it acts the way Toop described it, and then we can have lunch." After lunch, he thought, they could do one more manite test on the far side of the house to confirm that where the manites are going, and then they all could go home. It had already been a long, tiring day, and it wasn't even quite noon.

They set off again, through a somewhat higher area that looked as if it had been an affluent suburb; the water was shallower here, and there were even a few trees. On the way, Kimma produced a small noose-necked net from her reticule and used it to snare a frog – a dull green one, which she pronounced safe to handle. After a few blocks, Hox said he thought he saw a yellow house, and a few steps later they could all see it.

Jorac led them on a wide path around the far side of the house, and they found a small ruin to help get the darkness for the mana test. No one was surprised when the manites zoomed straight at the rise where the yellow house sat. They folded the little tent for what they hoped was the last time, talking in low, quiet tones.

They picked their way carefully to the yellow house, which looked exactly as described. It was on a little hill, so they could walk right up to it; the ground around it was rocky and mostly bare, with a few forlorn tufts of grass.

Jorac said, "Just stand back and look for now, and look at the other houses too. Don't get too close." The nods he got from the group told him that everyone was thinking the same – the swampie's story had them all spooked.

They walked all around the raised area, listening and watching, but all was quiet. The yellow house was in much better shape than most of the buildings in the general area, but there were a few mostly intact houses right around it, so it didn't look out of place. The house itself was rather small, but the steeply pitched roof was oversized and overhung the walls by quite a bit. They walked around it and saw that there was indeed just the one, wide-open window on the first floor, and around the corner, a bricked-up doorway. Upstairs were four windows centered under the high point of the roof, a pair on each end.

Back on the side with the ground-floor window, Jorac said, "Lets move well back, and toss in that frog."

They all moved away from the house, and Kimma opened the neck of the net. She grabbed the frog through the net and tried to toss it into the window, but it stuck to the net, so she missed rather badly. It flew in a high arc and hit the house between the two upstairs windows, a good ten feet above the ground-floor window she'd aimed for. There might have been a slight "zap" sound as it bounced off the house; then it fell to the ground with a plop and lay on its back with its legs making crawling motions, clearly stunned.

The group all looked at each other, puzzled and a little scared.

"Maybe it hit its head?" Hox said dubiously.

"Maybe. . ." Jorac was not liking this. He was almost ready to push the three eyes on his badge of office and summon a wizard, whether one arrived with a bad attitude or not.

Veseen spotted another frog not far away, and Kimma used her net to catch it.

She said, "I'll get it through the window this time. I'll use my hand."

Jorac said, "Not too close, please? Seems risky. Everybody quiet now, see if it lands inside."

She stopped three or four paces from the house and tossed the frog cleanly through the window. Jorac thought he heard a slight "swoosh" sound, but that was all – it definitely didn't hit the floor inside.

Jorac said to Hox, "Big Guy, what can you see inside there? You have the best angle – don't get very close of course."

Hox walked around a bit, looking through the window from various angles. "Leaves, mostly. Weeds blown in. Stairs going up, look wooden, kinda swollen and warped. Floor's too dirty to tell if it's stone or wood. Fireplace, benches nearby. Just the one room I think. Can't see any stairs going down." He craned his head a bit, but Jorac stopped him before he got too close.

"That's plenty. Come on back here."

Jorac looked up at the two windows on the second floor. One had closed shutters; the other was mostly open, with its left shutter missing and its right one hanging loose on rusty hinges. He said, "Remember how that first day, the wizard said we should have brought a wagon? What we should have brought this time is a big tall free-standing ladder. I want to look in that window up there."

Schrog snorted. "Yeah, I mosta time gots one in me back pocket, just fergot it today."

Jorac looked down where the first frog was still writhing. "But I don't want to touch that house, that's for sure." He looked at Hox, and Veseen, and the windows.

"Hox, do you think you could lift Veseen up enough to look in those windows? Have to stand further back. If you get unbalanced, you don't want to come close to the house."

"Hmmm. Should be able to. Could maybe lift him holding his ankles. Need to practice a little first."

"Veseen, you willing?"

"Sure! Sounds interesting. But grabbing me by the ankles would probably hurt – let's find a stick I can stand on, then you lift the stick. I can balance pretty good."

It took longer than expected to find a usable stick. They had to walk a few minutes to find a tree; there Hox reached up and hacked off an arm-thick branch using Jorac's sword.

While Hox was practicing lifting the branch and Veseen overhead, Dorrie had some practical advice. "We need to stand around and get ready to catch Veseen – break his fall anyway. We might get bruised, but we'd save him from breaking his head."

Schrog said, "Yeah, good idea. I'll stand in de middle, by de house, stop 'em from getting too close-like. You ladies on de sides, Jorac in de back."

And so it was decided. After a bit of practice, they were ready to try it in earnest. Hox held the branch at waist height, and Jorac and Schrog boosted Veseen onto it, sitting. Hox slowly raised the branch overhead and walked toward the house until Schrog told him to stop. After Hox widened his stance and steadied, Veseen was able to stand up on the branch.

Jorac, standing a few feet behind Hox, just barely managed to stop himself from asking "What do you see?" Veseen shaded his eyes with his hands and peered inside. He also moved from side to side on his perch a few times, worrying Jorac. Finally he started talking.

"There's a bed there, I can see the bottom of it. And a big ball of some kind next to it. Ball is maybe metal of some kind? Hard to tell. Room isn't dirty like down below, looks clean. How does the dust stay out? Bed has posts on the corners. Bed cover is all shiny white. I think there's someone in the bed, looks like it but hard to tell. Let me sit down here... Okay, can you move to the right a bit? Steady... Okay, I'm standing up now. Yeah, someone in the bed with a big beard. Can't see well enough to tell if he's breathing or not. Let me get closer..."

"No! That's enough. Come on down."

Hox lowered him gracefully, still standing, to a height where he could easily jump down.

"That beard looked like it would come down to his waist, but it was all spread out, over his shoulders and such. I think that ball is metal – it's kind of dark in there – but it's real big, taller than the bed."

"Okay, that's enough. I'm going twenty paces back. The rest of you stay here, so you won't get frozen while I call the wizard."

Jorac backed off, well away from the group, took out his badge of office, and pressed the three red eyes of the cow on its face.

Nothing happened.

He pressed it again, with similar result. He'd been hoping for a quick ride back to the city on a flying carpet, with powerful wizards checking out this obviously strange house, but it seemed he was too far from the city for the spell to work. Now they'd have to walk back to Kimma's, and it would be another day before he could get back to the city and make his report.

He walked back to the group and said, "No luck. For some reason it didn't work – maybe we're too far out from the city, or maybe it wasn't charged right last time."

Jorac could hear the smile in Kimma's old-lady voice. "I told ya about my luck, right? Bad, terr'ble, an' worse. We can walk back okay – anyt'ing else ya wanna do here?"

"No, I don't think so. You think you can find this place again, Schrog? I'm pretty sure our guide here could."

"Yeah, I knows where dis place is now."

"Okay, let me get a drink and. . ."

Suddenly, Jorac erupted in a sneezing fit – one head-shaking, powerful, rapid-fire sneeze after another, almost every breath. He looked at Dorrie and Veseen, but both looked at him and each other quizzically, then shook their heads.

"Veseen, can you – *achoo!* – try to shield me? *Achoo!*"

"I'm trying. I don't know what's going on!"

Kimma almost forgot the old-lady voice for once. "Why is he sneezing like that?"

In between sneezes, he waved at Dorrie. "Tell them. *Achoo!*"

"He's allergic to magic – makes him sneeze. That's why they made him the Wizard Constable in the first place."

By this time, Jorac was bending over, his body wracked. He sneezed once more, then suddenly felt better, and looked up at Veseen, who had his brow furrowed in concentration.

Veseen said, "I can't tell what caused that. Hox, can you just lift me up, so I can look in there?"

Hox immediately bent down and grabbed Veseen's ankles, lifted him up, and carried him to near the open window. "The bed is empty!"

Jorac shouted, "Back away and put him down. Let's get out of here!"

Hox turned away from the house and put the teenager down, and everyone started to run, heading back the way they'd come.

But they only got a few steps when they were paralyzed in place. What it felt like to Jorac was invisible ropes suddenly tying his entire body in place. He heard a crash of brick behind him, and tried to turn and look, but merely strained his neck muscles. Then he heard a hoarse, triumphant laugh behind him.

Chapter 12 - Sleeping Wizards Lie

Despite being frozen in place, Jorac could still move a little. He was breathing without difficulty, and though it hurt a bit, he could wiggle his muscles, pressing against invisible restraints. He could also turn his head a trifle, and could move his eyes to look around at his companions. Unlike him, they appeared to be completely frozen in position, the way Kullo and his cutthroats had been.

A voice came from behind him. "Allergic to magic casting, are you? Well, I've wrapped you up just so. The others, they just received that spell of yours I captured, but you get special treatment. Not sneezing, are you? I very much hope you appreciate the care I've taken." The mocking voice was so raspy it was hard to understand. The accent, however, was rather upper-class.

Jorac discarded his first few replies, which ranged from gibbering to screaming, and took a deep breath. He responded in as level a tone as he could manage, "No, I'm not sneezing. Thank you." He did his best to imitate the same upper-class accent, making it even more noble if he could.

"I've just hardened the air around your body – but not your face. No one else would have thought of it."

Jorac said politely, "I daresay you are right, sir wizard. I've never heard of it before." He paused a moment. "Not to be presumptuous, sir, but may I please ask whom I'm speaking to?"

"You may call me Wolburn. Wizard Wolburn. Has a nice ring to it."

"I've always admired alliteration, also. I am Wizard Constable Kellor. Under different circumstances, I would bow, or at least nod my head to you. Please forgive the lapse."

"Oh ho! He has a sense of humor!" The wizard giggled. "What a joyful day this has turned out to be. I say, Wizard Constable, if I loosen your bonds a little, will you agree to behave?" He giggled again; it didn't sound joyful, it sounded nervous.

"I certainly will try not to do anything foolish."

"Very well then. Just a moment."

Jorac felt the bonds around him move away; he wasn't sure if they'd been dissolved or merely pulled back. He turned around and got his first look at Wizard Wolburn.

The wizard was slight, a little shorter than Jorac and quite thin. His most striking feature was his beard, a huge salt-and-pepper mass covering most of his chest. His clothes, obviously just donned, were stiff and creased where they'd been folded. His face wore an arrogant grin.

Jorac said, "Pleased to make your acquaintance, sir wizard," and gave a formal bow, with his best outstretched hand and back-kicked leg, then continued, "How might I be of service to you?" In performing the exaggerated bow, his foot didn't feel anything but his hand brushed against something, presumably the "hardened air" Wolburn had mentioned.

"Ah, courteous too. It will be a shame to have to kill you, but of course I'll have to. That damned Council won't take me seriously unless I deliver a message in a manner they'll take heed of."

"Are you referring to the Council of Wizards, sir? I must then correct your misapprehension. I strongly suspect they'd scarcely take notice of my disappearance or untimely demise, and any notice they took would, I fear, be positive." This was stretching the truth, and Jorac realized he'd need to be more careful. It was best to be sincere when talking to wizards; they couldn't read minds, but some of them could detect lying.

"Oh, those stinking bastards don't like you? You'll have to tell me more. I've been, uh, indisposed for a few years." He giggled, sounding manic and not quite sane. Then he stopped suddenly and his face fell. "I hope you'll forgive me for my language. I've not been around gentlemen for quite a while."

"No apologies needed, sir; you were provoked. I know those – *individuals* – too." The venom he put into the statement was quite real, as he thought of all the problems he'd had with wizards like Ruejeo and Banloz.

He must have been convincing, because Wolburn said, "You know the Council? Who leads it now?"

"I believe it's Pergimtor, sir. He's an arrogant, surly fellow. Unfortunately he's the one who is the ultimate superior in my chain of command, in the position I currently hold at least. So I've had the misfortune to deal with him."

"Fascinating. You must tell me more. Come up to my room." This was said in tones of command.

Jorac merely raised one eyebrow slightly. He'd seen a noble do that once.

"Uh, if you please, sir," the wizard said, looking like a little boy who'd had his manners corrected in public. His sudden mood shifts were disconcerting.

Jorac tried to sound reassuring. "I would be delighted to accept your invitation, sir. I suspect we have much in common in our attitude toward the Council. And perhaps other things as well. First, though, might I offer you a drink of water? Your voice seems a little dry."

"Ah, thank you, but no, I have refreshments upstairs." He giggled at length, apparently having said something he thought very funny. Then he made a wide gesture and added, "Would you be so good as to follow me? One thing, though: I'd ask you to leave that sword on the ground."

Jorac could think of no way around it, so he said "Certainly, sir." He unbuckled his sword and laid it on the ground at his feet, with what he hoped looked like good grace. Then he gestured lightly toward his five frozen companions and said, "But what of my subordinates? It would be unseemly for me to abandon them here in this condition."

The wizards eyes narrowed in suspicion. "You aren't suggesting I let them go, are you? I thought you'd be reasonable about this."

"Certainly not. I wouldn't trust them out of my sight, much less to get back on their own. And if they returned without me there's no telling what sort of foul stories they might spread. I just thought we might transport them upstairs. You'll be asking me about them, and you'll want to see them for yourself."

This rationale sounded pretty weak to Jorac as he said it, but Wolburn's suspicious look faded and he smiled a little. "Ah, perhaps you're right. You're asking me to levitate them?"

"If you don't mind, sir. I could help you by carrying the females, or perhaps that tall thin boy."

"No, don't trouble yourself. I can do it easily," Wolburn said smugly, and started toward the corner of the building. "Right this way."

Jorac followed. He put out his hand in front of him, lest he bump into invisible walls surrounding him, but found none. When he went around the corner, he saw bricks strewn in front of the now-open doorway.

"Pardon my landscaping," the wizard said. "I've not been able to keep that up. It was all I could do to make sure no vermin came in to disturb me." He went inside, and gestured for Jorac to precede him up the stairs. The stair treads, which were open between like a ladder, seemed solid but were quite warped, and Jorac needed care to avoid tripping.

At the top of the stairs was a hallway with a closed door ahead and an open door to the left; this would be the room with the windows they'd looked in from below. Jorac looked back at Wolburn and pointed to the open doorway with a questioning look.

Wolburn was toiling behind him, hanging on to the banister as he laboriously climbed the steep stairs, breathing hard after a few steps. He was obviously not used to any sort of physical exercise, and Jorac wondered why he didn't just levitate himself up; maybe he didn't want to be distracted from watching his guest/prisoner. "Yes, that's the room," Wolburn panted. "Go ahead."

When Jorac got to the door he waited for Wolburn to catch up with him and go first. He was careful not to look around too obviously, despite his curiosity.

"Sit, make yourself comfortable," the wizard said rather grandly, sounding like the gracious host. "Over there, if you please. Just a moment. . ."

Jorac did as he was bid, and sat in a creaky chair in the far corner near the open window. Along the wall to his left was a huge sideboard that looked as if it belonged in a manor-house dining room. Across from it was a four-poster bed with a storage chest to its left and a small bedside table to its right. Nearer the foot of the bed was the big metal ball Veseen had mentioned, looking gigantically out of place there in the middle of a bedroom.

Jorac watched while Wolburn went over to the bedside table and picked up a tiny half-spherical silver cup, not much bigger than a thimble. Then he sat on the bed, reached over, and turned a small gold tap on the side of the large ball, which Jorac could see was a tarnished silvery metal. It was waist-high or a little taller, and the outside had round, raised ribs to provide strength. The tap disgorged a small stream of liquid, which was clear but nonetheless gave off a rainbow glow – Jorac thought it looked rather like the manites he'd been watching the past week, but in liquid form. Wolburn filled the cup and drank it, coughing a little, then a coughed little more. His face turned red.

Acting concerned, Jorac said, "Wizard Wolburn, here, have some water. It was put into the skin just this morning, and boiled last night." He unslung his waterskin and made to toss it to the wizard.

Hoarsely, Wolburn gasped, "No, thank you. That won't be needed." He gestured at Jorac in an off-hand manner, then waved both hands in a complicated gesture at the sideboard, which contained an inset copper bowl. In the center of the bowl, water started fountaining, rising up a handspan from the top of the bowl.

Jorac didn't feel the least need to sneeze; somehow the wizard had shielded him and started the fountain at the same time. He said, "That was the most impressive bit of wizardry I've ever seen. I take it that water is clean and well filtered, like the fountains in town?"

After another complicated hand wave at the sideboard, Wolburn said, "It is now. An excellent suggestion. Your pardon. . ." He took a larger cup from the bedside table, went over to the fountain, and drank several cups. "Ah, that's better. Would you care for some?"

"Why yes, please, if it's not an imposition. The water in my waterskin is safe enough to drink, but not flavorful."

"For a guest, it's the least I can do. Hmmm, no extra cups here; I didn't anticipate hosting anyone. One moment." He looked up at the corner of the room in an unfocused way and made some sort of magical pass that Jorac thought looked like pulling a rope, then snapped his fingers. A set of four glass goblets appeared on the sideboard.

Again, Jorac didn't sneeze. He'd have to ask why not, if he could, but right now he didn't want to distract Wolburn from feeling magnanimous. He stood and walked toward the sideboard, but halfway there ran into an invisible wall. He'd been half expecting it, and didn't hit too hard.

"What are you doing?" Wolburn looked highly suspicious again.

"Why, just getting myself a drink, as you bid. Sir wizard, you're obviously a little tired. You're a most gracious host, which is to be commended, but a thoughtful guest doesn't make his host keep to tradition if he's indisposed. I can fetch the water; it's no bother."

Jorac's open manner must have done the trick; the wizard's suspicious look faded away, and he grunted and waved a hand toward the fountain. Jorac walked over to the sideboard with no trouble this time. He rinsed a goblet – they were very dusty – and watched the magic fountain as the water quickly cleared. He drank a goblet full and refilled it, then filled Wolburn's cup and brought it to him.

"Here you are, sir." Wolburn took the cup with a nod, and Jorac noticed his fingers were soft and puffy and his nails recently and roughly cut.

Jorac returned to his seat and sipped his water. "Well sir, I imagine we have a number of questions for each other."

"Yes, that's true. There are several things I want you to tell me about."

"I'll be happy to, and then perhaps you can satisfy my curiosity. To start, I propose to explain how I came to be in the unlikely position of Wizard Constable, and with the motley group I find myself traveling with. Perhaps you can work at retrieving them while I expound?"

The wizard nodded, "I suppose I can do that. Pray, begin."

Remembering the wizard at his constable oath-taking, Jorac resolved to speak only the truth. "My father is a nobleman, a large landowner in the provinces, quite well off but, if truth be told, a bit rustic in his thinking. I'm the third son, and my eldest brother will inherit the estate. I received a good education, but my father and I didn't always see things the same way, and there were one or two little incidents. . ." He smiled wryly. "Well, suffice it to say, we agreed it was best if I departed. So I left for the wider world and sought a position befitting my station." All true, but he'd tried to make his father's ramshackle sheep farm in the hills sound like a castle, and make himself sound like something of a rake. He hoped he wasn't overdoing it, but so far Wolburn seemed to be lapping up his nobility act.

"All men must eat and drink, and we all want the finer things too. If our fathers haven't seen fit to grace us with an income, this presents a problem for men of our station. We can't just forget our birth and grub for money like a common merchant. Therefore I accepted a position offered to me in a foreign country, commanding an army." Again true, though the army was a semi-civilized tribe of barbarians.

"Really!" The wizard sounded rather impressed. "Go on, please." He'd floated Dorrie up the stairs and stood her in the corner beyond the window to Jorac's right; now he was moving Kimma.

"Our small army was undefeated, but it turns out that a successful army has its own issues. The time of battles ends, and keeping the troops gainfully employed can be problematic. So I took another position for a time, again leading fighting men, but this position also reached its end." His second army numbered only three, including himself, and might more properly be called a wagon guard.

Kimma was now standing beside Dorrie, and the wizard floated Veseen in and stood him nearby, filling up that corner of the room.

"Thus I was cast adrift after a few years, albeit with the finest references." The wagon owner retired, and Jorac still visited him occasionally.

"And so I came to the city. There my allergy became known, and I was persuaded by a Duke of my acquaintance to accept the position of Wizard Constable." The Duke, who was in charge of the Emperor's Domestic Service, had interviewed him for ten minutes when he was recommended for transfer from the constabulary to the Council. "He assured me it was at a social level equal to my station. And he was a man of his word; all the nobles and better gentlemen accept me graciously. But the wizards. . ." He paused and shook his head. "The wizards direct my tasks, but they seem to have as little idea what to do with me as a fish would a trumpet."

He peeked out the window and saw the wizard was lifting Hox – only Schrog remained. "Oh, please be careful with that large one! He acts like he doesn't have two brain cells to bang together, but there are some tasks sheer brawn will do best, and it would be a shame to damage him." Wolburn floated Hox in the door and up the stairs, but his arms were out to his sides and his legs spread front and back, so the wizard had to rotate his body halfway through the door to get him through. He found a place to stand him, in front of the window to Jorac's right.

"Oh, well done!" Jorac said, clapping his hands. When the wizard nodded smugly, he continued his narrative.

"I think my predecessor did things like adjudicate minor squabbles between the lower-ranked wizards and even the apprentices, but of course that wouldn't suit me, and they claimed they wanted someone with greater capability. Which of course they got, if I do say so myself, but in the main, my abilities are squandered... Oh here, let me move my chair – you can stick him in the corner there." Schrog, still holding the crossbow slightly behind his back, had been brought upstairs, and Jorac shifted his chair so that he'd be sitting right in front of him.

"Anyway, my job, such as it is, consists mainly of sitting in a tiny, dingy office and filling out useless paperwork. As an example, I once spent two hours discerning that a boat had been sunk by an explosion from within, not a fireball or some other attack from the outside, and then I had to spend two weeks writing reports on the subject! As I said, my abilities are wasted in pursuing trivia." He sighed heavily.

"Which brings us to my current assignment. Some wizard detected something vaguely amiss with magic in the rougher sections of town near the swamps, and sent me off to search for the reason. Some of those places are filled with the worst sort of ruffians, areas where an armed squad would scarcely dare go, and they sent me off there without a second thought. Or perhaps it was calculated to eliminate me; a friend suggested that to me."

He looked around the room and waved a negligent hand toward his frozen companions. "So I've been dispatched on this assignment, and have been given this assortment of subordinates to help me, if help is the word. Let's see here. Behind me is a city constable – apparently the only one they could spare. He's from the lowest class, and putting up with him has been a test, believe me. His accent grates on the ear, and his vocabulary is stunning in its lack of originality. I suppose he might be competent enough dealing with a squabble between a fishwife and a laundry-woman." Jorac's frozen companions could presumably hear his words. He hoped if they got out of this alive they'd forgive him.

"Still, he's a mountain of intellect compared to that big one. He's called Hox, though sometimes I think 'Duh' would suit him better. If you tell him what to do, clearly, several times, and supervise him, you may get something useful. Perhaps. But he's very strong – he could probably lift that big sphere, or at least shove it around." He mentally apologized to Hox, but hoped he was listening.

Hox's form blocked his view, so Jorac stood up to point to the other three in the corner. "Behold, the licensed wizard of the group. Despite her age, she's been licensed for less than a year, and uses what scant talent she has to fleece the merchants by finding their lost baubles and telling the strumpets who was the father of their latest whelp. You see what I have to work with?

"Then I have this skinny wizard boy. He's a mere apprentice, and claims to be excellent at a few tricks, but I've never seen them. His main contribution has been to whine about the places we have to go, and shield me from sneezing when the licensed one there tries something magical." Veseen had claimed to be excellent at starting small fires, and Jorac hoped he could figure out a way to give him a chance.

"And finally, the constable found us a guide through the swamps. She claims to know some herbs and such. She's lived out here for many years, doing minor healing of those called the, *ehem*, 'swampies'." He thought his snort before "swampies" was a good touch. Kimma, who was still covered with her concealing veil and lumpy costume, hardly even looked competent.

Jorac sat back down in his chair and said, "And that's our little group. Not so very impressive."

Wolburn frowned at him. "You left out one part. How did you come to look here in the first place?" He sounded suspicious again, but somewhat less so this time.

Jorac kept his voice amused. "Oh, that's simple. Word of your ingenious little man-trap downstairs has gotten around, in the dregs of what passes for society here. Some of the swamp-dwellers have been using it to remove their competition. I just thought I'd take a look at it – so often the description is inaccurate. How ever did you think of it?"

"My father taught it to me. He learned it from Aplath himself. It is good, don't you think? No messy bodies to clean up later."

"Most impressive." *Amoral, deadly, horrifying too. But certainly impressive.*

"You know, you haven't been lying to me. Everyone lies to me. All the time."

"Confidentially, sir, I might have shaded one or two items. But in the main, yes, all I said is true. A gentleman shouldn't lie to another, not without extreme cause. Otherwise, how would gentlemen differ from the common rabble? My father always used to tell me to act like a gentleman. I suspect yours did too."

"Yes he did. I'm surprised, astonished, to find a gentleman has been the one to discover my little nest. And one who feels as I do toward the Council. We might even be friends."

Good! Jorac thought, and tried to stay relaxed and non-threatening. "I am likewise surprised. Would you care to share the tale of how you came to stay out here for what has obviously been a number of years?" He paused to take a drink and added, "I'd offer you a bite to eat, if I had thought to bring anything decent – we were to be heading back by now. You must be hungry."

"I am a bit peckish. Let me see. . ." The wizard stared up at the corner of the ceiling again and waved his hands; a large tray of canapés and snacks appeared on the sideboard, near the fountain.

Jorac started sneezing.

"Oh, I beg your pardon. I forgot to set up the wall before I did that. I hope you can forgive me."

"Apology – *achoo!* – happily accepted, sir. Since I took my current job, you don't know how many times – *achoo!* – a wizard has caused me to sneeze this way, with only a sneer in return. It's so nice to deal with courtesy for a change."

Jorac pulled out his handkerchief and blew his nose, and said, "All better now."

The wizard went to the sideboard and took a small plate full of food. "Would you like a bite?"

"Perhaps a bit later – I had a large breakfast. I'm anxious to hear your tale."

"I don't know. . ." He hesitated. "Well, you're a gentleman. Can you keep it under your hat?"

"Certainly, sir. I'll not repeat it if that's what you wish."

Wolburn sat down on the side of the bed with his plate of food. He took a bite or two and seemed to be thinking. Finally he put his plate down on the table and began to speak.

"My father was an apprentice to Mad Wizard Aplath – oh yes, they called him that to his face, too, as long as you were smiling at him. He didn't mind, for you see he wasn't really mad, just the most powerful wizard in a hundred years. He didn't see why he shouldn't be commanding the country, instead of an idiot who inherited the throne."

Wolburn took another bite and continued. "As the most powerful wizard, Aplath became the head of the Wizards Circle, which was the governing organization at the time. Benneso the First had just declared himself Emperor, not King, and persuaded the Circle to create the Wizards Bridge, since the old wooden one was washing away. My own father was part of that bridge-raising, did you know? Lifting that much weight took every available wizard, and even the stronger apprentices like my father. That taught the wizards they could work and even cast spells together, and Aplath thought he'd do a better job than that fool Benneso. Most of wizards supported him, but a few didn't agree, and betrayed him. A great war and the destruction of the area around us was the result. I can speak of this without rancor, for the outcome of a failed rebellion is well known. It was a risk he took."

"What I cannot forgive is the way my father was treated. The wizards who fought with Aplath were mostly killed outright. Those who were captured had their wizard skill burned out of them. Imagine having your foot burned off, one layer at a time – that's what my father said it felt like!" His voice was getting shrill.

Jorac said, "Your father was an apprentice? Bound to serve, with no other choice?"

"Ah, you see exactly! He had no choice, none at all. He would have been a powerful wizard himself, so he was apprenticed to Aplath. Yet they treated him the same as the others. He was still just a teenager!" Wolburn was shouting at this point.

"I see," Jorac said quietly, and made a small show of drinking some water. His idea worked; Wolburn also paused to drink and seemed to calm down a little.

"My mother died when I was an infant, and my father raised me. When I was born he was already in his forties and working in the city – he was quite a good scribe. When I was twelve years old I started showing some signs that I would be a wizard, so he took me away, down the coast past the pirate isles, to a little fishing village in Parlund.

"There he taught me as he was taught, as best he could. He could describe what to do, but never show me. It was so frustrating for him!" Wolburn's fists were clenched, and he was almost shouting again. "They did that to him! The ones who now call themselves the Wizard Council. He would have been a great wizard, but he was just a child. They tortured him for something he didn't do!" Now he sounded almost on the point of tears.

Switching back to cold fury, he almost spat his words. "So we swore a great oath, my father and I. Before he died we swore to have revenge on the Wizard Council!" Then he spoke conversationally again. "It's been my lifetime's work, but it's been worth it."

Jorac, who thought the wizard sounded even scarier when he was matter-of-fact than when he was emotional, just smiled blandly and nodded.

"I spent some years – well, never mind, the details are mere commerce. I developed this – the Wolburn Sphere – and sat down to fill it with concentrated mana. It took me months to fill a much smaller one, but that gave me the power to set up this little house."

"It looks fascinating. How does it work?" Jorac didn't have to feign his interest, though hiding his fright of this powerful madman was a little harder.

"It's of purest silver, which as you may know reflects magic. Shaped into a perfect hollow sphere, it reflects magic back in on itself so that it becomes concentrated. At first I tried filling the inside with water to dissolve the mana in, but I found that concentrated spirits of wine works much better. This one spot is gold; that's where you can get mana in. Quite useful; I used to carry the smaller one with me everywhere.

"I was born a powerful wizard, you know, but I'm ever so much more powerful now. When I gather mana I can store it up indefinitely, and I can enhance my personal complement of power whenever I need to – I just have to take a little sippy." He giggled.

"Very impressive arrangement," Jorac said, trying to sound admiring. Wolburn nodded smugly.

"Of course, getting this huge silver sphere here was quite a challenge, because I couldn't use magic on it – that was when I first invented hardened air. And filling it up with spirits of wine was worse – I couldn't just borrow a little here and there and expect not to have it noticed. I finally borrowed a whole ship full of wine, and had to distill it myself."

Jorac wasn't sure how you "borrowed" a whole ship, and wasn't sure he wanted to know.

"Then came the hardest part. I had to fill it with mana without being detected, and I knew it would take a long time. I couldn't move my Sphere to the city, but I couldn't live here and have those – what did you call them – 'swampies' provide for my needs. Yet I had to be near enough to the Council to strike without warning when the time came. Has come!" He giggled again.

"So I went to the University library, incognito of course, and spent some time researching hibernation spells. I finally found a set of spells that would keep me slightly alert, enough to direct mana into my Sphere, yet slow my metabolism. And spells to preserve this room, too. Tell me, is the year now 608?

"609, actually. It would be just past mid-winter, if this city had seasons. I'm still not used to the climate, or what passes for it."

"I know what you mean – the village where I grew up had great storms off the sea part of the year, and sometimes a bit of snow in the winter. Anyway, so I thought I could fill this sphere in seventeen years – it took eighteen. As I filled it, I was gradually able to expand the area I pulled mana from, so it sped up near the end."

"Ah," Jorac said. That was probably when Darlora began to notice it.

"Now it's almost brim-full, and the time is almost here. I was waking before you came, but your appearance led me to tap a little of my mana and stop you. I hope it didn't too greatly inconvenience you."

Jorac waved his hand. "It's of no consequence. I didn't know you were the sort of person you are. Say, do you mind if I take you up on that offer?" he said, pointing to the food. He didn't want Wolburn thinking too much about the holes in his story, or the spell his badge had triggered that Wolburn had "captured." Delay was his friend; the spell freezing his companions lasted only about an hour.

"Be my guest."

Jorac went and looked at the sideboard and put a variety of snacks onto a small plate. It looked as if Wolburn had "borrowed" a snack tray from a mid-day party in the city, enough for a table of ten or twelve. The food was fresh and tasty; some poor servant was probably getting blamed right now.

Jorac sat back down and ate his food, though in truth he was too nervous to enjoy it.

"So, what are you going to do now? You must have planned this for quite some time." Jorac hated to ask this, but the character he'd been developing with Wolburn would ask.

"Wouldn't you like to know!" Wolburn sneered. Instead of suspicious, this time he sounded arrogant.

"Well yes sir, I would. I surmise it has something to do with the Wizard Council, but I have no friends there. In fact, I wouldn't mind seeing some of them get treated the way they treated me. Not at all."

"Hmmm. You mean that, don't you. Well, let me think."

Jorac had an inspiration. "Was the Wizard's Compound and Wizard's Tower constructed when you were last in the city?" He remembered it was fairly new.

"Wizard's Tower? No, I haven't heard of that."

"It's where the council now meets – many of them have living quarters there too. Would you like me to describe it to you?"

"Oh yes, please. Every detail."

"Well, it's in the old palace area. When they finally finished moving the new palace to the west side of the river, the old palace grounds became what's now called the Wizard's

Compound, and that's also where the Tower was erected. It's five-sided. . ."

Jorac launched into a long physical description of the tower, from the ground-floor rooms and the levels inside to its white stone façade and the 156 steps up to the meeting room – and how he'd had to climb them while the stronger wizards just levitated themselves up. He went on and on, with Wolburn listening intently to every word. If he could delay enough, his companions would unfreeze. Kullo and his men had all recovered at the same time, and Jorac was hoping for the same.

Finally, he ran out of things to say. "Well, I hope that proves useful to you. If you don't mind, I'd like to see it when you take them on. I'd not like to be too close, mind you – when the mighty beasts fight, the ants get trampled."

"Yes, perhaps that can be arranged. Say, I know, how would you like to be my bodyguard?"

Jorac was surprised, and rather horrified, but at least he seemed to be gaining the wizard's confidence. "Your pardon, sir wizard, but why would someone with your powers need a bodyguard?"

"I can't protect myself from some simple things like hard metal weapons, not without spending a great deal of mana on strong shields. And I can ward myself a good bit, but having someone who could detect magic being used would be quite useful."

"And who would I be guarding – that is, what role do you see for yourself?"

"Why, High Wizard of course. I'm sure the others won't object."

"The surviving ones you mean?" Jorac gave him a feral smile.

Wolburn grinned back at him, "Ah, you do understand. Yes."

"Not Emperor?"

Wolburn frowned. "The history of Etrombia is full of wizards who tried to take over as head of state. The people won't stand for it, whatever factions they are in."

Jorac smiled a crooked little smile. "The High Wizard sits on the Emperor's council. What does history say about wizards who leave the Emperor in place but somehow rule anyway?"

Wolburn's laughter this time was long, loud, and genuinely mirthful. "Ah, honorable Kellor, you are a treasure. I won't say I haven't thought of it, but one step at a time, eh?"

"Of course. I was just wondering if your ambition matched your power – so few people understand how you need both."

Jorac thought he heard the floor creak behind him. "Say, would you like a little more food? I think I'd like a little more of that ham."

"No, but help yourself. About the bodyguard, what do you say?"

"Well, if you were to take over the Council, I could scarcely find a better position in the city." Truth only. Any position outside of the city would be better of course, if this monster was leading the Council.

"Good then. I think I'll have a little more of this." The wizard took his tiny cup and once again filled it with the liquid from the large sphere.

Jorac needed a few more minutes – he thought his team was starting to move, and he needed to keep attention away from them. In desperation he said, "I say, would you mind if I had a small tipple of that?" Wolburn's brow furrowed in anger, but Jorac continued, "After you removed the mana from it of course. Aged spirits of wine is such a rare treat."

Wolburn said testily, "There's no need to remove the mana from it; you're a simple. If you ingested it, it wouldn't have any effect on you; it would just increase your regular exudation of mana until the excess was gone." He paused a moment. "Of course, it might make you sneeze. I doubt it, but it's possible, and that would be inconvenient if you're going to be working for me. Let's find out. Fetch one of those goblets and we shall see."

Jorac rinsed out a goblet and brought it to the wizard. Up close he smelled rather bad, like musty clothes, old body odor, and spirits.

Jorac held the goblet under the tap. "Just a taste, mind you. It wouldn't do to become lightheaded."

The wizard put some spirits into the goblet – he actually filled it half full, much more than Jorac wanted. The liquid looked like a jumbled rainbow of colors, fascinating to look at.

Jorac held it up under his nose and sniffed; it smelled like spirits, nothing more. "Apparently, being near concentrated mana doesn't make me sneeze," he said. "Now I'll try drinking some. If that triggers my allergy, then perhaps you can remove the mana from it and then we can try again."

He gingerly took a small sip. "My!" he gasped. "That is strong, and harsh on the throat." He fetched some water in the other goblet and rinsed his mouth. "I was thinking it would be aged and mellow. I suppose the silver inhibits proper aging. A pity."

"Yes, but you've given me another idea. I can just remove the mana from those spirits when I need it; I don't have to drink it every time. There are indeed times when a clear head is needed."

"Indeed. I often find a clear head is needed. Mind you, I like a drink or two as well as the next person. Among friends, or at a party. Perhaps this liquid could be diluted, or flavored with something to make it more palatable. Then you could enjoy it." Jorac was babbling now, running out of things to say. But he was standing in front of Wolburn, blocking his view of his group.

He turned toward the sideboard and took a little more of the food. Out of the corner of his eye he saw that Hox's arms had drooped down somewhat. Not stupid at all, Hox was trying to remain still in an uncomfortable position, but was now under his own control. It was time.

Jorac walked over to the corner of the bed and stood beside the bedpost. He said, slowly, "Well, what are you going to do. . . NOW!" He threw the remaining spirits in his goblet at Wolburn – he missed his eyes but managed to soak the lower part of his beard. Jorac hoped the element of surprise would be enough.

Hox rushed forward. He started a little off balance and didn't move very fast at first, but still got to the large silver sphere quickly. He bent over and slammed into it hard with his chest and shoulder, pushing it away from Wolburn.

Meanwhile, Veseen held out his left hand in an odd position and said a single strange-sounding word. Wolburn's beard caught fire. It crackled and burned with a bright blue flame where the spirits were.

The wizard shrieked and beat at his beard, then raised his hand.

Hox grunted with effort. There was a low wooden frame on the floor to contain the sphere, but Hox managed to overcome this and start it rolling. It rolled toward the sideboard.

"You can't trick ME!" the wizard shouted.

He made a simple one-hand gesture and struck Jorac with an invisible wall – it pushed him back a few steps, knocking him to the floor.

"I'll show you what happens to those who oppose Wolburn!" Jorac watched as Veseen was likewise struck, and then immediately heard Hox say "oof" and hit the floor.

From behind the supine Jorac, Schrog shot the crossbow at the wizard. It hit him in the middle of his smoking beard, at the center of his chest.

The bolt bounced off. The wizard grimaced a bit, as if he'd received a punch in the chest, then slammed a wall of force at Schrog. It knocked him hard into the corner and he dropped the crossbow.

"Fool, my shirt is bespelled. Nothing can penetrate it."

Jorac lay on the floor, trying to hold his breath so he wouldn't start sneezing. He looked at the corner where the two women were and noticed movement.

Kimma threw her waterskin at the wizard; he blasted it in the air with a firebolt. Water and steam sprayed everywhere. She too received a slam of invisible force from the wizard, bounced off the wall, and landed heavily on the floor, her hat and veil knocked askew but not completely off.

Standing beside her, Dorrie spoke up in her deepest, most serious voice. "Wizard, you claim. Ha! I have more wizardry in my little finger than all you command. Watch this!" And she pointed at him – and did the now-familiar Exercise Number Three, with the faintly glowing lights shooting a finger length off the ends of her fingers.

Wolburn waved his hands, presumably to put up some sort of magical shield; then he smiled a cruel smile. "I'll show you magic!" he said.

He twisted his hands and fingers in a complex gesture, obviously preparing a powerful spell. Fire gathered in his hands, and he reached back to throw it at Dorrie.

That was when Schrog shot him in the head with the second crossbow bolt. Wolburn slumped to the floor, and the fire in his hands sputtered out.

Jorac let out a gigantic sneeze. He stood up and looked at the wizard. There was a hole in his temple and brains were leaking out.

Schrog said, "Ya know, Kimma, you be right about dat. De second bolt do come in handy."

Chapter 13 - Sphere of Influence

Not one of them could stand without shaking. Dorrie was the only one not struck by one of the wizard's invisible walls, and she helped the others to sit on the furniture in the room. No one had broken any bones, but they were badly bruised, and Schrog and Kimma both had headaches from slamming into the wall.

Veseen said, to no one in particular, "Lucky he didn't start with the fireballs."

Jorac said, "I suppose he'd been using that 'hardened air' spell so much recently it was the first thing that came to mind. By the way, I'd like to apologize to all of you for the smears on your character. I wanted him to think you weren't a threat."

Schrog waved it away. "No matter. Kept 'im off balance, we did. Remember dat, Hox – surprise a guy and he'll do what he's used to, not what's best. Good job wit' dat, Jorac. Wasn't sure what you was up to at first."

"We did good together. All of us!" Jorac, knees still shaking, glanced around at his team and grinned, thinking how every one of them had contributed. "Now the only question is, what do we do with that, and that?" He pointed to the body, and the sphere.

They wrapped the body in the bed covers and rolled it under the bed. Jorac asked Schrog and Hox to go check the other rooms of the house to make sure there were no surprises, but they came back and reported they'd seen nothing but dust and cobwebs.

The small magic fountain had kept going after the wizard's death, but was obviously winding down, so they all had a drink of water and filled their waterskins, and those whose stomachs could stand it ate from the snack tray.

When everyone seemed to be feeling better, Jorac said, "There's something I'd like to try. Dorrie, would you do me a favor, and take a tiny sip of that magic liquid?" She nodded assent.

With all of them working together, they managed to move the Wolburn Sphere so that it could be tapped. It was immensely heavy, and they all praised Hox for having been able to move it by himself. They spun it so as not to crush the tap, and wrestled it back within its frame.

Jorac filled the wizard's little cup and handed to Dorrie. "Not even a mouthful, okay? It's pretty strong; you'll want some water to wash it down."

She took her tiny sip. "Echh, that is strong. Water, please. Thank you. Want me to try the manite thing again now?"

Jorac said, "Yes, please," and then, "Veseen, ready to shield me?" When the apprentice nodded, he motioned to Dorrie.

The manites shot across the room in a vivid rainbow pattern, and bounced off the far wall. There were four individual streams, one from each of her fingers, and when she spread her fingers, the streams spread out as well. She pulled the mana back to her with an astonished look on her face.

Veseen said, "Wow, Miz Velosp, that's amazing! We had a Council wizard show us that exercise one time, and he just got an arm's length, maybe a little more."

Hox said "Wow is right!"

Kimma said "Can we see that again? That was stunning!"

Dorrie obliged, but after a few more passes, her magic strength ebbed.

Jorac looked at his fellow adventurers – their expressions ranged from amazement to fear, sometimes in the same person. He held up his hand. "Not to be a spoilsport, but we need to think. What should we do with this stuff?"

Schrog looked at the ball with undisguised disgust. "Beggin' yer pardon Dorrie, but I'd sooner see dem swamp snakes comin' from every sewer in town as to see dem wizards get dis stuff."

Veseen said somberly, "There are wizards who'd kill for that much power – literally. Miz Velosp, you weren't an apprentice, so you don't know any of this. Kind of like the Constables, we get a clean slate, and we're supposed to judge each other on how much magical skill we have, not where we came from or who our parents are. This stuff would make anyone a Council-level wizard right away. Maybe lead the Council."

Dorrie laughed a mirthless laugh. "I don't think I want to run the Council, thanks. And I agree: this stuff is too dangerous."

Jorac said, "Okay, can we just open that tap and dump it into the swamp?"

Kimma shook her head. "Probably not a good idea. There used to be lots of monsters come from this area – Miz Madouve told me all about them. Glowing frogs, a cow that could breathe fire, and such. There was one oversized fly-trap plant that lived here, it could move around, and liked to eat people. Everyone figured it was the leftover magic from the old Wizards Quarters leaking out. It's mostly stopped now. Don't figure we want to start all that up again."

Everyone was quiet for a moment, and then Schrog said, "Don't want no wizard to get dis stuff, ever. So what we needs to do is spread it around, I be right? And not around here? Dat means we gots to get dis ball back to town."

After a moment Dorrie started giggling, then laughed out loud. Everyone looked at her.

"I know where there are a couple of boats. Good heavy ones. Not half a mile from here. . ."

Jorac looked at her, waited for an explanation, and finally said, "And. . .?"

She looked at Schrog and started giggling again. "What were the names of those people in Swampside? The ones the runners took messages to? Think they might want to throw a party? We'll supply the booze!"

* * *

"What do you mean, you want to borrow our boats? They aren't for sale, and they aren't for hire." Gleben was obviously annoyed at Jorac's effrontery for even asking.

He and his crew had been digging where Dorrie said, and had already brought up several of the glass and silver amulets; one even had a small gold chain, for wearing around ones neck. They were laid out in a row in one of the boats.

Jorac pointed to the collection. "How much money will you make from those?"

"That doesn't matter. There's also reputation to consider. A find like this needs to be examined and cataloged. This could make my career!"

Dorrie, in her deepest Madame Velosp voice, said, "Whose find is this, exactly?"

Gleben's eyes narrowed as he glared at her, but said nothing.

Miz Madouve said, "Hatlo, Hario, Toop. You be gettin' ten percent of dis. But you helps us out, what we gonna do is give you – you too, Mr. Gleben – ten percent of what we got. Den you come back for dese t'ings later."

Hatlo said, "Ten percent o' what?"

Gleben spluttered, "But you're working for me!"

Toop said, "You boss, not chief. When we wants to, we quits."

Hario chimed in, "But we ain't quittin', we just listenin'. Gots to listen."

Jorac spoke for the first time. "Gleben, you're an educated man. Imagine a metal sphere this big. . ." – he held his hand up at the middle of his ribcage – "hollow, filled with liquid."

Gleben said, "Yes, made from what? Bronze perhaps – iron would rust. It would be quite heavy, and why a sphere?"

"A sphere because that's what it is. And not bronze, silver. What do you think that metal would weigh?"

Intrigued despite himself, Gleben started mumbling to himself about diameters and metal strengths. He finally said, "I know silver bends easily, but I don't really know how strong it is. Say two hundred to four hundred pounds, as a guess."

Jorac nodded. "Here's our proposal. What's inside that sphere is all ours, no discussion. But the silver sphere itself, that's what we split. Ten people, ten percent each. You think twenty to forty pounds of silver might make you change your mind about those boats?"

Gleben opened and closed his mouth a couple of times, but nothing came out.

Jorac turned to Gleben's helpers and said, "We've been inside that yellow house. Lived to tell about it, as you can see."

Schrog waved his hands at their work area and added, "And we ain't talkin' to nobody about dis stuff. De fancies still be dere when you gets back. And Madame Velosp here, she keeps her mout' shut, too."

Dorrie nodded solemnly.

Gleben licked his lips and finally found his voice. "I'd like to see that sphere, if you don't mind. I might be able to more accurately estimate its weight. How tall did you say it was?"

* * *

Hox was waiting with the sphere when Jorac went upstairs ahead of the others. Hox reported that he'd found a suitable place in the swamp and sunk the wizard's body, for which Jorac was grateful – he didn't want to explain it to Gleben and his crew.

The fountain in the sideboard had stopped shortly after Wolburn had died, so the room where Wolburn had waited all those years looked fairly normal when the others came upstairs, except of course for the large metal sphere near the bed.

Gleben saw the sphere and walked around it several times; he rapped on it first with his knuckles, then with the butt of his dagger. "What did you say it held?"

Veseen, being the most unlikely member of their group, had been picked as the expert on the sphere's contents, at least as far as the treasure hunters knew. "A liquid," he said firmly. "That's all we need to know. We just need to get it to town. The liquid inside it is what we've already committed, to some very hard people, so we need to be careful with it."

Gleben said, "Hmmm. Let's say sixteen hundred pounds at the low end, and two thousand at the high. How do you propose to move it?"

Jorac looked at Hatlo, Hario, and Toop. "I thought we'd ask the experts here."

The three looked at each other in puzzlement for a few moments, and then Toop volunteered, "I knows where dere's a bunch o' rope. . ."

Gleben looked at the ball, looked at his erstwhile employees, and sighed. "Yes, I brought a good bit. I hope it's strong enough."

* * *

Wolburn had probably brought the sphere in through a window, but they could do nothing of the sort. Getting it to the stairs first required them to chop the doorway wider; that did no good to Jorac's poor mistreated sword, but they managed. When they pushed the sphere through the doorway, they almost lost it down the stairs, but Hox saved the day with a mighty push that redirected it up the hallway, where it got jammed. Veseen was the thinnest of them, so he crawled over the top of the sphere to carry the ropes around it. They chopped holes in the wall and floor until they found some beams holding up the second floor they could tie their guy ropes to.

Despite its being a ball, they didn't want to simply roll it; the strengthening ribs were considerably larger on the bottom and they feared crushing the top. So they tied it to two pieces of the wood from the bed rails, as best they could, and slid the bed rails down the stairs. With all the men on the ropes and the women spotting and directing, they slowly lowered it down the stairs, cracking each step as they went, but with no catastrophe. From the bottom floor it was a comparatively easy matter to widen the doorway and push the ball outside, still on its bed-rail cradle. The ground was soft, so they tore out the cracked stair treads to give them something to drag it on, and worked their way to the boats.

Gleben eyed the ball and his boats. The larger boat was no wider than the ball, but twenty feet long, a little bigger than most swamp boats. "I'm fairly sure the weight would sink the smaller boat," he said. "The bigger one might sink, too, but I think it will just ride low. But the main problem is the concentrated weight in the middle. We need to spread it out somehow."

Jorac said, "Yeah, it's going to be tricky. But let's wait and tackle that problem tomorrow; the sun's going down soon." They talked it over and decided to stay there for the night, since there were several semi-intact houses in the area they could sleep in. "Though not that yellow one!" someone said. When everyone seemed agreed, Jorac looked at the sky and said, "I think we have enough time before sundown to at least go take everything out of the big boat. Come on."

Hox said, "Let's start with the food, alright? I know where we can put that!"

* * *

Rolling the ball into the boat almost sank it, which would have been a disaster, but they recovered and by early afternoon, they had bailed out the boat and started back toward the city. With Hatlo, Hario, and Toop in the small boat (or sometimes wading in the water) and the other seven walking, they managed to steer the large boat down the flooded city streets. Navigation was a challenge; it was hard to look for the water path when they'd sought the dry path on their way here. At the edge of the flooded city the water and dry paths diverged, and the group had to split up. Hox went with Hatlo and Toop in the smaller boat (they'd learned to respect his strength, and Jorac privately thought it would keep them honest), and the three rowed across a long stretch of open water, pulling the heavily laden large boat behind them. The other seven walked, guided by Hario and Miz Madouve.

It had taken two hours to make the trip to the ruined city, but getting back took nearly two days. Even with four swampies in the group, finding a way to get the large boat through the densest parts of the swamp took extra time and some backtracking – and then all the people had to get to the same place as the boat, because Jorac wouldn't allow the group to stay split up for very long. Sometimes there was no nearby walking path, so two or three people crowded into the smaller boat for a series of trips to rejoin the larger one.

The first day they worked a little too hard and too long. By the time they camped on a grassy hummock, rather late, everyone was tired and nerves were fraying, so Jorac decided he wouldn't push too hard to get going the next morning. But at least they had enough food, thanks to Gleben's supplies. The two women slept in the small tent that had been brought to look for manites in, Hatlo and Hario claimed their small boat, and everyone else had to make do on the ground with makeshift bedding. Gleben had enough fine netting that everyone could cover their faces as they slept, and despite their damp clothes, sleep came to them all quickly.

The slow start the next morning gave them some time to talk, and the second day of pushing the boats through the swamp melded the group. They all learned that Hario was a whiner who could at least laugh at himself, while his brother Hatlo was quiet, and their friend Toop was relentlessly, if sarcastically, cheerful. Kimma in her Miz Madouve outfit again trailed the group carrying her crossbow. She spoke very little, but all her swamp advice proved good, and she seemed to know the dry parts of their pathways better than the others. Jorac found himself wondering, in odd moments, what she was thinking behind her disguise.

Toward the end of the second day they camped, exhausted, on another grassy hummock fairly near Kimma's house, and ate up most of the remaining food. They were only a half hour's walk from town, and it wasn't yet dark, but no one wanted to go any farther that evening. They set up sleeping arrangements similar to those the night before.

After supper, as the cooking fire burned down, Jorac excused himself and made a quiet visit to Wolburn's sphere, then found Veseen and led him a good distance away from the camp. While they were walking, Jorac told him what he had in mind.

"I've been thinking. When we go make our pitch in Swampside, I figure they won't believe our bare word; they'll need a demonstration of what that magic liquid can do. And Dorrie can't do it very well – you've seen her spray that light around, but that's about all she can manage. So if you're willing, I thought we could maybe try your fire-lighting trick. I'll give you a tiny bit of that stuff, and we'll see what you can do, okay?"

"Wow, sure." Veseen sounded eager to try it.

Jorac handed him a tiny silver bottle that Gleben's group had pulled from the swamp, which he'd now filled with spirits from the sphere.

"Take a sip of this – just a little bit. Here, wait until I get this waterskin ready; you'll need it."

Veseen drank from the bottle and immediately washed his mouth with water. He still choked a bit, but quickly recovered.

Jorac pointed at a fallen tree lying in some water nearby. It was perhaps twenty feet away, much further than Veseen's usual candle-lighting skill carried. "Pretend that's a candle, and go for it."

Veseen gestured at the fallen tree, and it blazed up brightly, with foot-high flames and billows of steam and smoke. Jorac held his breath, which helped at first, but he started sneezing as soon as he had to breathe again.

The tree's fire soon burned down and sputtered out. "It's waterlogged," Veseen said sadly. "I can't get it to burn completely."

Jorac said, "It was spectacular that you got it to burn at all! *Achoo!* And that far away, too. It's good to know – *achoo!* – that it works the way we figured." He slapped at a biting gnat, and then another one. "Want to try that bug-warding spell too? It might protect someone besides just you this time. Let me move away a bit first."

This time when Veseen cast the "bug-away" warding spell, Jorac could immediately tell it covered a greater area, since the gnats that had been bedeviling him were suddenly gone, and he sneezed some more. After another annoying minute sneezing, he recovered and walked back to Veseen.

Veseen said eagerly, "That is so cool. It's like I could push the bugs a mile away. I wonder if. . ." His voice trailed off, as he stared at the smoking log, thinking.

Jorac didn't like him thinking that way. He said, "What I wonder is what would happen if Master Radyry got his hands on this? Or another one of your teachers?"

"Uh. . ."

"Or someone worse? Any of your fellow students you wouldn't want to see drink it?"

Veseen was quiet for a time. Then he said, in a somber tone that brooked no contradiction, "That stuff is dangerous. If we can't talk them into getting people to drink it, let's just dump it, right?"

"Smart man. Let's head back."

Veseen looked pleased; Jorac decided no one had ever called him a man before. *Well, you act like it, so you can carry the name.*

* * *

Early the next morning, Kimma/Miz Madouve went to check on her house, and Schrog and Gleben walked into Swampside. Food was needed for the group, and these two needed to pass word to their families and employers that all was well. Jorac wrote another note for Master Radyry as well; their original one day trip was now five, but Veseen was still needed.

The rest spent the morning scouting for their next place to move the silver sphere. The night before, the group had concluded they'd come about as far as they could in the boats.

Normally people who wanted to move boats across the drier land nearer the city attached wagon axles to them and dragged them. Of course that only worked with empty boats; the wheels would quickly sink into the soft ground if there was much weight on them. So they'd have to find another way.

They decided what they needed was a narrow passage where the larger boat would barely fit and there were some large trees overhead to sling ropes from, and where there was good access to one of the main paths back to town. When Miz Madouve got back she helped them find just such a place, and within hailing distance of their camp, to boot.

So they steered the larger boat to the spot she pointed out, and then worked on levering and winching the sphere up to high ground, aided by some plain heaving and pushing. Toop had some sailing experience, so he took charge of the ropes, and it went better than Jorac expected. Once they got the sphere to a solid spot near the path, they used the wood that had been steadying it inside the boat to make a rough cradle to confine it. They were sitting around talking about what to do next when Schrog and Gleben returned, carrying a couple of large packs they didn't have before.

"How are things in town?" Jorac asked them.

"Eh, Swampside don't change much in t'ree days. It still be dere." Schrog unslung the pack from his shoulders. "Took us a while to find decent grub, but we gots it."

Gleben's pack held mostly food, while Schrog's had another tent and some camping supplies. The food was especially welcome, since everyone had spent an active morning with very little breakfast. After they ate, Jorac explained that his group needed to have a conference, and led them over by the silver sphere to talk.

"Any luck making contact with the Swampside chiefs?" he asked Schrog. "We really need their help. Without it, I'm not sure we can even move this thing into town, let alone throw a party with it."

"You be right. If dey don't agree, we be stopped. Ain't much happen dere if one of dem say it shouldn't." Then he added, "I sent 'em a message. Told Raah we needs to meet with him and Jimsley and Skowers and de Madame. Real important, big secret deal, need to meet tomorrow. Waited, finally get word back. Dey says okay but dis better be good, told de place and de time."

"Wonderful! Good work!" Jorac beamed at him, and then said wryly, "Now we just have to figure out how we're going to present our case. We can't afford for them to say no."

"Gotta show 'em," Schrog said. "Den dey'll see why."

Dorrie said, "Just let me swallow a shot of that stuff and I'll give a show they won't forget."

Jorac didn't mention he'd already thought of that; he just said, "And Veseen can do the same."

They worked out who should go. "We have to leave some people here," Jorac said, "we can't just leave this silver ball sitting around."

Schrog nodded. "And Gleben and dem swampies needs watchin', yer sayin'. I'm not disagreein' wit' you none." He counted off on his fingers. "Jorac gots to be dere, he de leader. Me, I set up de meetin'. And we needs you two wizards to show why we wants to dump de stuff. De rest gots to stay here and keep an eye on t'ings. Sorry, Kimma, Hox."

Jorac felt a flash of jealousy for Hox staying with Kimma, but he stamped it down. "Think you two can handle a day or two of guard duty?"

Kimma said, in her Miz Madouve voice, "Don't you worry about me none, sonny." Hox merely nodded his head.

Schrog said, "Hox, you keep an eye on dem, okay? Dis much silver, well, someone be t'inkin' about keepin' it all, just not sure who. I gots an extra sword mixed in wit' dat tent I brought. Gleben and dem don't need know 'bout it 'less dey cause trouble, okay?"

Hox deepened his voice and slowly said, "If they start trouble, I'll finish it." His "menacing" tone was definitely improving.

Schrog just smiled at him and nodded.

Chapter 14 - Meet the Chiefs

"What are you trying to pull, Schrog?" The Madame was a foul old lady named Revar, with ratty long gray hair and a shrill voice. "There's something you ain't telling us. Makes no sense, you giving away that much booze."

"Dat be de private part."

Jorac had been content to let Schrog handle the arrangements for the large room above the tavern and the initial negotiation with the area's four leaders, but he spoke up now.

"This is where everyone else needs to clear out. We'll only talk to you and Misters Raah, Jimsley, and Skowers. No one else."

Jimsley, a small crippled bald man who reminded Jorac of an ape, looked up from his wheeled chair and said sharply, "Dammit, no. Nobber stays." Nobber was the strong young man with a bad haircut who pushed Jimsley's chair. He was no taller than average, but Jorac thought he was almost as wide as Hox in the shoulders.

Raah said, "Nobber's always around. Jimsley vouches for him, trusts him." Jorac got the faint impression that Raah thought trusting anyone that much was a bad idea. *Must be the company he keeps*, Jorac thought.

Jorac's group looked a question at each other and shrugged.

"We can live with it if you three can," Jorac said.

Skowers was a dramatic-looking man dressed like a noble, with a black cape and fancy mostly-black clothes. He wore a wide-brimmed hat, even indoors. He looked quite handsome in a rakish sort of way. He spoke for the group.

"With the proviso that Nobber may remain, we don't object to confining this meeting to the four of us. But, sir, I didn't get your name. May we have the honor of knowing who we are speaking to?" His manner and accent wouldn't have been out of place in much better society, and Jorac wondered whether he was a swampie putting on airs, or a fallen member of the upper classes.

"A moment, please. . ." Jorac waited for the lesser servants to clear the room, then stood in the doorway while they filed down the stairs; he wanted no one lingering to listen at the door. He closed the door and went back to the group.

"I am Wizard Constable Jorac Kellor. At your service, sirs, madam. And I mean that quite seriously." The four chiefs looked back at him dead-pan; this wasn't going to be an easy sell. "First," he said, "I'd like to start by asking you a question. What do you think of dealing with wizards?"

They seemed puzzled, and no one answered. "Let me phrase it another way. No one will deny that wizards perform some very useful services. The weather here is nearly perfect, and the nearby farmers produce abundant crops because of it. The entire city has clean fresh water and a good sewer system, and the wizards who serve on the emperor's warships keep the pirates from the seas near here." There were some slight, grudging nods. "But would you also agree with me when I say that average wizards one might encounter – especially the powerful ones such as those around the Wizard's Tower – are annoying, overbearing, and treat those without magic as little better than something they might scrape off their foot?"

Raah spoke first. "I don't know. I try to stay away from 'em, best as I can."

Jorac nodded encouragingly to him. "Why do you stay away from them?"

"No telling what they might do. Could turn you into a frog, or make you drop dead, and no one the wiser."

"Exactly. So, let me tell you a story about a man with a grudge against those wizards and how he warped his son." His audience looked interested. "I suppose it started back with Mad Wizard Aplath. . ."

Jorac briefly sketched the story of Wolburn and his plan to store enough magic power to overpower all the wizards in the kingdom. He described the Wolburn Sphere and its contents, followed with the salient fact that he and his squad had now taken possession of it. He finished by saying, "So that's our problem. We can't just burn the stuff or dump it in the swamp. That much concentrated magic would warp any creature in the area into something dangerous; that's why the deep swamp has such a bad reputation to this day. The only safe way to get rid of it is to spread it out among people, so it will get gradually released like normal. That's why we're asking for your help. If we can throw a gigantic party here in Swampside, we can get everybody to just drink it up."

Madame Revar was obviously a suspicious sort. "A pretty story. But you two are constables; how do we know you don't just want to trap us into selling unlicensed booze?"

Schrog snorted, and said in an undertone, "As if you would know anything about that." At her glare, he continued, "Nay, I ain't sayin' nuttin'. One or two of you knows I used to live around here, but I ain't been back since I got my new job, you knows dat. I ain't never grassed on nobody, ain't gonna start. Mister Raah, he can tell you dat be true. And besides, we wouldn't bovver none wit' de small stuff. What we got here – it be dammed important."

Skowers raised an eyebrow. "Not to seem ungracious, but why should we assist you in this enterprise?"

Jorac said emphatically, "Because the alternative is just too scary to contemplate!" The four chiefs stared back at him noncommittally.

He motioned to Veseen to come near, and said to them, "I thought you might think we're over-reacting, so I brought along this fourteen-year-old wizard apprentice to show you what that magic liquid can do." He looked around at them. "How old do wizards have to be before they come into their full power?"

Skowers answered. "I've heard that they seldom reach their full power before about thirty years of age. But of course they can change their looks."

Jorac said, "Yes, that's true. Veseen, please forgive me. You're a young man who'll doubtless grow into a handsome fellow, but you're at an awkward age right now. Tall, thin, and – count your blessings – only half the pimples I had at your age."

Veseen turned red at this frank description and self-consciously put his hand to his face.

Jorac turned to the chiefs. "I put it to you, would any powerful wizard remake his image to this?"

They looked at each other, and then Jimsley said, "Nay, but what's your point"

"A small demonstration. Veseen's current primary talent as a wizard is lighting candles. Veseen, would you light that candle over there?" He pointed to a candlestick about ten feet away.

"It's a little far," Veseen said. "I can try."

Jorac walked across the room and opened the door to check for eavesdroppers while Veseen concentrated. Finally the candle spluttered into flame. Jorac felt the familiar tickle in his nose, but managed to suppress his sneeze.

Jimsley scowled. "Okay, he's a wizard, or a wizard-to-be, or whatever. What's your point?"

"Dorrie, would you show them what's in that little bottle please?"

Dorrie pulled the tiny silver bottle out of her pocket and showed it with a flourish, then walked over to the table, where there were several empty cups and a clear glass pitcher of water. She spoke in Dorrie the market-seller's theatrical voice, not Madame Velsop's deeper one.

"Ladies and gentlemen, may I have your attention, please? This is some of that magical liquid, the stuff you're wondering about. Watch closely and you'll see it actually glows a little. See as I pour it into this cup?"

She poured the liquid back and forth between two cups until everyone nodded. "Now, this is just a swallow or two, but it's plenty. You've seen that it glows in rainbow colors. What do you think it smells like?"

Someone said, "Booze," and she said, "That's right. Spirits, like you might get from a triple distilling process. Pure stuff, and strong." She carried the cup around and held it in front of each of their noses, including Nobber.

She went back to the table. "This pitcher here is pure water, brought up from downstairs. Anyone want to smell that? No?" She poured a cupful of water. "Okay, now I'll use it to dilute our liquid a little, so it won't burn quite so much going down." She poured a little water into the cup with the spirits and ceremoniously handed it to Veseen.

"Veseen is going to drink this, and wash it down with this cupful of water."

Veseen did as she said, and then stood there quietly, trying not to make faces or cough. Dorrie smiled beatifically and motioned to turn the proceedings over to Jorac, who was standing at the back of the room.

Jorac spoke to everyone. "Will all of you please move back here with me, away from that fireplace? No, come farther, please. Well back."

When they'd all moved far enough, Dorrie continued. "Now, this young apprentice, who you saw struggle to light a candle ten feet away, will light that fire. We asked the landlord to lay us a good fire, with some heavy logs, but not light it. Any of you want to go look at it, and make sure it's as we say?"

Jimsley nudged Nobber, who went over and poked at the fireplace a little. He brought back a small piece of kindling and gave it to Jimsley, who smelled it suspiciously, then passed it around. Jimsley grudgingly said, "Seems normal."

Jorac said, "Veseen, if you would," and held his breath.

It was really a fairly small explosion, as such things went. There was a flash of heat that felt as if it would singe their hair across the room, and several people cried out. The chimney was shaken, and a cloud of soot and ashes puffed into the room. A cloth napkin left on the table in front of the fireplace was charred and smoldering. The fire in the fireplace was burning briskly, all the tinder was gone, and the bigger logs were half consumed.

The puff of soot and cinders blew across the room, and several people started to cough. Jorac walked into the cloud, sneezing from both the magic and the soot. He grabbed the water pitcher off the table, poured a little on the smoldering napkin, and stomped out a few embers that had escaped the fireplace, while Schrog went to the door and reassured the landlord (who had run upstairs) that it wasn't really an explosion, they'd just decided they wanted a fire in the fireplace. The landlord was far from convinced, but left when the "chiefs" waved him away.

After things calmed down a little, and they again had privacy, Jorac spoke.

"The Wizard Council assigned me this apprentice partly because he's not arrogant enough for them to think much of him. That fact saved all our lives. Anyone who has that much power and as much ambition as most wizards would have just taken over the city, and don't think they couldn't do it."

The chiefs looked shaken. Veseen dramatically raised his hand and performed the now-familiar Exercise Number Three, spraying colored streams around the room. He spoke for the first time, his voice firm and serious.

"I'm the most powerful wizard in the city, for a little while. And I just drank a mouthful of that stuff. Jorac says we have at least two hundred gallons of it."

Jorac sneezed a few more times, then continued. "We could dump it in the river, and maybe not spawn man-eating fish or some other monster that would come up the river and eat you all. Maybe. If you four don't go along, that's what happens. But that's not the best way of handling it. The best way is to get everyone in Swampside to drink a little. That'll spread it out, slow down the release, and no one will ever get enough to do what Veseen just did."

The chiefs exchanged calculating looks. Schrog said, "Don' worry, if we hand out dat free booze, us constables ain't admittin' it. You chiefs gets all de credit, makes you real popular hereabouts. Us constables, we done our job, we jus' smile and go on home."

Jorac nodded. "It'll make everybody happy – except the big wizards when they find out. I'll get fired of course, but I can get another job. This way we don't end up with the wizards fighting amongst themselves, like Aplath's Rebellion. Or wizards running the country, like they do in Zargrona. When normal folks escape from there, we hear stories sometimes; I don't think we'd like it much."

Dorrie said, "I can't imagine this will be a good place to live if the wizards start fighting each other, do you?"

Raah said, "Swampside ain't such a good place to live anyways, but I gets your point."

Schrog said, "So, tomorrow we has us a big fockin' party, right?"

Chapter 15 - We're Having a Party

They quickly agreed to the party, but working out the details took the rest of the evening. They'd have to dilute the raw spirits enough for people to drink it, and flavor it enough to be palatable. Jorac estimated they'd end up with a thousand gallons or more of punch by the time they were through. That meant an average of eight thousand people had to each drink a pint of punch. Jorac thought there were perhaps ten thousand adults in Swampside, so they needed an excellent turnout.

They thought the punch should be sweet enough for everyone to enjoy, even those who normally didn't drink. But sweetness alone wouldn't be enough; it had to have some tartness, too, or adults would soon tire of it. Jimsley knew where some hogshead barrels full of vinegary apple cider could be bought cheap, payment later, but Jorac had to agree to pay up front for a few barrels of smuggled honey. (The emperor taxed luxury goods like honey at a higher rate, so good money could be made smuggling them; this was apparently Skowers' specialty.) The party could be held in the square by the city fountain; Madame Revar could arrange for the necessary festive accouterments (tables, cups, food, music, etc.) and for publicizing the event.

Jorac agreed to pay for these and all the other expenses for the party from his group's share of the silver in the sphere. Being city employees, Jorac, Schrog, and Hox couldn't officially keep their share, anyway – they'd have to turn it in and hope for a reward – so he didn't mind pledging a good bit of it for this enterprise. But this meant he'd have to arrange for the sphere to be cut up and divided as soon as it was empty. And of course Gleben and his crew would immediately want their share too. One more thing to worry about tomorrow.

The final stumbling block was getting the sphere from the swamp to town. It was awkward and gigantically heavy, and transporting it would take a couple of long, sturdy poles and a number of men who could be relied on not to ask too many questions. For the bosses of Swampside, men like that were easy enough to find, but they had to wake up a man who worked in a shipyard and get him to "rent" them some ship's timbers. Jorac was sure the shipyard owners wouldn't know about their timbers' temporary use, but he figured it would work out, as long as they got back the timbers back intact.

Jorac and his team finally got some sleep after midnight; they managed to find two rooms at a place Madame Revar knew, for just a few coppers (cash up front please). Veseen offered to drink the last few drops from Dorrie's bottle and do his insect-warding spell again; Jorac let him try it and hoped it would work against fleas and bedbugs as well as it had against flies and gnats in the swamp.

* * *

Jorac woke early, his head awash with the things that had to be done. His clothes smelled of the swamp, but he had no time to get them cleaned, or even shop for more, so he washed up as best he could, waking up Schrog and Veseen in the process. He knocked on Dorrie's door and went downstairs, where he was greeted by a man who said he was to fetch Raah as soon as he saw Jorac.

The rest of the morning was a whirlwind. It started by sending Raah, Schrog, and a crew of twenty-some with a lot of rope and the two long timbers down into the swamp. Schrog then fetched Hox to help them, along with Hatlo, Hario, and Toop, who explained that Gleben had gone back into town, leaving instructions that he was to be notified when the silver was divided, and that rather than cash, he wanted an actual slice of the sphere.

The sphere had been covered with branches and the small tent to camouflage its shape and hide the silver, and it looked like a huge odd lump. The expanded crew lashed the sphere to the timbers, using some of the wooden cradle and lots of rope. Then, with every able-bodied man shouldering part of the burden, they worked their way up the path toward Swampside. Miz Madouve, who had made a stop at her house, joined them part way there.

Meanwhile Dorrie escorted Veseen back to his dormitory. Jorac had thanked him again for his masterful performance at the chiefs' meeting, and he and the others sincerely apologized, but Veseen was really too young for this sort of party and they were already days late getting him back. Jorac wrote another flowery note to Master Radyry full of praise for Veseen's talent and mature resourcefulness, and Dorrie promised to meet with the wizard master and lay it on thick. Veseen clearly wasn't happy to leave just when exciting things were about to happen, but seemed resigned. Jorac could sympathize.

While she was in town, Dorrie had a chance to stop by her house and pick up some things, and then got back to Swampside before noon. There she met Kimma as Miz Madouve, who had come in along with the crew bringing the sphere. After lunch, they were supposed to talk to the Madame and set up the distribution side of the party arrangements near the fountain. Somewhere in the process Kimma would emerge from her disguise – Jorac was looking forward to seeing her dressed as a young lady.

Punch-mixing was the next thing on the agenda. Jimsley had arranged for the temporary exclusive use of an old boathouse on the edge of town; that morning one of his men had arrived there with a small, light wagon, overloaded and groaning with the weight of eight big barrels of apple cider. Skowers had brought some casks of smuggled honey to the same place, and was waiting there with a couple of guards when Jorac arrived. When the crew with the timbers got the sphere to the edge of Swampside, a guide sent by Jimsley met them and led them to the boathouse as well.

The crew carried their burden into the boathouse. Hox stood outside; inside, his head would have hit the rafters near the walls, and Jorac was happy to have someone on guard anyway. His strength wasn't needed when more than twenty normal-sized men were available for labor.

While the crew rested and waited, Hatlo, Hario, and Toop used the boards they brought from the swamp to stack up the same sort of cradle the sphere had rested on before. Then the crew all heaved together and hoisted the canvas-covered sphere up onto the cradle; it was heavy and they were tired, so it took a few tries to get it situated. The front end of the timbers hit the back wall of the long, narrow boathouse, but it worked well enough. While the rope was being untied and the timbers were being removed for their trip back to the shipyard, Jorac looked at their materials, and worried that they wouldn't have enough barrels to hold their mix.

When the timbers were freed and the men who carried them were ready to go, Raah had them roll in the barrels full of cider and stand them in the corner. Then he told them, "Pays you tonight, like we said. By de fountain. Big free party dere tonight, bring your pals," and sent them off.

Jorac asked Hatlo, Hario, and Toop to please wait outside with Hox for a few minutes while he consulted with the two chiefs. "Sorry," he said, "it won't be long; we just need to look at something."

Jorac and Schrog closed the big double doors and then removed the old canvas tent from the sphere. It was dim inside, but enough light leaked through the slat walls to let them see. Jorac was glad of that; he didn't like the idea of lanterns around so much strong spirits. He and Schrog, Raah, and Skowers all stood back and looked at their progress. Jorac said, "We might have more than two hundred gallons here. Our guy said it was a rough guess. Do we have enough mix, and enough barrels to hold it?"

Raah said, "If dis ain't enough cider, we can get plenty more. Dis place up nort' buys it cheap when it starts gettin' old, makes it into vinegar. Dere's a warehouse full of it up in Pigtown."

Skowers said, "I believe that a few more barrels of honey might also be available, but regrettably the cost will be higher, since I'll need to pay a forfeit to those they're currently promised to. As to the empty barrels, Jimsley was to deliver those; I suppose this was all that could be found on short notice."

Jorac looked around, and counted. "Schrog, do you think we have enough barrels?" There were about twenty barrels stacked against the wall, some so small as to rightly be called casks, not barrels.

Schrog make a quick count, then said, "Nope. Not even if we just fill dese barrels wit' de cider and de stuff, and den take 'em to de fountain and add de honey dere. But what we do is use dem big cider barrels too, as soon as dey's empty. Dat might just be enough."

Raah and Skowers nodded, and Jorac said, "Yeah, that's a good idea. So we'll just send barrels of concentrate to the fountain, along with the honey, and they can finish mixing it there. Right?"

Raah nodded. "Jimsley runs de fountain area, so dat part should be okay. And the Madame, she's lettin' all the girls come down when dey ain't otherwise occupied. Mostly it's a matter of gettin' the word out, and gettin' it all set up with tables and cups and such. For dat we're gonna need some cash."

Jorac thought of the few gold pieces left in his pocket; he'd spent all his smaller coins and hadn't had time to visit a money changer. He said to Raah, "You and the other chiefs are paying all those expenses now, but you're keeping account so I can pay you back, right?"

"Yup. With interest. Dat's what we agreed."

"Good," Jorac said, and pointed at the silver ball. "Let's see what we can do to get that thing emptied. Those three outside each get ten percent of the silver for bringing it out from where it was hidden, but they don't need to know what's inside it. Schrog, can you get them out of here for a while?"

Schrog cackled. "Sure. . . I knows, I'll get deir day started like it'll end – I'll buy dem a drink!"

* * *

Jorac's concern about the number of barrels available proved well founded, and what he didn't anticipate was how long it would take to drain the spirits out of the sphere. The small tap that Wolburn had installed was fine for filling a glass at a time, but Jorac was trying to fill barrels. Yet he didn't want to spill any, so merely hacking a hole in the side wouldn't work well either. He finally used his dagger and a mallet he found to drive a vent hole in the top, which he gradually enlarged as they filled the first small barrel.

Finally they had a large enough hole in the top of the sphere to dip a bucket into, and they started making better progress. As the level in the sphere dropped, they had to pause several times and enlarge the hole. Jorac was going to need a new dagger; treating this one as a chisel was doing it no good, but they managed to get the hole enlarged enough to let even Hox put his arm and shoulder inside, and Hox could reach nearly to the bottom of the sphere with the bucket in his hand.

After a while they all started feeling a little woozy, even tipsy, from the fumes. Jorac called several breaks and opened the doors at both ends of the boathouse to air it out. Skowers and Raah assured him the word had gone out to stay away from this area, but Jorac knew there was always someone who didn't get the message, so he worried about secrecy. He walked around the building several times, just looking, but saw no one.

They started by filling the empty barrels half full of spirits but ended up with them closer to two-thirds full. Then they added enough cider to fill the barrels to the top and put the lids on. The main thing Jorac wanted was to have enough cider in all the barrels to kill that eerie rainbow-colored glow; at least they managed that, but when they tasted a little, the mix was still undrinkably strong.

Finally, after emptying three of the cider barrels and refilling them with mix, they ended up with eight knee-high barrels that one man could lift, seven thigh-high ones that two men could barely manage, and three large barrels that would need to be rolled everywhere. They'd need to mix in the honey and add more cider, not just water from the fountain as they hoped, but their concentrated mix would do for now.

Jimsley's man Nobber showed up in early afternoon and said he'd drive Jimsley's light wagon to the fountain. On hearing they were almost done, he agreed to wait and go with the heavy main wagon that was to ferry the punch mix. He'd brought horses with him, and Hox and Jorac helped hitch them up; they were excellent horses, and Jorac privately wondered how they ended up pulling a wagon in Swampside, but kept his mouth shut. When the wagon was loaded with the honey casks and the five unopened cider barrels, Nobber pulled it up beside the boathouse and waited while they finished up inside.

After they sealed the last barrel, Skowers stepped out of the boathouse and gave two loud whistles. In a few minutes, a large wagon appeared; in the back was a small crew of dark-skinned, rough-looking characters with straight back hair pulled into pony tails. Jorac had never seen this type of people before, and he had traveled fairly widely before becoming a city constable. Skowers spoke to them in a language Jorac didn't understand, and motioned at the barrels.

Jorac said, "Schrog and Hox are going with those barrels. Let them know they'll kill anyone who tries to take any of them."

"Oh, these fellows are all right. They come from way down south; they don't care much for our ways here, or our trinkets. You don't have to worry about them."

"Let them know anyway, as politely as you please, but let them know. Wouldn't do to have them make an honest mistake, right?"

Skowers looked a little dubious, and was starting to say something when Schrog said in his best menacing tone, "Dead, accidental-like, still be dead. Best tell them."

Skowers sighed. "Very well, I shall inform them to leave these barrels alone, and the penalty for transgression." He spoke again, and motioned at Hox and Schrog. They were all smaller than Schrog, and looked to be in awe of Hox, so to Jorac they seemed properly cowed. Jorac pulled Schrog aside and told him to keep an eye on Nobber, too.

When the loaded wagons had left on their lumbering way, Schrog fetched Hatlo, Hario, and Toop from the pub where he'd left them. It was already past noon, and Jorac was left with two chiefs, three swampies, and a silver ball to dismantle and convert to cash.

Toop knew Skowers, and Hatlo and Hario knew Raah. The swampies were respectful enough, but hard bargainers. It took a little while before an agreement was reached, formally witnessed by a bemused Jorac. Each swampie was due ten percent of the silver in the sphere. Raah would arrange to melt it down; Skowers, with his upper-class manners, would sell it to jewelers in the better parts of town. The chiefs would then give each swampie eighty percent of what they received for that person's share. It might take a while to get their money but that was all to the good, Jorac didn't want people wondering about anyone's windfall.

Jorac promptly struck the same deal for the rest of the sphere. Gleben had said that he wanted a slice from the actual sphere, but Jorac was going to overrule him; he didn't want a wizard someday seeing part of the sphere and puzzling out what it was for.

He estimated in his head how much his own share was going to come to. Even with all his expenses and Dorrie's five gold a day, it looked like he'd be turning a profit on this operation. Working for wizards, he wasn't foolish enough to actually cheat on his expenses, but some creativity was possible.

Raah volunteered to handle the cash for the transaction, and give an accounting to each party at the end. When everyone else nodded approval, Jorac did also; Raah apparently had a reputation for fair dealing. After the agreement was concluded, with formal handshakes to seal it, Jorac laid down the law about not talking about the sphere. When Skowers and Raah joined in on the pressure, the three swampies agreed and formally pledged their silence. Their cover story would be that they'd found a gold bar, close enough to the truth but misleading enough to keep wizards off the trail.

The actual dismantling of the sphere was kind of fun. Someone found a good steel axe, and it was chopped into manageable pieces in short order. Hatlo, Hario, and Toop went with Raah and the silver to keep an eye on everything as Raah carted it away in a small wagon.

Finally, the preparations were in order, and Jorac and Skowers hurried to the fountain.

* * *

The fountain area was a little busier than normal; there were some large awnings being set up but no party was going on there yet. The two wagons with the barrels had been pulled up in sight of the fountain, and the area around them had been roped off. Hox stood beside them, and the small brown men were on guard around the perimeter. Jorac noticed Hox had his cudgel out. He gave Hox a thumbs-up gesture and went around the fountain where he'd seen Schrog.

He found Schrog talking to Jimsley and his companion Nobber. Jorac walked over to greet them, and asked about the ladies.

Schrog said, "Dorrie has t'ings handled. Dey're off wit' de Madame, gettin' stuff fer de party. Needs two bands, so's we gots music all de time."

Jorac raised his eyebrows. "Not that I'm questioning your judgment, but why do we need a band, much less two?"

Jimsley grunted. "You ain't never run a bar, dat be clear. Folks hear music, dey move around more, dance even. Makes 'em thirsty. Got a baker workin' on some salty snacks too. You got de money worked out?" By his suspicious expression, he expected someone to try to cheat him.

"Yes, but it's complicated. Let me get someone to explain it better. My assurances will probably comfort you little." Jimsley didn't seem to know what to make of that and said nothing. Jorac craned his head around and spotted Skowers some distance away, talking to a pretty lass who'd evidently been fetching water.

Jorac went over to get him. "Sorry to interrupt, but Mister Jimsley needs to hear that we have the money worked out."

Skowers waved a negligent hand. "You may tell him I said things are fine." He turned back to talk to the girl. "So, me darlin', are you going to be here tonight?" His clothing and manner wouldn't have been out of place even in the finest areas of the city.

Jorac smiled at the girl and said, "Everyone will be here tonight. Everyone. It's the social event of the year." He changed to his upper-class accent, and said, "Honorable Master Skowers, your immediate attention is requested and required, at the fountain. Master Jimsley has certain queries that you are best suited to answer."

Skowers did a double-take, and burst into laughter. "Well, with such an invitation, I can scarcely refuse. Lead on, lead on!" He winked and waved at the girl, and went with Jorac.

Skowers explained to Jimsley all about the agreement between himself, Raah, the three swampies, and the other parties who had a claim on the silver, and Jimsley seemed satisfied. The four chiefs of Swampside may have trusted each other somewhat, Jorac thought, but none of them expected the others to take their bare word for anything.

The first band appeared before anyone was ready for them, so Jorac had them put their instruments over with Hox and the wagons, and sent them off to try to find something that would work as a bandstand, or at least some sort of raised platform that would put the music above the crowd.

Shortly afterwards, a procession of women came down the street carrying tables, with Madame Revar in the lead. The Madame halted them and Jorac and Skowers went to meet them.

"You be gettin' de money straight?" were her first words. On receiving assurances from Skowers, she waved the procession forward. Jorac pointed toward a wide area in front of the fountain, and the women carried the tables there. By flattering Jimsley and his bar-running skills, Jorac got him to agree to supervise setting up the tables for mixing and serving.

"Where are the two ladies?" Jorac asked the Madame, and received a laugh in response. "They be getting' ready. Never you mind, they'll be here before too long. They both needed fresh clothes. Yer Dorrie, she told me to find sump'n fer de t'ree of you men to wear too. My girls be bringing it – even got sump'n to fit Muscles there." Jorac figured anything clean that roughly fit would be better than the swamp-stained clothes they were wearing.

The Madame leered at him. "De girls was fussin' over which one gets to measure you – 'specially de trousers." She cackled. "Oh, you should see de look on your face. You prolly t'ink dat scar makes you ugly, right? Not half, sonny boy, not half."

Jorac was faintly alarmed by the conversation, and left to check on the cider, with her laughter and a few bawdy calls from the painted ladies following him.

Raah went to look for what was holding up the delivery of drinking vessels – leather jacks and simple clay mugs. Most people would bring their own, but some would need them, and Raah was going to sell them cheaply, encouraging drinking and making a small profit for himself in the bargain. Anything that helped the dangerous liquid disappear safely was fine with Jorac.

Two pairs of middle-aged women arrived, each carrying a large wooden tub between them. With their arrival, the actual mixing could begin. Jorac worked with Hox to roll a cider barrel and the first big barrel of concentrated mix off the wagons and over to the tables. He helped open both barrels, and they started mixing punch.

As far as the mixing ladies were concerned, the cider/spirits mix from the barrel was just an extra-strong version of raw hard cider. They and Jorac experimented with it and found that the best way of getting it drinkable was to add two full cups of cider for each scant cup of mix, plus a generous dollop of honey. With less honey, they had to add more cider or some water to hide the strong flavor, and that didn't taste as good. They agreed they'd save that strategy for later, after the drinkers' tongues were a bit numb. Skowers had sent someone off to get more honey, but they had enough to get started, so the four ladies started mixing punch in the big tubs on the tables, using buckets full of ingredients.

Hox, Schrog and Jorac took turns changing into clean clothes (they turned out to be rather fancy and well fitting) and watching the mixing and taste-testing the punch. Though the sun wasn't yet down, the band started playing some warm-up songs, and the first few people came up, wondering what the occasion was and if they were invited.

"Everyone's invited," Jorac told them. "Bring your friends. Come back with your cups, have a free drink."

"What are you celebrating?" one of them asked.

Schrog said loudly, "Kullo be dead. From now on, no more slavers hereabouts. Chiefs say so. Big party to celebrate."

They repeated this scene a few times, and within minutes people were arriving and being served punch. If it seemed an odd excuse for a party, no one was looking a gift horse in the mouth.

Jorac and Schrog surveyed the scene. On the long serving tables in front of the tubs there were a dozen or more pitchers of punch tied with long ropes – they could be refilled from the tubs without untying them but couldn't be taken away. Various people assigned by Jimsley kept the pitchers full, occasionally having to go out into the crowd to stop a squabble. More people arrived and crowded around the tables; the drinks were flowing quickly, but the mixers and pitcher-fillers were keeping up. It looked as if it was going to work.

The first cider barrel was nearly empty, and the barrel of mix was going down fast. Leaving Schrog to watch it, Jorac poured a half mug of punch and took it over to Hox, who was still standing guard at the wagons. Just a taste, Jorac explained; they still needed to keep an eye on things.

Hox took a swallow and said, "Tastes okay, I guess. With all that bother, I was thinking it was going to be something special. This seems kind of, well normal. We might have something like it at harvest festival."

Jorac grinned. "Glad to hear it. We had trouble getting it even this good." Then he added, "They're starting to run low on ingredients over there, so we need to take them some more barrels. Once all our mix has been turned into punch, we can have some ourselves."

Nobber rolled an empty cider barrel over toward them. When he got there he said, "Looks like we're going to need more cider pretty soon. I'll go get some. Need to take back the empty barrels too. Let me know when they're ready to go."

Hox said, "Well, if you'd help unload these full barrels off your cider wagon, we'd be ready sooner."

"I guess so. Be right back," he said, and went over to talk to Jimsley.

Hox and Jorac – well, mostly Hox – unloaded the cider wagon, rolling the barrels down some strong boards off the back of the wagon, and Nobber came back to help them unload the last one. Nobber helped Hox lift two empty barrels onto the wagon, and said, "As soon as we get one more barrel emptied, I'll go. Right now I think I'll go have a drink." And that's what he did; Jorac saw him drinking and talking to one of the men tending the tables, and keeping an eye on his boss.

Jorac walked once around the outskirts of the fountain area, and found nothing specific to be bothered about, but he was still worried. He was anxious about Dorrie and Kimma, and worried about a wizard showing up. He didn't know if wizards could sense mana in this form, but if so the area would fairly reek of it, and there would be trouble.

He wandered back toward the fountain, and watched as Nobber single-handedly carried a large empty barrel to the wagon, lifted it onto the wagon bed, and tied it down. An empty barrel wasn't so heavy, but in this size it was an awkward load.

Maybe by carrying it alone he wanted to show up Hox. Nobber looked strong and muscular, but Jorac doubted he could match Hox, who was not only strong but much larger.

His musings were interrupted by a loud, appreciative whistle, which drew his attention up a side street leading to the square. Two ladies were approaching, dressed in finery and lace. One was Dorrie, with a thin, polite lady's walking stick, a large, fashionable hat, and a long lavender dress set off by a rose-colored cape.

Dorrie he recognized, so the other one must be Kimma, but she looked ten times as good as the swamp girl from the days before. Her dress was amazing: Jorac normally didn't notice things like that, but this was striking. It had a lacy white skirt with a dramatic red slash down the left side, and a tight, low-cut pink and red bodice, made more modest by the addition of a wide rose-colored chiffon pouf over her shoulders. It was set off with a lightweight fringed white cape that hung down to her knees in the back, and rustled and swayed as she walked. Her wide white hat had a matching red slash; it wasn't as big as Dorrie's hat and was meant to complement the dress rather than be an item of attention. In all, the look was devastating, and by the time she'd walked just a short way, all eyes were on her – especially all male eyes.

At first her steps seemed a little hesitant, but Jorac could see Dorrie say something to her, and she pulled her head higher and stepped out with confidence. It was a fine sight to see.

He was mentally preparing suitable remarks when he saw Nobber and the wagon cross in front of him, and something clicked in his head. He yelled, "Stop that wagon! Hox, Schrog!" He started running after the wagon, but it was already across the square from him.

Nobber whipped the horses into a faster gait, and Schrog and Hox jumped to follow him. Jorac waved Schrog back – they still had other barrels to protect, and Schrog didn't move as fast as Hox.

Jorac and Hox chased the wagon, but it was already outrunning them. Nobber again whipped the horses to still greater speed and turned up the street the ladies were coming down.

Jorac yelled "Wolburn!" and pointed at the speeding wagon. The front two barrels were visibly bouncing in the wagon bed, but the third one was obviously heavier than the others.

The two ladies quickly stepped to the side, out of the path of the wagon. Kimma whipped off her cape and flung it at the horses – it hit one of them in the face, causing it to rear and pull the wagon closer to their side of the street. The horse quickly shook off the cape, but the wagon had slowed a bit.

As the wagon passed in front of them, Dorrie stepped forward and stuck her thin walking stick into the spokes of the back wheel. As the wheel turned, it yanked the stick from her hand and flung it against the wagon. Jorac wondered what on earth she was doing, but the elegant carved wooden cover broke off the stick, revealing a stout metal bar inside. The bar initially locked up the wheel, then one of the spokes let go with a crash, followed by another and another, and soon the wheel broke entirely, and that corner of the wagon was down.

Nobber whipped the horses to greater effort, but they were now badly aimed and pulling an uneven load. They were excellent horses, probably very fast, but not used to hauling wagons through city streets. When the left side horse tried to push the right side one into a building, the right side horse reached over and tried to bite the other one. Meanwhile the rope holding the barrels had let go and they were now rolling around the back of the wagon, further spooking the horses.

All the commotion gave Jorac and Hox time to catch up. Jorac jumped up on the back of the wagon and had started to climb forward to grab Nobber from behind, when he saw Nobber launch himself at Hox.

Nobber must have thought he could knock Hox down, but Hox was too quick. He simply sidestepped, grabbing one of Nobber's arms. Then he just squeezed and bent the arm a bit, breaking it. Nobber's forearm looked nasty, with the bone poking through the skin. All the fight left him, and he lay on the ground whimpering.

The whole thing had taken only thirty seconds or so, and the few people who saw it had made themselves scarce; this was Swampside, after all, and it didn't pay to notice things here. Kimma calmly picked up the slightly bent metal bar – it still had the elegant handle, and proved to have a sharp point on it – and rested it gently on Nobber's chest. He wasn't going anywhere. Jorac smiled a big smile at her and said, "Good job!" Meanwhile, Hox and Dorrie did their best to settle the horses, who were still trying to get away and take the wagon with them.

It was a few more seconds before Raah and Skowers came up, along with a few of their guards.

"What the hell!" Skowers accent slipped a little – was that a Swampside accent Jorac heard?

Jorac was catching his breath. "Hox, can you lift that barrel? The one in the back."

Hox walked back, reached over the side of the wagon, casually put his arms around the big cider barrel, and lifted it out. "It's not that heavy, but it has something inside it." He pried the top off with Jorac's maltreated dagger; inside was one of the middle-sized barrels with the mana-filled concentrate, the size Jorac thought it would take two people to lift.

Jorac said, "I think this needs to go back with the other barrels, don't you?" Hox nodded, and when Jorac turned to Skowers and Raah, they nodded vigorously too. Jorac marveled as Hox picked up the barrel and walked off down the street with it. It wasn't a one-hand load for him, but it didn't seem to be a great strain.

Jorac said to the men behind Raah, "Can one of you take care of the horses, and Nobber? I'd like to thank the ladies who probably just saved all our lives." Raah nodded assent, and the men quickly did as he asked, freeing Dorrie and Kimma to join him.

Jorac went and picked up the cape that Kimma had thrown at the horse, then walked back and presented it to her. "Dear lady, I believe you dropped your handkerchief?"

Kimma started laughing, and it was infectious. Dorrie joined in, and soon the whole group was howling with laughter. It had been a long, stressful day.

* * *

They were still giggling when they got back to the party. Because the band kept playing, few people had even noticed them leave, and seeing them come back with smiles on their faces was reassuring. The chiefs' smiles disappeared when they found the Madame and confronted Jimsley. One of Raah's men pushed Jimsley's wheelchair to an area on the other side of the fountain, ignoring the crippled man's protests.

Skowers waved everyone away, and those nearby made themselves scarce. But when Jorac shook his head in a determined fashion, he was allowed to stay. He felt he had a stake in this operation, and they apparently agreed. Doubtless, he thought, he was the first constable to sit in on a meeting of the Swampside underworld leaders; not that he'd ever mention it to anyone.

Raah glared at Jimsley and said in a furious tone, "You vouched for dat bastard. And then he tried to run off with one of dem barrels. I ain't bowin' to no damned wizard because you can't pick a guy to push dat damned chair."

Jimsley glared back at the three chiefs and Jorac; he looked scared, angry, sour, but not giving up.

"I didn't have nuttin' to do wit' it."

The Madame said, "Don't matter none. You vouched, dat's de same as you tried to steal it. You steals from us, you know what dat means."

Skowers was equally angry. "These two are quite right. You could have sent him out of the room. You can't say you didn't know what the penalties are."

There was silence for a moment and then Jorac said, "I'd suggest you leave him alive. The wizards may want to question him." While that was true, Jorac also didn't want to see any more violence tonight. Nobber's compound fracture and probable early demise was plenty for one evening.

Raah said, "Oh? Whats you want us to do wit' him, spank him like a baby?"

Jorac said, "I imagine he has quite a bit of wealth, correct?"

They thought it over for a few seconds. Skowers said, "*Had* quite a bit."

Raah said, "All right, had. Best deal you gonna get. Lucky I gots a soft heart."

The Madame agreed, "Had. He works fer me, room and board only. We split his business, t'ree ways."

The group looked at Jimsley; cold, hard looks one and all. It wasn't so much defeat as bitter acceptance on his face. "All right, dammit. If I could still walk... never mind. But tonight I'm going to get drunk." He reached for the mug of the punch, and downed it in a gulp.

Jorac wasn't sure he'd done a good thing consolidating the power in the district, but he could worry about that another time. What was important was that they were still on track to get rid of the mana-filled spirits, tonight. He went back to the barrel storage area and, with Skowers interpreting, talked to the guards and made sure they knew the only place the barrels could go was over to the mixing station.

* * *

As the evening wore on, torches were lit and the bands kept playing. Jorac had the punch mixed up a little stronger now, and he watched it disappear into the large, happy crowd. The bar owners were the only unhappy people around, but even they were making some money hawking food, and all the regular street vendors were doing great business. The Madame's many ladies all showed up for a cup or three; some of them left with a customer on their arm, so it was probably a good night for them, too.

The few people who knew the real reason behind the party each took turns watching the barrels, but they tried to do it casually, without drawing too much attention to them. By the time the final barrel of spirits was rolled over to the punch mixers, it was several hours after midnight. Jorac thought it had been eight or ten hours since they started, but the party was still going. The serious drunks had shown up early and mostly gotten their fill, and now many of them who passed out earlier were staggering back for a second go. There were a few people who had vomited, but they were near the fountain and a few buckets of water washed things away; since the area wasn't known for a lovely odor to start with, no one seemed to mind. The two bands had gotten too tired to play, but amateurs had taken over their instruments and were playing on, with less skill but greater enthusiasm. Their music was good enough to dance to, and a few tireless souls were still dancing, or something like it.

Kimma and Dorrie were sitting with the punch servers, and taking turns themselves. Jorac walked over to them and said, "Dorrie, Kimma, you both look so great tonight."

Kimma said, "You said that before," to which Dorrie giggled. Dorrie was giggling a lot since she'd gotten a few drinks inside her.

"You know what I like best about those dresses?"

Dorrie said, "No, Jorac, why don't you tell us?" and giggled some more.

"I like those little mud stains. Shows you know how to save the day, no matter how you're dressed. I like that in a woman."

Dorrie pretended to slap him, and giggled. Kimma just laughed. Jorac liked her laugh.

Chapter 16 - Pergimtor's Reaction

Jorac stood in the council room, while Pergimtor glowered, and considered what he said. He'd demanded to speak only to the Head Wizard, and had eventually gotten his way. *Oh well,* he thought, *this job paid better than most, but I can get another job. If Pergimtor doesn't blackball me, maybe Cerom will take me back with the constables.*

"So, let me get this straight. You took that mana-filled liquid – spirits of wine – back to Swampside?"

"Yes, High Wizard. It took us three days to get that ball back there. It was quite heavy."

"And then you gave it away?"

"Well, we threw a party with it. Schrog talked the bosses there into hosting an area-wide celebration, and we volunteered to make the punch. It lasted until dawn, and the residents drank up all the punch. That's where most of the silver we found went, too, to buy things for the party, pay guards and such. Most of the mana came from Darlora's area, so back there it went."

"I see. And the silver ball – what you call the Wolburn Sphere?"

"Well, that was what he called it. We broke it up with an ax, and it will get melted down for jewelry and such. We owed the swampies some of the silver, for helping us get it out of the swamp. A lot of it we spent on the party." Jorac had carefully arranged not to have an accounting from Raah yet. He didn't want to lie to a wizard.

The wizard sat down slowly and sighed. "Well, what's done is done. You should have come to me, dammit! What I could have done with that liquid. . . I'll expect a report tomorrow."

"No, High wizard. A thousand pardons, but no."

"No?" The wizard wasn't used to hearing that word, and got a little upset. "No?!"

"High wizard, I believe you are the most powerful wizard on the council, correct? If I wrote that report, and someone with lesser power read it, how long before he had made a similar sphere?"

"Erm. . ."

"And all over the land, in caves and secret hideaways, those who would always be second or third rate wizards would hole themselves up, slowly gathering immense power. . . You see my point. No report."

The wizard closed his eyes and sighed a deep sigh. "All right. No report. You may go."

"You'll want to speak to the scholar Gleben, to make sure he doesn't talk about this too much. I did what I could, but you know the scholar's mind."

"Yes, very well. Anything else?" The wizard was impatient, but for him, this was polite.

"No, High Wizard, thank you."

He walked to the door and said, "Oh, one more tiny thing. If you could ask the accountants to merely glance at the figures on my expenses, please. I promised my helpers some rewards, and left out some details. An audit might raise questions we don't want asked."

"Yes, yes. Have them send it directly to me." He turned to a scroll, where he started drawing something round, then scribbled it out.

Jorac left, and closed the door behind him. He almost skipped down the stairs, all 156 of them.

* * *

Dorrie and Kimma were waiting in his office, a little anxiously. "How did it go?"

"I seem to still have a job. I even got him to agree not to look at the expense report too closely."

Dorrie said, "Jorac, that's great! Now we can get Kimma set up properly. She's going to stay in my guest room for now."

Jorac looked at Kimma. "What about Miz Madouve's business – and your customers?"

Kimma said, "Hario and Hatlo are going to buy me out. Their ma knows the plants and potions too, and they think they can keep her out of trouble out there. Harder to find booze in the swamp."

Jorac smiled and lowered his voice a little. "Barring the occasional giant silver sphere full, of course. Anyway, the best part is I got Pergimtor to agree that there won't be any report on this. You should have seen his face – I don't think anyone has said no to him in years. Which means, ur, well, I won't be stuck here in the office tonight. Um, Kimma, would you care to have dinner with me? At a nice place, I mean."

Kimma smiled at him, then Dorrie. "Dorrie thought you might be asking me. She says I'll need a chaperone. She wants me to play the Noble Lady for her, help her get a better class of customers. Sounds like fun to me."

Jorac turned to Dorrie and bowed. "Dorrie, are you free tonight?"

"I thought you'd never ask." She grinned, and there was something like satisfaction in her tone.

"Go ahead, Kimma, tell him the other part."

"Jorac, you know I grew up – well, you know, in a bawdy house. Anyway, I never – that is, I wasn't. . ."

"You don't have to worry. We'll just start with when we met, okay?"

He could still see the doubt in her eyes.

"Kimma, I grew up on a sheep farm. And despite some of the jokes you hear, I never had my way with them, either, okay?"

Her laughter, and Dorrie's, were music to his ears.

Kimma said, "Okay then," and her bright smile made him feel happy, for both of them. "Okay."

Chapter 17 - Jorac is Confused

Six weeks later, Jorac got up early and walked to Dorrie Velsop's shop.

"Hi Dorrie. Your new sign looks good." She had a freshly gilded sign out front, with the "Licensed Wizard" part even more ornamented and prominent than before.

"Thanks, Jorac. Kimma isn't here. She's down at the market; she'll be back in a couple of hours."

"I know. It's you I wanted to talk to. Do you have any appointments?"

"Not this morning. We try to keep Moonday free for shopping and such. What's up?"

"It's Kimma." Jorac hesitated a little, then went on resolutely. "I really like the girl, you know." He paused, awkwardly.

"I know that. I like her too." Dorrie was amused, and Jorac could see her trying to keep from smiling. "I'm glad to see you're coming out of your shell a bit, at least."

"I'm trying . . but Dorrie, you're, well, cramping my style. I can't talk to her the way I want to, when you're there all the time. And she's. . . well, she's. . ."

"She's what?" Dorrie's eyes narrowed a little, and the smile started to leave her face.

"She's. . . confusing."

Dorrie's smile came back, and lit up her whole face. "I was afraid you were going to say she was a strumpet's daughter, and I was trying to figure out how I was going to slap you."

Jorac shook his head. "I never think like that. She's a hero, to you and me and lots of folks from the swamp, even if some of them have never seen her face. But I don't know what she's thinking half the time. Or even less than that. I think she likes her new life with you. But how would I know?"

"Good question. Okay, I see your problem. Tell you what. If she agrees, I'll upgrade you to a 'prospect,' all right?"

"What do you mean by that?"

"Well, it's sort of the nobles' way of letting two people see if they can get along, without too much risk. It technically means the family has checked you out, and you're an acceptable candidate, marriage-wise. Don't worry, it's not a promise or anything. It just means the aunties – meaning me in this case – have decided that perhaps you'll do – just perhaps. Which means that you and she can occasionally take luncheon alone, if she's willing. Nothing after dark, mind you."

"Do you think she'll agree to me being a prospect?"

Dorrie smiled a secret smile. "Oh, we'll have to see. I'd have to say I like your chances."

Jorac felt unexpected glee at this. "I know you're trying to do everything properly for her. Did I tell you my father is a member of the nobility? A baronet. That makes me in line to be Emperor. Somewhere near the end of the line, of course, but I'm in the line."

Dorrie laughed. "I know how many nobles there are in this city. If everyone in front of you dies, I think we'll have bigger problems than an Emperor Jorac. But, as her stand-in auntie, I'd say it's a point in your favor."

Jorac said "Hmm," and waited for as long as he could – maybe ten seconds – then asked, "So, are you going to need Kimma at lunchtime today?"

Dorrie laughed, and waved him out the door. "Be gone, you. Come back around noon, and ask her yourself."

* * *

"... So," Kimma was saying, "with the reward money from your wizards and such, I've got some money saved, but no income to speak of. And Dorrie wants me to play the snooty young noble lady, just in off some farm. That's kind of fun sometimes, but I keep thinking they'll catch me at it, and they'll know I'm not Kimathea Ravensclough." Kimma took a quick look around the outdoor dining area in the market square to make sure she wasn't heard. The square was empty this early afternoon, with the morning market over and shut down.

"I thought I knew most of the noble names. I know Ravensclaw and Riverclough – is it supposed to be something like that?"

Kimma put on her finest noble accent. "An old family, not without tradition, but one that produces mainly girls. I believe my late father was the last of the line." In her more normal "city" voice, she added, "Dorrie looked it up and everything. The name is in some old records, but she thinks it's just a writing mistake."

"Dorrie is a humdinger sometimes. Always has an angle. Do you want some more bread?"

"Thanks, but I've had enough. I'm watching my figure. I haven't been walking nearly as much as I used to, and my clothes don't fit like they should."

Jorac wiggled his eyebrows, and in a comically exaggerated leer he said, "I'm watching your figure too, dearie."

Kimma flushed, and sat in embarrassed silence. After a little while, she said, "That's one of the things Dorrie doesn't understand. When you say something like that, I know you're just joking, but I don't know what to say back. I missed that time growing up, with people my own age, and it's like. . . like everyone knows the steps to the dance but me."

Jorac considered a little and said, "Well, if you like it, you say something like, 'Aw, hush up, now,' but in a way like you don't mean it. If you don't like it, you just sort of stare in a cold way, or turn your back. Then I won't do it anymore."

"Well then, hush up now." She giggled a little.

"Yes ma'am." Jorac smiled back at her. He still liked her laugh.

* * *

Jorac went back to his office and looked for something to do. He was expected to spend several hours there each day, "just in case," but he'd even caught up on his petty paperwork, and no new jobs had come from the Wizard's Tower. When he first started the job, he'd refused on principle to discipline the older apprentices, which had seemed take up most of his predecessor's time. It was too late now to start dealing with them out of sheer boredom.

He sighed. *I'll go on patrol, I guess. Maybe I can go find someone doing something bad to a wizard, or more likely the reverse. Probably not, but at least I'll get a walk. I wonder what Cerom is up to. . .*

Cerom was finishing up his shift by the time Jorac got there. After they'd exchanged greetings, and bantered about Jorac looking bored, Cerom said, "Hey, Jay. You ever going to tell me the real story of what Schrog and Hox and you did in that swamp?" He'd asked before.

"Not today, sorry. Wizards' secrets and all that. And don't ask them too much either, okay? This one is touchy, best to keep it quiet. We just happened to be there when some treasure was found, and we were around when the good folks in Swampside had an impromptu party to celebrate." That was the official story everyone on Jorac's team and in Swampside had agreed on. That was the whole story; no other details were offered or available. It frustrated people like Cerom who were good at seeing beneath the surface, but it couldn't be helped.

"Yeah, right. I know those 'good folks in Swampside' too, but okay, I can leave it alone. You couldn't pull a word out of Schrog with a mule team, and he's teaching Hox too. I'll give up."

"So, how's our young giant shaping up? He seemed to like being a constable, even after seeing the more, um, quaint parts of the city."

"Well, he took those trips with you and almost got killed twice in a week, once by an axe-wielding bandit, once by a poison frog, and he tells me he's never had more fun in his life. I hope standard patrolling doesn't get too dull for him. I don't want to lose him to some private guard."

Jorac sang part of the introduction to a bawdy drinking song. "'*Oh, to be young and full of joy; A day in Spring should last forever. . .*' I better stop before I get to the 'midnight's pleasure' part. Hey – he's just nineteen. He'll grow out of it. Try to keep his jobs varied, I guess. Say, can I buy you a beer when you're done here?"

"Not today; I promised the missus I'd get right home. Speaking of that, I hear you were out with a lady, I mean a real fancy one?" Cerom's tone was friendly, not leering. He knew the constables had trouble meeting decent women, those who weren't for sale or didn't want something from them that went against their oaths.

"Yeah. She's . . . nice."

"Nice?"

"Yep." *Beautiful, and deadly with a crossbow, and at home in Swampside but trying to learn to fit into noble society. Too much detail. . .* "Pretty pleasant, actually. She's staying with Dorrie Velosp – you remember her. Dorrie acts as a chaperone, mostly."

"Oh, a chaperone. Um." Cerom said this knowingly; only "good" young ladies (or noble ones) had chaperones. Having one was good and bad; it made things a bit more serious for the man involved, but the young woman was more likely to be worth the effort.

Cerom shrugged. "Well, good luck to you, however it works out. Worse comes to worse, I may still remember a few tricks for escaping from the minder – my wife and I dreamed them up, before we were married."

Dammit, it isn't fair. I don't know how serious Dorrie is about this chaperone business, and I don't know what Kimma thinks most of the time, and I'm not even sure about how I feel about her. Damn.

"Thanks. I may just take you up on that, someday. Right now. . ." he paused.

"Chaperone." Cerom finished.

* * *

The next week, Jorac had a day off, and talked Dorrie into letting Kimma lunch alone with him again, partly by promising that the three of them would go out for dinner that night, at one of the fancy places across the river.

Part of Dorrie's grand plan for Kimma's Makeover was her wardrobe. She was never to be seen in anything a noble lady wouldn't wear in similar circumstances. Luckily, noble ladies dressed down to go to the market, and so she wore a simple brown dress with large pockets, with perhaps just a bit more trim than usually seen in Dorrie's working-class neighborhood.

Like most clothes, Jorac thought it looked good on her, and he told her so.

"This old thing? Well, thank you." Kimma smiled as she said it. Jorac knew that the dress was new, just delivered this week, with other fancier outfits to follow.

He grinned back at her. "You've been practicing. That sounds properly hoity-toity. But if you want my opinion, you could use a little more astonishment that anyone would mention these practical clothes."

"*This* old thing?"

"Much better."

She laughed, and took his proffered arm as they set off down the street.

She leaned in and said quietly, "It's better than any dress I ever owned before. I'm afraid of getting it dirty."

"Just give it to the laundry woman."

"We don't. . . oh, I guess I'll have to think like that. I'm so used to doing for myself."

"Knowing how to do things yourself is good, but not having to is more fun. Like today: we're letting someone else cook us lunch."

Jorac led her to a tavern near his rooms. They ate a spicy fish stew and fresh bread, and drank far too much tea, as Jorac told Constable stories. Some of what the constables dealt with was bloody and frightening, not a good topic for ladies at lunch, so he told only the funny stories, or those with happy endings. There were plenty of those too, and Jorac wasn't getting tired of her smile. Kimma was using her upper-class accent, and it seemed to get them slightly better service, though Jorac had been here many times before.

They lingered longer than the usual mid-day crowd, and the restaurant was mostly empty when they finished.

"Kimma, do you have to get back right away? I'd like you to look at my place."

She frowned. "I don't know. . . I think Dorrie would. . ."

"With an escort I mean. I've just got a tiny room over a stationer's shop. I wanted to show you that, and then ask you to help me look at some bigger places. I saw what you did with your little house. . ." he stumbled. "I guess I want it to be a place you'd like."

Kimma looked at him speculatively. Finally she said, "All right."

The tired-looking, middle-aged scullion came to clean off their table, and Jorac asked her to come back with the owner, after reassuring her it was nothing bad.

"Pajlo, can I borrow your lady here for an hour or two? I'll pay you and her a couple coppers each."

Her eyebrows raised to her forehead. "Now listen here, young sir. I don't know what you think, but I'm not the kind to run off for an hour for money, and what would your lady here say? That's just. . ."

Jorac interrupted her. "No, no, no. And because you're not that kind, that's why I want you to be the escort for the young lady here, all very proper. I'm going to ask her to go look at my room, and then go look at a few more places, and of course a chaperone is always needed for a young lady. I ask nothing strenuous, nor ungentlemanly. Or gentlewomanly."

Her face broke into a wide, crinkled smile. "Oh, a proper escort. I've done that in my time, yes indeed. Mistress Nuff, at your service. Pajlo, since he's paying you too, you can clean up, right?"

"Aye, Nuffie, go ahead. You watch now, see how the upper-class act, all right?"

"Let me clean myself up, won't be two shakes!" She left the dishes on the table, and almost ran back to the kitchen.

Pajlo, amused, took the dishes from the table (and Jorac's coppers) back to the kitchen.

Kimma said, "So you really liked my little house?"

"It was great. Nothing fancy, but nice. Welcoming, kind of. You had colors there – all my stuff is mostly brown or gray. I want you to help me find a place like that, one you'd like. I mean, a place you'd like if you were there yourself. Or would want to visit with Dorrie." Jorac couldn't help think, *or all alone... for hours and hours...* but he hoped that thought didn't reach his face. "I just don't want a cave like my place now. It's quiet, but it's cheap and it's ugly, I know that. I want something nicer, like..."

"Like what?"

"Like you." Jorac reached out across the table, and took her hand, softly.

Kimma squeezed his hand, and smiled at him, and said quietly, "Aw, hush up now." The look she gave him made his blood rise a little.

Then, as Nuffie and Pajlo returned, she pulled her hand back and stood up. "If we are to embark on a little quest, I believe I should, uh, adjust my coiffure first."

"Right this way, mistress. I figured that, so I cleaned it up nice."

Jorac made a tiny questioning gesture to Pajlo, and received a tiny rueful shrug in return. Upper-class ladies didn't want to hear that the toilet was ever anything but spotless; Nuffie still had a bit of education in front of her. But Jorac appreciated the attempt.

* * *

They looked at several places, and decided the nicest one was a red brick house, complete but tiny, hidden behind an older house that was now a candle shop. It had a small sitting room, a large and small bedroom, a small kitchen and bathroom, but the private toilet (rare for any house this old or small) was what decided Kimma, and Jorac was willing to be instructed. The fact that it was between the Wizard's Tower and Dorrie's house was a bonus; he'd be only a ten minute walk from either place.

Kimma said, "We need to ask Madame Velosp to survey this residence. She would know what furniture you should seek to obtain."

"I was thinking the same thing. Mistress Ravensclough, Mistress Nuff, I shall return shortly; I believe I heard the landlord just outside."

Nuffie said, "Take your time, good sir. A pleasant afternoon, 'tis." If it wasn't quite upper-class, at least she was trying. Jorac turned away to hide his smile, and quickly settled with the landlord. He'd pay a little extra so the cleaning lady would visit his new place twice weekly, and was given a set of keys. He could move in anytime.

* * *

Later, when Jorac and Kimma had gotten back to Dorrie's, she'd just returned with some groceries.

Kimma said, "Dorrie, you've got to go look at the little house Jorac's rented. It's so cute! He'll need your help picking furniture. I saw where he lives now – don't worry, we had a proper escort – and he needs just everything. I was looking at rugs in the market on our way back. . ."

It took many minutes for Kimma's excitement to run down, and Jorac was happy to see her so animated. He was too much of an old campaigner to care much what his furnishings looked like, so if someone wanted to pick things for him, it was all to the good.

Finally, Jorac got a word in. "So Dorrie, when do you think you can look at the place?"

"Not tomorrow; I have appointments all day and evening. The day after, maybe."

"Perfect. Tomorrow morning I need to do some reports, and then the Council meets in the afternoon and they usually have something for me to do afterwards. Kimma, what about you? Are you going to work with Dorrie?"

"Onc't the morrow, good sir, I shall assist the Madame in the light of day; howsoever I believe my instruction in Deportment is scheduled for the morrow's eve." Kimma giggled – her parody of noble language was as good as her serious efforts.

Dorrie added, "It turns out Skowers offers instruction on getting along in noble society, when he's not passing there himself.

"Ah, good." Jorac wasn't sure it was good, knowing Skowers was rather a ladies' man, but he could keep an eye on things and warn Kimma if necessary. He didn't want to disturb her needlessly.

But still he felt uneasy. After a pause he said, "Where's all this going, anyway? When Kimma is accepted as a noble lady, what then?"

Kimma and Dorrie smiled at each other, and Dorrie said, "Simple, we've got a foolproof plan. For now, Kimma will be my assistant. It's a little unusual, but it's a respectable job for a gentlewoman, since I'm licensed and all. Then when she talks to the nobles, she tells them the truth about what I can do, as simple as it is, and I increase my prices eightfold, and we split the increase. The value of the lost trinkets and jewelry in those circles ought to more than pay for it."

Jorac was almost convinced. "And the knack you have for learning who the father is, they'll need that too."

"True. But there's other wizards do that, after the kid is born at least, and I don't want to make them mad. I'll stick to finding the baubles, mostly. The other only for special clients, at special rates." Her smile was avaricious. "We're going to go through them like a hot knife through butter. It'll be so much fun!"

It wasn't Jorac's idea of fun, and he wasn't so sure about Kimma either, but he couldn't think of any arguments against it. He thought he ought to be happy they were looking to move up in the world. And it really wasn't any of his business. Best to keep his mouth shut.

"Now Jorac, you run along. Come back in an hour, or better yet two, if that's not too late. If we're going to that fancy place you told us about over in Westmire, we need to dress properly. You're lucky, your fanciest constable uniform is correct anywhere."

"They're open past midnight, so don't worry. I'll wipe the crumbs off my uniform, and see what I can do about the gravy stains. Maybe I can find a dog to lick them clean?"

Dorrie laughed, "Get along now," and started up the stairs. She and Kimma slept in the rooms upstairs.

Jorac turned to Kimma, and said, "Thanks."

Kimma looked surprised. "For what?"

"For helping me with the new place, and, oh, for being nice." The last bit came out a little hoarse, a bit forced. Jorac wondered how it sounded to her.

She flushed slightly and gave him a crooked smile. "Oh, um, you're welcome. And-you're-nice-too." Then she bounded up the stairs two at a time.

Jorac let himself out, and whistled a bit as he walked home.

* * *

The dinner at the fancy tavern was good, even excellent, if you liked tiny servings of dozens of dishes. Jorac would have rather had larger portions and fewer choices, but he wisely didn't mention that, and the ladies seemed to enjoy themselves. Afterwards they were all a little over-full and welcomed the walk back. When they got to Dorrie's house, she told Jorac and Kimma to relax, and walked to the door leading into the kitchen.

"Now I need to put away the rest of the groceries. No, Kimma, I can handle it. I think it'll take me several minutes. I'll probably bang some pots and pans, so don't mind me." She turned and left, with a backwards glance and a wink at them both.

Kimma looked a little surprised, but Jorac reached out and took her hand. "I think our chaperone is giving us a few minutes alone."

Kimma said, "Ah." Then, smiling a shy smile, said "Ah!" again.

Jorac bent down to kiss her, and a bit clumsily, she responded. After a few light kisses, she banged her nose into his. She hugged him close and buried her face in his shoulder.

She murmured sadly, "I can't even kiss right."

Jorac whispered, "Practice makes perfect. . .", and within a minute or two her technique had definitely improved. Jorac stopped before things got too heated; they were both conscious of Dorrie in the next room. Instead he held her close and stared into her face. If she wasn't the best-looking young lady in the city, she was surely in the running. But her skill with a crossbow attracted Jorac even more, and someday he'd try to figure out why. For now he just enjoyed it.

"Kimma, I know Dorrie wants to work the nobles like a barker working a crowd – she loves that sort of thing. But you need to decide if you want it too. Don't let her make you into something you aren't, okay?" He suddenly wondered if he was being too paternalistic. He had no right to tell her what to do.

She seemed to take it okay. "I used to know who I was. I had a life in the swamp, not too far I could rise, not too far I could fall. I guess I'm not sure what I am here in the city – at least not yet. I guess I'll learn, though."

"Well, however that turns out, I like who you are, deep down, and that won't change, okay?"

She nodded, smiling a wry little smile, and said "Okay." Then the smile warmed and she very quietly said, "You said. . . practice?"

They had to step apart quickly when Dorrie came banging her way into the room a few minutes later. If they both seemed a bit flushed, Dorrie had the grace not to mention it or smirk. Well, not smirk too much anyway.

Chapter 18 - An Assignment

The next afternoon, Jorac was loitering in the big open room at the base of the Wizard's Tower when the council meeting ended. He could always tell because of the rush of air that meant several wizards were coming, flying down the 156 stairs that he'd probably have to climb soon. Though he'd had nothing important to do for weeks, a council meeting often produced an assignment, or at least some questions for him to answer.

He sauntered toward his office at a slow pace, and was rewarded by arriving at his door just as a rolled-up piece of paper winked into existence just above the circle on the floor near his desk. He sneezed, just once, and resolved next time to walk even more slowly.

To his surprise, the scroll said, "Wait there – will be down soon – Perg." As far as Jorac knew, the head wizard had never been to his office, or anyone's office. People visited Pergimtor, not the other way around.

The head wizard entered a couple of minutes later. "Honorable Kellor, so good to see you. I wanted to commend you on your job in the swamp." He put his hands together. "Upon reflection, I'm convinced that what you did was best."

Jorac was surprised. He'd thought Pergimtor had been severely annoyed at what he'd done with the Wolburn Sphere.

Pergimtor continued, "You didn't tell any other wizards about it, did you?"

"Veseen knows, but he's an apprentice, and he isn't at all the power-hungry type. And Dorrie Velosp knows, but she's probably the weakest wizard in your guild, and happy with what she's got. Both of them have no reason to talk about it, and plenty of reason to keep it quiet."

"Good, good. I was just wondering. Some people have enough power, and more might be bad for them, if you know what I mean. Keeping secrets is. . . tricky."

Jorac didn't know how Pergimtor thought, so maybe his comment was innocent, but maybe not.

Jorac chose his words carefully. "There are five people in Swampside who know about the liquid and the sphere, and two other constables. They all know there could be a big fight between the wizards if the news got out. But if something starts happening to them, if they start having accidents or something, then the news is sure to leak. No sense in keeping a secret that might kill you."

Pergimtor said, "Hmm. Well, we aren't all like Wolburn, don't worry." Jorac couldn't tell if Pergimtor had discarded an idea, or if his warning had just given the wizard a new idea. He still didn't trust wizards – in fact, when a wizard was nice to him, he worried. And Pergimtor was being nice.

"Anyway, your efforts were noted and appreciated, and the council has agreed to double your salary."

Jorac was startled at the salary announcement, but didn't get to react, because Pergimtor continued, "But I really came to see you about a different matter. What do you know about the rebellion in the north?"

"Respectfully, sir, there's *always* a rebellion in the north. Has been ever since Benneso the Great took over the little kingdoms there one by one, eighty or a hundred years ago. Every summer, it's fighting season, and there'll be some province, sometimes just one town, trying to regain its independence. Usually it gets stomped down, and made poorer for its trouble."

"So you don't know that the province of West Luverna has declared independence, rallying behind Ozifaj the Sixth, the great-grandson of their last independent monarch? And that East Luverna claims to oppose them, but seems to be doing nothing to stop it?"

"Sir Wizard, I don't pay much attention to it anymore. The army marches north each spring and puts down whoever is rebelling this year." Jorac used to worry about such things when he was a wagon guard, because you had to know where the trouble might be coming from, but during his years in Vaggert he'd lost interest. But he was wondering why Pergimtor was concerned about this minor rebellion.

"The advance scouts tell their commanders they think there's a wizard working with the West Luverna army. They say the enemy guesses right too often about their movements, and fights much too well in the dark. They don't think the rebels have enough training to fight like that on their own, but there are some wizard spells that would account for it. They may be right, but spells like that require considerable power. Out in the provinces there are occasionally wizards like your Velosp woman whose abilities aren't detected in adolescence, but they're all quite weak. An unknown local wizard who's that powerful is unlikely, but we've been asked to investigate."

"Why would it have to be an unknown wizard? Why not a known wizard who chose to go there?"

Pergimtor frowned. "Now you're getting into guild knowledge, but I suppose you have a right to know, so long as you don't repeat it. Let's say there are certain incentives for a wizard to stay here, or at least stay loyal to the emperor – social, logistical, and magical incentives. It's not a coincidence that the only wizard training schools are here, for example. But it's certain that no wizard as powerful as they claim was trained here. We've checked, and all the reasonably powerful wizards who prefer to live in the provinces are accounted for. There may some weak, self-trained wizards in the countryside who hide themselves very well, but not many, because we do search. I believe Wolburn was an aberration – it took his ex-wizard father to train him, and he was more crafty than truly powerful."

"You said you search, sir. Can't you send a wizard out with the scouts to check?"

Pergimtor sighed. "Jorac, if you never get involved in Court politics, you'll be a happier person all the days of your life. As you know, I sit on the Emperor's Council. The Emperor is a cheerful, earthy sort, but some of the council members are. . . well, never mind. Count Danak Melsim is the general of the army, and he has specifically asked the Council and the Emperor to order me not to send a wizard with the army this year. The Emperor has complied with his request."

"I see." *A general who distrusted wizards, I'm not surprised at that, but him being able to exclude them from his army, that's surprising.* "So you want me to search instead. What would you expect me to do?"

"Go with the army, of course, and report back to me. I did manage to ensure that you weren't under that idio. . . under General Melsim's command."

So I can do your bidding and not his. I'm probably the only "simple" you can trust. I'd better check up on this Melsim.

"You'll be a detached auxiliary observer – it's a recognized position. You're supplied by the army, but you report to no one there. You're allowed to bring a servant, or assistant, whatever you choose to call it. Some observers bring their wives, or, ahem, *ladies* with them. There are generally a half dozen or so observers in each campaign."

He means they bring whores along. That probably causes all sorts of problems. I better check on the "observer" position too. "I see. When does this operation start?"

"Unfortunately, I think the army is scheduled to leave in just two or three days. Spring is breaking in the Outside areas, where we don't stabilize the climate, and the roads should clear soon. Or so I hear."

Crap. This sounds like a whole bucket of snakes. And he's giving me practically no advance notice. No wonder he doubled my salary before he told me about it. "Well. . ." He paused, discarding various swear words that came into his head, until he could come up with something sensible. "How long would I be expected to remain with the army?"

"Only until you can establish whether or not there's a wizard with the opposing forces. You can leave whenever you have an answer." The wizard waited a moment. "Any other questions for me?"

Jorac shook his head, mainly to stop himself from saying something stupid. He'd learned when he was very young not to say the first thing that came to his mind when he was upset, so he didn't blurt out a string of curse words followed by "I quit!" Instead, he said, "I need to think, and I'll doubtless have some questions tomorrow. Am I to assume that you came down here for a reason, and this shouldn't be discussed. . . well, upstairs, or anywhere outside this room?"

Pergimtor smiled. "Ah, you're perceptive. Yes, that would be best. Drop a vague note for me in the message box tomorrow; I'll know what it's about."

"Very good, sir. You might wish to have a draft of your orders for me then. So we're both clear on what you want." *And so my ass is covered. A secret cat's-paw for the head wizard is NOT what I signed up for. I wonder if I should just try to get another job. . . it might be hard to find one that pays so well. . . I wonder what this Melsim is like. . .*

Pergimtor pursed his lips, but then nodded. "Perhaps that will be best. Until tomorrow then." He strode out of the room, while Jorac's head spun with the variables of this new assignment. He walked up and down his long, narrow office for a bit, then got out a fresh piece of paper and started making a list. The very first thing on the list was "Kimma!"

* * *

Jorac was hanging out just down the street from Dorrie's later that evening. He'd put on simple, dark gray clothes with no ornamentation at all, and strolled up and down, trying to watch her front door without being conspicuous. There was light foot traffic in the area, so it was fairly easy to not be noticed as long as he didn't stay in the same place too long.

When he saw a covered carriage pulled by a pair of matched horses come trotting up to the house, Jorac walked quickly toward it. He arrived as Skowers turned away from the departing carriage, but before he reached the door.

"Psssst. Skowers."

"Who. . . Oh, Constable, how pleasant to see you again. Your pardon, but I'm expected inside."

Jorac put himself in front of the door. "It's about that."

Skowers drew up, a bit wary, and stayed several paces away from Jorac. His hand drifted down to his hip, where a weapon might be concealed. "What might I do for you?"

"I heard Schrog say this one time. We've done business, and done it square, right?"

"Go on."

"Well, you're doing business here. Not my concern. But it stays business, right?"

"I'm not sure I take your meaning." Jorac was pretty sure Skowers did understand, but he'd spell it out as clearly as necessary.

"How about I say it this way. At some point you'll be teaching about courting customs. I expect decorum and appropriate behavior at every turn."

"Why sir, decorum is just what I'm teaching. What else would you think?"

Jorac was tired of his verbal dancing, and still had things to do tonight. He rose to the balls of his feet and stared Skowers straight in the eye. In his best "menacing" tone of voice, he said, "Okay, one more try. Hands off Kimma. I find out you've been bothering her I'll cut your balls off. This one ain't business, it's *personal*. Got it?"

Skowers took a half step back and looked at Jorac as if seeing him for the first time. Then, to Jorac's surprise, Skowers laughed, a genuine mirthful laugh. "Ah, my good sir, again you surprise me. Now I understand you. I'll admit that perhaps I did have some, well, some notions in that direction, but no more; it shall be as you say. It may be that later I find a different teacher for the young lady – a female one perhaps. Would that suit you?"

Jorac felt relieved that the confrontation had gone as well as it had. "Admirably. I thank you for understanding."

"Not at all, sir. Now if I may enter?"

Jorac stepped aside and gave a sweeping "be my guest" gesture. On a whim he asked, "So how would a true nobleman say that? My father has a noble's title, but he runs a sheep farm in the hills. Not much noble talk there."

Skowers chuckled. "Very close to the way you said it. Perhaps he might say 'geld' instead, but perhaps not. It's more in the tone. And your tone was – quite believable, actually." And with that he knocked on the door, while Jorac backed away swiftly, so as not to be seen.

Jorac briskly walked to Constable headquarters, but found neither Cerom nor Hox there. He knew Hox was from a farm in the north and wanted to ask him about it, and he wanted to talk to Cerom about taking Hox as his assistant. But all he could do tonight was leave notes for both, and see them in the morning.

Chapter 19 - A Journey Planned

The next day, Jorac met with Cerom and Hox early, then went to Dorrie's and briefly outlined the situation he was facing. Dorrie postponed an appointment so she and Kimma could talk it over with him.

"I don't see how you can refuse to go," Dorrie said. "The strongest wizard in the city isn't a good enemy to have."

"I don't know that he'd become my enemy."

"And you don't know that he wouldn't. Maybe he'd just speak his displeasure and someone else would do something, just to curry favor. Your choices are to take the assignment or leave the city. I don't like it, but it comes down to that."

"I don't like it either." Kimma looked distressed. Jorac was distressed too, but one part of him was unreasonably happy, to see that she'd miss him.

Jorac said, "And I don't like it either, but I have to agree with Dorrie. Cerom said some of the same things. And he said Hox was getting bored here, so he didn't yell too much when I asked him if Hox could go with me. When I talked to Hox, he said he'd jump at the chance to go back home – well, near there anyhow – and show off his new uniform."

Kimma said, "Hox is a good egg. I never once heard him complain when that frog poisoned him."

"And he saved our ass a few times during our little game with the big silver ball. I'll just need to make sure he has enough clothes – nothing standard will fit him – and enough food."

Kimma said, "I thought they were supposed to give you food?"

"I've heard it's pretty bad – enough to live on but not much more. That's probably where they can most easily skim money from the army. And Hox can eat."

Dorrie added, "And eat, and eat some more."

"Right. So I'll have to check out this observer business. Cerom knows someone I can talk to."

Kimma said, "Sounds like you've thought it through."

"Well, sure, but there's my new little house, maybe I can give you some money to outfit it, and... I just don't... I'm not sure what you'll... Oh hell." It was hard enough to talk to Kimma when they were alone, but with Dorrie here it was nearly impossible. He just stared at her, trying to get his face to convey what his words couldn't.

Kimma's look back was at once pensive and smoldering, and Jorac knew he'd remember that look for a long time... But then Dorrie spoke up.

"I'd love to watch you two get tongue-tied for the next hour, but we don't have the time. Kimma, you'll wait for him, right? Not fall for a rake like Skowers, or one of the pretty noble boys, right?

Kimma looked a bit shocked, but nodded and said, "Of course. I..."

Dorrie interrupted her. "And Jorac, you'll be good while you're on the road, far away, right? Not dally with some pretty milkmaid or something, right?"

Jorac nodded silently, still looking at Kimma.

"Well then, it's settled. Come back tonight after supper. But now, I've missed one appointment and I'm going to be late for the second. Kimma, go upstairs and get your costume on. Jorac, I'll let you out the back door." Dorrie stood up, which stirred the others into motion.

As Jorac was leaving, he told Dorrie, "I'll bring some groceries, right? What would you like?"

Dorrie looked at him in puzzlement for a second, then cackled in understanding. "Anything that'll take a good long while to put away will be fine, scallywag. Go!"

* * *

Pergimtor said, "I thought the army would supply your needs?"

"Well sir, I talked to a young man who was an observer a few years ago, and he had some most colorful descriptions. I wrote them down so I wouldn't forget. . ." Jorac pulled a scrap of paper from his pocket and read his notes. "Food: flavorless, watery gruel twice a day. A few scraps of meat in there that came from no animal you'd want to admit eating, mixed with stale horse fodder. Blankets: moth-eaten scraps you could read a scroll through, not fit to keep you warm nor keep biting flies from you. Cartage: none unless you know who to bribe, and if you don't do it correctly, your pack mysteriously falls in the creek or into the fire."

Pergimtor's eyes narrowed. "The army wouldn't put up with that. The men would desert."

"Yes sir, but the observers aren't really in the army. No one with any power cares about their daily welfare. Things are better for the regular soldiers; you'll note that the chain of command runs two ways, both up and down the chain – or for observers, doesn't run."

"So what did your man suggest?"

Jorac consulted his list again. "At a minimum, a sturdy wagon, with a cloth cover set up for sleeping. Some cooking and camping gear, like that made for traveling merchants. Some dried food, but mostly spices and flavorings that will pack small. And plenty of coins, coppers and silvers, not just gold. You can't take enough food for the trip, but you can buy it at the villages on your way through."

"So what would all this cost me? This is coming out of my own pocket, you know."

Jorac had checked some prices, so he said, "About two hundred and twenty gold. Perhaps a bit more, sir, but in that range. And another hundred or so for supplies during the campaign." He was padding his estimate, but not a lot.

Pergimtor said, "That's too much. This is coming out of my pocket, not the treasury. What could you do with a hundred and fifty?"

Jorac was distracted, and short on sleep, and answered with a curt, annoyed, "Fail." Then he was aghast at what he'd just said. That was NOT the way to talk to any wizard, much less the most powerful one in the land. *Don't you ever learn, idiot? Pick your words carefully, or keep your mouth shut!*

Pergimtor glared for a second, and then to Jorac's relief and surprise, barked a laugh. "Ha! Fairly said. Alright, shop carefully, but get what you need. Here's a hundred now; bring me receipts or owe-notes and I'll pay for your gear. And you say the huge young constable is going with you?"

Jorac accepted the pouch from the wizard and said, "Yes sir. He knows the country in the north, and isn't as dumb as he plays. He's young, but he'll get over that."

Pergimtor sighed a little. "Yes, we all get over that." The wizard looked like a man of late middle age, but you couldn't tell with wizards, and he suddenly reminded Jorac of a much older man. "I'll have your orders tomorrow. But you should get your supplies quickly; I believe the army is almost ready to depart."

"Yes sir. Anything else?" Jorac was impatient to get started; he already had some shopping lists made.

"Well, yes, there is one more small thing you might look into when you're in the north. Last month, I got a note – a paper note, delivered by a merchant. See what you make of this." He handed Jorac a yellowed, wrinkled piece of paper.

The note was written in a good clear hand, with thick letters in faded ink. It read, "Perg – ran into a spot of bother here in Labblox. A Simple thing needed, don't you or your pals visit, just send some help – Lartimaparian."

"Who's Lartimaparian? And how was this delivered?" Jorac handed him back the note.

"The only one I've ever known with that name was a teacher of mine. If it's the same person, he must be ninety or more years old by now. He wasn't a bad sort; he taught Ethics, and D&S – that's Divination and Scrying. A runner-boy brought this from the river gate; he said he didn't remember the sender – some merchant type."

"Is he asking for non-wizard help? That word 'simple' is seems to be emphasized."

Pergimtor looked at the paper again. "It could be. Actually, this note probably means nothing – my name gets used many times for things I know nothing about. But since Labblox is in East Luverna, I thought you could ask around for an old man by that name if you get there. He might be in his dotage; if so, bring him back here and we'll take care of him."

"Yes sir. Best put that in the orders too, so no one in the army will question me leaving. I know they get testy about keeping the army together." It had taken the ill-equipped observer that Cerom put him in touch with several weeks to find a chance to desert, but that was a detail Pergimtor didn't need to know.

"Very well. Tomorrow, then."

* * *

It was late the next afternoon when Jorac and Hox pulled their large wagon up outside the Wizard's Tower complex. They'd found a converted ore wagon, big enough for both Hox and Jorac to sleep inside in bad weather, and a pair of large, older horses to pull it. They were still rounding up supplies but were running out of time; they were scheduled to leave in the morning.

Pergimtor came down from the tower and gave them their official orders, a small cask full of copper coins, and a purse with silver and gold pieces in it. Jorac was now carrying more money than he'd made the entire previous year, but he didn't feel rich; mostly he felt the weight of the coins as an anchor. Hox, never disrespectful, was exceedingly polite to the head wizard and said as little as possible.

After Pergimtor dismissed them and went back inside, Hox urged the horses into action. The oversized wagon wasn't easy to maneuver, but Hox handled the job well enough, and they worked their way through the streets and soon arrived at the market area near Dorrie's house.

Jorac climbed down and handed Hox the list of supplies still needed. "Dorrie and I asked some of the sellers here to stay late for us – there's one now. Buy anything else you want that's small – any spices you like. And we still need to get some oats for the horses too."

"Where are you going?"

"I need to take some groceries to Dorrie. Long story. I'll be back in an hour or so."

* * *

Kimma answered the door and gave Jorac a long look that warmed his heart and curled his toes.

Dorrie came downstairs and greeted him. "You've got everything you need?"

"I think so. Hox is loading the last of the food. Kimma, I know you offered that double crossbow, but we've got two normal ones and I'd worry if you didn't have it. I used to guard a traveling merchant, so I know what we need. I think we'll be okay."

Kimma said, "Alright. But I worry anyway."

Jorac smiled at her and said, "Good. I worry about you too. Oh look, Dorrie, I found this nice bag of dried beans."

Dorrie smiled a knowing smile as she took it from him.

Jorac added, "I'm afraid the different types all got mixed together."

"Well, gosh. How inconvenient. I guess I'll just have to go sort them out. That'll take a while. I'll be in the kitchen. Don't disturb me, I'll need to concentrate to do this well." With that, she left the room.

Kimma rushed to his arms, and the half hour that Dorrie spent in the kitchen was well spent. They finally got to talk privately, in quiet tones, between kisses. Jorac felt better after hearing Kimma's sweet and loving words, and he thought she looked happier too, hearing his. But too soon for either of them, Dorrie started making noise, then came back into the room. This time, they didn't step apart but continued to hold each other's hands. It would be their last chance for several months.

Dorrie said, "I hate to break this up, but Jorac has to go. There's only so much Hox can do by himself."

"I hate it when you're practical, and right," Jorac said. "But I do need to go."

Kimma gave him a fierce hug. Finally she let go, whispering, "Come back."

He whispered back, "I will. To you."

And before everyone's emotions spilled over, he let himself out, and hurried back to the market.

When Jorac found Hox, he was haggling with a foul-tongued merchant, and Jorac wrenched his thoughts from Kimma to practical concerns. After a few more hours of haggling and loading, they got their wagon supplied with the essentials for the trip. Jorac had wanted more and a better variety, but they could get by on what they had for at least a few weeks.

And that was all the time they had. Hox took the wagon to the constable quarters, while Jorac went to his new house and tried to sleep. Sleep was a long time coming.

Chapter 20 - A Journey Begins

When they pulled their wagon out of town the next morning, they found the area outside the city gate a teeming mob of wagons, horses, and people. Dust was everywhere, and there were officers galloping around on horses, yelling at people, trying to organize the mob into a marching column. Jorac presented his orders to four different people before finding someone to tell him that his place was at the back of the column, and (sneeringly) to keep out of the way of real army men.

Eventually, they found the area that should become the back of the column. They parked the wagon, and Jorac asked Hox to spend some time rearranging the supplies. They'd packed in a hurry, and would want room to sleep inside the wagon in a few days. Outside of the weather-controlled area, it was spring, and they were heading toward the even cooler Northlands.

Meanwhile, Jorac walked around and checked out the nearby wagons. A few sported a large tag with an "O" that he learned meant "observer"; he was told he'd be issued one soon. The other wagons weren't actually part of the army but were planning on following it. Jorac wandered among them, watching to people renew acquaintances from the year before and do last-minute loading. He saw some suspicious types who looked at him appraisingly, while others seemed to be friendly, salt-of-the-earth merchant types.

At one wagon, he met a fat, cheerful older woman who sold cooking oil and spices and had a greeting for everyone who walked by. She wasn't doing much business, but it didn't seem to worry her. Jorac's rubbernecking attracted her attention.

"First time out, dearie?"

Jorac nodded. "I'm a new observer. Still trying to figure out how this whole thing works."

"Well, come sit down and talk to me. You're a nice-looking young man, and I don't mind telling you what I know." She smiled and patted the folding chair next to hers, so Jorac sat down gingerly.

"Relax," she said, "we won't start moving until this afternoon sometime, anyway. I'll have no business today, but I'll sell out in a week, and head on back." She pointed around at the wagons in the area. "Lots of these folks will follow the army right north, all the way to the northern border, but not me. I don't mind a week or two out of town, but not three weeks there, a bit less coming back empty."

"The northern border? I thought that was way up at the cold, treeless country that no one much wants."

The woman laughed a little. "Oh, you *are* new at this. Well, if you don't mind listening to an old lady natter on, I'll explain it. The army lets us follow until we get to the *old* northern border, not the current one. No one in Old Etrombia is fighting us, so it's nice and safe. But once they get close to the town of Norfort they send the followers packing, and just the army folk go on from there."

"And you say that takes three weeks? I could ride there in a week, or less if I pushed it."

"The army never moves very fast, at least down south. You'll see. Sometimes it's the weather, or a bad section of road or something, but it's always something. I turn back when they bunch up to cross the Japrees river; that's about a week from now. Most of the other folks go further along; they just follow the Broxna river road, all the way to Norfort. The army supplies go by river barges, of course; it takes a lot to feed an army this size, but they get it done."

"What sort of folks are here? I mean, what do they do, and why are they following the army?"

She started counting them off on her fingers. "Well, there's the wives, of course. Some soldiers are married, but not so many. There's rules against prostitutes, so there's lots of 'extra workers' – cooks who can't cook, laundry ladies who don't wash, and so on. Real laundries for those without real wives. Armor sellers, sword makers, all sorts of soldierly crafts – the army has its own of course, but some soldiers will pay for something a bit fancier. Some folks sell talismans, good luck charms, and the like – they won't sell much until the last day or two. A couple of wagons sell liquor, but they keep it quiet and package it like lotions and potions and such, because selling liquor to the regular soldiers is against the rules too.

"And a few like me, selling the things folks should have bought in town. Each day out I increase my prices a little, but it still sells. Oil is heavy and I can't carry much, but I do alright with it. Up north they use mostly sheep-lard, and most city folks don't like the flavor it gives, so they're glad to pay me. And it makes for a nice little break from the shop each year."

Jorac thought a moment. "You know, I'm not sure I brought enough oil either. I guess I should buy some while it's still cheap." He knew the sheep-lard flavor well, and didn't miss it.

In good humor, she smiled. "Ha! The old sales trick worked. Tell you what, there's a couple of cases I haven't packed away yet. That one there – see if the lid is loose on it."

It proved to be, and soon Jorac had exchanged two silvers for a large jug of cooking oil. She grinned and said, "I'll be getting triple that in a week, and folks will be glad to pay me too."

He thanked her and carried his purchase back to Hox, who said he was almost done arranging the wagon.

"Here you go, some extra cooking oil. How's the wagon space looking?"

"I think it'll work out fine. I can sleep across here, kind of diagonally, and I think you'll fit across the back. I may want to get some more blankets or something to level it out."

"Well, grab a handful of coppers and ask around the wagons back that way. They aren't the army, they're the army followers. Some of them remind me of the folks in Swampside, so watch yourself."

Jorac busied himself making a place for the jug of oil, and watched the column gradually getting assembled. When Hox came back, he had some blankets under his arm and word of a recent acquaintance. "Madame Revar was asking for you."

Jorac raised his eyebrows in surprise. "Did she say what for?" He didn't think he had any business with the biggest lady pimp of Swampside. He hoped not, anyway.

"No, she just asked if you were around. She was trying to teach some of her girls how to do laundry. They were bending way over into the wash basin, and bouncing up and down. I thought any woman that age would already be taught to do laundry by their ma, but I guess not." Hox's eyes twinkled with knowing good humor. He played the country bumpkin well enough, but his understanding of city ways had grown tremendously in the few months he'd been a constable.

"Well, I better see what she wants. Are you okay here?"

"I'll work on our beds. I saw some of the other Swampside types too, so one of us should stay with the wagon."

"Yep, good idea, at least until we can find out how to get a guard we trust to watch our things. I won't be too long. The oil seller told me we won't be moving until this afternoon anyway."

Madame Revar greeted Jorac with a false smile and camaraderie even more false. "How's my favorite Constable?" Her Swampside accent was missing, he noticed.

Jorac nodded coolly. "Madame. What can I do for you?"

She tried to look hurt, but on her pinched face it looked more like indigestion. "Is that how you greet me? Merrie, Joy, meet Jorac. He was the one who had the idea for that nice party a couple of months back."

One of them said, "Ooh, you didn't say he was handsome, too!", while the other just giggled.

Jorac folded his arms and nodded to the voluptuously smiling laundresses, then turned to their boss and said, "Miz

Revar, did you want something? Or did you just want me to meet your, um, migrant workers?"

"Now Jorac, is that any way to act? I need to go back to town, but my friends here are going with the army, to wash clothes and the like. Ladies like this, out all alone, might want to know some strong man is looking after them. They'd be *very* grateful."

"If I thought there was any chance you didn't have someone watching them, and your coins, every minute of the day, I might take you more seriously. Would you care to get to the point, or are you just wasting my time?" Jorac turned a bit, as if to leave.

The old whore-mistress sighed and shook her head. "I might have known. We'll do it your way. Palork! Come here! Bring 'em all!" The Swampside accent was suddenly back.

At her call a greasy, short man came from behind the laundry wagon, with three more young, fairly attractive if hard-eyed ladies. "Jorac, Palork. He works for me, just keepin' an eye on things. You don' gotta worry about him doin' nothin' else. Palork, Jorac. He's a constable, but he can keep his mouth shut if he wants to. He's one of those too-damn-good ones, so don't try nothin' bent with him. Dere. Dat suit you?" She looked at Jorac challengingly.

Jorac didn't like her much, but he had to admire her brass, and honesty. He gave her a half smile. "Better. But why are you telling me all of this?"

"Ask Jimsley, he be a kitchen scullion now. Or Kullo; he's dead. You done dat inside a month. I needs to know what you doin', so's I stay outta de way, right?"

Jorac nodded, considering. His mission wasn't a secret, but she didn't need to know exactly what he was doing, so he said, "I'm not looking into the laundries, or any camp followers, okay? My business with the army is north of the old border. I don't think we need to bother each other this trip."

She nodded, satisfied. "Good enough. But if you change your mind, Palork wouldn't mind some extra help keeping an eye on the ladies." She turned to one of her stable. "Sweets, show Jorac here how you wash clothes, when they're *extra dirty*."

Jorac spent only a few seconds watching the young strumpet "accidentally" splash water on her ample bosom, turning the thin blouse she wore translucent, then bouncing and jiggling up and down as she rinsed some old clothes in a laundry barrel, performing a lascivious imitation of a normal laundry-woman's task. Jorac chuckled and walked away smiling, and not without a few backward glances. *Cute one, but Kimma is at home. Doesn't hurt to look, though. . .*

* * *

After he and Hox had a light lunch, Jorac killed some time by taking a little tour of the nearby wagons with the "O" tag on them. He thought he might find someone he could ask about the ins and outs of being an observer, but saw no one to talk to except one middle-aged man who was obviously drunk, even though it was barely past noon. So he gave up and went back to the wagon. He and Hox moved a few boxes, and found a place to hide a crossbow just behind the driver's seat, and made a few other adjustments. He found himself increasingly impatient, and sternly told himself to relax and just let the day come to him. He was idling in the shade of his wagon when a dried-up, scarred old man on a sway-backed horse rode up and yelled, "Observers! To Me!"

After motioning Hox to stay with the wagon, Jorac went toward the man, joining people emerging from other wagons nearby. Five other men and one woman gathered and looked up at the rider.

"For those who don't know, I'm Sergeant Zemak. I gotta ride ass-drag this week. You stay in front of me, and that rabble" – he pointed a thumb at the camp followers – "stays behind me. I got two badges for each of you. Put the big one on your wagon if it doesn't already have one, and show the small one to the cook if you want to eat, or the supply master if you want standard stuff. Don't get your hopes up too high there, if you catch my drift.

"There are some rules you gotta follow. They're all written down on the papers I wrapped your badges in. Read it." Then he pulled out a sack of small packets and began to read out the names on them. "Okay, Dembo, Laldo, Berich, here you go." He clearly knew these people, and handed packets to the red-faced drunken man, a small somber man whose face was lined with frown lines, and a paunchy, bald man who immediately examined his badges carefully.

"Mistress Gompel. That'd be you," he said, looking at the one woman. "The rest of you, let me know. Scholar Burnwright... Honorable Kellor... Mister Ekedior..." Jorac and the other two accepted their packets. "That's it then. We should be ready to go in a few minutes. I'll be back." He turned away and walked back up the column.

Jorac thought he recognized the woman, and walked over to her. "Haven't I seen you somewhere before?"

She turned and glowered at him, and snarled, "I don't think so." She was quite good looking in her own way – short-haired and stocky, perhaps thirty years old, and like everyone else, dressed in trousers.

"Sorry, I guess that sounded rather trite. I didn't mean it that way at all. Didn't you used to play music with Robin and his group last year, at the northeast Fireday market? You played tambourine and hand drum, right, and sang a bit?"

She relaxed a bit, and said, "Yeah, that was me. That was year before last, I think. You like music?"

"I like the way you play it." Her glower returned, and he quickly added. "Oh, damn, I did it again. I'm not trying to chat you up, honest. I just remember you playing there, and you were pretty good. I was a constable. I stopped there fairly often; your group drew a crowd and we had to watch things. Robin, he knew what he was doing, but you held the rest of them together – you kept them in time. Some nights I think you were the only sober musician there."

She smiled a wry smile. "Some nights I think I was the only sober person in the whole town. I never liked drinking much. Anyway, that's all over. Robin and me split up after a few months working there. Women trouble."

Jorac said nothing, just raised one eyebrow.

"We both wanted the same birdie, and I won." She stared at Jorac challengingly, seeming to dare him to disapprove.

Jorac grinned a crooked grin at her. "Ha! We have that in common – I like women too. Well met! I'm Jorac." He extended his open hand to her.

Seeing Jorac's reaction, she relaxed a little and shook his hand – she had a firm grip – and grinned back a bit. "Call me Nellie."

"What are you doing here? Seems like a musician wouldn't have much to do as an observer?"

"I'm working for a scholar who wants me to write down the army drinking songs – the bawdier, the better. He thinks because I'm a woman I'll have a better chance to hear them. His money's good, even if he's a little crazy, and it sure beats juggling on a street corner to try to get some extra coin. Let alone take a real job."

"Interesting. I know a few songs like that. Some evening I'll see if you already know them. I probably have to be drinking myself to remember. Let's see. . ." He named a couple of songs, and they talked about music for a bit. When Nellie finally seemed to be getting comfortable, he said, "Say, what do you know about the rest of this group? I got this job at the last minute, and don't know much about the other observers, or being one myself. We seem to be an odd lot."

"I was trying to figure that out when I was here last year. I decided there's just two main types, scholars and remittance men." Jorac must have looked puzzled at her second category, because she explained, "Those are the ones the family pays to stay away. They go down the coast to the islands in the winter, and up the river in the summer, or travel with the army. They're the type that can't be disowned, but can't be kept around Vaggert either. I think that one" – she pointed over her shoulder and mimed drinking a bottle – "is one of those. The scholars are easier to spot; they ask so many questions. So that's you, right?"

"Not exactly. I'm the Wizard Constable. Sort of a scout for the wizards, I guess."

"Oh. You work for the wizards?" There was a hint of distrust in her tone, and Jorac didn't blame her. Wizards were hard to trust.

"I'm afraid so. Remember what you said about the person who hired you? – the money is good, but he's a little crazy? Well, replace that with dangerous and scary, and you'll know what it's like working for wizards. Better than walking a beat, though."

"Yeah, I bet." She shrugged. "This observer gig isn't so bad. The regular army treats you like shit, but you can go anywhere and ask anything. The worst they can do is tell you to go away." She stopped and looked around; some people nearby were starting to stir. "We better get ready now. Zemak said he'd be coming back soon. Talk to you later."

Jorac went back to the wagon and told Hox about the scholars and remittance men. While they waited for Zemak, the two of them entertained themselves looking at the other observers' wagons and trying to guess why they were here.

The "few minutes" Zemak had mentioned ran on and on, but by mid-afternoon they were finally on the road. The road here was wide and well kept, and the seven observer wagons went along in two columns, with Zemak at their rear. The whole gaggle of camp followers came behind him, and Jorac could sometimes see them jostling and yelling at each other since they had no Zemak to keep their wagons in line. They only went two or three hours before they found the groups in front of them halting and pulling off the road; it was late afternoon, not yet early evening. Zemak pointed the observers to an area inside the guard lines that were being set up, and disappeared. Their first day's travel had ended.

Nellie parked her small wagon and turned her horses over to the army hostler (Jorac noticed her pass a few coins as well); then she hurried toward the main camp without unpacking anything. She paused just long enough for Jorac to introduce her to Hox, then went on her way, saying "Plenty of drinking this first night. I have to go – they'll start singing early."

Jorac and Hox found a level spot for their wagon and hailed the hostler, who told them the standard fee to take the horses, feed them, watch them, and deliver them back in the morning was four coppers each, since each man who handled the animal got a copper. It was technically against the rules to charge money for their care, but the hostler was open and matter-of-fact about the practice and its price.

Jorac paid eight coppers cheerfully enough, but he wondered what the broken rules said about the army. It seemed inefficient at best; from what he'd seen, it was no match for the tribesmen he'd gone to war with. But it was certainly big; despite the disorganization, they had enough troops to overwhelm any group of provincial rebels or desert tribes that could be assembled, so he supposed it served well enough. But the lax attitude still grated on him.

Jorac and Hox went through their supplies, selecting a few items to cook for their first meal. The small spirit-fueled stove Hox had bought was tested and found weak but serviceable, and they cooked an indifferent meal of pan-bread and fried meat. The plan was to normally use a metal fire-ring and cook their dinners over wood fires, but it was good to know that if it was raining they had an alternative. It was still early when they'd eaten, and they were curious about. . . well, everything.

A steady stream of young soldiers hurriedly passed their area, heading for the civilian area nearby; when they saw a pair of older soldiers moving more slowly, they got them to stop and talk for a minute. The pair were headed to the FAB ("Family Assigned Bivouac"), not the VAB ("Vendor Assigned Bivouac," or "Vice And Bitches" as one of them called it). Apparently the mothers of the real families enforced some order in the setup process, ensuring that the vendors set up near the family area were legitimate, and that the gamblers and shady businesses like Madame Revar's "laundry" were kept away from their children.

Jorac and Hox watched the traffic for a while, but soon grew tired of that. They took some time to make up their beds and finally crawled into them, but it was the first night out and the noises from the VAB area were loud. Jorac lay on his side and put a pillow over his top ear, resolving to try to set up further away from them the next night. It was late before they finally got to sleep, and the morning light came early, but though they lay in bed for some time and got ready rather slowly, they still had to wait more than an hour before Sergeant Zemak arrived and called to the group to move out.

The second day's travel was much like the first, except they managed to leave by mid-morning. They encamped just as early, and Jorac and Hox found a vendor to buy a cooked meal from – Jorac wanted to hoard their supplies of food as best he could. The third day they left a little earlier in the morning – Jorac supposed the plan was to gradually accustom the army to a decent pace. But when they stopped even earlier in the afternoon, he decided he'd been wrong, and he was simply with the laziest army he'd ever heard of. He also noticed they always stopped far away from any towns along the road; he supposed the soldiers – and the V.A.B. – brought enough trouble with them.

The area they stopped at was near a small river, apparently the standard third day's stop. Jorac and Hox each spent a little time shopping in the V.A.B. area, which was already growing familiar, while the other watched the wagon. After they'd cooked a simple dinner and cleaned up everything, it was still early. Jorac wanted to visit the army – they were here to observe them, after all. He told Hox, "I'm going to go find the fighting men. There must be some in this damned army, even if we haven't seen them yet. I haven't had any decent sword practice since I became Wizard Constable."

Hox waved him away. "Let me know what you find. I'm going to dig into the food we just bought. A sweet, or bit of fruit would suit me."

Jorac grinned at his companion and said, "Growing boy like you needs his nourishment. I'll back before dark."

Chapter 21 - Training Recommences

Jorac held his observer badge in his hand, ready to show it to anyone who asked, but no one did. There were guards around a few tents and wagons, doubtless belonging to high-ranking or rich officers, but the guards looked fat and bored, not alert. Jorac wandered in and out along the crooked paths through camp until he heard the distinctive rhythm of swords clashing.

When he found the source, he saw a group of about twenty men he thought looked like "real soldiers" standing and watching a mock duel. A couple of beefy young men in light armor were practicing with wooden swords and light shields in a marked-off circle. They both had the big arm muscles of blacksmiths, but they were agile for their size and moved well. As Jorac approached, they closed again and grunted with effort as they swung their swords.

In the circle with them, watching them closely, was a smaller brown-skinned, black-bearded man who seemed to be keeping score. "Blocked, both."

The two circled a little; then one managed to push the other off balance with his shield, and swung his sword inside the other's guard, giving him a sharp rap on the side of the helmet.

"Dead!" called out the score-keeper. "He could hit neck with that blow. Plorg know we in training, hit helmet, I so say. Good, you two. Good."

The two men stood panting, while the brown-skinned man talked to the assembled men. "See, shield not only block. Plorg watch, he push when Granko has weight wrong. Granko, he think shield protect so he shift weight wrong. He learn. You learn too. Form pairs, try push, try sword, too."

The men formed up in good order, and as Jorac continued to watch, the men began their drill, trying to push each other with their shields to force openings for sword blows.

The brown-skinned drill-master walked around a little, watching the men, then saw Jorac. He came over to him and said, "You go away. Soldiers only."

Jorac showed him the observer badge, drawing a grimace from the drill-master.

/*May the seven hundred gods preserve me from beardless, buggering fools!*/ he said. It was in a language Jorac knew well; he'd spent two years with a desert tribe that spoke it, and they used nearly the same words in dealing with outsiders.

He waved Jorac back. "You go. Don't bother soldiers." /*Probably wants to find himself a bed-partner.*/

Jorac replied in the same tongue. /*The seven hundred gods won't help you in this far land. And I like women for my bed partners, if you don't mind. Although I have had to break the arms of a few of The People's buggering fools to convince them otherwise.*/

He grinned at the man's shock, and continued. /*What brings you to the Wet Lands?*/

The drill-master briefly returned his gaze to the fighters, calling out a suggestion to one of them. Then he looked back at Jorac. /*A lovely young woman, her ugly brother, and a fast horse brought me here. How did you learn The People's language? Some traders know a little, but you know it well. There is a story here, I think, one worth hearing.*/

/*I was with the Aboji for two summers. I learned much there.*/

The drill-master looked at him more closely. /*You say you broke some arms there? How did this come to be?*/

Jorac replied, /*One man, both arms, when he would not believe that I was not a zarch-man. But in time, the tribe learned that I was a fighting man, even though I found the beard I grew hot and itchy in the summers.*/

The weapons trainer was definitely interested now. /*Are you. . . Forgive my rudeness, I am Brozadam, son of Borzandar the Strong-armed, son of Borzedden the Smiling. The use-name they called you, was it Shiar?*/

In the desert culture it was the height of rudeness to flatly ask someone's name, but Brozadam had done it acceptably. He only asked Jorac what others called him, and only the nickname, after offering his own.

/Yes, that was so; that is the name they called me. My birth name is Jorac, son of Widdel, son of Widdel the Black. You are welcome to use my name. Now I have a job that makes me sit and get fat, so I was drawn to the sound of fighting men, being wishful to practice. It is a sound that makes the ears happy./ The language of The People lent itself to flourishes like this.

Brozadam bowed to him, in the manner of meeting a respected equal. */Ah. I have heard stories of you. Some are quite remarkable. It is said. . . But no, stories are for later. It would be an honor for you to use my name, though those here call me 'Brownie,' which I do not mind. You are wanting to practice, yes?/*

Jorac returned the bow. */I would be obliged to you. Please though, I was not being un-boastful when I told you I was fat and out-of-shape. It was the bare, sad truth, so please help me start slowly./*

/It shall be as you say. First, though, a practice match to see your skills as they are?/

/If you can find a fat, out-of-shape man like me here./ Jorac looked around approvingly. */I don't see any like that, which means that you are doing your job well./*

/I hope so, but there is one here. . . The stories I heard said you preferred two blades. Is this still true?/

When Jorac nodded, he continued. */This youngling, he has had much training, and can win many practices through speed and tricks and new moves. He becomes lazy, and arrogant. I talk, but he does not listen./*

/If you have no beardless youths, no old crippled men, I will practice with this one. You wish a lesson to be taught to him? Since I am fat and out-of-shape, you must tell me how he fights if I am to win./

/He favors his right hand, and wants to circle to his left. He likes two swords also, to feint with one hand and attack with the other. Often he takes a short step back first. He is very quick with his hands,

so here he can beat these stronger men. But in a real fight they would be cut and he would be dead. Here, put on this padding; I will return./

After Jorac donned the practice armor, Brozadam called the exercise to a halt, and said, "Taj, you come here now. Practice fight for you."

Jorac's opponent proved to be a slight young man, a little shorter than Jorac, who had the sardonic look of a bored nobleman. Jorac noticed the other fighters were moving in to surround the ring, murmuring about the newcomer.

Brozadam looked at the audience and pointing at Jorac said, "This man – I hear his name before. I hear he fight before. We see."

Brozadam selected light wooden swords from the practice rack and had the rest of the men step out of the practice ring. At his signal, Jorac started moving.

It took him over a minute of standing and watching Taj feint at him – and striking a few slow, easily-blocked strikes – for Jorac to mentally get into the fight. He started looking at his opponent's cues – the footwork, the center of his chest, his eyes. After Jorac returned a half-speed strike with a faster one of his own, Taj's eyes gleamed a bit and they both speeded up.

They started moving faster, then faster still. Taj jumped back at one point to disengage, and started circling to his left. Jorac waited for the expected attack, and when it came, beat Taj to the counter, giving him a sharp rap on the wrist.

Brozadam yelled "He cut!"

Taj's eyes narrowed a bit, and he started moving in tiny steps, looking for an opening. He then switched his style from a feint-and-strike to a weaving attack, but Jorac knew that style too. The switch actually helped Jorac, as it made him begin to concentrate in earnest. He started moving smoothly in a slight crouch, seeing dangers, openings, targets in a way he hadn't done in years. In a near-berserker rage again, he stopped thinking about the training circle and the onlookers – the only things he felt were the swords in his hand, his opponent, and the need to *attack!*

He blocked a looping strike with one hand and a short off-hand thrust with the other hand; this let him move past Taj's side, and while passing he hit Taj hard with a low strike on the back of his leg, below the knee. Taj stumbled forward and turned to face Jorac, but it was too late. For all his speed and sword-learning, he wasn't very good at close-up defense, and after a flurry of blows, Jorac struck him hard at the side of the neck. Taj fell to the ground in pain – and the shock of being beaten.

Jorac stood over him, a part of him wondering why there was no blood, and glancing around for the next opponent to fight. With an effort, he wrenched himself out of his trance. He put down his swords and helped Taj to his feet. He found himself dripping sweat, breathing hard, and his wrists and shoulders were tired. He needed more basic practice, not practice duels. He felt a little ashamed about hitting Taj in the neck so hard, but Brozadam came up and put his arm around both fighters.

"See! He fight, not play. He fight as soldier fight. Taj, you quick. You learn, too, you be good, too. Now we done, put swords away."

Jorac formally shook Taj's hand, and quietly said, "You're good."

Taj wryly grinned and shook his head, wincing in pain as he did it. He said, "Not good enough," as they walked toward the gathered fighters. His sardonic look was gone, replaced by a much more respectful one.

"Not good enough today, but there's tomorrow. That's what practice is for."

"I suppose. But I think tomorrow I'll be sitting out practice with a bruised neck."

"Sorry about that."

One of the other fighters said, "Don't apologize. Brownie never lets us apologize for training bruises. Says we ought to thank the guy who gave 'em to us." He was a bit taller than Jorac, and had much broader shoulders and stronger arms – obviously he practiced daily.

Jorac smiled. "I think that's going a little far, but I see his point. I've sure had my share."

"Brownie's been warning Taj he'd get his too, but none of us had the speed. I'm glad to see it. Stinkin' snooty nobleman." He grinned at Taj, taking the sting out of his words.

In the same joking tone, Taj replied, "Someone's got to teach you guttersnipes a thing or two."

Turning to Jorac, the large fighter explained, "He's the only noble-taught who made the Guard this year. Learned different than us. I'm Poznoy, by the way."

"I'm Jorac. You said you're in the Guard?" Jorac could hear the capital letter in Poznoy's tone.

Taj said, "The General's Guard, of course. Nobody else would be dumb enough to be practicing the first week out. Everyone else takes it easy the first few days, shakes out the kinks."

"I was wondering about that. I thought this was the slowest moving army in history – well, the one with the shortest daily marches, anyway."

Poznoy said, "Tomorrow we get real weather back and we'll start moving a bit faster. Of course the Guard could have made it here the first day."

"Remember I'm new here. So, who are you guys, anyway? I've spent the last few years as a constable, and we mostly stick to the city."

Poznoy said, "The guard is two dozen of the best soldiers, picked by the Emperor's Chamberlain himself, after the winter tournament." He said this with some pride.

Taj added, "You should come out to the tournament next year – or maybe not. I might be the one you beat out." His expression said he didn't think so, but Jorac knew a good solider needed confidence and just smiled.

"No tournaments for me. I spent a couple of years with the tribes over the mountains, near where Brownie comes from, but I left the serious fighting behind me years ago. Now I've got this damned job working for the damned wizards, and I just need to get into some sort of shape – they have me sitting behind a desk far too much, writing stupid reports."

Poznoy said, "You say you work for the wizards?"

Jorac nodded, "I'm afraid so. My title is Wizard Constable. They heard rumors the rebels have a powerful wizard working for them, so they sent me to look. That's why I've got the observer badge."

Jorac saw the guard's face cloud in concern, so he added, "Not that I trust them – maybe they were just trying to get rid of me for a while. I almost quit instead, but I figured if it was true, then we should know about it."

Poznoy shook his head. "The General hates wizards."

"I don't like them much myself, truth be told. At least they pay well, and right now I take their coin."

"The General *hates* wizards. Hates them. I'm not sure why, but I heard his sister had something to do with some wizard who got her in a family way, then walked out on her. We don't even talk about wizards when he's around. Just a warning to you. You observer types will be seeing him around more than we will."

"You guys are the General's Guard and you don't see him?"

"Once we get up north we will, you bet. Until then we'll spend most of our time in training. We don't mind, see. He has a bunch of fat and fancy types around him, map carriers and report-writers and such."

Jorac smiled. "Hey, didn't I just tell you I got fat writing stupid reports?"

Taj grinned back. "Yeah, but you didn't get *that* fat, and those guys don't call them stupid reports. They think reports are great, and if they ever had to fight, they'd be in big trouble."

Poznoy said seriously, "Now, let's be fair. Faced with a dangerous opponent, Kezert could sit on him. Squash the life right out of him."

Taj and Jorac grinned and shook their heads. While Jorac was thinking up a proper rejoinder, Brozadam came up to them. "You wash now? Cloth, water, there."

The men went over to the wash area, and Jorac cleaned up as best he could. He'd gotten used to frequent baths while living in the city, and even stripping off his clothes and rinsing with a clean wet cloth was a great comfort.

Brozadam said to him, /*You are welcome here each night. We train just after camping, before dinner. I would be pleased to dine with you soon, and to hear the story of how you came to live with The People, if you should wish to tell it. If not, I would not wish to intrude.*/

/*You certainly shall have the story. But I have eaten tonight, and I need to return to my companion. May I bring him to train, also? He has just nineteen summers, and has a height – I do not give any but the truest facts – this high.*/ Jorac reached up on his tiptoes and reached for the sky.

Poznoy looked amused and imitated the movement. "Is this some sort of stretching exercise?"

"I was telling Brownie here how tall my traveling companion is. I'd like to come back tomorrow and bring him. He's nineteen, and not long off the farm, but he's fairly quick, and we always joked that he's eleven-teen feet tall."

One of the other guards overheard and said, "I saw him – on the observer wagon, right? He's huge. Yeah, bring him, so long as Brownie says it's okay."

Brozadam said, "Bring him. I can boot him away, if I need. Tell him no whine, no sulk, no try to bully. Bring him, can teach some these big mans how to fight with man more big."

"He'll enjoy it, I think."

A low chuckle from the nearby Guard members told Jorac that Hox might not enjoy it as much as he might expect to.

* * *

When he got back to the wagon, Hox was learning to juggle. Nellie Gompel was teaching him the basics, and he seemed to be picking it up quickly.

She saw Jorac first, and caught the cloth balls she'd been demonstrating with. "What ho, Jorac – where have you been?"

"I found some real soldiers. Hox, they said you and I can practice with them. They're an elite group, and they've got a regular trainer, so we should be able to learn a lot. Just the thing after sitting on a wagon seat all day."

Hox looked pleased. "Sounds good! These little balls are good for the hands and eyes, but not the muscles."

Jorac said, "I think they'll take care of the muscle exercise there, don't worry. Anything new here?"

Nellie said, "You missed the fun. General Melsim was here, with all his staff, looking all full of pomp."

Hox added, "They were full of something, that's for sure. There was one guy I thought would break his horse – no taller than you, and at least double your weight."

Nellie said, "They asked us observers what we were doing here – each of us. They were a little skeptical about the song collection, so I showed them the orders, and now I get to go to one of their parties in a few days. Makes my job a lot easier, that."

Hox said, "Me, they just asked who sent me here. Then I showed them the orders and they asked if I was Jorac. It was a little strange – like they were angry at me or something, and I never even met them before."

"I just found out that General Melsim hates wizards. So he probably hates us too, by transference. I guess we should hope he stays away."

"He said he was looking forward to meeting you."

"Somehow, I doubt it."

* * *

As the days went on, a routine developed. Jorac and Hox exercised in the evenings and then bought their way into the General's Guard mess (and finally found people who ate as much as Hox), so didn't have to rely on their own indifferent camp cooking. It made for a full, satisfying evening, after the boredom of a day's wagon ride.

The army traveled only five days out of seven. Starday was spent working in camp, repairing their kit and drilling. Sunday the soldiers had to themselves, and Jorac was bored, so he spent his time writing letters to Kimma and Dorrie. He used words like "curious" and "interesting" to describe the army's daily habits, and had to figuratively bite his tongue to keep from writing "lazy." He knew all his correspondence would be read by the army censor, and perhaps Pergimtor as well, so he just filled it with a description of the weather (lots of cold rain, a novelty to those in Vaggert), their practicing with the soldiers, and brief descriptions of the farms and forests they passed through. He posted the letters with the biweekly messenger back to Vaggert, and wondered when they would arrive.

Twice, when they returned from their nightly exercise, they learned that the General had been by the observer's area, but since they usually left for their soldier practice right after camping and didn't return until after dinner, they missed him. From what was said, and not said, about the man by the General's Guardsmen, Jorac didn't count it as a great loss.

One sunny, lazy Sunday morning, while Hox was shopping and Jorac was hanging his laundry, Nellie Gompel came to Jorac, looking vaguely troubled.

"Hi Nellie. What's up?"

She smiled wanly. "I had a bad dream last night, and I just wanted to talk to somebody rational." She took a deep breath. "See, I get a bonus if I stay with the army through the whole campaign, and I've been trying to decide whether to do it, so I must have had it on my mind. Anyway, I dreamed we went with the army on beyond Norfort, and the rebels attacked us and slaughtered us all. And they were horrible, big and ugly. . ."

She shuddered a little, then took a deep breath. "So I decided to stop acting like a child and ask you. You've been talking to the army guys. Do I need to worry about the rebels?" She shrugged and smiled. "If I'm going to get a bonus, I want to live to spend it."

Jorac looked at her – for all her confident exterior, it couldn't have been easy to be one of the few women in the midst of the army. "Well, I can tell you what I've pieced together. Mind you, this is all second-hand or worse. The rebels are usually a mixed lot – some of them are fools or lunatics, some are decent fighters with bad training, and some are just cutthroat scum, like you might find in Swampside. They aren't too well organized, either. They make a few careful, smart attacks, but then follow that with a mistake a second-year army man wouldn't make. So, by the end of the campaign the rebel leaders end up dead or in hiding, and their troops – the ones that survive – sneak back and lead their normal lives."

"So if we're behind our Etrombian army, it's not likely we'll. . . I mean, we probably won't see enemy soldiers ourselves?"

"Our army outnumbers them a good ten to one. The only ones you'll probably see are the ones waving to you from the farm fields. The emperor's policy is to drive the rebels back to their farms, not kill them all. Some of the guys I talk to seem to think that's kind of foolish and short-sighted, but they're smart enough not to say so."

She took a deep breath. "Okay, thanks. That makes me feel better. I guess I'll stick with it."

"I think you'll be fine. Park your wagon next to ours, and if you hear any disturbances at night, stay near your wagon. Once we get further north we'll start camping near the center of the army, with guards on the outside."

"Thanks Jorac." Some of her confident swagger returned. "You ever need something, you let me know, okay?"

* * *

After three weeks, they reached the old northern border at the town of Norfort. The town was a strange one, a small core of permanent residents serving the local farmers, a larger number of traders, and (at this time of year) even more traders to service the army. Everything a soldier could get in the V.A.B. area was available here, and more. Jorac was told the army would spend two days here, then set off north under much more strict discipline.

They encamped as usual in an area just outside the town. Hox was content to rest in the wagon and nurse his training bruises. He never complained, and was learning fast, but in truth he lost most of the practice fights each evening. Jorac went into town and found some dried meats and preserved vegetables to add to their larder. The town was full of soldiers, but most of them seemed to be drinking and carousing; inside the shops he had little company. When he returned carrying his packages, there was a young man waiting for him at the wagon.

As Jorac approached, the young man reached out his hand with a piece of paper in it. "Constable Kellor, this is for you."

Something about the young man's attitude reminded Jorac of Zarl Leganwei, the young noble lout he'd stopped from robbing a laundry-woman. Jorac's hands were full, and so he walked past him and his outstretched hand and started putting his packages into the wagon.

"I said, this is for you!" He thrust out the paper again. Jorac didn't much care for his tone, which seemed to expect him to obey without question.

"I heard you the first time. And you saw my hands were full. Patience, it's a virtue, yes?" Jorac untied a package and started handing some items to Hox in the wagon. It only took a minute, and Jorac felt a little guilty pleasure as he saw the messenger's consternation.

"Now, what can I do for you?"

"General Melsim wants to see you and your assistant. *The General.*" The messenger was literally bouncing with impatience, bobbing up and down on his toes.

Jorac took the paper, which, with flowery words and perfect penmanship, asked to see him and his assistant. Jorac recognized the careful wording – his position as observer meant he couldn't be actually ordered, but this was the closest thing to it.

Jorac handed the paper to Hox, and turned to the young man. "Did he say when we're expected?"

The messenger was nonplussed. "Right away. It's the *General himself,*" as if that made all the difference.

Jorac took the time to wet a rag and wipe his face; the day had turned fairly hot and the trail had been dusty. He also took the time to find and don his fancy scabbards, those with silver scrollwork and glass jewels. Officers seemed to care about that sort of thing – Jorac had always figured that it was the quality of the steel in the sword that was important, but he knew appearances were important too. He wished he had time to put on an actual uniform, but the everyday trousers and dusty tunic he was wearing would have to do.

The young messenger was practically tapping his toes in impatience by this point, but managed not to say anything.

"Alright. Let's go, Hox. General Melsim has requested the pleasure of our company. Lead on – Ensign, is it?"

"Ensign Leflurery, at your service. This way, please." He led off at a brisk pace toward the main army camp. Jorac and Hox had always skirted it before on their way toward the Guards and their nightly practice.

Jorac fell back far enough to quietly tell Hox, "Don't say anything – nothing at all – unless I tell you to."

Hox nodded, his brow furrowed a little in worry. Leflurery looked back and paused for a little while to let them catch up, and soon they had were in an area of better-looking tents, a few quite fancy. They stopped in front of the largest one, with a guard standing under a deep red, gold-tasseled sun-shade in the front. Leflurery, in a loud voice, announced "Observer Kellor and his assistant are here to see General Melsim, as order. . . as requested."

The guard, a paunchy, middle-aged fellow in very fine clothes, poked his head inside the tent, then returned and nodded. He said, "This way, gentlemen," and opened the tent flap. Jorac could detect faint sarcasm on the word "gentlemen," but it was too subtle to make an issue of.

General Melsim proved to be a vigorous white-haired man of perhaps sixty years. In the tent were several others: two young men in well-tailored uniforms seated on chairs by the walls, an obvious clerk or secretary seated to his right, and a grossly fat man to his left. The fat man whispered something in the general's ear; the general nodded and turned to Jorac and Hox.

Without any preamble, the general spoke – he had a surprisingly high-pitched voice. "Observers, are you?"

"Yes, sir."

"That means observe, not meddle, right? I want to make that clear. Very clear. The damned wizards have to have their spy in my army, I know. That's you, but don't think you can lord over us like the damned wizards do back home. This is *my* army."

"Sir, we're merely observers."

229

Melsim replied with a derisive sniff, and continued, "I've tried to visit you, several times, but you've been hiding."

Jorac said levelly, "We have been exercising each night."

"Yes, yes, I know how you observers are. The Vice and Bitches area is right next to your camp; I'm sure you've been getting lots of exercise there. That's all coming to a stop now, and you can turn back with them if you want. Wouldn't want you to miss your pet slit, now."

Jorac glanced at Hox to see if he was going to have to quiet him, but the young giant had his jaw visibly clenched.

"Sir, we'll follow our orders, and remain with the army. As you know, we're here to determine if the rebels have a wizard with them – a powerful one. That's our only reason for being here."

"So you say. Just stay out of the way of fighting men, and try not to tell too many lies to the sodding spell-casters."

Jorac took a deep breath. "Sir, I work for wizards, but not because I love them. At the best of times they're uncomfortable to deal with. But I'm here to answer a specific question, and report that one answer to a member of the Emperor's Council."

"So you say. But of course, the sort of man who'd work for the damned wizards would say that. *You* might say anything."

Jorac looked around the room; no one there seemed surprised at the general's words. He looked back at the general, and asked in a quiet, dangerous voice, "Sir, when a gentleman says another doesn't speak the truth, what response is expected?" Jorac's hands were resting comfortably near his side, which were also near his swords, and he "accidentally" brushed the hilts so that the scabbard slapped his leg. He wasn't about to attack this buffoon, but neither was he going to be called a liar in public without any response at all.

The obese man spoke for the first time. "I'm Colonel Kezert. I'm sure the general didn't mean to impugn your honesty." He whispered something in the General's ear.

Melsim curtly nodded to Kezert, then turned back to Jorac. "No, I didn't call you a liar, and wouldn't. A man may be duped after all, or bespelled. Still, you work for the damned wizards, do you not?"

"Officially I work jointly for the Wizards Council and the Vaggert City Constable service. In practice, I work for the damned wizards. And I call them the 'damned wizards' too, if not to their face."

Melsim seemed not to hear the last sentence. "Well then. This is how it shall be. You will not interfere with my army in any way. You will go where we tell you, when we tell you, and do what we tell you. Is that clear?"

Jorac nodded agreeably. "So long as it doesn't conflict with my observer's orders, I shall be happy to oblige you." He'd read his orders carefully, and they specifically said he didn't have to obey any army command; thus his agreement was completely empty.

The general nodded, looking somewhat mollified. "Kezert, anything to add?"

The obese man spoke again. "No, General. I would however ask Constable Kellor what he thinks of our army so far? I hear you've been a fighting man, even a commander, eh?"

Jorac was surprised. He'd told his story a few times, but not recently (except to Hox and Kimma), unless talking to Brozadam in the language of the desert tribes counted. If it hadn't leaked from there, then Kezert had done research on his past back in the city, during the short time between his assignment and the army's departure.

"I have much to learn about an army this size. I've learned there are reasons for many of the actions I first found strange. I expect it to continue that way." That was safe, and true, if not exactly enlightening.

"Yes, we all have much to learn. Does the young giant speak?"

Jorac turned to Hox and gave the faintest of nods.

"Yes sir, I speak." Hox was on his best behavior, acting very formal.

Kezert asked, "Anything you want to say, or to ask?"

"No, sir."

The General laughed at this. "Teach you a thing or two – eh, Kezzie? Damned if he couldn't. Knows when to shut up, he does, and not carry on with a bunch of useless questions."

Kezert gave Hox and Jorac a smile that didn't reach his eyes, and nodded to Melsim. "That's all I had."

The general turned to the man on his right and looked at a paper, and with his left hand waved toward Hox and Jorac. "You may go."

Jorac knew the general expected a salute of some sort, or at least a "Yes, sir," but he was annoyed enough to simply turn and leave silently. It was a minor snub, but one he couldn't bring himself to regret.

The man outside the tent was listening to what was said inside, and was startled by Jorac's sudden lifting of the tent flap. Jorac merely raised an eyebrow at the guard, who looked away sheepishly.

Jorac strode off, with Hox following. Neither spoke a word until they got back to their wagon, but Jorac could tell by Hox's determined stride that he was still angry.

When they reached their wagon, Hox let loose. "That idiot!" he roared.

"Keep your voice down."

Hox looked around, but no one seemed to be listening.

He continued at a lower volume. "That idiot commands this army? All he did was insult you and not listen to a word you said."

Jorac said mildly, "What did you think of Kezert?"

"Him? He's so fat. Seemed smarter than Melsim."

"I agree with you. But of course it's all political. The gossip says Melsim wasn't put in charge for military reasons – he's related to half the families in those fancy houses near the castle, and his wife is the emperor's third cousin. But he's a good cavalryman, aggressive in a fight, good at rallying the troops. I've heard he looks very fine in his fancy uniform, up on Virack, his big gray stallion."

Hox looked disgusted. "I'll bet. I can just see him now."

"On the other hand, Kezert is very sharp, but he's fat and lazy, and a poor example for the troops, so he's the General's Aide or something. He has a high rank, but no soldiers report to him – they wouldn't respect him. But he's good at logistics and even battle plans – at least he's made good enough plans for Melsim to beat the rebels for the past ten years. They say he knows every officer and sergeant by name, but I've heard grumbling that he still thinks of his troops as just little toy figures he maneuvers on a battlefield. Almost every year, though, one of his tricky little plans works and completely surprises the enemy."

Hox said, "Hmm. What if he guesses wrong? You can't always figure out what your opponent will do next." That had been one of the lessons that the drills with the General's Guard had been teaching them – sometimes you need to just react, not think ahead.

"Sometimes he's wrong, but we outnumber any likely band of rebels by at least ten to one. The general likes to keep the army together, so it doesn't get picked off in pieces. It's worked for the past ten years, in four different northern provinces."

Hox was a good bit calmer now at least. "Humph. I'm still glad I'm not in the army except as an observer. What if Melsim doesn't listen to Kezert, or Kezert is wrong?"

"That could be a problem."

Chapter 22 - A Surprising Side Trip

When the army moved out of Norfort, it had a different feel to it, as if the time for games had passed and they were now getting serious. The observers' wagons were moved to the center of the column with the clerks, cooks, and others who weren't expected to fight. Observer Dembo acquired a helper from somewhere, a teetotaler, so in the afternoons when he got too drunk to drive his wagon he wouldn't be a hazard.

They camped early the first afternoon, and the entire army was called to practice fighting, a few in small groups, but most of them in one long line. Jorac and Hox walked over to where the General's Guard was practicing, but Brozadam (in his native language) told Jorac this was show-practice and the General was expected to come watch them. So Jorac and Hox merely walked around the camp and observed. The army was starting to act like one, and Jorac was glad to see it. There were two or three support people for every true fighter, but even the hostlers and clerks did some weapons training on Starday.

Now that they were beyond Norfort, Jorac had begun thinking about the side trip Pergimtor had asked him to make. Before they pulled out the next morning he said to Hox, "I need to find someone with a map. When we get to East Luverna, we're supposed to go to Labblox and look for what's-his-name, the man who might be Pergimtor's old teacher. Remember? I need to know if we're going to go there, or how close we're going to get."

"Well, I wouldn't recommend asking the General to explain his plans to you," Hox said wryly. "But one of the scholars probably has a map."

It turned out that Scholar Burnwright was indeed tracking their daily progress on a map, and seemed glad to display it for Jorac. Assuming they kept going north on this road, in about two days they'd meet the main east-west road. At that point they could turn right and go east to Labblox, turn left toward the rebellious West Luverna, or keep going north toward Marpo's Keep, the capitol of East Luverna.

"What do you think they'll do?" Jorac asked the scholar.

"I couldn't say. Either they wish to ensure that East Luverna continues to support the Empire, and will therefore take a few extra days to visit the capital and ensure their continued good behavior, or they will turn west and strike straight for the rebels. I have an appointment with Colonel Kezert this very evening. It will be very exciting to watch the decision process, for that is just the sort of thing I hoped to see when I sought the appointment."

Jorac thanked the scholar and took the news back to Hox, who was putting the horses in harness, preparing for the day's travel.

Hox said, "Huh. I'd go find and fight the rebels, and not worry much about what they think here."

"Me too. Which probably means they'll do just the opposite."

* * *

Two days later, their words proved correct. The army camped just past the crossroads and prepared to leave the next morning for Marpo's Keep. That was when Jorac and Hox decided it was time for their little side trip. As slowly as the army moved, they were confident they could visit Labblox and return before the ponderous machine had gotten back from Marpo's Keep, turned, and made much headway toward West Luverna.

Early the next morning they hitched up their horses and threaded their wagon through the encampment and back to the road. They got a little hassle from the perimeter guard, but they showed him their written orders and were passed on through the lines. In a short time they reached the crossroads and turned east, toward a bright sunrise.

For the first time in weeks everything was quiet, and for a while the novelty kept their attention. The land was good flat farming land, and they could see that some fields they passed had been newly planted. There were a few other travelers, but none going their way at their pace, so they were mostly alone. Certainly travelers in a lone wagon needed to watch out for bandits, but there were no places to hide nearby and they received no reports of trouble from farmers they passed. So they gradually relaxed.

"Hox, isn't your family somewhere in this area?"

"Well, it's a day or so past Labblox, down this road and then a bit north. I thought we might be able to make a quick trip there, so I sent them a letter from Vaggert before I left saying I might or might not make it up to see them for a day. I wasn't sure how this journey would go."

"We can probably work that in. I think our horses are quick enough to catch up with the army, even with a couple of extra days."

Hox snorted. "Huh. Unless we trade them for turtles, we can catch up."

"Turtles need too much care, and finding them big enough to pull a wagon might be difficult."

"True. Maybe giant snails instead. Easier to feed, though harder to water."

"Not so good on a rough road... and think of the trail they'd leave..."

They spent the rest of the morning this way, thinking of the many ways of moving faster than the army, each more outlandish. At noon they stopped to water the horses and give them feed bags with good grain, agreeing they'd gotten spoiled by having someone take care of their animals each night and bring them to their wagon each morning. They'd need to do more horse work or stop at local stables.

After they'd eaten lunch and set off again, both Hox and Jorac started yawning. They'd been getting up at first light the past few days, and not getting to sleep early enough. After Hox's third yawn, Jorac found himself growing too drowsy to pay attention to the road. "Tell you what," he said. "It's supposed to be a day and a half to Labblox. Let's make it a longer day tomorrow, and stop the next place we find, okay? You're as sleepy as I am."

"I won't object," Hox said. "I bet we can find an inn or way-house with a couple of beds."

"Sure, and one for me, too." Jorac and Hox grinned at each other. Hox wasn't the easiest traveling companion to provide for, but with his strength and temperament, Jorac was still glad to have picked him.

Soon they went over a small rise and saw a small settlement just off the road to the right. It looked like a farmer's village, but being so near the main road it would no doubt have some places that catered to travelers. They pulled off the road into the village, and found a clean-looking inn called Woper's Sun near the village square. When they pulled their wagon into the yard, a young boy of perhaps eight or ten years came out to help with the horses.

"You'll be staying for a time, sir? I could feed and water your horses, sir, for a few coppers each." When Jorac nodded, a tall teenaged boy came out of the barn. They quickly settled on eight coppers for the two horses for the night, the same cost as in the army camp. From a look the boys exchanged, Jorac thought he could have talked himself into a better deal, but he consoled himself that keeping the same rate would make his expense reports simpler. Hox and Jorac spent a few minutes dropping the hoops that held up the canvas that covered the wagon when they were inside, and tying it tight. They parked the wagon inside the barn, where they were assured it would be safe.

They went inside the inn and looked around. By then it was past lunchtime, so there were only a few loungers around, sitting idly at tables by the walls. A quick look satisfied Jorac that he'd chosen well, and no one was looking at them with avarice in mind. In fact, no one seemed to pay them much attention, except for the usual glances at Hox's height.

When he turned back to Hox to ask what he wanted first – food, bath, or bed – he saw him looking across the room, literally dumbstruck, his mouth agape. Quickly turning to see what had Hox's attention, Jorac saw a large-boned, pretty blonde serving girl, a good bit taller than he was, carrying pitchers of drink to the customers. Jorac thought she was the tallest woman he'd ever seen, but she wasn't looking at him. She was standing there, staring back at Hox, a smile flitting on and off her face. Jorac turned back to read his friend's face.

Hox didn't say a word, but he slowly closed his mouth. Jorac turned back to the girl, who was doing the same. Much later, he reconstructed the moment for the two of them, to much laughter all around:

"You are the most entrancing sight I have ever seen."

"Oh, you're so handsome, and not small like these locals."

A glance to her ring-less hand, an eyebrow raised in faint question said, *"Are you unmarried yet? It cannot be!"*

A smile, the faintest of nods. *"Have you no one? Then let it be me!"*

A more thoughtful look from Hox. *"Ah, you cannot be serious. Toy with me not."*

A friendly, open look, with her face rounding into intelligence. *"I would not lead one on this way. Serious, I am – if you are?"*

"Yes, I'm serious. My love, I am serious."

"My Love! Let us plan our lives together."

At this point, Hox turned to Jorac and said something completely unintelligible, probably even to him. He immediately turned back to the serving girl and started staring again, returning her look. She put the pitcher down on the nearby table, without turning her eyes from Hox, nearly spilling it in the process. Jorac thought he'd better step in. He firmly took Hox by the arm and walked him across the room to stand in front of her.

"Good lady, this is my friend Hox Tormand. He is of good family, and of stout heart, and as you can see he's tall and strong. We live in Vaggert, but are currently observers with the army, temporarily detached on a task in Labblox. Would you like to come with us?"

Even Jorac wasn't sure where the last sentence had come from; he'd had no thought other than to introduce the two. He'd heard of love at first sight before, but never expected to see it. Unnerving, that's what it was.

"I'm Monrae, daughter of Chirtsen and Mirdeu."

A soft "Monrae" escaped as if unbidden from Hox's lips.

Hox walked over to her and sat on the table, so their faces were at the same height, and started talking in a low tone. His hand and hers reached out at the same time, and soon they were holding both their hands together in front of them.

Jorac just stood back and watched them for a few minutes. If the other patrons of the tavern saw, they didn't pay attention, so Jorac had the scene all to himself. Their talking continued, and soon their hands were intertwined between them, more hand-fondling than mere hand-holding.

Finally a tall man of wearing an apron came into the room from the kitchen. He was forty or fifty, with the same look as Monrae (though a little shorter) – she was obviously his daughter. Ignoring her and Hox, he asked Jorac, "What can I do for you?"

"We want rooms for the night. I already talked to the boys – your sons? – about caring for the horses."

"Good, good. I let the younger boys run that part of things; teaches them how to handle business. Beds in the common area are six coppers, a room of your own is a silver, and dinner is eight, or more if you want something special."

"Good standard fare is fine with us, so long as there's enough of it. My friend can eat." Jorac gestured to Hox, who the owner saw the first time.

"No problem – my boys eat a good bit themselves. Monrae, what are you doing? That pitcher's about to spill."

"Father, I'd like you to meet the man I'm going to marry. Hox Tormand, meet my father, Chirtsen Woper."

For the second time in just a few minutes, Jorac saw someone's mouth drop open in surprise.

* * *

It wasn't that simple, of course, but Monrae was remarkably placid about the ruckus she caused. Jorac finally delivered the pitchers of beer while she and Hox held hands and stared into each other's eyes, when she wasn't glaring at her father. She made short, tart answers to her increasingly upset sire, while Hox said little to him beyond, "Yes, sir, it's what I want too. That's why I asked her."

Finally, just before actual yelling started, Jorac pulled the elder Woper into the yard for a private talk. Jorac wasn't completely sure Hox was in his right mind, but he was going to support him in this. At least as far as he could tell, Monrae seemed perfect for Hox – and then there was that eerie love-at-first-sight thing that you only heard about in stories.

Woper glared at him. "Okay, I'm here. Now talk. Who are you, who is that young giant, and, and. . . What have you done to my daughter?! She was always the levelheaded one, and now this!"

Soothingly, Jorac explained his Wizard Constable role at some length, concluding with, "and in precedence, the position ranks me with a Duke. It's a very prestigious and unique role. Now as to Hox, he's a City Constable, and the one I selected as my assistant for this trip. I'm helping with the army – apparently your neighbors to the west are causing trouble. I had over two hundred constables in the service to choose from, and I picked Hox. He's already distinguished himself by twice saving the day in a rather delicate operation. He's young and healthy, and good natured. He likes to work, gets drunk only on feast-days, and he doesn't complain. You could do worse, much worse."

"But. . . but. . . she's just eighteen!" Chirtsen Woper had a deep voice, but it was very nearly a whine at this point.

"Hox turns twenty this summer, so that won't be a problem. He's got a good job, and I know he's already set aside some money from it – a bonus from that delicate operation I was telling you about. He knows farming too, if it comes to that, and he's good with horses. They won't go hungry."

Jorac pulled closer, and lowered his voice. "Tell me, man-to-man, haven't you worried a little about her getting a good husband? She's taller than most men. Where else will she find a man who can put his chin on top of her head, or carry her to the marriage bed?"

"Well, tell the truth, her ma and me, we talked about it some. She'll be back in an hour or two; we'll see what she has to say. I suppose. . . Let me talk to him."

* * *

Monrae's mother had a much calmer reaction, and was mainly concerned with grilling Hox about his prospects and family – she didn't know his family, but knew and seemed to approve of the area he came from. Jorac thought she certainly must realize her daughter's prospects for finding a decent husband locally were limited. Apparently she was satisfied with Hox's answers, because after that she joined Monrae in talking her father into accepting things.

Monrae's four brothers immediately seemed to like Hox, especially when he started telling jokes at his own expense about his height; the oldest boy was Monrae's height and had heard a few of his own. With Hox's plain farmer's good sense and Monrae's simple conviction that she was doing the right thing, no one but her father still retained doubts. The clincher came late that evening, after he made a particularly foolish objection.

Monrae said, "Father, tell Brother Darmon to get the wedding bower ready. I'm leaving with Hox in three days. I'll do it as his bride or his doxy, but this is the man I'm going to be with."

That had finally shocked the father into silence, and in that silence, Jorac claimed everyone's attention by counting out silver and copper coins onto the table. He paid for dinner and ale and breakfast, and for two separate rooms – a minor extravagance, but he wanted to sleep, not listen to Hox all night saying how wonderful Monrae was. (He thought that this night at least, her father would make sure she stayed in her room – but all bets were off after that.) As soon as he could manage it, Jorac slipped Hox the purse with the remaining coins. There was more hidden in the wagon, and Hox needed to make a good impression right now.

Before Jorac could politely leave and go to his room, Monrae's mother brought out her wedding dress, a lovely shiny green and light blue thing with many layers and much fancy beadwork and embroidery. She said, "Monrae dear, we'll need to do a few minor alterations, but I think we can make this work."

Monrae looked down at her mother, a short woman, and started to laugh. Pretty soon everyone was laughing and cracking jokes: "Sure, nothing to it, only takes a couple of stitches – just let it out a foot or two."

To Jorac's surprise, though, they seemed to be serious about the project. Their tradition was to remake the same wedding dress for each daughter, and Monrae's mother could point out the beadwork her grandmother said had been done by *her* granny, five generations back. It would take more than a "few minor alterations," but if they could get enough hands working on it, Jorac supposed it could be made to fit Monrae.

It was probably close to midnight when he finally got to his bed. As he lay there, he considered the past few hours. *Well, that was certainly unexpected! Flat-out astonishing is what it was. I sure hope Hox doesn't quit. . . I'll have to talk to him; we can figure out how to travel with Monrae along – at least she seems pleasant enough. I'm happy for Hox, though. And to think we stopped here so we could get to sleep early. . .*

Chapter 23 - Jorac Runs an Errand

The next morning, Jorac borrowed a horse from the eldest Woper son and set off for Labblox. Hox was staying behind for a few days, planning his wedding and figuring out how to get a wagon barely big enough for two to hold three. Jorac would have liked to stay around and watch things develop, but he knew that Hox – and Monrae of course – could handle things. Meanwhile, his orders said they were to rejoin the army as soon as he'd determined whether this Lartimaparian existed, and if so, needed help.

The horse was an ugly-faced, piebald beast with long legs but, as described, it proved to have a long, comfortable, ground-eating stride. Still, Jorac had been riding a wagon, not a horse, and was fairly sore by the time he got there.

He made good time, arriving in early afternoon. Labblox proved to be a dusty mill and metals town built into the side of a steep hill. There were long-established gold and copper mines in the mountains above, and a swift-flowing stream ran next to the town. Jorac found a stable near the road, at the bottom of the steep main street. He had an exact copy of the note to Pergimtor, made by some magical means, and Lartimaparian had a unique name, so should be easy to find.

But after stopping at several taverns and shops, and checking with the local tax collectors (there were quite a few here, monitoring the mines), Jorac was puzzled. No one had heard the name, and the last shopkeeper he talked to said she was born and raised in the town and thought she knew everyone. The only suggestion she had was to try the workhouse, a few hundred yards outside the town proper. "Workhouse" was really a misnomer, since it was a series of small huts inside a fenced area. Apparently it served as a prison for both vagrants and debtors, and had a separate area for orphans.

Jorac cleaned the dust from his clothes as best he could and donned his Wizard Constable badge of office, plus his army observer's badge; he hoped the combination might help prevent some petty bureaucrat from giving him a hard time. He mused as he made his way there, *It's possible an old man could end up there, I suppose. Maybe he got into money trouble. I wonder how much it will take to spring him.*

By then it was late afternoon, but he was told they would be open; the mines were often open around the clock, and the workhouse supplied some of the mine labor. He walked to the workhouse complex, and got a clay chit and directions to the office from the guard at the gate.

The office was one of the larger buildings; as he waited for the mousy clerk to finish with another customer, Jorac read the placard on the wall. The labor-hire rates for each type of inmate differed by age and skill, but none were very high. Adults could be hired from sunup to sundown, but children only from sunup to mid-afternoon, and lunch had to be provided. With the fence and heavy doors, this didn't seem to be a pleasant place.

Jorac gave the chit to the clerk, and asked, "Do you have a person here named Lartimaparian?"

The clerk opened a narrow drawer and started thumbing through the cards inside. "Let me see... Lan, Lap, Lartimaparian. Oh. Oh. Just a moment." He took a card from the drawer and scurried into the back room, and immediately returned with an older woman with tidy, graying hair. She looked brusque and competent.

"You asked about Lartimaparian? May I ask why?"

"And you are...?"

"I'm Mistress Osena Uydes, the day manager here. And you?"

"I'm Wizard Constable Jorac Kellor."

She looked at his badges as he spoke, and something about his title made her face fall. "I see. Well. You must understand that so many of the boys lie to us. Many grew up without any parents at all, or parents they're better off without. So when we hear a story like that, well, we don't believe it, that's what. Vagrancy is vagrancy, no matter what story you can tell."

Jorac's confusion must have shown on his face, because she continued.

"Yes, we have a boy named Lartimaparian here – he said he had just the one name. He said his uncle or someone from Vaggert would be coming to fetch him, either a wizard or someone sent by them. I take it that's you?"

Jorac was confused because he was expecting an old man, but wasn't going to say that just yet. He confined himself to facts. "Yes. I can show you my army orders, if you'd like, for authorization."

"That would be best, yes. Ardo, go fetch the boy if you would. This time of day, I think he's in the schoolroom." She turned back to Jorac. "He's much better educated than most boys his age – in fact, better than most of the adults we have here – so he helps out there. We give them schooling, you know, several hours a day." She sounded defensive.

Lartimaparian proved to be a typical-looking boy of about twelve years. He had an unruly wave of light brown hair in front, and hadn't yet started a growth spurt. He was boy-shaped, neither fat nor thin.

"Did Uncle Pergimtor send you to me? I've been awaiting your arrival with some hopeful anxiety. I dispatched a number of messages, but I wasn't sure any of them completed their journey." His voice was a boy's, but his accent was definitely from the upper classes of Vaggert and his language was quite adult.

"Yes, he sent me." Jorac knew Pergimtor was unmarried, and he'd once mentioned he had no siblings, but if this lad wanted to claim the head wizard as his uncle, Jorac wasn't going to object.

The boy nodded gravely, and said, "Thank you. May I ask who you are?"

"I'm Jorac Kellor, Wizard Constable of Vaggert, currently assigned to the army on temporary duty." He added, "My orders are to bring you with me." Even if this setup was purely a scam, he wasn't going to leave a youngster so resourceful here. This was looking interesting.

Jorac showed his orders from the army and from Pergimtor to Mistress Uydes; the boy asked to see them too, so Jorac complied. After she did some paperwork, Jorac signed a large journal that said he was formally taking charge of the boy; he hoped he did a good job of hiding his surprise and amusement at this turn of events. Mistress Uydes gave them each clay chits that would let them out the front gate, and sent Lartimaparian to fetch his things.

The boy proved to have very few possessions, just a change of poor clothing and some rolled-up artist canvas with some paintbrushes and a few fancy pens. Jorac helped him stuff them into a small cloth sack. As the pair prepared to go, Mistress Uydes said, "Lartie, we'll miss you. You've been a great help."

He turned to her, and said sternly, "Mistress Uydes, your inattention could easily turn this place into a hell-hole. You'd better watch Kwuvik; he's stealing from you. And Gospurt: he didn't get that black eye from hitting a door; he's a pederast, and we caught him trying to sneak into the boys barracks. Again. You'd best learn to police your staff, or someone with greater power than I have will most assuredly see that you lose your position and perhaps your liberty. Now, good day to you."

With that, he marched out the door, and Jorac followed. A backward glance showed the manager standing there, staring at the retreating pair with a pinched, worried face.

Jorac and the young man walked out of the front gate, surrendering their chits to the guard. The lad stopped and stretched. "It's good to be free of that place. I thank you for freeing me. I'd like to go on to Vaggert by myself, but I fear that someone of my age and appearance would be in danger along the way. Could I impose myself upon you until we return to the city? I could see that you were suitably rewarded."

Jorac looked over the serious young man. "How did you come to be confined in that place?"

"I was merely walking down the main street of town. I fear I was a bit scruffy in appearance, and my clothing didn't quite fit, but before I could find a suitable shop to outfit myself, I was seized by a man who said he worked for the town council, and I was sent to this prison for vagrancy. I've heard about such places; this one seems to be better run than most, but it's no idyll by the sea."

"So, how did you come to be walking down the main street in town looking scruffy? And come by your obvious education? And where are your parents, that would leave you to be alone in a remote mining town?"

At that, the young man stopped, looked at Jorac and his Wizard Constable badge, and sighed. "Now, that's a long story. I'm really not at liberty to divulge the details to anyone except Uncle Pergimtor. I'm sorry. Perhaps you can trust me until we get to Vaggert."

"Sorry to disappoint you, but we can't go straight to Vaggert. I have a job to do with the army in West Luverna first. However, you may feel better if you read this." He fished in his pack and retrieved a personal letter of introduction from Pergimtor; the head wizard had provided it for reassurance in case the elderly wizard Lartimaparian was suspicious about being rescued by a stranger with a funny badge. In formal language it said Jorac was Pergimtor's personal representative and should be treated the same as Pergimtor himself. It also included some nonsensical-looking phrases Jorac assumed were wizard code, and was sealed with a shimmery wizard seal.

The young man read it over twice, very carefully, then gravely handed it back to Jorac. "Yes, thank you, I feel somewhat more at ease now. I'm willing to put myself in your hands until we can reach Vaggert." He paused a moment and then added, "As you may have surmised, he's not really my uncle. You see, my parents died in a wagon accident when I was very young, so I was raised by my namesake, the wizard

Lartimaparian. He was a kind old man, but not rich. I didn't know it at the time, but he was working on some magical research, and also acting as a small-town wizard to the miners and such around here."

Jorac was suddenly alert. The last time he'd heard "magical research" it was related to the madman Wolburn.

"I'd certainly like to hear the whole story."

The boy sighed. "It's not one I really wish to tell, though I suppose if anyone has the right to ask me about it, it's you." He paused. "You don't suggest we leave town this evening, do you?"

Jorac shook his head.

"Good. I propose we first find a place to spend the night. I've heard there's at least one honest boarding house in Labblox. I could do with a decent meal. I've managed to retain a few resources, but tonight I'll need to impose upon your kindness. Tomorrow we can arrange transportation – you have just the one horse? And once we leave this place, I'll lay it all out for you. Is that suitable?"

Jorac didn't know what to make of this young man. He looked at him, considering everything. Something strange was going on, and it might involve magical research. It was clearly his duty to hear the boy's story, and besides, he was bursting with curiosity. "I'll agree to that, provided I hear the truth from you. All of it."

"As long you can keep quiet about it, agreed."

That was quite a pronouncement from a lad his age, but Jorac merely nodded.

"And what am I to call you? Lartimaparian has six syllables, not the sort of thing you want to try to say in a hurry."

"A good point. Lartie will do; I've grown accustomed to hearing it these past months."

"Do you know the name of the honest boarding house?"

"No, but I've heard where it is: next to The Ox, a tavern with a reputation for a good meal. Shall we go there?"

Jorac's "Lead on, young sir," was meant semi-ironically, but the lad took no notice and merely nodded and started walking toward town.

* * *

Jorac learned no more during dinner, where young Lartie kept glancing around as if people were listening to what they were saying; nor at the boarding house, where the walls between "rooms" were just canvas partitions. He was content to wait for the boy's story anyway; it had been a very long day and he was tired.

The next morning they ate breakfast at the boarding house, where Lartie was still silent about his origins. He then led Jorac to an assay shop down the street that served the independent miners who scrounged for metals in the hills above. Jorac saw signs in the window that advertised "Fair weights!" and "Best assay in town."

"Would you be good enough to don your Wizard Constable badge? I think it may ease matters inside. This shop is apparently the best of a bad lot."

As Jorac took out the badge and put it around his neck, he said, "All right, but what are we doing here?"

"I'm not destitute. I merely need to convert some of my assets to a more useful form." He led them into the shop.

Inside, he walked over to the weigh-in counter, unrolled his artist canvas, and selected a pen. He twisted the end off it and tapped it on the counter until a tiny round gold cylinder fell out. He placed it in the pan of the scale.

Of course, this attracted the attention of the proprietor, who watched carefully. When Lartie looked up, the man smiled and said, "How may I help you?"

"I have some pure gold here I'd like to sell."

The proprietor looked at him, and at Jorac and his badge. When Jorac just nodded, he replied to the lad. "Ah? Well, this is the right place. What have you got?"

"You'll find it's wizard-pure; there will be no need for the lower-purity tests."

The proprietor was definitely more interested now. "Ah? Well, since you have it on the scales there, let's see what it weighs."

"Very good. But if you don't mind, let's all do it from this side of the counter."

Jorac was puzzled, and the proprietor stiffened defensively. "What do you mean?"

Lartie said nothing. He just looked slowly, meaningfully down at the bottom of the counter, then at Jorac's constable badge, and then back at the proprietor.

Something in the proprietor's eyes looked a little guilty, and he said, "Ah, yes, well, if you wish, I'll join you over there. Anything to make a customer happy."

The little cylinder of gold was weighed and assayed – it proved to be wizard pure, as stated – and Lartie was handed a rather heavy purse filled with silver and copper coins. He handed it to Jorac, who put it away in his pack, and they left the shop.

"Mind telling me what that was about?"

"Not at all. His scale itself is dead honest, so it passes any checks, but he's got a foot pedal back there that can move magnets around under the counter, and that's how he cheats. He can make it look like the pointer is just a little to one side or another, or hold it right in the middle. I heard about it from some of my former work-mates."

"Fascinating. I never heard of that method before."

"Neither had I, until recently. The old saying still holds true: every day you learn something is a day you didn't totally waste. Let's go buy me a horse. I think you might be the better one to do the bargaining there, and probably without that badge showing."

* * *

Horses here proved quite expensive, and they were mostly tough little ponies bred for mine work. However, they found a small two-wheeled passenger cart that two could ride in for much less than the price of a horse. The Woper horse proved to be well-trained, and after they adjusted the cart harness, it seemed content to pull them along. By mid-morning, they were on their way, headed back the way Jorac had come. They'd bought gear for the boy and food for the day, and within a few minutes out of town were alone on the road.

Jorac couldn't contain his curiosity any longer.

"Well, young sir, I believe it's time I hear your story. All of it."

Lartie said, "Well. You're not a wizard yourself, correct?"

"No. I just work for them." Jorac wasn't going to mention his allergy, at least not yet.

"Good. First, I'd like to ask for a pledge of silence on this matter. I saw that Pergimtor trusts you, and my uncle trusted him, but neither of them is here. It's not something to bandy about."

"Well, hmm. I'll go this far: provided it doesn't affect my other oaths, or the safety of the realm, I'll keep it quiet. But I'll be the one to decide that." Jorac was very curious now to learn what deep secrets a boy of twelve might have.

Lartie sighed. "That will do – I guess it will have to. I was thinking on how to say this last night; I believe straight and simple is the best." He took a deep breath. "I lived alone with my great-uncle Lartimaparian. He transferred all his knowledge to me just before he died. It's a little-known spell, quite forbidden, because it doesn't *copy* what the person knows, it *moves* it. That's the research he was doing, trying to improve that spell. I didn't know it at the time, but he was killing himself in the spell-casting, though he would have lived only a few more months in any case. So I have most of his memories, and for a time it made me rather confused. I can see why the spell is forbidden – an unscrupulous wizard might be able to take over a young mind. But that wasn't my uncle's intention; he didn't have a lot of money so he wanted to leave me what he knew. My mother was a wizard too, and he thought I might become one, and he wanted to help me."

"You know all this?"

"I think I know just about everything my uncle knew, but he was a bit scatterbrained near the end, and I think that came over too. Sometimes I think I've got a whole library in my head, with lots of it mis-filed."

Jorac paused to think it over. "So how did you get into that workhouse?"

"The first time I went to town alone, I was picked up and put there. As I said, I was a bit confused for a time, and that likely had something to do with it. But I couldn't have stayed where I was. My uncle's house started falling down shortly after he died – I remembered him telling me he used magic to build the house, and now I know that if a wizard isn't there to put magic into a thing, it will decay back to its original state.

"So I followed the plan he worked out if anything happened to him. I got the pens with the hidden gold you saw, but I never had a chance to change it for honest coin. I was going to make my way to Vaggert, probate my uncle's will, and redeem his investments."

"Then what?" Jorac wasn't quite dumbfounded by this young man's situation, but close enough.

"I thought I'd spend some time in the University Library, maybe learn something about fishes. I've always liked fishing, ever since I was a little boy, and my uncle didn't know anything about them." Lartie had gone from serious to an animated, enthusiastic boy in a heartbeat.

"I used to catch lizards when I was your age. Too dry where I grew up for much fishing."

"Lizards are neat too. I caught one with blue stripes a few weeks ago!"

"I know those; they're fast." The boy was charming, but Jorac wasn't done asking him serious questions, so he changed the subject back. "Do you know if you'll be a wizard?"

The serious Lartie returned instantly. "My uncle didn't know, so I don't know either. It'll be at least a year before I'll see any sign. If not, at least I'll know more about wizards than most people. In Vaggert, I'm pretty sure that would help me, whatever business I find myself in."

Jorac thought a few moments. It certainly wasn't Lartie's fault that his uncle had done what he did, and the boy seemed to have a good attitude – for instance, he'd helped with teaching at the workhouse when he could have just sulked. But his plans might need some adjustment.

"Maybe you should reconsider the part about going to Vaggert, at least until some preparations have been made. If someone your age suddenly turns up in town with an elderly wizard's credentials, questions could be raised you wouldn't want to answer. Especially if a wizard inspects you closely."

Lartie frowned in concentration. "You have a point. But I'm afraid it's just going to make things more difficult for you. If you're willing to have me accompany you during your army assignment, I can certainly wait longer to go to Vaggert. But I may then request your help in preparing my way and settling my affairs once I get there." He thought a moment. "Of course I'll compensate you when I can."

Jorac nodded. "It's a deal." He liked the boy and would have helped him anyway, but an offer of compensation was a nice gesture. "You go with me first, and then we'll work out how to get you settled. But for now, I need to backtrack and join up with my associate – I'll tell you about him in a minute. And on the way let's work on what we're going to tell people. I think you need to remember to act a bit more like your age – not your uncle's age."

Chapter 24 - A Quick Wedding

It was mid-afternoon when they topped a rise and saw the village where he'd left Hox; Jorac explained to Lartie that he didn't even know its name. He'd been gone just two days, but since Hox had gotten engaged in less than five minutes, Jorac wondered aloud what he, and Monrae, could accomplish in two days.

Lartie said, "Wow! At that rate, they could have a family of four by next Windday!" It was the first attempt at humor Jorac had heard from him the boy, and he thought it was a good sign.

"Heh. Good one. Best not mention that to her father, though; he took the most convincing. I think he believes his little girl is still about your age, even though she's a head taller than he is."

When their cart pulled into the bustling village square, they were almost ignored. It seemed that everyone from the farms surrounding the village had come to town to view the young giant and his bride-to-be. Jorac asked a passer-by, and was told the wedding was to be tomorrow noon.

When Jorac and Lartie pulled into the yard at the Wopers', they were met by Hox, Monrae, and a gaggle of local women. Hox looked as blissful as he had two days before, and Monrae looked just as happy but a little less stunned – she was showing the women where to set up the food tables.

Jorac introduced his young ward as Lartie, a nephew of Pergimtor's now-deceased sister-in-law. That made the exact relationship to the chief wizard hard to pin down, which was all to the good. The story they told was that a manservant who was to watch over him had absconded with their belongings and left him alone in Labblox; from that point they could continue with the true story of his rescue from the workhouse. It was a good enough explanation, and anyway, everyone was more interested in Hox and Monrae.

Before he could finish unhitching their horse, Jorac was cornered by Monrae's mother, who was vastly relieved that he'd gotten back in time. Hox had sent a letter to his family, but it wouldn't reach them before the wedding, so Jorac would be expected to stand with Hox at the ceremony. Jorac immediately drafted Lartie to stand with them too; with two attendants, it would make a respectable groom's party. Monrae's mother, looking pleased, sent one of the nearby middle-aged women to search the town for suitable clothes the boy could wear to the ceremony; she agreed that Hox and Jorac could wear their dress uniforms.

As Jorac returned the borrowed horse and stowed the cart in the barn, he heard all about the wedding arrangements from a younger brother's point of view. Apparently Monrae had firm ideas of what she wanted – a short and simple service on the village green, just after mid-day, and the wedding feast to follow immediately. No one had been able to make a dent in her resolve.

The older boy asked, "So what is Hox really like?" From the stiff way he said it, Jorac guessed he'd been pushed into asking the question. That was confirmed when the rest of the stable stopped work and listened to his answer.

"I had a choice of two hundred constables, and I picked the one that was the hardest to outfit, and eats enough for two or three. That answer your question?"

"Uh. . . I guess. Does he talk much?"

"He can talk plenty when he wants. I think that he's just trying to be nice here, since he doesn't want to offend anyone in town. And as a constable, it makes his job easier if he's thought of as a big dumb hunk of muscle, so he keeps quiet and listens a lot. But when he talks, it's usually worth listening to."

Jorac had variations on that conversation twice more in the next hour. He sat on the shaded porch in front of Woper's tavern and watched as Hox and Monrae conducted a kind of goodwill tour, visiting most of the houses in town. The entire village would be there to witness the wedding, and though some may have been shocked by the speed of the thing, it seemed clear that no one was truly angered. Townspeople who spotted Jorac kept coming up to introduce themselves and talk to him, as if he were a minor celebrity. They mostly ignored Lartie, who sat shyly by his side and said little.

When the middle-aged woman arrived with an armful of boy's clothing and took Lartie off for a fitting, Jorac went inside, sought out Chirtsen Woper, and gave him a single suggestion. "Water Hox's ale tonight. Everyone will be buying him drinks, and you don't want him dropping his breakfast in the middle of the wedding."

"Aye, good idea." By this time, Monrae's father looked more resigned than upset. "I knew she was too big for this village – not just her height, either. You keep an eye on her too, alright?"

"I'll do that. And speaking of buying rounds, here's the first one." Jorac handed him a pair of gold coins. "That should buy a mug or two for most of the folks in town. I was thinking we could start it early this evening, so we might get to bed at a reasonable hour, but I'll take your advice on that – I wouldn't want you to run low on drinks for the wedding, so you might want to set some aside for tomorrow."

Woper's business sense hadn't left him, despite his worry about his daughter. "I already thought of that. Tomorrow morning we're getting ale brought in from everyone who brews around here. So, thank you, and I'll do as you say – we don't see much gold here. If you'll help me move some tables here first, we can get started."

After rearranging some tables, Chirtsen Woper went outside and started banging on a metal frying pan with a stick. It made a ringing sound that carried across the town square, and people started coming over toward him. After a few minutes of banging and gathering, he spoke to the crowd. "This gentleman has offered to buy you a drink – he's buying the whole town a drink, he said. And I'm next in line to buy drinks after that. So, go eat your dinners, then come on back. We'll be waiting for you."

One of the men in back said, "What about now?"

Woper said, "Or have a drink now, that works too. But remember, my daughter insists on a noon wedding. We're closing early tonight."

A dozen or so, all men, went inside for a drink, and the rest went back to their houses. Hox and Monrae showed up shortly after that, with the group of women who'd been following them around for the past few hours, and the party started in earnest.

* * *

Jorac shared the largest guest-room with both Hox and Lartie that night. The inn was packed to well beyond capacity. Spring planting was past by then, so all the farm families within distance of the news had shown up. Woper was a friendly and open-handed man, and the sudden wedding of his tall daughter to a stranger – a full head taller than she was, too – was something that no one wanted to miss.

Jorac got less sleep than he liked – despite what Woper had said, they hadn't closed early at all. But early the next morning he found Hox awake and sitting on the bed, reading Jorac's orders by candlelight.

"Look here. Lartie can be an observer!"

"Uh, good morning. Bleah. 'Scuse me." Jorac hadn't quite gotten drunk the night before, but he'd definitely been drinking, and was a bit woolly-headed. He went over and used the chamber pot, then came back to Hox. "What were you saying?"

"Lartie's an observer. It says if you find him, he's to be carried as an observer. That means he gets his own wagon, right?"

"Meaning we don't have to try to pack four of us into our one wagon? Let me see that."

"I was worried that they wouldn't let Monrae come at all – I wouldn't want to quit on you. We talked about maybe getting her signed up with one of the other observers as an assistant, like a cook or something for one of the scholars. Even with Miz Gompel, if she was alright with it. But Lartie is an observer himself – it says so right here."

Jorac was glad that Hox didn't want to quit, but he also knew Hox wouldn't abandon his new bride. They'd had a quick word about travel arrangements before Jorac left for Labblox, but since getting back he'd been too busy with Lartie and the wedding preparations to give it much attention. A thought flashed through his head – sharing a wagon with a newlywed couple whose physical desire for each other would be obvious to a blind man would be, um, challenging – and he nodded gratefully.

Jorac read the orders again. They were a bit ambiguous – "... if found, said individual shall be carried in the army as Observer under the above orders..." – but you could argue that Hox was correct. You could also argue he was wrong. One more thing to worry about.

"I think I understand. Lartie, you awake?" Jorac nudged him politely.

"I am now. I'm an observer, you say?"

"Yes, an army observer under orders, and so you can have an assistant. Monrae Woper, soon to be Monrae Woper Tormand."

"A neat solution." Lartie sat up on the bed and thought about it. "What do assistants do, anyway? Can I tell her to cook for me, do my laundry, shine my shoes, and the like?" His smile at Hox took all the sting out of the question.

Jorac wasn't sure how Hox would respond to the boy, but Hox just grinned and said, "She's already offered to help with laundry. I told her about the V.A.B. laundry women, and she said I didn't need to visit them. Then I told her about the *other* laundry women there, and she said I didn't need to visit them, either, but she'd help out my companions with the first, but not the second. She's got a great sense of humor." The smile on Hox's face was sickeningly sweet.

Jorac laughed, and then had to explain to Lartie about the laundry women who did no washing of clothes, now departed from the army. If his boyish eyes were a little too wise, it was probably only Jorac's imagination.

* * *

After a leisurely breakfast, they went back to their room to Get Ready. Somehow, Hox and Jorac's best constable uniforms had appeared, pressed and spotless, the evening before, so getting Hox dressed was simple enough, and Jorac followed with his own uniform. Jorac lent Hox one of his two fancy scabbards, though they had to redo the mounting so it would hang on the right side. (It was tradition here for the groom to be armed, and Jorac felt more comfortable that way anyway.) Lartie had been given an outfit that outshone their uniforms, and so he swapped the multi-colored shirt for his own best shirt, a simple tan one. With Jorac's largest knife hung on his belt, he looked like he belonged to the groom's party.

Then came the waiting – they sat on the beds, trying not to sweat too much or wrinkle their clothing. Lartie was having trouble not fidgeting, and Jorac could see that not all the sweat on Hox's brow was coming from the stuffy room.

When they faintly heard Monrae's voice yelling, "Mother, it's MY damned wedding!", Jorac suggested they go outside and talk to the arriving guests, an idea that was immediately seconded by Hox and Lartie. Their ostensible purpose was to find someone who'd take the small cart Jorac had bought in Labblox, plus some cash, in trade for a second large wagon. They didn't try very hard at it, just a few words passed to some of the arriving guests, but it gave them a believable excuse to stand in the shade of the stable. They got one of Monrae's brother's to run inside and tell the rest of the family where they were. Jorac had Hox drink some water and kept up a running conversation about horses and wagons and other trivia to help calm his nerves.

When Brother Darmon arrived, he proved to be a heavyset, sober-looking older man with braided white hair, wearing a headdress of leaves and a sky-blue gold-embroidered apron-like garment over plain farmer's garb. The wedding attendants followed him to the small village green next to the town to receive their last-minute instructions. There an elaborate bower interlaced with wheat sheaves and small flowers had been set up at the top of a small rise; flanking it were small flowered trellises. The groom's party was told they mainly had to stand under one of the trellises and wait for the bride's father to bring her. Even someone more nervous than Hox could manage that.

Noon was approaching, and Jorac watched as the townspeople began to wander toward the village green. He was interested in seeing the wedding; he hadn't been to one since his own. (He didn't remember much of his own ceremony, just the hangover he'd had after being toasted into oblivion the night before.) This time he just had to stand beside Hox and keep an eye on the ring – matching wedding rings had been hammered out of two of Pergimtor's gold pieces, and Jorac wasn't going to let Hox lose his.

Monrae's wedding dress that had been mostly green and light blue before was still that color on the top, but now had a whole new skirt-piece in green and yellow. Jorac had caught a glimpse of her wearing it in the tavern after a test fitting, and was amazed to see that it now fit her perfectly. All the fancy embroidery and beadwork had been moved to the new version, and it looked part of the dress, not an afterthought. Hox had said that Monrae's friends and family had been working on the dress night and day, which was believable.

When people had mostly gathered, Jorac saw Monrae come out of a barn next to the village green and call Brother Darmon to her. She whispered something to him that made him turn beet red. He turned and walked smartly to the bower, looked around at the crowd, and loudly cleared his throat. As people gathered around and quieted, he waved his hands in a "move-aside" motion, clearing a path through the middle of the crowd. This was the cue for Hox, Jorac, and Lartie to move up beside the bower and stand still at an angle to it.

There was a low box at the back center of the bower, and Brother Darmon climbed on it and bellowed, "Gather to me! Gather to me. For here, today, a wedding will be. Gather!"

Monrae and her father walked up the green through the parted crowd, not wasting any time. As the crowd closed behind her, Jorac sneaked a look at Hox's face. It wasn't yet too late to back out if Hox looked stricken, but he didn't; he looked happy, excited, almost lustful. A very good start, Jorac thought.

Monrae took her place near Hox, and nodded at Brother Darmon, almost challengingly. When she turned to Hox her look was much softer.

Brother Darmon had a good deep voice that carried well. "These two loving young people stand before us in the sight of all. Horxien and Monrae have come here today to be joined as one in marriage. We can hope to bolster them with the knowledge that love confers strength, and the anticipation that time confers wisdom. Monrae, is it true that you come of your own free will?"

Monrae barely waited for him to finish before loudly saying, "Yes, it is true."

Jorac was mildly surprised at the free-will question; where he grew up, weddings didn't include that.

Brother Darmon said, "Who presents you, and whose blessings accompany you into marriage?

Chirtsen Woper said, "She comes with me, and all her family will accompany her into marriage – I mean all her family's *blessings*."

The crowd chuckled, and even the solemn holyman smiled a bit. He held up his hands for quiet, then started to speak in a slow, serious voice.

"Please join hands with your betrothed and listen to these blessings."

May the Goddess who watches over the fields bless these two.

May the God who watches over the stars bless them equally.

261

> *Above you are the stars, below you are the stones; as time doth pass, remember:*
>
> *Like the stones of the earth, may your love be firm;*
>
> *Like the stars in the sky, may your love be constant.*
>
> *Let your strengths bind you together,*
>
> *Let the power of love and desire make you happy,*
>
> *Let the power of your conviction make the two of you as one.*

After a short pause, he continued. "Horxien Tormand, if it be your wish to wed Monrae, say so at this time and place your ring on her finger."

Jorac slipped his hand under Hox's, in case he dropped the ring, but despite a little trembling, Hox did a fine job of putting it on her finger.

Without moving his lips, the holyman whispered, "Loud," and Hox complied.

"I wed thee, Monrae Woper, with glad heart."

Brother Darmon turned to Monrae. "Monrae Woper, if it be your wish to wed Horxien, say so at this time and place your ring on his finger."

She said, in a loud, clear tone, "I wed thee, Horxien Tormand, with a glad and happy heart." The ring she put on his finger was very thin; hammering a gold piece into a ring to fit Hox's big finger hadn't been easy. Hox looked down at it with undisguised pleasure.

"With these vows you have sworn, by the God and Goddess, to be handfasted and married, each to the other. As you wish it, so be it. The union of one and one has now created a new one. Horxien, you may kiss your new bride."

At the weddings in Jorac's village, the first kiss was a lusty affair, but here theirs was short and chaste, as the crowd yelled their approval.

After some seconds of cheering, Brother Darmon again raised his arms for quiet, and eventually got it.

He began again in his deep voice. "This is a couple, and let all who witness work at making this couple happy and safe. It is said. . ."

Monrae turned her head ever-so-slightly, and Jorac could hear a hissing sound from the corner of her mouth.

Brother Darmon went on with only a slight break. "It is said that the wedding day is for the bride and groom. I've never seen a happier couple, nor a taller one. Let us pray a moment in silence for Monrae and Horxien."

Twenty or thirty seconds later he said loudly, "And may this marriage be blessed for all time. I believe there is a feast nearby; enjoy the bounty and bless the new couple. It is Done."

A hearty "Well done!" came from the assembly, and they broke for the tables.

Chapter 25 - A Rejoining

It was early morning when their observer party set off two days later. They'd come with two horses and a wagon; they left with five horses, two wagons, and one cat.

The Wopers had challenged the town to outfit their departing daughter with everything she needed at a fair price, and they'd come through. If anything, the wagon was over-full. It was a bit smaller than Jorac's first wagon, but it had enough room for the newlyweds to sleep inside.

Pulling the smaller wagon was a pair of draft horses somewhat lighter and younger than Jorac's original pair. Monrae also owned a beautiful little dun mare called Sunbeam that she didn't want to leave behind. Jorac mentally checked his finances and decided they could stand another four coppers a day, and anyway, a spare riding horse was often useful. So along came Sunbeam, walking between the two wagons.

The cat was a complete surprise to Jorac; it appeared in Monrae's lap when they were an hour outside of town. He wouldn't have seen it then, except that he called a stop at a wide spot in the road, just to check their rig and gear.

"Monrae, where did that thing come from?" The gray tabby cat was idly batting at the reins that Hox held.

"Falcon? She must have been in the wagon." The answer was a bit too blithe for Jorac. He was going to have to do something now before things got out of hand.

Jorac got down from his wagon and walked over to Hox and Monrae. He spoke loudly, so Lartie could hear. "Okay, group meeting. Lartie, keep an eye on the horses, okay? Now listen. We're going into a war zone with an army. That means discipline is needed. When I tell you to do something, you do it first and ask questions later, right? It might save your life. Got it?"

He waited until he got agreement from everyone, then continued at lower volume.

"This one is a little delicate, but I have to say it. You two newlyweds can do whatever you want in your wagon, but quietly, right?"

Monrae and Hox both blushed, and she quietly asked Hox, "Did they hear us?"

Jorac couldn't avoid grinning as he answered, "The whole town heard you. Your windows were open, weren't they? Don't worry, everyone was happy for the two of you. But noise can sometimes be dangerous, so I have to say something, okay?"

The two nodded at Jorac, looking abashed, and he hoped he hadn't been too crude about it. But when Monrae whispered something in Hox's ear that made him laugh and blush again, he knew they'd be alright.

Jorac raised his volume again so Lartie could hear, and pointed at Falcon. "Now, on to that thing. There'll be no time to chase lost cats. What do you feed it? I know they have to eat meat most every day. There won't be a granary to attract mice, or birds for it to hunt."

"Falcon has been to Labblox and Marpo's Keep, both. She likes to travel, even more than Sunbeam does. And she's good at hunting mice and birds when we're on the road, so we almost never have to feed her."

"That won't do. We'll be camped in the middle of an army. The army will scare away any prey, and if any soldier sees her slinking about, he's likely to take a pot-shot at her just for fun."

"She'll make friends with them. Don't worry. Falcon likes people."

Jorac looked at the sky. Finding no answers there, looked back at Hox, Monrae, and Falcon, trying to decide what to say next. Only Hox truly was under his orders, and they were civilian orders, meaning he could quit if he wanted. Jorac didn't want to force his friend's hand.

The cat in question sat calmly licking her paw. Suddenly she froze, then with a powerful leap, launched herself out of the wagon and across the roadside field, chasing a mouse toward its hole. It wasn't quite quick enough, because Falcon came trotting back with it between her jaws. She jumped back up on the wagon, dropped it in Monrae's lap, and looked up at her expectantly. Monrae giggled, and holding the mouse by its tail, carefully put it down on the floorboards. Falcon started eating it, purring loudly.

"See? She'll even feed us first. Don't worry about Falcon."

Jorac knew that with that mouse delivery, he'd lost the argument. "Well . . . keep an eye on her. We need to make good time until we catch up to the army. We can't wait on a cat." Jorac felt helpless, as if he'd lost control of the expedition, but since he felt like whining, not yelling, he didn't say anything more.

* * *

It was afternoon when they got back to the crossroads where they'd left the army six days before, and Jorac half expected to see them there again, newly back from Marpo's Keep. A passing tradesman in a large wagon told them that the army had already come and gone, heading west at the crossroads just this morning.

So they pressed on, and though it made for a long day, they saw the smoke from the army's cooking fires before sunset. Jorac called for a brief rest and a conference.

"Lartie and I have been talking about how to make this go smoothly. We don't want them reading our orders too closely, so we'll want to misdirect them a little. Hox, you come over to my wagon, and Lartie, go sit with your 'servant' and fill her in. Okay, now, here's what we need to say. . ."

The guards on the road had parked a wagon as a makeshift roadblock, and watched Jorac approach without any special caution. He was walking his tired horses slowly, and of course he'd put on his Observer badge. He didn't know any of the guards personally, but word had gotten around and there was no one else in the army who was Hox's size.

"Hi guys. Sorry I'm back so late. I brought another Observer back with me. Can you find someone to show me where to camp tonight?"

"Let's see your orders." The guard was bored but following his procedure. No one entered or left the army without written orders.

"Here you go. Read section 7, that's where they come in. I need to find the horse wrangler. We've had a long day, and we've got five that will need some care."

With a shrug, the guards pushed their road-blocking wagon aside and pointed vaguely off to the right. "The General is up on that little hill there, so your group would set up someplace nearby."

Jorac stood in his seat and turned around. "Lartie, give the reins to the lady. She can drive that wagon as well as you can, and *she* can follow orders."

Jorac casually jingled his purse a little as they threaded a careful path through the army. He quietly called out to a few passers-by, "Need the hostler. We're late, so we pay extra."

"I'll fetch 'em, sir, for a little sump'n." The man had a Swampside accent as strong as Schrog's.

Jorac tossed a pair of coppers to him, and said, "You'se gotta deal – but, swampie, you cheats me, I finds you, right?" in an imitation of the same accent. Jorac grinned when the man grew round-eyed and nodded, then ran away, calling "Horseman!"

As they got near to where they should camp, they found they wouldn't actually fit inside the rope that delineated the Observer area. So they found a spot nearby, then spent a few minutes helping an agreeable young man move his tent so they could park the two wagons close together, side by side.

The man from Swampside led the hostler to them, and hung around while Jorac bargained with him – the swampie had probably also made a deal with the hostler to get a cut of tonight's bonus pay. Five silvers was the final deal; by the time they'd reached agreement, a small crowd had gathered to watch, and Lartie's whining voice could be heard from inside the wagon.

"But I'm hungry *now*. You were hired to take care of *me!*"

Hox fumbled around inside the back of Jorac's wagon, while Jorac walked over to the other wagon. "Master Lartimaparian, a word with you." Jorac pitched his voice a good bit louder than he normally would.

"I'm busy!"

"*Now.*"

The boy climbed out of Monrae's wagon and said, "She won't even start cooking. What are you going to do about it?"

"I will do the following. Mistress Monrae, you don't work for this prattling fool any longer. You will now take your orders from my man, Horxien Tormand. And if this young dolthead gives you any trouble, see me about it."

She said, with a gleam in her eye, "Thank you, sir! Master Hox seems to be a good man, from the few days I've known him."

Turning to Lartie, he said, "Young man, I have my orders too, and you won't interfere with them. You'd best learn when to keep quiet, and don't think you're too old to be taken over my lap and spanked."

Lartie was the very picture of a spoiled, outraged lout of privilege. "You can't... You wouldn't..."

Jorac said distinctly, disgustedly, "Try me."

"Hmmph." The boy sat on the ground near the wagon with his arms folded. After some seconds of silence, Jorac nodded in satisfaction, then looked around. He found everyone in earshot had been watching the little drama unfold. He stared at them until they moved away, self-consciously.

Lartie didn't say another word that evening. He took his dinner silently and with ill grace, and shortly climbed into Monrae's wagon. The little show had been his idea – he'd admitted to Jorac that he'd probably draw suspicion if he didn't talk, but if he did talk he'd have trouble sounding like he was twelve years old for very long. For a few minutes' mummery they now had a good reason for him remain mostly silent, and for Hox and Monrae to be together. If people saw that the tall woman and the taller man became close over the next few days, they'd just be seeing what they probably expected.

It was full dark before they were through eating, and they quickly rinsed their dishes and climbed into their assigned wagons. The wagons were parked so close together that a person could raise the canvas sides and climb from one to wagon another, as long as someone on the other side raised the canvas as well. This was not due to chance.

The next morning, after some more quiet climbing around, everyone emerged from the correct wagon. As Jorac had half expected, General Melsim made an appearance while Monrae was cooking eggs on their small spirits stove. There were five or six men with him, murmuring amongst themselves.

"What's this young turd doing here? And who's that slubberdegullion doing the cooking? I had to accept two of you damned wizard spies, not four of you!"

Jorac replied chidingly, "Sir, you misspeak about the lady. She is both neat and proper." He then put every ounce of feigned disgust into his voice, and continued, "But your description of the boy, I will not comment upon. Lartie! Come over here!"

The boy slouched into sight from behind a wagon; his tunic was dusty and his hair was a mess.

Jorac said, "You wished to say something to the General?"

As if his arm was being twisted behind his back, the boy forced out, "Thank you for, for the, um, honor of being an observer in the, uh, your, uh, army." He looked down, then to the side, but never up at the General.

The general glared at Jorac. "Where did you find him?"

"In Labblox. He was part of my orders. Damned wizards."

"Heh! Well, carry on then. Keep him out of the way, mind you."

"He will usually be confined to the Observer area, sir."

With a nod, the General stalked off, with his entourage in tow.

Jorac winked at Lartie, who flashed the briefest of grins. Any order Jorac didn't like made the general happy; he'd now accepted Lartie and Monrae as another Observer team. It had been a hell of a week.

Chapter 26 - Casualties

Jorac and Hox had one more early morning of weapons practice with the General's Guard. (If the man who came to get them noticed them climbing out of separate wagons, he didn't say anything.) After their warm-up exercises the group was told there would be no more practice sessions; the rebels could strike at any time, from any direction, so the Guard was going to be scouting from now on. Their trainer Brozadam wished them all luck, then spoke to them individually, reminding most of them about something they needed to work on or think about. His task was done, for this year anyway, and he'd be heading back to Vaggert soon.

Jorac was grateful to have had the chance to come to their sessions, but somehow felt as if he'd missed an opportunity. Though he'd tried, he never had been able to get the soldiers to talk about the army's methods. Sometimes they'd talk about individual fights, but never overall enemy tactics.

Luckily, Brozadam was more forthcoming. Hox left with the others when the class was over, but Jorac lingered a while. He and Brozadam leaned against the trainer's wagon, looking out at the army as it slowly got ready for the day's travel.

/I have heard only a little of the enemy we are to face. What should a fighter-man expect to see when they are found?/

/There are mostly three types of these rebels: fools, idiots, and dangerous men. The fools fight for glory and so they can tell their grandchildren they fought against the invaders. Therefore they make a show of attacking us, then run away like the swift rabbit. They are sometimes many, but easily turned back into farmers, which is what the Emperor wishes. This is why the army fights as it does, in a large group with a strong charge at the enemy, to produce quick, overwhelming victories. So it is said, so I hear, so I tell you./ The last phrase suggested he didn't necessarily agree with the tactics.

/Surely some of their fighters are more serious?/

/Yes, they are the idiots. They believe that the empire can be broken up by a few dozen or even a few hundred men. They are the type who will fight for what they believe in, even at hopeless odds. They will charge even when it is clear they cannot win, and most of them die early. A few fight well and kill some soldiers. Some of these are merely shrewd, or lucky; only a few are battle trained./

/Who are the battle-trained ones?/

/Each year is different. Sometimes a group from Rabakht can be convinced to come to these cold wet lands and fight for a season, or perhaps another outland group will come. But most of the trained fighters we see are from these very northlands. Perhaps they guard a mine or merchant in better times./

/Are these the dangerous ones?/

Brozadam shook his head once. /They know when not to fight, and will quickly seize any advantage. But if you do nothing foolish, if you are prepared, they pose no risk to a fighting man./ He said this in a tone that implied "like us." Jorac was glad to be accepted as an equal to this man.

/But there is another small group of men. We see them year after year. They are not rebels, more like vultures. Or like jackals, and they will attack the weak wherever those are found. Any small group that goes against them fares poorly, for they fight together. This is what I have been trying to teach the men you train with./

/You have taught them well. I have seen it./

Brozadam bobbed his head a little, acknowledging the compliment. /I thank you for your words, I receive them from a man who has seen true fighting, so I know they are not empty. I hope I have done enough. Last year in fighting them, two Guardsmen were cut off from the army and never got back to camp. All we know is their armor was sold in Vaggert, even before the army returned, and the source could not be traced. The jackals who fought them, these are the dangerous men. Some few of them may fight because they are simply fighting men and know no other life, but most are karknk without honor. They are the ones to avoid./

/This group of jackals – what is their sign?/

/It is only a double handful of men, so it is not easy to say. They have excellent armor, but that is not enough to mark them, since many of the fools have money for armor too. We have seen a few in battle, fighting together as a group, and fighting very well, but they mostly lurk on the fringes. Granak, he has been in the Guard many years. He says he can tell them from the style of their sword-blows./

/I thank you for your insight. Though I may see no battle this year. I am here only to look for wizards, then head back to the city if they are found. When do you go back to Vaggert?/

/I am to escort the first fast dispatch rider, who will leave after the General has an estimate of the foe. It will be only a few days, I believe, now that we are in the rebel lands. I will visit you then to ask if you have any messages. You do not talk much about this 'Kimma,' but I see your eyes./

Jorac turned and looked more fully at Brozadam and bowed a little in the fashion of the tribes. */You are a man of wisdom, as well./*

/Ha, were I a man of wisdom, I would not have taken a woman over the mountains to the Wet Lands. I am a fool, like other men. But men are fools, it is our fate./

/As a fool, then, I thank you. I will work on a letter for her eyes alone./

Jorac had sent back a short message to Dorrie and Kimma with the oil-seller, and had sent formal letters to Pergimtor and chatty ones to Dorrie and Kimma – but those were all to be read by many others. He'd need make the most of his chance to write to her, privately.

* * *

With that, Jorac took his leave and went back to his wagon. Their horses were delivered late that day – in fact, everything was late, because this was the first day the army switched to battle tactics. Jorac wasn't particularly impressed with the tactics: A core group consisting of about half the army stayed in the center – all the infantry and senior officers were there, along with the wagons and spare horses, plus the observers and all the other non-fighting personnel. Surrounding the core was a heavy armored guard, with a wide screen of outriders and scouts beyond them. It looked more like a gigantic caravan than an army, but this configuration had the advantage – a questionable one in Jorac's mind – of keeping the entire army together.

After their late start that morning, the ponderous caravan started moving, slowly, toward Tilville, the West Luverna capital, where Ozifaj had his headquarters. Unless he surrendered, they intended to occupy the town, or if needed, raze it, to put an end to the rebellion. At the rate they were going, Jorac estimated it would take them at least two more weeks to reach the town. No point in getting impatient, he told himself.

He and Hox continued to work out in the mornings, but doing it by themselves was more work and less fun. Still, they managed at least to get their blood pumping every day before having to sit on the bumpy wagon seat. And the seat was bumpier – the roads here weren't up to the standards of the south. The army was moving more slowly and carefully but making up for it with longer days.

Jorac privately told Lartie he still acted far too much like an old schoolteacher much of the time, and asked him to go seek out some of the boys his age around the camp and try to have boyish fun. Finding fish and lizards in the middle of an army was impossible of course, but maybe they could find things to play with.

Monrae had become fast friends with Nellie Gompel, despite their different backgrounds, and the two women spent most of their idle time talking and playing with Monrae's cat Falcon. With Monrae cooking and Hox doing most of their food-buying (from unofficial army sources or the local farmers), they were eating quite well and not dipping into their food reserves at all.

* * *

Two days later, the first attacks came. Jorac heard trumpets in the distance and saw a cloud of dust rise from some nearby hills. The whole army turned toward the skirmish, and the infantry formed columns and moved toward the sound at a trot. Most of the mounted men also turned that way and galloped forward. Meanwhile, Jorac noted, some of the General's Guard immediately went toward the senior officers.

By the time Jorac finally got to the battle area, the fighting had been over for more than an hour. He was told there were about twenty dead rebels on the ground, while the Etrombian army had lost only three men dead and ten wounded, plus a larger number of horses. This rebel group had fancied itself archers and launched a few flights of arrows at the soldiers; that was what had caused most of the wounds and equine causalities.

Jorac overheard a grizzled-looking army man who summed it up. "Just the usual fools. Should have run after they shot the arrows, they might have had a chance. Maybe a hundred or so ran away – Plambo's squad's trailing them. Hope they head toward Tilville, make our job easier."

Jorac had seen the aftermath of a battle before and had no desire to look too closely. Two of the scholar-observers ran onto the battlefield and came back looking very queasy, though still trying to write in their notebooks. Hox kept Monrae with the wagon, away from the bodies, and Lartie had no desire to go look either.

That night, Jorac gave Brozadam the letter he'd been writing to Kimma, and watched as the trainer put it in his boot, separate from the other dispatches. Jorac's letter to Kimma was several pages long; it had been written in short little heartfelt paragraphs over the past few days. When he read it back he thought it was disjointed and sappy, but it was what he'd felt when he wrote it, so he just signed and sealed it. He told Brozadam how to find Madame Velosp, and included a short note for Dorrie, too. In it he described more factual things, including the news that Hox had suddenly gotten married to a tall woman who seemed to suit him, and that Lartimaparian had turned out to be a youngster. He asked Dorrie to share the letter with Kimma. He realized Kimma would probably show her more personal letter to Dorrie, too, but thought at least he wouldn't be there to be embarrassed by it.

* * *

Over the next few days, there were a few more of the smaller skirmishes and raids. The rebels always seemed to run off away from the road, slowing down progress toward Tilville as the army had to follow them. Jorac thought they were making glacial progress, but his army contacts thought the campaign was going well and they might even be back home by the end of summer. On a happier note, Hox and Lartie managed to switch wagons without a discouraging word being said by anyone, and when Nellie Gompel said, "Say, those two got together pretty quick, didn't they?" it was all Jorac could do not to laugh. She had no idea how right she was.

Late the third night, there was another cursory attack. The army's outriders, as usual, headed toward the attackers, so at dawn they were out of place for a flank attack from the other side. The General himself mounted his stallion and headed the counter-attack, handily beating off the rebels. But some of the outriders from the night attack didn't return, so a full company was sent to look for them. Jorac noticed Taj of the General's Guard went with the company when it left – he'd learned they rotated field duty with time spent actually guarding the senior officers.

The company returned at midmorning, with tight, angry looks on their faces. They brought back a few riderless horses, and a few more with bodies slung across the saddle. One of the bodies was partly burned. They drew to a halt in a field nearby and began stripping off their horse's gear.

Jorac ignored the angry looks from the soldiers as he pushed forward to find out what happened. He showed his observer badge, and got there in time to hear most of the story first-hand.

"Twenty-six dead, a few more missing. Arbleft – he was alive when we got there. Said there were a couple of dozen, maybe, but damned good – it was like they could see in the dark.

Arrows took down a bunch until they dismounted, then there was some hand-to-hand stuff. Nothing good."

One of the soldiers pointed at the burned body and asked, "What happened to him?"

"His horse got it worse, that's all I know. Burned all up, like he ran through a big fire. Ugly."

Another of the returning soldiers spoke up. "Some sort of a flame-bomb, maybe. Rock oil, a fuse, a clay pot – I heard about those, maybe six or seven years back."

A senior officer came down from the General's tent and escorted the company leaders away, but not without a sharp "Report to your duties!" to the assembled group. The men quickly dispersed – everyone there (except Jorac) was supposed to be somewhere else. As they were leaving, Jorac caught Taj's eye, but Taj just shook his head very slightly. Whether he couldn't talk or disagreed with the report, Jorac didn't know.

That night, Jorac received a summons, even before he'd finished setting up the wagon for camping. "Observer Kellor is hereby requested and required to attend General Melsim immediately, alone." Jorac looked at the note again – technically the general couldn't require anything of him, but he could certainly request. The man who gave him the note wasn't a clerk; he looked more like a soldier, and was utterly silent. Jorac walked over and handed the note to Hox, then turned to the soldier and said, "Lead the way."

The General was in the tent with only a few men; Kezert wasn't there today. He wasted no time with greetings. "You were told to leave my army alone. What were you doing today? Bothering my wounded men, or staring at the dead like some sort of blood-leech?"

"I was observing, as per my orders."

"Dammit, leave my soldiers alone. They have enough to worry about without a damned wizard spy getting in the way. I won't tell you again."

Jorac was getting angry, despite himself. "Sir, I have my orders. And they didn't come from you."

`"You pathetic flunky, listen to me. You'll do what I say! I had to let you come along, but remember, I'm in charge here, not any fool in Vaggert."

Jorac was red hot and ice cold at the same time. He slowed his words, and put on his best noble accent. "I'll remember that, sir. I'll write it down, if you like. You say that you're in charge, not any fool in Vaggert. I wonder if the rebel leader – Ozifaj, was it? – said something like that recently?"

The general turned bright red and almost started spitting. "You! You . . . Get out of my sight!"

Jorac drawled, "Yes, sir. I'll be about my duties now." He turned and sauntered out of the tent. He felt that it was childish and immature to gloat. He also couldn't help himself. But his grin had faded by the time he got back to his camp, thinking of who was in command of the entire army.

* * *

That day, and the next, the army made almost no progress toward Tilville – large squads combed the countryside looking for rebels, but to no avail. Jorac and Hox spent some time with soldiers scouring the hills where the ambush had taken place, but found nothing useful. Jorac was interested in the small burnt scar on the hillside near the remains of a burned horse. There were some broken clay shards there, so it could have been the flame-bomb that he'd heard about that morning. But Jorac also remembered Wolburn and the fireballs he could throw. Jorac sniffed a bit of the burnt pottery and didn't smell much of anything – no active magic, and no rock oil smell. Maybe some sort of spirits that evaporated quickly were used? He didn't like it, but all he could do was shrug and keep looking.

Jorac tried to get someone in the General's Guard to talk about the flame-bombs from past campaigns, but all they would say is that the General himself had told them not to talk to Jorac.

And no one else he could find had been on that campaign, so he learned no more.

The army started making cautious progress toward Tilville the next day. No more groups split off the main army, especially not at night. Small attacks continued each day, but were mostly on the scale of someone shooting arrows at extreme range and running away. One morning, they saw a whole ridgeline filled with rebels, several hundred men, but by the time the army got to the area, they'd moved off. Jorac wasn't sure what the rebels were trying to accomplish with the show – it was puzzling, but they might have had internal reasons he couldn't guess.

Four days later they were out of the farmland and into sparsely forested hills. They were two day's fast ride to Tilville, or a week or more at this army's pace.

Their first night in the hills brought Jorac some amusement. As Hox and Monrae finished dinner and started making eyes at each other, preparing for another early retirement to their wagon, the man who came to take their horses that evening had another man with him who introduced himself as Poshert, the head of the hostlers.

He spoke to Jorac in an apologetic tone, saying, "Observer, we got a problem. We got a deal, right enough, but that fancy mare, she's riling up the others something fierce. She's ready, if you get my meaning, ready for little companionship in her life."

Jorac looked pointedly at Monrae and said, "That would be your Sunbeam, I think." He tried not to smirk.

Poshert said, "Your pardon, missus, but that's why we don't like to have mares along – when they get into season, there's no telling what they'll do. The stallions get to fighting, and the biggest one wins, but the others are all beat up and worn out."

Jorac giggled a little to himself, but said to the hostler, "So, what do you propose? We can't keep her in camp here. We have enough going on without a broody mare in our midst."

"Well, sir, there are a few others who need constant watch. We've got two corrals set up, on either side of the big herd, and we keep Virack – that's General Melsim's stallion – and the officer's horses on one side, and the ones like your Sunbeam on the other. Most of the stallions are fine amongst the geldings; it's only when the mares get acting up that we need to separate them. There's a few geldings we're doctoring, and one or two other mares we can keep with her, so she's not lonely. It's another six coppers a night, but it'll mean we can keep a boy or two on watch with her all night. I don't want you thinking this is a cheat-em deal, mind you. Army hostlers, we have a good name, and want to keep it. But your Sunbeam, she's extra work, like, and that's the facts."

Hox and Monrae nodded to each other, and he said, "Well, that seems fair enough."

Jorac nodded too. "The horses have been well cared for so far, so I think your good name is safe. How long do you think, a week or so?"

"Like as not, yes. Maybe a day or two more; we'll watch her and not leave her there longer than needed."

Jorac said, "It's a fair deal – I'll fetch the coppers."

He returned and paid Poshert, who no doubt wondered about the grin Jorac couldn't hide. After he left, Jorac turned to his companions, pointed to Monrae, and said, "So, she's ready for little companionship in her life, is she? And the biggest stallion wins?"

Hox just started laughing, while Monrae took off her slipper and threw it at Jorac. Her aim was terrible, because she was laughing too. And if Jorac and Lartie heard some giggling and whinnying from the next wagon that evening, and if it creaked a little more than normal that night, they were too polite to mention it in the morning.

* * *

Another slow-moving day brought them closer to Tilville – the scouts reported the hills behind the city could be seen from the treetops nearby. Within a week or so they would be at the city gates, either being admitted by the inhabitants or storming the walls if they stubbornly refused. It wasn't a large enough city to have very strong walls, but sometimes pride won over common sense.

That afternoon, there was a bustle of activity in their marching column when a scout returned at a gallop. Jorac managed to talk to him after he left the commanders' tents – it took both his observer badge and some persuasion to get him to speak at all, and four silvers to get him to spill everything, but he finally told Jorac what he saw.

"It looks like they're tired of running. Going to put up a fight, finally. They're at the top of a ridge, two hills over to the west, looks like they're digging in. About time we got a good fight."

"How many do you think there are?"

"Two hundred, maybe three hundred tops. General, he'll charge out with the horses, with the ground-pounders right behind him. Whole thing won't take half a day."

"Won't they prepare traps and such? Seems like we're fighting where they want, on their ground." To Jorac, the whole setup stank. If someone ever taught a course in lulling an army into complacency, this whole campaign would be a case study.

The scout grinned. "That's where we come in. We go in now, and again tonight, check it out real good. Then the General makes the final plans, him and Fattie. But they always like to end it with a cavalry charge, even if we have to spend a few days clearing them out first. A big charge helps for next time, they say. Anyway, I gotta go. I'll probably need to go out again right away."

Jorac was worried enough to tell the guard, "Come see me when you get back. Any time, day or night, okay?"

"Errr. . . I'm *supposed* to go straight to the General's tent." His tone implied that there was another option, if only Jorac would suggest it.

"Stop by here on your way and there's a couple more silvers in it for you. I need to know what you find – it's part of my job, okay?"

The scout was torn. "Well. . . my captain, he don't mind a little enterprise, as long as it don't hurt the army. . . and he gets his cut."

"Okay, three silvers." Jorac knew by now this army ran on small bribes – one of the many things he'd change if it were up to him. "But you come to me first, right? I'll be around those two wagons there. Come over and give me a quick rundown – what traps or whatever you found, what the enemy strength is, what the land looks like and such. Try to figure out why they stopped to fight there, okay?"

"Okay, gotcha. Will do. Gotta go now."

Jorac watched him leave, then went back to his wagon and told his team about the development. He was hoping someone had some idea about why two or three hundred rebels were digging in at the top of a ridge, but no one did.

Monrae said, "Maybe the men have been calling the leader a coward, so he has to turn and fight, even if it doesn't make much sense."

Jorac replied, "They're supposedly led by Ozifaj the Sixth; that's a famous name to live up to, so you could be right. But – no, somehow. I've seen stubborn soldiers before, and these have run too easily."

Hox added, "Or maybe they'll pull out again when we get close. They've done that before, more than once."

Jorac answered, "Yes, or maybe it's an elaborate trap of some sort. I just don't like it much – something's wrong here, but I can't really tell you what."

Lartie listened and frowned. "I think you're right – there's something we don't know. I wish . . . well, I wish we could know more, some way. I guess the scouts will have to tell us." Jorac knew he missed his uncle's scrying ability, though he hid it well.

The daftness of sending the army out with no wizards still grated on him.

* * *

The army stopped early the next day and regrouped a bit, leaving the observers with nothing to do. Jorac napped a little in the shade of the tents, while Lartie spent some time with the horse-boys who were his age and read a book he'd borrowed from the scholars. Hox and Monrae sat quietly on the back of their wagon and chatted with Nellie. They watched the messengers hurry back and forth around the command tents, and tried in vain to see what troop movements the orders resulted in.

It was just after dawn when the scout returned, quietly appearing next to Jorac's wagon. The scout was good; he'd moved so quietly and blended in so well that Jorac hadn't noticed his approach. He was wearing dusty green-brown clothes, and carrying a small knapsack.

"Hsssst. You, observer. I'm back."

Jorac took a quick glance around and walked between the wagons, out of sight of most of the camp.

Jorac handed him three silvers, and asked "What did you find?"

"The whole field is in high grass – easy to sneak around if you're careful. It's big, probably a valley that burned over a few years ago, kind of like a long bowl shape. Nothing that would stop a charge there that I could see. They put a line of ground spikes about halfway up the field on the far side; we cleared out a path through the middle, and we'll pull the rest of them out as soon as it gets dark. There's a trench of some sort up near the top – maybe spikes at the bottom, or maybe they'll set a fire in it, but we have some little bridges we can throw over it. It doesn't look bad, overall."

"Hmm. Looks perfect for one of the General's charges, doesn't it?"

"Yep, I'd say so. He can wipe 'em out if they stand – and if they turn and run, it's decent country for pursuit. Not many trees around."

Jorac thought a moment. "I'm not saying anything against you, understand that. But did you miss anything? You know what you can and can't see – anything you couldn't see?"

"Hmm. Well, you ask it that way, it's a maybe. That tall grass could hide lots of stuff, but nothing big, understand? You could hide a few people out there, but spread out. If you bunch them up they'd knock down the grass and be easy to see, right?"

Jorac nodded. He was glad this scout at least knew his limitations.

"The only weird thing out there was a bunch of these old pots." He reached down in his bag and pulled out a worn-looking clay pot, squat and ugly, about a foot high. "I found a hidden way to get me up there, behind some bunch-grass, so I crawled up near the trench at the top. I didn't make it all the way to the trench, but close. I found this one in the field there – there were a lot of them laying around up there. It's empty, just some old dust inside, probably been laying there for years. There are some old wagon wrecks up there, seems like some sort of road runs atop that ridgeline. Not worth picking up a bunch of old pots if they spilled, I guess. I wouldn't give you two coppers for it."

Jorac turned the pot over in his hands, looking at the curious design. "I would."

The scout grinned and said, "I hoped you'd say that – I grabbed two of 'em. There's gotta be a couple of hundred of them up there, maybe more. Keep that one – I gotta go now."

The scout took the extra pair of coppers Jorac handed him and dropped them into his boot-top. With a quick "I wasn't here, right?" he ducked under the wagon and disappeared.

* * *

Jorac's team gathered to cook breakfast, and he described the scout's finding to them. They were beginning to share Jorac's apprehension after he explained how the General had been using the same tactics for ten years, and the stage seemed to be set – set far too well – for him to repeat them.

The pot was the only thing they had to look at, and it didn't look like much. It was thick-walled and almost round, with a wide opening; you could see how it could have rolled down the hill. Its style was old, and it was cheaply made and badly fired, but somehow it didn't look old. It was dirty but it hadn't been sitting outside for years; a season at the most, because it hadn't been colonized by insects or filled with rotting vegetation. It had some random-looking squiggles painted on it in a blood-red color, but nothing that made sense to anyone.

They put the pot down and ate a quiet, nervous meal. Jorac idly stirred the fire in the firepit, and in doing so knocked a stray spark at the pot – some of the squiggles burned off it in a fizzle of sparks. There was now a definite pattern to the remaining squiggles, more like writing. Jorac reached for the pot, but Lartie shouted "Don't!"

Jorac snatched his hand back as if something bit it.

Everyone looked at Lartie expectantly.

"I think I recognize something. I'm not really sure. . ." He knelt down and carefully peered at the pot without touching it. After a bit, he went to the wagon and took a torch from their supplies and lit it in the firepit. He walked around to the other side of the pot, stood back as far as he could, poked the torch near it, and was rewarded with another fizzle of sparks. Then he examined it closely again.

"I recognize the language, I think. That writing is demonish." His quiet, matter-of-fact manner was most convincing.

Hox, Monrae, and Jorac looked at each other in puzzlement. Jorac said, "Okay, what is demonish writing?"

"Put simply, if you. . . I mean, if you're a wizard and you want to communicate with denizens of the nether planes – demons – you can talk to them, provided you know their language or can cast some sort of translation spell. But some of the more powerful demons also have some written language – more like pictures than letter-wise writing. Writing them instructions is said to be a more precise way of getting them to do exactly what you want."

Hox and Monrae looked at the boy as if he'd gone completely crazy.

Lartie said, "I've had a good education, you know, uh, I mean for someone my age, so don't think I'm making this up."

Jorac said, "I believe you. What does it say?"

"I remember that third glyph – I Command. And that one there, the chain, is supposed to link things together. The rest I don't know. I think they're starting to fade – can we find some paper?"

Jorac quickly found some paper and pens in the wagon and gave some to each of them – he figured four copies would be better than one. By the time they'd finished their sketches, the hieroglyphs had almost completely faded.

They compared their four sets of sketches and found they mostly agreed. There was one figure that looked very much like a horse, another two-legged figure that could be a man or a bird, and a number of strange, curling symbols.

Lartie said, "I wish I'd read that old book more." He pointed to the sequence of symbols. "Something – a name? – I command – something, something – the horse symbol – six more symbols – linked to – two symbols – that bird-thing – two more, then command end. See, that last one is like the third one with this extra cross on the end. Not much help, sorry."

Hox asked, "Do they have horses on the nether planes?"

"I only know of dogs. So you think that symbol might really mean a horse?"

Jorac said, "Remember hearing about that burned horse from last week? Didn't I tell you?" He quickly relayed the story of the successful ambush, and the few words that told of a dead horse and rider, both badly burned, from something that seemed to be harder on the horse than the man.

Monrae said, "What kind of cruel person would treat a horse like that?"

In the silence that followed the question, they heard a tiny, high-pitched sound like escaping steam. The pot had started smoking and making a sort of boiling sound. They all stared at it in alarm and started to back away, except Lartie who walked up to it and hit it hard with the torch he still carried, breaking the pot into pieces. A large red spark jumped from the pot and flew on a swift curving path to the front of the wagon, where it hit the wagon tongue with a loud pop. Another, blue-green spark spiraled around their wagons a few times in a widening circle, before petering out quietly.

Jorac sneezed one mighty, violent sneeze.

Chapter 27 - A Glimmer of Dread

After his sneeze, Jorac looked around to see if there was anyone nearby, but all was calm. None of the other observers were in sight, and none came over at the small noise. He didn't have the urge to sneeze anymore.

Hox and Monrae said nothing, just looked at him with worried expressions, and the broken pot in fear. Lartie poked around the pot shards with the torch, but nothing happened. All their senses were on edge, but they looked around the camp and saw nothing unusual happening, and Jorac didn't sneeze anymore.

"Uh, good thinking there, Lartie. I guess. What was that?"

"I don't really know. Some sort of spell, I suppose."

After a quiet minute, Monrae walked to the front of the wagon, where the spark had landed, to see what happened there. "Smells like burnt horse hair," she reported.

Jorac sat down on the edge of the wagon and started mumbling swear-words under his breath.

Hox looked at him strangely. "What are you saying? I can't hear you."

"Just as well, you wouldn't like what I was saying. How do we tell the General there are a bunch of horse traps up on that hill? Magical, fireball horse traps. That we think we just managed to trigger one of them, somehow, at least partly. But we broke it, and now it just looks like another broken pot. . ."

Hox shook his head in disgust, and said, "I told Monrae about the General."

"Right, he hates wizards, and doesn't trust me. Oh, and for evidence we have some scribbles on paper, and a young boy – a known lout (sorry, Lartie) – who says they're demon writing. But the original writing is gone now; it was on the clay pot we broke. What do you think the General will say?"

While Hox merely looked concerned, Lartie looked ashen, and said, "Before you talk to them. . . I read a book about traps once, too. The first pot a horse gets to won't spring the trap, or else the lead horse would be the only one who got caught. There's probably a trigger near the top, one that won't be reached until all our horses and troops are in the area. That or they have a wizard watching over it all the time, to set it off when they want. But if there's fog or a dark night, that wouldn't work, so it's probably automatic. Maybe they have a wizard for backup, in case the lead horses don't set it off in time."

Jorac glared. "I keep hearing how the general loves a great, final horse-borne charge, so the enemy knows it too. And somehow he's been talked into keeping wizards out of the army. This thing stinks, stinks like a rotten fish."

The group was silent. Finally Hox said, "I guess you've got to try to talk to the general."

"I'm afraid you're right. The only thing that might help is finding that other pot the scout brought back, so I'll try that. He's going to laugh me out of his tent, so see what else you can come up with while I'm gone."

* * *

The next morning Jorac used his observer badge to bully his way past the first line of guards and up to the officers' area. He walked up to the general's fancy tent and spoke loudly.

"Observer Kellor needs to speak with the general and his aide. It's very important."

The guard outside the tent looked at him with a disrespectful glare, and said, "Huh. If the general wants to see you, he'll ask for you. Now be gone. And don't bother waving that observer badge, it won't work here." He shifted his staff to a ready position, in case Jorac tried to push his way in.

Jorac increased his volume even more. "Where's Kezert?"

"*Colonel* Kezert's whereabouts are none of your concern, observer."

As Jorac hoped, a pair of the General's Guards he'd been working out with walked up to him. One said, "Hey, Jorac, what are you doing, trying to stir up a hornet's nest?"

"Hi Taj, Poznoy. I ran into something that may have to do with your business, not mine. I figured I needed to talk to Kezert, at least."

Poznoy said, "No can do, sorry. He and the general are off somewhere, I think they're looking at where the rebels are digging in. They want the whole army – the fighting part, I mean – up there at dawn tomorrow. Anyway, we're not even supposed to talk to you."

"Damn. Well, tell them – well, read this note." Jorac handed over a short note he'd written, explaining that he feared the hillside was a trap, and why.

Taj read it, frowning. "Pretty thin. One busted pot you say had disappearing writing on it. And a spark from the fire that hit the wagon." Jorac had left off the part about his allergy and the sneeze.

"I know it's not much, but we all saw it – sparks don't curl like that. I was just hoping that someone could look into it more. If it's true, the general's famous charge is going to be a problem."

Taj was unconvinced, but willing to go along. "Yeah, okay. Poz and I can talk to Kezert about this when he gets back."

Poznoy added, "But don't expect too much. They like the plans they make themselves, if you catch my drift."

Taj's eyes went past Jorac to something behind him, and he said, "Now, observer, you'll have to leave."

Jorac turned around and saw a well-dressed aide coming toward them; not wanting to get the Guards in trouble, he nodded and quickly left. He'd done what he could. The rest was up to General Melsim and his team. Jorac's hopes weren't very high, but they couldn't say they hadn't been warned.

When he got back to his wagon, Monrae was talking and Lartie was taking notes.

Monrae was saying, "Maybe Nellie would help us with that; I'll ask her."

"Help you with what?"

Lartie handed him the notes he'd been writing, and Monrae said, "Well, we don't like it much, but with the time we've got, it's all we could think of. We've got a full moon, which should help. But we'll need to start right away. . ."

Jorac read the notes while they explained. He didn't like it either, but at least it was something they could do, and the alternatives were worse. They talked it over, and refined a few points. They just had to wait until General Melsim and his group came back.

* * *

It was mid-afternoon when Jorac stood near the horse corrals and watched as a dozen horses rode up. You could tell it was the general's group from afar by his fancy salt-and-pepper colored stallion and the immense form of Kezert on a large draft horse. When they arrived, Jorac was standing with a group of men near where they dismounted. Jorac tried to get the general's or Kezert's attention, but the press of men around him was too much – there were a dozen or more aides and orderlies waiting for them, seemingly all speaking at once. At one point he was physically pushed out of the way by a few other supplicants. He managed to catch Kezert's eye for a moment, but the look of disdain on Kezert's face told Jorac his cause was probably a lost one. He gave his note to a man from their group who said he'd see that Colonel Kezert read it, but as he left he saw the note get pushed into a satchel with dozens more.

Jorac grimly turned back toward the camp. When he was beyond the corrals he waved, and in a few minutes Monrae walked up. As the horses that had just come in were being cared for, Monrae and Jorac walked slowly up the row of tents nearest the horse corrals. Most of the horses were in the big center corral, which was portable, made of three ropes tied to widespread spears in the ground. There were over a thousand horses in the main corral, but they were used to their accommodations by now and in took relatively few men to watch over them.

There were two smaller corrals, one on either side, with the General's stallion and other pampered steeds in one, and some wounded horses and a few mares, including Monrae's mare Sunbeam, in the other. Each group had boys watching them day and night.

"Hi boys – we need to take Sunbeam for a little while. Monrae needs to show her to a possible buyer. Sorry to bother you."

"That's okay. It gets a little boring here, except at feeding time. Do you need a saddle and bridle?"

Monrae said, "A halter is fine, thanks. You're doing a good job with her, she looks happy." The boys beamed with pleasure.

When Sunbeam was haltered, Monrae and Jorac led her out past the big corral, and just past the other small corral too. The general's stallion Virack had been curried first, and was now loose in the small corral as the horse-tenders finished with the others. Jorac had to admit the stallion was a strong, fine horse, with excellent lines; he pranced about the little corral proudly.

They paused with Sunbeam in front of the small corral for a little while, checking her hooves. Sunbeam started wiggling her behind to Virack, who came over to the edge of the corral ropes. When she started spreading her legs a little, getting ready to urinate, Jorac moved her over right next to the corral to do her business. The stallion went a little mad, calling to her and pushing on the ropes, and the boys who were watching this group of horses had to come over and hold the corral ropes.

To the horse-boys, Jorac said, "Sorry, fellows. We better get her out of here."

One of them said, "Yes sir, you better. Virack will be breaking out soon."

It took the combined force of Jorac and Monrae to pull Sunbeam away, but they managed. They led her back to their wagon, where Hox and Lartie were waiting with a large tub of cool water, poured from a cask they'd filled just that morning. Leading a horse to water won't always make her drink, but it worked this time, and she slurped noisily. Hox and Lartie tied her to the wagon, and Monrae went to talk to Nellie Gompel.

* * *

After dinner that evening, they met Nellie near Jorac's wagon. Nellie was dressed oddly, with leather slippers, ballooning green trousers that fastened at the ankle and a colorful, short-sleeved shirt with oversized, flapping elbows. She was carrying a lumpy cloth bag at her side, which she handed to Hox.

She turned around and said, "I haven't worn these clothes in almost a year. Good to know they still fit. I know it's what folks expect, but I always thought I looked like a fool in this outfit."

Monrae said, "Nonsense. You look fine. Perfect; they'll never have seen the like."

Nellie said, "Are you sure this is needed – and will work?"

Monrae said, "Oh, it'll work. As for the need, well, we explained about that."

Nellie nodded, and visibly steeled herself. "Okay, I believe you. Let's go."

Lartie consulted his notes. "Monrae, you move your horse. The bucket is over there. We need to go." Monrae nodded curtly, picked up the bucket, and left.

Hox and Nellie set off, with Jorac and Lartie trailing more slowly. By the time they got to the horse corral, Jorac was well behind; he stopped beside the nearby tents and watched.

Nellie and Hox set up their juggling practice area in the tramped-down area in front of the corral. She took out her cloth balls and started into what was obviously a practiced routine. Soon she started tossing the occasional ball to Hox, too. He'd been practicing with her a little, and threw the balls back so that they were in her pattern. She didn't have a great deal of pure skill, but was lithe and looked good at what she was doing, like an acrobat or a dancer.

By this time all the returning horses had been brushed and put into the corrals, and only two boys were left watching the small corral with the fancy steeds. They immediately stopped what they were doing to watch the jugglers, and Jorac and Lartie moved closer. Jorac stopped at the intersection of the small corral and the large one, while Lartie walked over and greeted the two boys.

Lartie said, "Hi guys. This is the lady I was telling you about. She said she'd teach you too."

Nellie smiled engagingly. "You're Graxie and Lenafird, right? It's okay, Lartie explained it to me. I owe him a favor, so he asked me to show you how to do this juggling. It takes a lot of practice, but I can teach you the basics." She looked around. "We can't do it here; there are too many horse-apples around. But there's a clear area up by our wagons – want to try it up there?"

One of the boys said, "Wow, great! Lartie, can you watch the horses for us?"

"Well. . ."

"We'll let you ride the general's stallion tonight! Come on, please?"

The other boy added, "Yeah, and it won't be very long. All you have to do is watch, and call someone if anything happens. They just came back, and we gave them grain, so they'll be quiet."

"Well, okay, go ahead. It's pretty fun. I've been learning, too. We can try juggling together after you learn how."

"Cool! Let's go!"

The boys fairly vibrated with excitement, and set off with Hox and Nellie. As soon as they were out of sight, Jorac and Lartie quickly set to work. The general's stallion was still over where the mare had been, sniffing at the ground; the other horses were cleaning up the last of their nightly grain, set in piles on canvas in front of them. Jorac walked up quietly and put a halter on Virack's head, and after a tug or two, was able to lead him over to Lartie.

Lartie said, "He's a big one, isn't he? Are you sure all the rest will follow?"

"They're herd animals, so if we stay calm and keep them quiet we should be okay. You lead, take the path we talked about. I'll go behind and keep them bunched. We're just following orders, so act a little bored."

Lartie dropped the gate to the rope corral, and led the stallion out of the gate. The other horses followed when Jorac walked among them with a long stick, touching them lightly on their rumps as needed. As soon they were all underway, Jorac went back and closed the small corral gate, then untied the ropes between the large corral and the small one. That was Hox's idea; he thought it might give them a little extra time before anyone realized the horses were truly missing.

Jorac quickly caught up to Lartie and the small herd. He looked back once or twice, and saw some of the remaining horses entering the small corral, where there was better food. Though the camp was still moving, most people were eating their evening meal, and they saw no one watching them. Maybe they were going to get away with it.

* * *

They led the horses on a roundabout path to the west side of camp, and gathered them in a little bowl in the hill they'd scouted earlier. Hox was already there, tying some rope into horse halters.

Jorac asked him, "How did they take it?"

"They were pretty unhappy when I had to tie them up. I feel bad for them. They wanted to do something quite different with Nellie than sit there bound and gagged in her wagon."

"Well, at least they'll be released unharmed. It's a good lesson for them, but I know what you mean. I hope we can make it up to them, somehow. Both with the army, and, you know, personally."

Hox said, "Well, I think so too. But they're boys; they'll probably outgrow it."

Jorac nodded. "I'm still going to have to apologize to them, and their bosses – all the hostlers in fact. If I stay out of jail, I mean."

Hox had a stubborn look on his face "I saw that pot, and those sparks-that-weren't-sparks. This has to be done. Now I need some help with these halters."

Jorac and Lartie both had a little trouble putting the halters on some of the horses, so Hox did most of them, but soon they had all the horses in halter, or at least had a rope around their neck. Altogether, they had nineteen horses, which was more than a handful for three minders.

They held the horses with them in the small bowl until it the sun had gone all the way down and it started getting dark; then they set out. By tying the halter leads in a line behind the stallion, they found they could manage the herd, if they took it easy. Jorac would have liked to tie them all in proper halters, but they were out of rope.

They led the horses over the hill and toward the top of the next one, following a path the army had beaten by repeated trips to the staging area for the next day's attack. As they approached the top, they met a large squad of army men coming back down the path, their packs clanking with cruel spiked caltrops, meant to stop charging horses. Jorac didn't even have to ask them; they volunteered with some pride that they'd cleaned out the field and the general would have a clear path tomorrow.

Jorac and his crew went on past the squad quickly, trying to look like they belonged. Jorac in the lead busied himself with the horses, and Hox bent himself over in the middle of the herd to hide his height. Lartie brought up the rear, chivvying along the laggards with a switch, using the slang he'd learned from the horse-boys. In the semi-darkness, their raggedy line of horses must have looked like a normal-enough operation; at least no one questioned them.

In a short while the squad was out of sight, and they topped the hill that looked over tomorrow's battlefield. A rising full moon showed them a shallow mountain valley with a few scrubby trees at the bottom, and beyond that a wide grassy meadow rising to a prominent rocky ridge on the far side. Presumably the enemy was dug in not far beyond that ridge – and the traps were set just below it on this side. They tried to keep the horses quiet as they crossed over the hilltop and were briefly silhouetted against the sky.

They began looking for Monrae as soon as they'd crossed over and started down the hill, but they didn't find her until they were nearly to the tree line at the bottom of the valley. She was standing there impatiently with a covered wooden bucket in her hand, holding Sunbeam's halter rope with the other. There was a small pile of gear nearby, and Sunbeam was wearing a light saddle.

"Took you long enough," was her greeting. Hox shrugged, and she went on. "Good thing there are no clouds. The full moon ought to be enough light. These two need to see each other."

She pointed at Virack, who'd definitely noticed Sunbeam. Hox had to grab and pull at the stallion's head with all his strength to hold him back. And the mare seemed just as interested – she nickered and made soft trumpeting sounds. Jorac was worried someone might hear, but he didn't think anyone could see them at this distance. They were probably midway between the observers from both the rebels and the army, who were no doubt on the top of the hills nearby. *Only fools would be halfway between two armies in the dark, the night before a battle,* thought Jorac. *So what does that make us?*

Hox stood firmly holding on to Virack while Jorac and Monrae dragged Sunbeam away, with Lartie following. By the time they'd reached the far side of the trees, Sunbeam had calmed down a little, and Monrae insisted on riding her, despite

Jorac's intense misgivings. She aimed the mare uphill, toward the traps, while Lartie followed with the bucket.

Jorac watched them go. He wanted to call out "Good luck," or "Be careful, Hox will kill me if you get hurt," but he didn't dare. Instead he turned and walked back to Hox and the horses. He said, "They've gone," and in the moonlight he could see the tense look on his friend's face.

They led the horses through the trees to the base of the meadow, and stood watching them while they began happily eating the new growth among the tall grass.

Hox said glumly, "Now comes the hard part. Waiting."

"Yeah." Jorac made a face. "The fate of our whole army rests on a boy with a bucket of horse piss. Well, that and the mating instincts of a stallion, and the herd instincts of the rest of them. You sure Virack will follow that scent-trail?"

"The stallion will do his part, if the boy does his. A horse can scent a trail almost as good as a dog, so he'll follow where Lartie leads him." He paused a moment. "Why'd you let him do it, anyway? I know you're not afraid for him, don't take it like that, but he's maybe not as good at you as moving around in the dark. And he's just a kid."

"Well, he really wanted to. But the main thing is that he's read all those magic books – you know he's related to the head wizard. If there are more traps up there, a different type maybe, I'm hoping he can spot them."

Hox seemed satisfied with that. "He's not really a little lout, I know. But he's weird; sometimes he almost talks like an old man. I'm still trying to figure him out."

Jorac didn't want Hox thinking on that too much. "Don't worry about it. I had a long talk with him on the way back to your wedding. He's a good kid; he's just been isolated in a funny group for a while – all educated adults, not kids his own age." *That's one way of putting it.* "I think he's been learning to fit in, though."

After a time, Hox said, "The general is going to have our necks for this, you know. Or try to, at least."

"Our orders say the worst he can do is kick us out, and try to get us arrested back in Vaggert. But who knows what he might do. I don't think so highly of his ability to reason when he's mad."

Hox snorted. "Or when he's not."

* * *

Outside in the dark, they had no accurate way to measure the passage of time and could only estimate it by the moon and stars. Jorac kept looking up across the meadow – Sunbeam's light coat didn't really stand out among the long grass, but perhaps he caught a glimpse of her here and there.

If things went according to plan, Monrae would stop Sunbeam before she reached the pots, but Lartie would keep on going from there, carrying the bucket to the area where they thought all the horse traps were. He'd volunteered for – nearly demanded – that part of the operation. If it was going to work, both Monrae and Lartie would need to be quiet and careful – and lucky. Jorac was worried about them, and he could see Hox was too.

Finally, after waiting for what they thought was almost an hour, Jorac and Hox led their nineteen horses down the row of trees to the spot where Sunbeam had stood. Virack sniffed and pawed and fidgeted, but they untied and released all the other horses first. Finally they released Virack too and shooed them all uphill, hoping they'd keep on moving in that direction. The stallion was clearly interested in going somewhere, and seemed to be tracing the mare's path and the scent of the slightly leaky bucket of her urine. And the other horses seemed to be more or less following behind him up the hill. So far, so good.

Jorac and Hox found a spot near the edge of the meadow where they thought they might have a better view of the top. They watched the horses go uphill, but quickly lost sight of them.

Jorac sighed. "You know, if we're wrong, the rebels will get some very fine horses. They'll just need to go round them up."

Hox said, "Yeah, Monrae and I talked about it. We'd be disgraced, a laughingstock, probably in jail. But I figure we could live with that better than we could live with watching the army run into a whole field of those traps." He shrugged. "There are lots of other jobs in Vaggert."

"Yeah, I thought I'd be looking for another job after that little episode in the swamp, but instead they gave me a raise."

Hox nodded. "Yeah, and I got that bonus." He gestured nervously. "I just hope this all works out. . ."

* * *

They'd found a log to sit on, but it wasn't very comfortable. They were too nervous to be really sleepy, but they didn't want to admit their worry, and since they had run out of other talk, they mostly just sat quiet with their own thoughts.

Jorac kept checking the sky, but the stars seemed to be moving much slower than normal this night. They kept listening too, but after three hours they'd still heard nothing. Hox had started to fidget, and Jorac wanted to join him. It shouldn't have taken this long for Monrae to get back with her mare – after nearing the top, she was supposed to ride swiftly to the side of the meadow, then come back down the hill.

A half hour later, they heard whinnying high up on the hillside, but could see nothing. There were no voices, no noises, no explosions, so they just waited and fidgeted and worried some more. They couldn't go investigate because they'd promised to stay here. Monrae and Lartie had been of one mind, and had made Hox and Jorac swear to wait where they were until first light at least – it might take a while to position things properly, and having two more people on the hillside in the dark was more likely to hurt than help.

An hour later Jorac was beginning to have a sick, sinking feeling in the pit of his stomach. Hox looked up at the sky and asked, "Is it getting lighter?"

"Not quite yet. Soon. Maybe we should start putting our gear on. We'll need to move very quietly." They slowly donned their swords and gear, and kept looking up at the sky. It had just started to turn a deep purple, in preparation for the rose colors of dawn. They decided they'd try to find Monrae and Lartie as soon as they could see their way.

They actually left a bit earlier than that; they could barely see where to put their feet. But they hadn't gone very far into the meadow when the first light of dawn actually came and they saw Monrae and Lartie walking toward them. When they got closer, Jorac could see that Monrae had been crying. She ran up to Hox and threw her arms around him.

"I had to leave her up there!" Her voice was thick with emotion, with sorrow and anger fighting for supremacy. "I raised her from a wee filly, and now I just killed her, for a bunch of men I don't even *like*. Oh, I know it had to be done, and I did it. But Hox-my-man, we're not going out with this army ever again, right?"

Hox held her in his large arms while she continued. "I ran into the first of the pots before I knew it – she almost stepped on one of them. I got off to see what it was. Lartie told us he thought all the traps would go off together, once the key trap was triggered. So I didn't dare let her move very far. Whenever I let her go where she wanted, she ran toward that damned stallion – he was busy prancing up and down on the hill below us. So finally Lartie and I tied her there and ran for it. I think we scared the horses a little, but that stallion will figure it out soon enough. And one of them will get close enough to the trigger, and, and. . ." she turned her head and cried into her husband's arms. Hox patted her hair and murmured quietly in her ear.

Lartie seemed very subdued, maybe a little frightened. Jorac put an arm around the boy's shoulder and looked up across the meadow to see if he could see the horses – it was hard to tell, but he thought something was moving up near the top just below the ridge. They kept looking up the hill as the sun crept over the horizon, and kept squinting up toward the ridge looking for movement or changes. But suddenly he was distracted by the thunder of hoof beats behind him. General Melsim and his staff were riding down the trail from the hilltop.

The general's group was in the lead, but he'd seemingly brought the whole army with him. The base of the meadow began to fill with mounted men, who started forming into fighting formations.

The general and his aides stayed in a tight formation, and Jorac saw that most or all of the General's Guard were with them. There were about thirty or forty in the group, all riding rather ordinary-looking horses. The general was on a large brown gelding of no particular quality. Kezert was absent, Jorac noted – finding a horse to take his bulk must have been difficult on short notice. The whole group seemed to be looking around intently, some straining their eyes up the hill, some peering around the meadow. When someone spotted Jorac's group and pointed, the general cried "There he is!" and spurred his horse, galloping toward Jorac. The others followed close behind.

The general had to fight his horse to a stop. After trying in vain to make it turn to face Jorac, he dismounted and stopped a few feet in front of Jorac. Red-faced, legs apart, fists clenched, he thundered, "What Have You Done With Virack?!"

If Jorac was an artist, he would have drawn steam coming from the general's ears and perhaps sparks from his hair. He was composing himself to speak, but Monrae stepped up and planted herself in front of the general.

"Saving your miserable life, that's what he's done with it. And your whole stupid army as well. You may be too stupid, too pig-headed to take a wizard with you, but others aren't. So your god-dammed stupid stallion, and the beautiful mare I raised with my own hands, is up on that hill, setting off a trap meant for your whole army. And I hope you choke on it, you and your fat fool!" Hox walked up and stood protectively behind her.

Jorac thought that if a man said this, the general would probably slap him or worse, but hearing it from a woman left him looking nonplussed. "What sort of nonsense are you talking about?" He shook it off and turned to his aides. "Never mind, you heard them admit it. Butrin, arrest them. Horse thievery will do for now; we'll see about treason charges later."

A slump-shouldered, middle aged man dismounted and started toward Jorac, reaching for his sword. A few of the Guardsmen jumped off their horses; one ran up to the man and stopped him. "That won't be needed. Just a misunderstanding. Jorac, you'll come along quietly, right?"

"Right. My best behavior," Jorac said. He didn't want to fight anyone in the army, even this fool of a general, much less the (very competent) Guardsmen he'd been practicing with. Jorac carefully unbuckled his sword belt and handed it, with its two swords, to Lartie.

Monrae was the only one nearby not watching this little drama. She was scanning the hillside above, and so she was the only one to see it start. When she shouted, "Look!" and pointed at the top of the field, Jorac turned his head in time to see a flash of flame cover the whole upper end of the meadow, expanding out from the center in a steady, roiling wave.

The wave of fire reached almost halfway down the meadow and petered out – the grass there was merely smoldering. But clear across the top there was an active sheet of flame. Even at this distance, they could see it was many feet tall and burning strongly.

And then the sound of the explosion hit them – a rumbling thunder that went on and on. Suddenly a wave of something heavy hit Jorac, and he sneezed an explosive, coughing sneeze and fell to the ground. The last thing he remembered was feeling like his head was going to explode.

Chapter 28 - Jorac Awakens Alone

Jorac awoke alone in semi-darkness. He felt terrible, hot and sweaty and weak. He tried to speak, but it came out a worthless croak. Gingerly, he raised his head a little and looked around. He was lying in his bed in the back of the wagon. Someone had left a waterskin nearby, and he managed to unstopper it and take a drink without spilling too much on himself.

He tried to yell but it came out more like a moan. At least it had a little volume this time, and he heard the comforting sound of Hox's voice saying, "I think I heard something back there." Suddenly there was more light, and the sound of someone poking their head into the back of the wagon. Jorac turned his head toward it, but that was all he could manage.

A woman's voice said, "I think he's waking up." Jorac's brain was working very slowly. *Right, that's Hox's new wife. . . Monrae.*

As he heard someone climbing off the front of the wagon, a small cat walked up his bed, stood on his chest, and then started licking his chin. Jorac tried to pet the cat, who promptly sat down on his shoulder and started purring. He was shocked at how heavy his hand felt, and let it fall.

The flap at the back of the wagon was raised, and he could see Monrae standing outside the wagon. "Falcon found you first, I see. How do you feel?"

Jorac found his voice. "Terrible. Weak, tired. What happened?" He waved his hand, but not his arm. "Tell me everything."

"Drink this first." Monrae climbed into the back of the wagon and poured some thin, lukewarm soup into a bowl. She helped him sit up and put some pillows behind him. He tried to feed himself, but she wouldn't let him, so he let spoonful after spoonful of soup enter his mouth and just swallowed.

Lartie poked his head in the wagon. It took Jorac a few seconds to remember the boy's name, and a few more seconds to remember his unusual history, but it slowly came back. Jorac lifted a hand to him and was rewarded with a small grin.

The nourishment made him feel better, and soon he was sitting up and eating unaided – well, drinking the rest of the soup. After another long drink of water and a wobbly-kneed trip to the latrine, partly held up by Hox, he started to feel human again. He came back to the wagon and sat down on the back of it with the others. He started to notice things, like the fact that it was mid-afternoon, and the nearby army camp was busy, but not full.

"Okay, I think I'm back among the living. How long was I out? And what the hell happened?"

While Hox and Monrae looked at each other, Lartie spoke up. "You've been out since yesterday morning. That was the largest release of magic I've heard about since Aplath's Rebellion! The fire up there burned for a good five minutes, even after there was nothing left to burn."

Monrae said, "And there you were, lying on the ground, while that idiot Melsim still tried to arrest you. Luckily Hox set him straight, didn't you, husband?"

"Sweetie, I think your calling attention to what would have happened to the army made most of the difference. Mind you, I don't like to hear language like that from a lady, but I'll grant that you were provoked, and that it worked."

The newlyweds paused for a short hug, and Hox continued. "I was really trying to pass on word to the Guard to look for the wizard, or any wizard-like things. It's pretty clear they have orders to avoid us, but they were standing around there and couldn't help but hear me."

Jorac digested all this. He would have liked to have seen General Melsim getting screamed at, but he had more immediate concerns. "So how did the fighting go? Did the rebels stand, or run, or what? Did we find the wizard?"

Monrae said, "The general led the soldiers on a glorious charge. The history books will speak of it with awe." This was said in the flattest, most sarcastic tone Jorac had ever heard.

Hox grinned. "Everyone was scared, because I told them it was probably another wizard trap. They'd seen saw you fall down, and I was trying to keep them from grabbing you, so I made up some nonsense about you being the last person to touch the horse that triggered the trap. So they were being real careful, and their charge up the hill was barely a walk. The horses didn't like the smell at all, and some of them balked; some of the troops even had to dismount and lead them. Glorious it was not." Monrae snickered, and he smiled at her. "But I'll give them this, they did it. They got their horses to the top and finally fought with the rebels and won."

Jorac said, "Well, that's a relief! Do you know how the fighting went? Did you find out anything about the rebels?"

"Oh, yes." Monrae sounded smug. "Hox and I showed our Observer orders, which are very specific in that area, so the general couldn't really stop us from interviewing our returning troops, and we even got to talk to some captured rebels."

Lartie remarked wryly, "The general wasn't feeling very assertive at that point."

Hox said, "So we found out what went on up there. Our troops got up to the top of the ridge where the enemy was, even while arrows and stones were coming at them. We don't know how many rebels ran away while we were approaching, but it wasn't many, because they'd put trenches and a log wall all the way around their area, and it was just as hard to get out as in. There was some fierce fighting up there for a little while, and then our troops kind of got mad and attacked again without waiting for orders. The log wall the Rebs had built could be climbed, and in one spot we got some ropes on it and pulled it down. That finished things, and it was over pretty quick after that. The second attack on top of the first one must have surprised them."

"What happened to their leaders? Did they get away?"

"Most of them we killed or captured – we took almost a hundred prisoners. And Ozifaj the Sixth is dead. You can be sure General Melsim will talk that up. What's left of their regular troops are probably hiding in the countryside up there, trying to get back home and pretend they never left – we found lots more weapons than men."

"Did the prisoners say anything about wizards?"

Monrae said, "Well, we only got to talk to six of them, and they were just ordinary soldiers; volunteers mostly."

Hox said, "I told them there'd be wizards, powerful ones, asking them the same questions later, and if their answers changed, it would be the worse for them. I'm fairly sure they told us all they knew."

"Which didn't seem to be much," Monrae added.

Hox went on. "None of them had heard about any wizards being around. All they knew was that Ozifaj had some outlander advisors, who were good fighters, well armed, but kept to themselves, had their own cookfires and such. I think they were scared of them. One guy said he saw the bottom of a wagon that had two layers of those cheap pots in it, but they chased him off."

"But we think those outlanders got away," Monrae said.

Hox nodded. "According to our troops, when they were closing in, a group of about twenty skedaddled on fast horses. Some of the General's Guard and cavalry are chasing them. Last I heard, they were heading west toward the mountains. If they don't catch them before they get there, they'll likely get away."

Jorac said, "Hmm. . . I don't have anything except Brownie's story to base it on, but I'll bet those are the ones who've been stirring up rebellions for the past few years. Mercenaries, maybe."

Monrae said, "I hope they catch the bastards. Sorry, husband, those scoundrels. Their horse trap was the meanest thing I ever saw."

Jorac had seen worse, but he tried not to think about it; this was cruel enough. "I hope they catch them too. But we've done our part. Now I think we need to head back to Vaggert. We've found the answer to the question we were asking – they definitely have a powerful wizard."

Hox nodded. "Yep, we've started planning the trip back. Right now, we need to go talk to Nellie."

"Thank her for me. And ask about the horse-boys."

Monrae said, "We'll do just that. Lartie, you stay here and keep and eye on him, right?"

* * *

When they'd left, Jorac turned to Lartie, speaking quietly. "What happened out there – what about their wizard? And what happened to me?"

"Well, the second one is easy. Spell shock. My uncle saw it many a time in apprentices, when they overdid their casting. Nothing to worry about with them; probably affect you the same."

"Spell shock? I'm no wizard. Just the opposite, I'd imagine."

"Well, no. See, there are two distinct traits you need to be a wizard: you have to be able to both shape mana and store it. The ability to shape mana is reasonably common; many people don't know they can do it because they don't have any stored, so there's none to shape. The rare trait is the ability to hold on to mana and store it up for later use. The more you can store, and the better you can shape what you store, the more powerful wizard you are. Virtually everyone who can store mana can shape it."

"But not me?"

"Probably. This is all guesswork, of course. A wizard would need to examine you over several days to be certain, but it all fits. I think you store mana all the time, but since you can't shape it, it leaks out – it has no place to go."

"Except out my nose?"

"As you say. The organ that stores mana is somehow related to the sense of smell – nobody knows the details. Anyway, when you fell over and your hands started twitching a little, I figured it was simple spell shock and you'd come out of it okay. Your headache should go away pretty soon, too."

"That's good to know." Jorac closed his eyes for a moment and decided the headache was a little better already. "So, tell me what you think about their wizard. Powerful, wouldn't you say?"

Lartie paused, then said, "Well, not necessarily that powerful, but at least clever and patient. We can't tell how long it took to charge all those pots with a flame trap. A weak wizard could do one or two a day, a strong one several dozen. And I believe they also get baked in a hot fire as part of the spell. That speaks of long preparation."

"Is it a spell everyone knows? I mean, how well trained is he?"

"Well, I've certainly heard of the spell before, or its relative. As for his training, there's no evidence to support even a guess: We've seen just the one spell." Lartie had adopted a lecturing tone, sounding like the teacher his uncle used to be.

"Of course you're right. I'm still waking up. Any idea how many pots were there?"

"I went up there this morning and looked around – I think there were three to five hundred. I think they've turned into ordinary pots now, or at least the broken ones have. I found a couple of unbroken ones, but I left them alone."

"Wise of you. Do you think they had more than one wizard?"

"That's hard to tell for sure of course, but I'd guess not. It looked as if all the pots were triggered at once, which would mean they were part of a single spell, and that argues for a single caster. It's hard for wizards to work spells together, at least without long preparation and practice together."

Jorac thought a moment. "As soon as my headache goes away, I guess I should start on my report. I certainly have enough material now to write one."

"I hope you'll be lavish in your praise of Monrae and Hox. They really did perform superbly in this situation."

Jorac smiled at him. "I might add that you did too." Lartie smiled back shyly.

Jorac went on, "I'll show you what I write and see if you have anything to add. Meanwhile, see if you can think of anything else that might help us find out more about that wizard. Or better, stop him."

"The latter, by preference. I saw what was left of the horses too."

* * *

Jorac did some slow stretching exercises and went for a brief walk through the camp nearby, just to get his blood flowing. Previously he'd been ignored among the soldiers, but now people pointed at him, and one or two waved at him with a smile. Jorac waved back, and wryly compared it to what General Melsim's attitude would be.

When he got back to his wagon, Hox was looking for him. "There you are. Come on, hurry. We need to go hide in Nellie's wagon. I'll explain later."

Puzzled, Jorac did as Hox bade. It was a tight fit, and her small wagon became stifling hot when the canvas door was dropped. Hox started to whisper, "The guardsmen have orders not to talk to us, and. . ." but was interrupted by a sharp double-knock on the wood side of the wagon.

Jorac heard Nellie's voice say, "Hello, Poznoy. Thanks for coming by."

"Hello, Miz Gompel. Say, Jorac's not around, is he? I have strict orders not to talk to him."

"No, he's nowhere in sight." Jorac heard a slight tap on the wagon.

Jorac could hear the broad wink in his voice. "Good, good. Wouldn't want to disobey orders."

Nellie said, "So, what did you find? Did you catch up to the group you were chasing?"

"Aye, that we did. A sharp chase, it was, and they had some fine, fresh horses. We kept them in sight, but they were starting to outrun us, so we slowed down to spare our horses. Finally we started just walking, leading our horses. We walked most of the night – our horses were spent, and we nearly were too, but at dawn we found where they were pulling out of camp. It's open country there, just below the mountains, not much cover, so we left our horses behind and snuck up on foot. We got as close as we could, then shot arrows at them before they saw us. We even managed to hit a few."

"But the rest got away?"

"Well, that's where it got interesting. We were running at them by that point. We had fifty on foot to their twenty on horseback, and if they'd stayed to fight it would have been a tough one, but they all ran off. All except for one rider. We ran up to him and found out he was dead – a lucky shot had pinned him to the saddle, and his horse kept stepping on its reins and finally just stopped altogether – it was a good horse, well trained. The other riders circled back and tried to pick him up, but we'd gotten there first, so they rode off. Twice they came back and tried to get him, but we weren't having any of it. We killed a couple more, and they nicked up a few of ours. Before they ran off for good, a few of them tried shooting arrows at us. Taj caught an arrow in the arm, just a flesh wound, but it was the damnedest thing – it seemed like they were really aiming at their horse. Good thing they weren't very good shots; they put an arrow through the hair of its tail, but that was it."

"So, was it the wizard on that horse? And what was he carrying?"

"We don't think it was the wizard, unless he was a muscular man with sword-calluses on his hand. But we were very careful, as you might imagine. I made everyone else stand well back from the horse and used a long stick to open its saddlebags. One was empty, but there was a thin-walled glass bottle tied at the top of the other one, and a bunch of papers inside. We untied the bottle very *very* carefully, and took out the papers. The bottle broke in someone's hands right after we untied it, but it just held water. The papers are really fragile; they start sticking to your fingers if they're even a little damp. I think the idea was that dropping the saddlebags or having the horse fall over on them would break the bottle and ruin the papers."

"So they're important. What do they say?"

"We couldn't understand any of the writing. The pages all look like they were written by two or three different people, and most of the letters make no sense, much less the words."

"My goodness, that sounds like a job for scholars." She paused a moment. "We have some here amongst the observers, you know. Maybe they should look at the papers?"

"Yes, we thought of that, though of course we can't suggest anything like it. Observers have wide-ranging rights to, well, observe things. But Jorac and his group, and that young boy related to the head wizard, should stay away. The general can't stop them from looking, but he can stop people from cooperating, or even talking to them."

"Right; I understand. You know, Jorac's leaving soon. He needs to get word back about the wizard here."

"Yeah, we're leaving too. We'll be marching on Tilville tomorrow or the next day. I think there might be an army scribe copying the papers right now. He might even be making an extra copy; he might have gotten his orders confused."

"I think the scholars here should take a look at those originals right away. If that paper is so fragile, a humid day might destroy it."

"Hmm, perhaps so. I could even take them there, if they're around."

After a moment Nellie said, "Wait here." Then Jorac heard her walk away.

Jorac risked saying a low "Thanks."

"Did I hear someone say thanks? Must be my imagination. If it wasn't against my orders, I'd be the one saying the thanks to Jorac, if he was around. And I'm not the only one; everyone who saw that hillside go up in flames thinks the same. And once the campaign is over, and we aren't under the general's orders anymore, I don't think Jorac will be able to buy his own drinks as long as there's a Guardsman around. Hmm, I should really stop talking to myself out loud. Folks will think I've gone crazy. Crazier, anyway."

Hox's well-muffled laughter made the wagon shake a little.

Soon, Nellie returned with two of the scholars, and after they went away with the solider, Hox and Jorac went back to their wagons. They explained to Monrae and Lartie where they'd been.

Jorac said, "After what we just heard, I think we should pull out tomorrow morning if at all possible. Hox, Monrae, can you speak to the cook from the General's Guard and see if you can talk him out of some extra food? I want to move fast, and the more supplies we have the fewer stops we'll have to make."

Monrae asked, "You don't think they'll give us the brush-off – or worse – after what we did to their horses?"

Hox smiled, and said, "From what Poznoy said, the army, and especially the Guard, was smart enough to figure out what would have happened if we hadn't." He went on to explain what they'd heard. Jorac added details where needed to make sure Lartie heard the part about the captured papers.

Monrae listened with interest, then said, "We've been staying in the observer area, but I guess we didn't have to. I thought the army would be upset about their horses; I'm still sad about poor Sunbeam – and angry, too." She smiled at Jorac. "Of course, we had to keep an eye on you too. Lartie was sure you were okay, that you were just sort of asleep, but we couldn't wake you up. When you started snoring, we felt better."

"Snoring?"

"Loud. Don't worry about it; Lartie said it was a good sign."

Jorac shrugged sheepishly. "Well, I do feel groggy, like I slept too long, but it's getting better now. Lartie, would you please talk to the scholars when they get back? I'm going to go talk to the horse-boys, maybe try to clear it up with their boss. I can walk there slowly; that's about my speed today."

* * *

Jorac walked to the area where the horses were kept, but didn't see the two boys he'd tricked. He asked where Poshert the head hostler was, and was pointed to the far side of the large rope corral.

It was a hot day, and Jorac was sweating by the time he got there. To get some height, Poshert had climbed a small tree that formed one of the stakes of the corral, and was scanning the herd of horses and talking to some men below.

Jorac called up to him. "Honorable hostler, I'd like to talk with you a bit, if you have a few minutes."

He looked down at Jorac in surprise, and nodded. "Yarbo, get up here. It looks quiet for now, but keep an eye on the sorrel; we may need to move him again."

Poshert came down and walked along the rope fence, and Jorac followed. "I've come to apologize. It was a dirty trick I played on those two boys – what were their names? – and I'm really sorry about the horses, too."

Poshert stopped. "Well, now, you put me in a tough spot. A real tough one. Half the army thinks I was in on your little stunt, and wants to make me a hero for it. Colonel Kezert is sure I was in on it, and wants to see me in jail. So I told Graxie and Lenafird to say nothing, and I've denied knowing anything. Which I don't – what did you do to those boys to get those horses away?"

"They're what, ten or twelve years old? We got Observer Gompel to lure them away by showing them some juggling and offering to teach them how. They left their new friend Lartie to watch. The horses had just been ridden, and were tired and quiet, just eating their dinner. The boys were supposed to be back in a half hour or so."

"Ah, good, they didn't just run off. They didn't say where they'd been, and I didn't push them. I've had them mending harnesses since then, so I can keep an eye on them. I didn't really punish them, because I didn't know what to think."

"No, they didn't run off. They were probably too embarrassed to tell what happened, at least without some prompting. They got tied up and stuck in her wagon, and she watched them until after midnight. By that time the horses were up on the meadow, where the traps were." Jorac explained the operation with the horses, to an attentive audience of one.

"Canny, that. I've heard of leading a bull to another field that way, using urine from a cow in season, but never a horse. It's a plain shame it had to be Virack and the other officers' horses, but I guess you didn't have much choice."

"We didn't think we did. We had to grab what we could get quickly and quietly. The mare was one Monrae raised with her own hands, and we had to leave her up there too. A cruel trap, hard on the horses. But if it had worked the way they wanted, it would have been hard on the whole army – in fact, there wouldn't be much army left."

Poshert nodded and thought a moment. "So, who else has heard this story? No one in the army has; there are too many rumors going around. Your folks carried you back yesterday morning, and just stayed there by your wagons since then, and we were told to stay away from there."

"We haven't told anyone. But you deserve to hear it, you and the boys. You decide how you want me to tell your part of it, and that's what I'll do. I'm going to try to talk to General Melsim after this, but he hated me before because I worked with wizards, and now he probably hates me more. I don't know if he'll listen."

"He's a mule-headed one, right enough. Just say you distracted the boys to grab the horses, and leave them guessing, okay? I'll do the same, and things may calm down."

"Sounds good. Tell the boys I'm sorry, okay?" He stopped abruptly. "Say, I just got an idea. Suppose I try to talk Nellie Gompel into coming down here and giving them some real juggling lessons? You could watch her do it so they feel safe. If they still want to, that is."

Poshert nodded. "That should help. I'll tell them your story, or parts of it, so they'll know what the stakes were. That should help too. Folks send their boys with me so they can learn to handle horses, but it looks like those two get to learn some more. A good bit more."

* * *

Jorac wasn't surprised when General Melsim refused to see him – more properly, when the man standing guard outside his tent told him to go away. Despite the thick walls, Jorac could hear yelling from inside the tent; it sounded like the general and Colonel Kezert were arguing. Jorac dropped off the very brief report he'd written – three bare sentences explaining that they'd determined the rebels had a wizard and thus they would be returning to Vaggert. Part of him wanted to see the general's face again, but he wasn't sure he'd get any real satisfaction from it.

When he got back to the wagons, Lartie was deep in discussion with the scholars, and Hox and Monrae were putting away food.

Hox said, "The food sellers wouldn't take our money. In fact, we had to beg off taking more than we asked for. We came back with three sacks full as it was."

Monrae nodded. "Goes to show that some people in this army have some sense. Some of this fresh meat we'll have to cook tonight. Maybe we can get Nellie to help us eat some of it."

The meal was wonderful, and even after they all had seconds, they ended up inviting the scholars and Dembo the Drunk (as he'd come to be known) to come over and help them finish it. Everyone was fairly groaning with satiation and satisfaction by the end.

Despite having slept around the clock, and probably helped by the huge dinner, Jorac tired early and crawled into his bed. As he drifted off to sleep, he could hear Lartie engaging the scholars in a discussion of the coded papers; Lartie was getting better at keeping his words like those of a boy, and only slipped occasionally.

* * *

Jorac awoke in the middle of the night when someone knocked on the side of the wagon with a stick. A man's whispering voice said "Psssst – Jorac!"

Jorac said, very quietly, "Here." He sat up. Out of habit, one hand was on his sword, but he doubted a robber would call his name first.

The voice said, "We got the papers copied, for all the good in the world it will do that fat fool. We're giving him one copy we made, but here's a second copy. He just said not to cooperate with what you asked, but this was our idea, not yours. We'll say the originals started to dissolve after that, so we threw them away. Really, we put them between two sheets of paper each; we think that will save them. The scholars think they're related to wizards somehow; maybe you can figure it out. Here they are too."

The man took care to keep his face out of sight, but Jorac saw an ink-stained hand reach around the back of the wagon and hand him a thick stack of papers tied up in twine.

"Anyway, this didn't happen. Go back to sleep."

Jorac called out "Thanks" to the departing footsteps. After a little while, he took the advice and went back to sleep. He felt better than he had in weeks. The army was badly led, but it had some good people in it. And he wouldn't have to stay with it any longer, and he'd get to go back to Vaggert. And Kimma.

Chapter 29 - Heading Home

The next morning they pulled out early and headed their two wagons down the road toward home. After they were an hour away from the army and the trip was getting boring, Jorac let Hox and Monrae's wagon pull a bit ahead, and then asked Lartie to look at the papers.

"Study the copies as you want, but we have to be careful with the originals. They're extremely fragile and have be kept absolutely dry, so they shouldn't be handled."

Lartie started examining the pages of the copy, and made some wordless sounds of interest.

After a few minutes of that, Jorac couldn't stand it any longer, and asked, "So, what do you think? Ever seen anything like that before?"

"I recognize the alphabet, at least. Let me see if the copy is good..." Lartie carefully unwrapped the top page of the original and, without touching it, compared it with the corresponding page of the copy. "It seems like the copy is good enough... But, oh, look here!" He pointed at the original. "See this thin line around the edge of the page? It joins these tiny little symbols in the four corners. This is a magic circle of sorts." He carefully rewrapped the original while he went on talking. "There's a spell where one wizard gives up control of his hand to another; you can use it to do remote writing. If you have one wizard who's left-handed and one right-handed, you can carry on a proper chat from quite a distance, but normally it's one person at a time. It's rather tiring, though, so messages are usually short. I believe this document was created that way; that's probably why you see different handwriting on the same page."

"Fascinating," Jorac said impatiently, "but what's it *say*?"

"I don't know, actually. It's in either Zargronian or Parlundian; it would take an expert to tell for sure. See, Parlund separated from Zargrona before Etrombia was founded, but they kept the same alphabet and general language structure. My uncle saw Zargronian sometimes, but seldom Parlundian, because they think any land with wizards is highly suspect. Their writing is similar to each other but quite different from ours. It's not *this* different, though. I recognize many of these letters, but I should also recognize some of the short words, and I can't. This is probably in code."

"Should I get a wizard to look at them, or some scholar or historian?"

"Probably both. A good wizard – a good one, mind you, with proper divining technique – could probably see traces of the magic left over, maybe even learn something about the writers."

Jorac thought a bit. "So now we have two spells this wizard knows. And perhaps a third – some soldiers once said it seemed like the enemy could see in the dark."

"I wonder. . . It could be that Zargrona and Parlund are at it again."

"At what?"

"Trying to use us to fight each other, or just take us over somehow. It's happened before." His academic lecture voice had returned. "As you learned in school, Etrombia is in between them, and much smaller than either. Zargrona is on the east side of the desert, and is run entirely by wizards; apparently it's not so pleasant to live there if you aren't one. Parlund, off to the southwest, was founded by rebels from Zargrona; they outlaw wizardry on pain of death but have a large population and a well-trained army. Either one would like to add us to their territory. And then there are the historical reasons of course – they both think of us as traitors."

"How can that be? We don't owe allegiance to either one. Etrombia was independent even before the Founding. Or so I learned from my tutors."

"Well, it goes back to that very Founding, well over two centuries ago. Zargrona was in turmoil, with various factions of wizards fighting for control, so lots of people were leaving, especially those who had no magic. They'd hire or steal boats and take off to the western frontier – what's now Parlund. Sometimes the wizards would chase them, sometimes just let them go. Then one day a flotilla of five well-stocked ships went out, and were soon chased by three ships full of wizards. The interesting thing was that the three ships of wizards had their families with them."

"And those were eight ships of the Founding? The famous Sprint, the Kelp Master and the others?"

"That's right. People have been wondering ever since how they got together to start a new settlement. If it was all set up before they left, or something happened at sea, we don't know – they did a very thorough job of hiding all the evidence. But within a couple of months, there was a tidy little village called Vaggert started as far upriver as the eight ships could sail. When the local lord came by, he saw a new fortified village on his land. You've heard the story from there."

"Sure, they managed to parley, and within a year there was a new kingdom called Etrombia, with the wizards swearing support to the lord, who became King Wafeloc the First."

"Correct. So Parlund believes those ships should have gone to them, and Zargrona believes trained wizards would never have been legally allowed to emigrate so those ships should have been caught and returned to them. Luckily for us, it was a number of years before either side figured out we were here, and by then they were busy fighting each other. We've tried to stay strictly neutral ever since. We have trade and diplomatic ties with both, but they hate each other and try to find excuses to fight. Mostly they fight over those tiny, useless outer-sea islands inhabited mainly by pirates, but each has tried to invade the other's inshore islands within my... er, in the past sixty or so years." He dropped his voice. "Within my uncle's lifetime, I mean."

"So you think they're behind this? Or at least one of them?"

"Well, they're both larger than we are, and either would love to take over Etrombia. But we have geography on our side – that nasty swamp downriver, desert to the east, tall mountains to the west, and icy mountains in the far north. And we have wizards at sea, keeping our shipping safe from pirates and the like. We've always been careful to tread a fine diplomatic line, making sure we stay as neutral as we can. Otherwise, one or the other would have managed to conquer us by now."

Jorac thought a bit. "So, if wizards are secretly involved in our rebellion, like those papers show, it's probably Zargrona, right? Unless the Parlundians are willing to give up their principles."

"Zargrona is usually more direct than this, but Parlund does outlaw magic. So it could be someone else. Renegades from either place. Freebooters. Mercenaries. Genuine rebels who found a wizard they could hire. Those papers may tell us, but maybe not, too. We won't know until we get to Vaggert."

Jorac nodded. "And we probably won't know then. If we deliver the papers to the government or the Wizard Council, they'll disappear into some bureaucratic hole and we'll never see them again." He thought a bit. "But maybe we can figure out a way to direct the research so we can learn what the answer is. I hate not knowing what's going on."

Lartie said, "Me too. I'd just love to help you figure it out – but then they'd be bound to wonder how I know what I know." He sighed. "In fact, I'm afraid I should just stay out of Vaggert altogether until you tell me everything's settled down. Do you suppose there's some place I can stay until then? I have enough money to live on for a few months."

"I was going to talk to you about that. Yes, let's keep our eyes open and see if we can find you something suitable on the way." He smiled at the boy. "Maybe someplace where you can catch fish and chase lizards?"

* * *

It took them a week to retrace their path back to Norfort. They might have made better time by finding smaller roads that were a more direct route, but they didn't want to chance a wrong turn. Even without pushing too hard, they moved much faster than the army had. They camped alone at night, in farm yards or small groves of trees, and avoided talking to other travelers when possible. Jorac knew Hox would be noticed wherever he went, and if anyone remembered him as he went north with the army, they'd ask about the war as he headed back. Jorac didn't want to be the one spreading news about the war, especially news about the wizard. If he could quietly enter Vaggert and get the information to people who could do something about it, he'd consider his job well done.

In the evenings, Jorac busied himself writing reports for Pergimtor. He covered everything related to wizards in extra detail; the bit about the demonish writing he attributed anonymously to "another army observer." He reported that Lartimaparian had turned out to be an intelligent older boy, an orphan probably related to his old teacher, who'd written because he'd been imprisoned in a work camp; Jorac had rescued him, so the matter could be considered closed. He also prepared an accounting of the coins he'd been given, and boldly entered the gold he spent at Hox's wedding as "wedding gifts"; he assumed that entry would be challenged, but he was feeling contrary.

In addition to his reports, he drafted a letter to the scholar Gleben, requesting his immediate attention to an undefined matter of some urgency. And he tried to write a brief note to Kimma, but with a pen in his hand he felt tongue-tied. He didn't know what she thought about the last letter he'd sent, so he finally gave up. It would only be another week or so before he'd see her again, he told himself. They could have tried to find a fast horseman to deliver his letters and reports, but it would save at most a day or two, and be rather insecure, so he tried to be patient.

Four days south of Norfort, they reached the lands where the wizards controlled the weather, and in another three they began to see signs that they were nearing the city. Jorac found a friendly-looking farmer going back to his small village, which was well off the main road but just a half-day's ride outside Vaggert. For a few silvers, Jorac arranged for Lartie to stay with the farmer's family there, explaining that the boy had been raised by a bookworm of an uncle and needed someone to look after him for a few weeks.

To Jorac's relief, Lartie seemed pleased with the arrangement. Earlier, he'd given Jorac four names to talk to in Vaggert, and some signed papers and pass-phrases to get them to talk. What remained of his uncle's estate was anyone's guess, but Jorac promised to return in a few days or weeks when he had answers.

Jorac also talked Monrae into leaving Falcon in the village. She was reluctant to do it, but Hox convinced her it was only until they could get a proper house in Vaggert. A village-bred cat would be much safer in a village than in a strange city. Besides, Lartie had grown fond of the fluffy little beast and would take good care of her.

After they waved goodbye to Lartie and got back to the main road, they had a final brief conference before heading in to town. Monrae, who'd never been to the big city of Vaggert, was obviously starting to feel happily excited, and it was contagious. On the last stretch toward home, it was all Jorac could do to not whip the horses into a trot, or even a gallop. Hox and Monrae were in the other wagon, and he was alone with his thoughts of Kimma, the wizards, the war, Kimma, the horses, the wagon, Lartimaparian, Dorrie, and Kimma. And Kimma.

Chapter 30 - Trouble at the Gate

Their good mood lasted until they reached the city and found the main gate closed, with a hundred or more wagons milling about outside. The road to the gate was clogged with wagons, and they'd pulled every-which-way into the hard-packed area outside. Even when the gate was opened, it would be some time before they could get through this confusion.

"What do you mean, quarantine? Quarantine from what?" The speaker was a barrel-chested farmer with a loud voice, but he spoke for them all. "I have six wagons full of wheat here. What do you folks in that city think you're going to eat?"

The guard yelled back from the tower above the gate "It's not a quarantine, it's just an inspection. There's a plant plague loose, out in the farmlands to the west. You can either wait for the wizard, pay for your own wizard, or go back home." He raised his hands helplessly. "Our wizard is tired. We've gone to fetch another, so you'll have to wait. As soon as your wagon gets checked over, we'll let you in."

Another man yelled, "We don't have any plants – we're down from the mines."

"Everybody gets the inspection. You passed through farm country, right?"

The general grumbling from the assembled wagons rose in volume.

The guard was obviously near the end of his patience "Look, it only takes five or ten minutes, but everyone gets inspected. Think we like it? Think we do this just for fun? Just hold your britches, and as soon as we get a wizard back we'll start letting you in."

Jorac could hear annoyed words from the nearby wagons. Apparently this inspection had only started this morning and wasn't particularly well coordinated. A rumor that a plant-plague was loose wasn't good, but Jorac had other things to worry about.

He thought it over, and then signaled Hox, who climbed off his wagon and walked over. "Sorry to do this, but I'm grabbing those papers the army scribes gave us and heading in. I'm going to pull rank on them. Meanwhile, can you put on your uniform and try to get these wagons straightened out – put them in order, give them numbers or something?"

"Sure, no problem. Try to send some more constables out if you can."

"I'll try – but it sounds like they mostly need more wizards. Meet me at Dorrie's tonight, okay?"

"Right. Once they let us through, Monrae can drive your wagon and follow me in." He strode purposefully back to his wagon.

Jorac quickly donned his second-best uniform, two swords, and his two badges, and stuffed his reports, letters, and the packet of captured papers into a satchel he slung over his shoulder.

He pushed his way up to the front gate, and called "Hey, soldier!" A harried guard there snapped "What do you want?" Then, looking at Jorac, he said in a quieter tone, "Can I help you?"

"I'm Wizard Constable Kellor. What can you tell me about the plant plague?" He showed the guard the ugly badge that proclaimed his rank.

"Oh, hello, sir. The wizard this morning said it's affecting all the grains and some of the fruit as well. Makes their leaves wilt. It's catching, and they think it's some sort of a spore or something, but it might be worse, a true wizard-plague. I guess if you're a wizard it's easy to spot, so they're having wizards inspect everyone and everything until they get it sorted out."

"I need to get into the city right away. I have to meet someone; it's quite important." *Kimma's there, and I'm stuck out here!*

"Sorry sir, we have strict orders, no one gets in, not if he were the emperor himself. Not until they get inspected."

"Fetch your wizard, please."

"Uh, sir, he's kind of asleep. The first one this morning lasted about two hours, then called in for his replacement. This one took over, and after about three hours he just fell over, with his hands still twitching. Now he's out like a light. We tried waking him, but no go – that's why we had to send a runner for another wizard. We hope we can get one soon! There's a hundred or more wagons full of food out there, waiting to get in. Do you know how much this city eats, every day?"

"I see. . . I'll be back in a bit."

Jorac walked along beside the stone wall until he was well clear of the wagons. At intervals there were towers jutting out from the wall, and he walked around to the far side of one. Then he lifted his badge of office and pressed its three eyes. He was rewarded, if that term fit, with another nasty sneezing fit – at least he knew the spell worked this time. There was no one nearby to freeze (he hoped there was no one up on the tower, or inside the wall), but this should produce a wizard quickly.

A few minutes later, a figure appeared, levitating over the wall and settling near Jorac. It was Banloz, a wizard Jorac had last seen threatening and bullying in a tavern that didn't allow wizards.

Banloz looked Jorac over with a sneer. "What do *you* want?" The tone might have been used describing something the dog left in the yard.

"Sir – it's Wizard Banloz , right? – I need to get into the city. I'd like you to come with me and help me get past the guards there. They're inspecting all the wagons."

"You called me for *that*? Fat chance! Wait until I report this – it's the last time you get to use that badge, fool."

Jorac had had enough of wizards sneering at him. He turned and walked closer to the wizard. "You will call me sir. Then you will come with me to the guard tower over there and convince the guards that I'm not carrying the plant-plague that they're worried about. And then you'll stay there and inspect wagons until your relief comes."

"Listen, you simple simpleton, I don't take orders from you, or any of your ilk." While he was saying this, he shook his hands free from his robe.

Jorac grabbed the wizard by his collar and slammed him against the wall, pinning one arm against the wall with his knee. He drew his dagger and showed its broad edge in front of the wizard's face. It wasn't the most effective way to use a dagger, but it was very showy.

In a low growl, he said, "If you want to die, dog, a wizard dies as easy as any. Easier. They didn't pick me as Wizard Constable because of my manners; they did it because I get things done. I report to the Council, and you don't – the Council is waiting for my report right now, that's why I called you. You do what I say, they pat you on your head. You don't, they kick you, and you know how hard they can kick. Or you can try casting something, and die right here." Jorac shook him again, just for luck.

All arrogance had left the wizard's face by that point; it was replaced by stark fear. Jorac was still in control of himself. He wasn't really going to do more than rough Banloz up a bit, even if he tried casting spells, but it was obvious the wizard believed him.

"Sir wizard, I mean Sir Wizard Constable, I shall do as you command."

"All of it."

Banloz nodded several times. "Yes sir, all of it. I'll inspect the wagons until relief comes." His voice was quavering, and he was swallowing hard.

Jorac released him and stepped back, sheathing his dagger. "Do it well, and my report won't mention this part. Shirk, or insult the farmers who keep this city fed, and it will. Your choice. Now let's go."

The farmers gave a cheer when Jorac yelled to them, "I brought us a wizard!" Jorac hoped the inspection was something that all the wizards knew how to do – or that Banloz could rouse the other wizard long enough to learn how.

Jorac marched up to the gate with Banloz, and ushered him inside. Then he turned to the jumble of wagons right in front of the gate and tried to get them at least a little organized. He finally got the farmers there to agree on what order they'd go in, which would clear the immediate area. He hoped Hox could do something with the rest.

He spoke to the farmers in front and said, "This wizard dropped what he was doing to help us out here – this isn't his job. So be polite to him, okay? Pass the word, if you would." He didn't know how long it would be before Banloz's usual terrible attitude returned, but he wanted to keep him civil and functioning as long as possible, hopefully until Hox and Monrae could make it into the city.

In a few minutes, when the gate was finally opened, Jorac was first in line. The actual inspection proved to be simple, and he didn't even sneeze. Banloz merely gazed at him and let his eyes grow unfocused for a few seconds, then announced, "He's clean."

Jorac replied punctiliously, "Thank you, sir wizard. I'll tell the council how helpful you've been in this time of trouble."

The wizard's face was warring between its usual arrogance and residual fear of Jorac, and he just nodded.

Once clear of the gate, Jorac found a man with a two-wheeled cart and a sleek horse who offered to take him to the Wizard's Tower for a silver piece. Jorac half-heartedly bargained him down to seven coppers and climbed into the cart. He tried to calm his mind on the trip there, but he wasn't very successful. It was getting to be late afternoon and he hadn't eaten since breakfast, but he still wasn't hungry; he was running on nervous energy.

At the Wizard Tower, he poked his head in his office. There was a layer of dust on everything, which he thought was a good sign. He put the copies of the captured papers in a drawer and set the packet of originals in the circle on the floor where messages from Pergimtor always appeared. He spent a few minutes updating his official report, adding that he'd used his Wizard Constable badge to summon help at the gate, and why. Then he walked to the base of the tower, dropped the many pages of his report into the message box, and literally ran out of the building. He didn't want to be delayed by Pergimtor or other wizards asking him a bunch of questions.

He hurried up the main street toward Dorrie's. His new little house was almost on the way, and he considered stopping there, but he thought it would just delay him. Soon he entered the familiar neighborhood he'd patrolled back when he was a normal constable, and finally came to Dorrie's house.

The sign on her door said, "Communing with the Spirits," which meant she had a customer, but Jorac knocked loudly, then barged in. Dorrie's eyes got big when she saw him. She apologized to her client and quickly hustled him to the kitchen.

Before he could say anything, she said, "Kimma's at your house. Didn't you stop there?"

"I came straight here – well, I dropped off a report for Pergimtor and ran away before he knew I was there. What's she doing there?"

Dorrie put a hand on her hip and looked at Jorac in exasperation. "Don't you know? You were the one who wrote that letter to her. She let me read it, once. The rest of the time she keeps it with her. She's been working on decorating your place – I try to help some. She sleeps over there sometimes; says she feels closer to you that way."

Jorac was embarrassed, but secretly very happy too. "Oh. Um. Yeah, that letter. I can see you're doing well" – he gestured to the client in the next room. "Is she okay?"

"Other than acting love struck, she's fine. How are you? You look good. Where's Hox and this new wife of his?"

"They're bringing the wagons in. They should be here tonight, and I'm fine. Well, sorry to interrupt you. I best be getting along."

"Yes, you had. Stop back here tonight, I'll cook dinner. Now shoo."

"Yes, ma'am." Jorac shooed.

* * *

Jorac didn't quite run to his house (that would have drawn too much attention), but he didn't think he'd ever walked quicker. He fumbled at the lock – his hand wasn't as coordinated as normal – and opened the door. When Kimma saw him, she squealed, "You're home!" and launched herself at him. They stood in the doorway, wordlessly holding each other for a long minute. When Jorac finally bent down to kiss her, he saw she was crying and grinning broadly at the same time. She looked just as he remembered her, except that her dark hair had grown longer and cascaded down her shoulders in loose curls.

"You came back. I knew you would." She gave him a brief, hard kiss, then stepped back a half step, still holding his arm. "Dorrie's been helping me decorate." With her other arm, she gestured at the room.

"I just talked to her. I went there first." He looked around. He remembered the front room as stark and empty, but it had been transformed into a comfortable gathering room with colorful soft chairs flanked by small tables. There were now curtains on the windows and a thick rug in the center of the floor.

"It looks nice. I mean, really nice." He turned to her, and said in a breathier voice, "You look nice too. I'm glad you're here." He drew her close again, and this time it was longer before they let go.

"Let me show you the place. I found this love seat here – I got it partly because I thought it would work for Hox as a chair, and then he went and got married. I wonder if his wife will fit in it with him – oh well, we'll find out. Dorrie picked out the rug, it matches the wood on the windows. . ." One by one she showed Jorac the things she'd selected for the house, pointing out this and that with one hand, while never quite stopping from touching him with the other, or bumping into him with her torso. Jorac didn't mind in the least.

". . . And this is the bedroom." When they got there, Jorac noticed Kimma's face was getting flushed, but she was still holding his hand, pulling him along. After admiring the furnishings in the room, Jorac sat on the footboard and pulled her close and started kissing her in earnest. She responded eagerly, running her hands all over his back, and they were both breathing heavily, almost panting.

Things were about to get very interesting indeed when a loud knocking interrupted them. Dorrie's voice came from outside. "Jorac, Kimma – are you in there?" Jorac heard Hox's voice also, calling his name. "We have your wagon. The man from the stable is parking it out back."

Jorac smiled and said quietly, "Think we can tell them to go away?"

She kissed Jorac lightly and shook her head. "I don't think so. We have plenty of time, now that you're back safe." She went to the door and let them in.

"Monrae, this is Kimma. Kimma, meet Monrae. Hox, you got here fast – how are things by the gate?"

"Once they got two wizards, things went quicker. We were inspected by that wizard you saw in that pub that doesn't allow wizards – he was actually cordial to us."

"He stayed even after the second wizard came? I had to bully him into helping out in the first place."

"Hmm, I didn't know that. Everyone was thanking him for helping out – someone told me he didn't have to be there and was just helping to be nice. I figured a wizard being nice was something to be encouraged."

Monrae added, "We thanked him too. He seemed very pleasant. He's the first wizard I've ever met to talk to; I hope they're all that nice."

Hox and Jorac exchanged a look.

Hox said, "I hope you only meet the nice ones, dear."

* * *

Dorrie cooked dinner that night with ample portions, and announced that her payment for feeding them would be a full accounting of everything that had happened since Jorac and Hox had left for their trip north. Since there were five people (two of them rather over-sized), they ate at the big table in her front room that she sometimes used for séances. Hox and Monrae sat close to each other, and Kimma sat even closer to Jorac – they were at a corner of the table, and held hands under the table when they weren't eating.

Jorac let Hox tell most of the tale, with a couple of exceptions. His drawn-out description of Hox and Monrae seeing each other the first time reduced everyone to tears of laughter. And of course he was the one who had to tell about finding Lartie, but he skipped over the truly interesting parts of that tale. He explained that the boy was only vaguely related to Pergimtor but had used his name to escape the work-camp; they'd left him at a farm on the way in because he wasn't sure of his reception in town and was waiting for Jorac to feel things out for him. Jorac tried to make it all sound like a minor, routine matter. Then he turned the storytelling back to Hox and didn't interrupt again.

By the time Hox had gotten through the dramatic story of the horse traps and was telling about the trip back, Jorac was hardly listening; he was too busy staring at Kimma and wondering what excuse he could find to take her off somewhere and (at least) kiss her thoroughly. And he thought she was feeling the same way, which made him happy – and excited, mentally and physically.

Before the night got very old, Hox and Monrae left; they'd be staying in the Constable quarters tonight and had to arrive there at a decent hour. After they'd gone, Dorrie whispered something in Kimma's ear that made her giggle. Kimma turned to Jorac and said, "Be right back," then bounded upstairs.

"Dorrie, what's she up to?"

"You'll see. She's been learning to be quite the lady. Don't worry, Skowers sent a lady teacher after that first time. She taught her absolutely everything about how a young lady of good breeding and high standards acts. She's learning deportment and etiquette and dancing, and we've arranged for her to be introduced at the Harvest Ball in two weeks. It's not the traditional Spring coming-out party, but this way she'll be recognized when that comes."

"Balls? Dances? What are you doing to her?"

"Jorac, all the nobles are expected to attend these functions twice a year, in spring and fall, plus of course the Emperor's birthday in mid-summer."

"I know she'll do okay, if she wants to. But does she want to? She's Kimma, not. . . not. . ."

Dorrie moved her head closer to Jorac, and dropped the perpetual half-grin that made her face wrinkle with smile-lines. Rather sternly she said, "Jorac, I think you have too narrow a view of that young lady. She's grown."

A voice from the top of the stairs said, "Dorrie, I heard that. Jorac, don't believe her – I still fit this dress." Kimma was grinning as she swept down the stairs, wearing a fancy cream-colored gown with much lace and fine bead work. It had many thin layers of cloth, and rustled as she moved. She looked fabulous in it.

"This is a practice gown for dance lessons – it's almost like what I'm wearing to the Harvest Ball." She looked at Jorac for approval.

Jorac gulped twice before he found his voice. "You fit it very well. Or it fits you. Or both. Or I'm babbling."

Dorrie laughed. "Only a little. Turn around, Kimma."

She did, showing off the large ribbon bow in the small of her back. She turned back and pointed to a lace semi-circle in the front of the dress. "This part is supposed to be an apron, like a farm-woman would wear. It doesn't look much like one, but that's the fashion."

As she showed off other points on the dress, Jorac made agreeable sounds that weren't quite words. He didn't know much about ladies' fashion, but he knew what he liked, and he liked this.

Kimma said, "You're coming to the ball, aren't you? We won't be able to see each other until after luncheon – they separate the ladies and men to start the day – but we can get a dance together. Maybe two." She batted her eyes and pretended to fan herself coquettishly.

Dorrie explained, "If a young maiden wants to show a young man he's favored, she grants him a second dance that evening. She's supposed to be fair to everyone, that day. That's why it starts so early, and runs long into the night."

Kimma said, "You've just *got* to come. I think dancing is about the stupidest way to waste time I've ever seen. If I have to spend a whole evening doing it, I need someone to talk to."

Dorrie shook her head and gazed heavenward, as if to say, "Where did I go wrong?"

Jorac's head was spinning. "Uh, I don't remember any dances. I haven't had any instruction since I was a teen-ager, and I was no good then."

Dorrie said, "We have plenty of time to teach you one. Or two."

Kimma said, "Two. The Kalzie, for one. It's just as stupid as the others, but it's slow and only has a few steps to learn."

Dorrie laughed. "How'd I know you'd suggest that one? You never let go of his hand all dinner, so that's the dance for you two. Anyway, enough about dancing; Jorac is tired and needs to go.   I'm sure the Council will want him early tomorrow."

Jorac was tired, but frustrated too. He didn't want to leave – at least, not without Kimma. He turned to look at Dorrie, who was looking at Kimma.

"Remember, dear, what I told you about propriety."

Kimma grinned at her and said in a happy tone, "Yes, auntie. I'll just see our guest to the door."

Jorac was puzzled as he was led to the door and ushered out. The step down put his and Kimma's face at the same level, and he was expecting – hoping for – a kiss. But instead she pecked him on the cheek, while whispering, "Leave your door. . .," then switched to the other cheek, ". . .unlocked."

Jorac could see Dorrie smiling as she hovered behind Kimma in the doorway. "That's fine, dear. Quite proper. Constable, it's been a great pleasure, please come again. Come inside, Kimma."

The door closed, and Jorac stood there for a few seconds, trying to wipe the grin off his face. Then he hurried back to his little house, where the wagon that had been his home for the past four months was parked. He'd only unpacked a few things, but he wanted to find his soap.

* * *

Jorac had bathed and dressed in clean clothes; he was toweling off his hair when a faint rap came on the kitchen door, and Kimma slipped in. Her hair was covered by a dark shawl, and she was wearing a gray cloak. She looked like just another working-class young woman, out running errands.

Jorac stepped forward and gave her a quick kiss, then stood back and smiled at her. He pointed to the water in the nearby tub. "It's been a long, hot day, and so I took my bath here, since the kitchen floor is stone."

Kimma smiled and said noncommittally, "Wise of you."

"I closed all the curtains in the house first. I just finished washing my hair." He toweled his head again briskly, then hung the towel on the back of a chair and turned back to her.

Kimma nodded, and took a small step forward. "Um. . . I used to help bathe Mistress Madouve sometimes, when her back was hurting."

Jorac put one hand on his back and reached the other out to Kimma. "Come to think of it, my back hurts."

"I think I can help with that. . ." She stepped forward again, reached toward the bottom of his shirt and slowly, tentatively started lifting it.

* * *

In the morning, Kimma was still a virgin. Technically. Barely. But though they hadn't explored the Greater Secret, they'd sated themselves on more than enough of the Lesser Secrets. Kimma had wanted to try many things she'd only heard about, and Jorac was more than happy to oblige, and return the favor. At one point, Jorac had worried a bit until he realized her small noises were just little chuckles of delight, and he relaxed and enjoyed himself – a lot.

When the sun came up, they were comfortable and happy and naked together in the bed. They had time, now, and didn't need to rush things. Jorac reached over and started stroking her hair; she responded with something like a purr and snuggled closer.

"So tell me, what did Dorrie say about propriety?"

Kimma chuckled. "She said a young lady of good breeding had to always maintain the appearance of proper behavior. But – this was the important part – not to confuse the appearance with the reality."

Jorac laughed. "Well, if she asks, I'll tell her you've done everything very properly."

She moved closer to him, running her hand lightly down his body.

"Oh, yes, there. Very, very properly."

And so the Greater Secret was also explored; afterwards Kimma, cuddling next to Jorac, suddenly started giggling.

When he asked her why, she said, "When Dorrie asks about last night, I can tell her the truth – we decided to wait. I just don't have to say how long we waited."

Jorac smiled and pulled her closer. "Almost ten hours. Downright virtuous if you ask me."

Chapter 31 - The Investigation Begins

A few hours later, Jorac got up and quietly dressed. He woke Kimma only long enough to tell her he was leaving and to go back to sleep, and then went to his office.

As he expected, there was a note awaiting him. What he didn't expect were the contents: "Busy all morning. Drop a note for me in box this afternoon – Perg." The originals of the papers he'd brought back from the north were still there, as were the copies he'd put in his drawer.

He found himself rather annoyed; if the papers showed foreign interference in Etrombian affairs, they could be urgent. *Okay, it's up to me, then,* he said to himself decisively. He hung his badge of office under his constable tunic, put the copies of the papers in his satchel, firmly closed his door, and left. After a quick stop to let Cerom know he was back (and arrange lunch), he set off to find Gleben – he'd expected to have to send him the note he'd already written, but now he could come in person. If Gleben couldn't puzzle out the strange writing on the papers, he'd know who could.

Gleben wasn't easy to find, as it turned out. All Jorac knew was that he lived near the library in the university area, a section of town Jorac had never explored. He crossed the bridge and followed the main road west past the palace, to the edge of the district.

On his way, he happened on a jeweler selling delicate hand-beaten silver necklaces. One in a butterfly pattern caught his eye, so he bought it for Kimma. He thought it would look nice on her neck, on that delicate skin, above those luscious breasts – he wrenched himself back to the task at hand, put the necklace away, and asked the jeweler for directions. The man didn't know Gleben, but said most scholars lived around on the other side of the library, and told him how to get there.

The area turned out to be a maze of narrow, twisty streets, where all the buildings were two stories high and had dark brick walls and small doors. Jorac had to ask passers-by twice, and when he finally thought he was on the right street, he still wasn't sure which house it was, so he just started knocking on doors. The first door was answered by a gray-haired older lady who was rather formally dressed despite the early hour.

"Your pardon, madam, but can you tell me where I might find Scholar Gleben? I was told he lives nearby."

Her nostrils flared a little at the name. "Another one, are you? *Master* Gleben lives next door, sadly enough. Though he's seldom there. He spends most of his days at the library, when he's not cavorting with riff-raff from the dregs of society. Now good day to you." She closed the door in Jorac's face. He shook his head and when he got no answer next door, turned around and headed back to the library, which he'd passed on the way here.

Since this was going to be an official request, he pulled his Wizard Constable badge out from under his tunic before he presented himself at the front desk. It raised a few eyebrows but got him prompt attention. The clerk suggested the map room would be the first place to look for Scholar Gleben, and showed him the plan of the building. He also gave Jorac a bright red "all-areas" pass that he was told to pin to his tunic. Apparently such a pass was rarely granted, and he drew some second glances as he walked the halls, following the clerk's directions. As he approached, he could see from the hallway that Gleben was indeed in the big map room, with his head down studying a huge piece of yellowed parchment.

Jorac entered the room and spoke in a loud voice. "Honorable Gleben, the Emperor's Constable Service needs your scholarly assistance. Again. Might we find a quiet place to talk?" Jorac was hoping to provide a salve to the scholar's reputation, since he'd been sworn to silence about his last adventure. The raised heads around the room, and the gratified smile on Gleben's face, meant he'd hit his mark.

"Of course, constable. Let me return this map, and I'm at your disposal." Gleben soon escorted Jorac down the length of the long room, nodding to everyone who looked up. Jorac felt a bit like a game-bird on market day, with everyone sizing him up; he responded by walking beside Gleben in a lithe, agile gait his old fencing-master would have approved of.

Gleben found a small side-room, with a small table and some chairs, and closed the door behind them.

"Ah, Jorac, it's good to see you again – here, sit, be at ease."

Jorac grinned at him. "Sorry I made such a splash in there, but I thought you might like a little recognition for a change."

"Yes, thank you, that was a masterful stroke. Actually, you have no idea how much that will help. There's talk about – they're beginning to say I'm turning into a mere adventurer. There was a particularly difficult time after a tough-looking, scarred old man showed up here. He talked rather like those two brothers I'd hired, and dropped a rather large bag of silver coins in my lap, saying I'd know what it was for. And earlier I'd received a private visit from High Wizard Pergimtor himself, warning me not to talk about our time in the swamp, so when I was among my colleagues I had to say nothing to even their most pointed inquiries. It was rather uncomfortable."

Jorac nodded sympathetically. "I tried to find you at home, and ended up talking to your next-door neighbor. She didn't think much of the company you kept."

"Oh, yes. Widow Haddon is very good at minding other people's business. Well, she'll hear of this, and find another target soon enough; I thank you again. Now, what can I do for you?"

Jorac moved his satchel to the table and pulled out the papers. "Well, you can't ask where these came from, and they're copies of course, but we need to find out what they say. They're in some foreign language, and I've been told they're also probably in code."

Gleben looked over the first few sheets, with their odd glyphs, and shook his head. "Hmm, well. I'm not your man, I'm afraid. I know maps as well as anyone, both old and new, but codes aren't my area of expertise. Nor foreign writing, in the main, except for some mapping terms. Would you like me to introduce you to the proper people?"

"I was hoping that you could handle the project yourself, getting their help and directing their inquiries. You'd know who to ask, and how to ask them."

Gleben stacked the papers and nodded. "Ah, that I can do. I do know many of the people who frequent this building, and their specialties. I presume there's some haste desired here?"

"You're correct, scholar. The sooner the better. I don't know what's written on these papers, but I know that a number of men died trying to keep them out of our hands – you won't hear that again, and I'll ask you not to repeat it unless you must. Please keep the results as quiet as you can. I know you'll need to talk about it amongst yourselves, but do your best."

Gleben's round, well-fed face turned grave. "Constable, I shall indeed do my best. I'll first talk to Sharfo; he likes puzzles, and is well-liked by everyone. Shall I call on you when I know something?"

"How about if I return in two or three days?"

"That might be a bit too soon – but perhaps not. Very well, come back on Fireday. Make it late in the day, if you would. I can't promise you anything of course, but we may have some information by then."

"I can't yet say what I can pay for this. You'll have the Service's and my thanks, at least – I can't promise anything else, but I'll see what I can do."

"You just proved you know the best-loved coin for a scholar, which is recognition of your efforts by your peers. Though of course this is no different from other professions, except perhaps in degree. So I shall ask this much of you: if I and my colleagues are successful in deciphering these papers, let us trumpet our success in some manner, even if we must obscure the details of our task. The last time I worked with you I made out very well in coins of metal, so I have nothing to complain about, but I'll be asking for help from those who possess, how shall I describe it, a purer sense of scholarship."

"That's fair enough. If we can be vague about the details, I'm sure I can arrange something suitable." He stood up to go.

"Very well," Gleben said, "I'll leave it to your discretion." He picked up the stack of papers. "Might I retain this satchel as well? It will keep prying eyes away, and keep the papers together."

"Of course. I have an office in the base of the Wizard's Tower if you need me for anything."

Jorac turned toward the door, then stopped and said, "Would you like – well, I don't want you to take this the wrong way, but would you like to parade me across the room again?"

Gleben chuckled a little. "Ah no, thank you, the one trip we took should prove sufficient; I saw enough of the right people paying attention. The door behind me will let you out into a small hallway, and two right turns will return you to the front desk. I'll expect you on Fireday."

* * *

Jorac's lunch with Cerom was relaxing, if slightly frustrating. He didn't want to say anything interesting about his time with the army, at least until he'd talked to Pergimtor, so he confined his talk to trivia, plus Hox and his new bride. He'd told the story of their first meeting a few times by now, and was getting good at it.

In return, Cerom recounted the news and gossip in town – what happened while Jorac was away, and what was going on now. The newest rumor, he said, was that the inspections of incoming wagons were about to end; apparently the threat of widespread plant plague was a false alarm. Jorac was surprised when Cerom told him that virtually all the crops grown in Etrombian fields were wizard-enhanced, and that a plague affecting multiple species was possible. It had happened a century ago and no one had forgotten it, which probably accounted for some of the overreaction.

Cerom let him go only after getting his promise to tell him "what he could, when he could."

Back in his office, Jorac found nothing new from Pergimtor, so he wrote a quick note to the High Wizard and dropped it in the message box, watched it disappear, and waited.

And waited, and waited. He tidied up his expense report (he was honest with the figures, but fairly creative with some of the descriptions), dusted his office (he sneezed a good bit, but was pretty sure it was the dust, not nearby magic), and waited. Finally, when he could hear the clerks and other day-workers leaving, Pergimtor walked into his office.

"Constable, it's good to see you again. So, did you find wizards in the rebel army?"

Jorac waited a full second, until he'd mastered the urge to yell "Didn't you read the damned report?" He said evenly, "Yes, sir. The details are in the report. They laid a large fire trap of some sort on a hillside. Luckily we were able to trigger it prematurely with only the loss of a few horses; otherwise it would have come close to wiping out the army. But the army was proceeding toward the capitol of West Luverna when we left, and was expecting little opposition."

"Hmm, really? I suppose I'll need to read that report then."

Jorac picked up the packet on his desk and handed them to the wizard. "Yes, sir, please. Here are some captured papers that we believe came from their wizard; they're in a code or a foreign language, perhaps both. They're very delicate, and from the effort the enemy made to keep them from us, seem to be quite important. We believe they need to be examined by experts, wizards good at scrying. I was careful to stress this in the report, sir." That was about as far as Jorac felt he could safely go in criticizing Pergimtor.

"All right, I'll read your report tonight – I apologize for not reading it earlier, but we have the Conclave starting in just two days. I have to preside over it of course, and this year I have extra duties as this year's Terwilger, meaning I have to do some sort of buffoonery-laced skit for the assembled wizards as well. Rather tedious, I'm afraid, but it's tradition."

"Conclave, sir?" Jorac had no idea what he was talking about.

"Don't tell me you haven't heard of it – well, you didn't grow up here; perhaps you haven't. Every third year we get all the wizards we can together and teach each other what we've learned. It's part of the process that binds us together, and to Etrombia. Every wizard who's passed his apprenticeship is invited, and most show up. 'See and be seen, talk and listen, cast and observe' – that's the unofficial motto. The real motto is fancier, but says the same thing."

"I hadn't heard of it, no sir. Will they be gathering here near the tower?"

"Yes, all over the Wizard's Compound. There'll be daily seminars and contests, and parties too of course, and we on the council have to make sure things don't get out of hand. Every large room will be used, as well as the square out front when we gather the group as one."

"I see, sir. So perhaps, with my allergy, I should stay away?" Jorac tried to sound dutiful, not too hopeful. He could use a nice paid rest – especially one he could spend with Kimma.

"That might be best, yes. In ten days it will all be over."

"Yes, sir." Jorac was happy to avoid wizards at any time, especially this gathering. He changed the subject. "There's something else I need to ask you about, sir. I heard of a plant plague yesterday. It was causing a little unrest – or to be more accurate, the testing for it at the gates was causing the unrest. Is there anything I can tell people? It seems the inspections have ceased, at least."

"Ah, Darlora had to go out there – the initial crew wasn't sure what it was, and they sent in a rather alarming report. She's just returned today. A single cloud-cotton tree somehow developed a plant toxin in its seeds, so when this year's seeds started blowing around, all the plants they touched wilted. We were worried it was a return of the general plant-plague of evil days past, the one that nearly starved this city, but it turned out to be just the one tree that was a problem, and it doesn't seem to be contagious except through the seeds. In fact, Darlora brought some of the cotton puffs back to study – what do you make of these?"

He took a small box from a hidden pocket and opened it up. Inside was a mass of wispy bits of near-white plant material, rather like thin cotton. Jorac had seen cloud-cotton seeds many times before; some years they'd covered the whole landscape around some of the trading roads he had traveled. At the center of each cottony mass there was always a tiny seed, but instead of the usual solid dark color, these had minuscule red spots.

He leaned in for a closer look, and sniffed the box, but didn't touch the seeds. "That smells odd. I've seen these before, but not with the red spots, and I don't remember that odor. You say they wilt other plants?"

"Yes, exactly, by a mere touch. You've traveled a good bit more than I have: does anything come to mind?"

Jorac thought it over. "No, sir, sorry. I can ask one of the scholars, if you'd like."

"That's already being done. Why don't you make yourself scarce for a while, starting tomorrow? Carry that badge with you – as long as you have it, I can find you."

Jorac took the badge from around his neck handed it over. "It will need recharging, sir." He told about summoning Banloz to get into the city quickly, but only part of the reasons why. Wanting to see Kimma was none of Pergimtor's business.

"All right, I'll have someone recharge it. Pick it up here tomorrow. Anything else?"

"My expenses, sir. I have a small portion of coppers to return." Jorac showed him another stack of papers. He expected Pergimtor to tell him to give it to his clerks for inspection, or at least skim over a page or two, but the wizard merely flipped to the back page and signed it.

"Not the type to cheat, are you." It was more a statement than a question.

"Not too badly, sir. Nothing extravagant."

Pergimtor chuckled a little. "Honest, too. Don't let this go to your head – next time I might scan every line. Give this and the leftover coppers to my clerks; you'll have a few months' pay to pick up too. I'll see you in ten days – no, make it two weeks. When you come back tomorrow, empty out this desk. I can put four or five clerks in here while you're gone." He turned to go.

Jorac spoke quickly – he was worried that Pergimtor didn't understand what happened, and wouldn't read the report. "The enemy wizard – he probably escaped."

Over his shoulder, Pergimtor said, "Yes, well, we can look for him later – maybe we can use him for the scrying competition. Until then, the army will have to deal with him themselves." And with that, he was gone.

Jorac stood there for a few moments, trying to sort out his jumbled feelings of exasperation, worry, relief, and excitement. Finally he shook his head, spent a few minutes emptying his desk contents into a box, and wrote up a whimsical schedule for the next two weeks. It had "Work" crossed out and "See Kimma!" written for each day, plus "Collect Pay" for tomorrow, "run errands" the next day (that was code for "scout for Lartimaparian's creditors"), and "visit Gleben" for Fireday. He'd enjoy showing the list to Kimma.

* * *

Jorac went to his house, where he found a note from Kimma telling him to go to Dorrie's and let himself in the back door. The note had beautiful penmanship, but slightly awkward grammar – he remembered she'd had a hit-or-miss education, and was happy she wasn't illiterate like much of Swampside. It also had some rather naughty endearments that made him feel like skipping up the street on his walk to Dorrie's.

He quietly let himself in the kitchen door and listened to the women in the next room. Apparently Dorrie had a female client and Kimma was acting as assistant. The client was being told to look for her missing necklace under a bed on the top floor of her house, where the servants quarters were. Jorac was rather impressed at the mention of live-in servants; Dorrie's scheme to get a better grade of clients seemed to be working.

When the client had gone, Dorrie and Kimma joined him in the kitchen.

"Hi ladies. I got the papers to Gleben, and I just talked to Pergimtor. Here's my schedule for the next two weeks." He showed them the schedule he'd written.

Kimma rewarded him with an exaggerated kiss. Dorrie looked amused but said, "Propriety, dear."

"Oh pooh, auntie. Jorac's house has access to three different streets, and no one notices a poorly dressed working-class girl carrying a bundle of old clothes."

"They might, if you're not careful. You mind you wear that floppy hat. Maybe get a couple more, too."

Kimma said, "Let me see that schedule." She found a pen and added "Dancing lessons" on three evenings and "Dinner at White Swan" on a fourth. A week from next Fireday she wrote "Harvest Ball!" across the whole day.

"There, that's better. So, why did you get the time off? Some sort of reward for your trip?"

"There's something called the Conclave starting day after tomorrow, where all the wizards gather in the wizards' compound for ten days – I got Pergimtor to let me off until it's over. Dorrie, will you be going to the Conclave?"

"I suppose I'll have to, at least for the first day and the big dinner at the end. When I joined the guild, they talked like attending the Conclave was a great privilege, but it sounds like a fairly large snooze to me. Most of it will be over my head, but what can you do?"

Jorac grinned at her. "Better you than me." I'd be sneezing at people."

She looked at him quizzically. "At people?"

"Yes, from now on I'm going to sneeze *at* someone. At whom? At-*choo*!"

Dorrie pretended to slap him, while Kimma just laughed.

* * *

Dorrie had one more appointment that morning, but Jorac managed to get Kimma alone for a late lunch in the market. He picked this time – in the daylight, when people could be more sensible – to ask something that had been worrying him.

"Kimma, remember when you first moved to town, I asked you to make sure you're comfortable going along with Dorrie's plans? It's still none of my business, but I still don't want you to be pushed into anything you don't want to do."

"I've thought about it. Actually, I kind of like the idea. You know where I started out, and that I'm not really – her voice dropped – "Miz Madouve, or" – in her noble's accent – "Kimathea Ravensclough." Then she went back to her normal city voice, "But I think when I'm plain Kimma I'm really kind of dull. When I put on the accent and the clothes, and become someone else, then I'm free, sort of. It's fun."

"The Noble Lady does suit you."

"As the Noble Man does you." The look she gave him was past smoldering and well into incendiary, and he knew they were both wanting to make a quick detour toward his bedroom, despite the early hour.

"Well," he said hoarsely, "as long as you can accept 'dashing' and not 'suave.' I'm better with sword work than a dance step. I don't think I'll ever learn to dance smoothly."

She leaned down to him and whispered "But your sword work is simply wonderful." Then louder, she said, "Propriety," and giggled.

Jorac growled, "I've heard of it. Scrumptious vixen, I've heard of it." Still, he managed to keep his hands to himself, except for a quick pinch of her knee below the table.

* * *

The next morning, Kimma left Jorac's house early in her plain clothes, but Jorac slept in – he thought he was developing a cold, because his head felt stuffed up and his nose kept running. Still, he dutifully went down to the Wizard's Tower to finish emptying his office and collect his pay and the recharged Wizard Constable badge. People in the area were running around distractedly, preparing for the Conclave opening, and he was glad to get out of there and home again.

His cold was still with him that evening, when he went with Kimma to his first dancing lesson. He found the footwork very dull until he turned it into sword-work exercises in his mind, and then he made rapid progress. After an hour or two he thought he could learn the routines well enough to at least keep from embarrassing himself, or Kimma.

By the third day with nothing much to do, Jorac was beginning to get bored; at least his cold was getting better. He did get to have lunch with Kimma while Dorrie went to the opening ceremony at the Wizards Conclave, but the only other thing he accomplished was finding an investment house that not only admitted they still had Lartimaparian's accounts but agreed to start the elaborate process of transferring the assets to Lartie, the old man's heir. Jorac counted that as a minor triumph, but he was also beginning to feel vaguely anxious.

That night, Kimma asked him what was bothering him. He looked at her in surprise. "I didn't know it showed." He thought a moment. "I don't know, I guess I don't like it that there's so much going on at once. There are foreign wizards trying to interfere with Etrombia, and the army's late getting back from the north, and all the wizards in the country are having a big party and not paying attention to anything but themselves. It just makes me nervous."

She frowned thoughtfully. "Yeah, I see what you mean. It does seem a little odd, doesn't it? It might be harmless, might not. Maybe you'll find out more when Gleben tells you what the captured papers say. Then we'll know whether we ought to be worried or not." Then she playfully pushed Jorac toward the bed and said, "But meanwhile... we should practice our dancing."

"Dancing?" Jorac was puzzled, given her attitude toward the activity.

"Yes, If we have to do the damned thing, we may as well get it right. I thought up a variant of the Kalzie. Hold your hand out, there you go."

They spent perhaps a minute practicing formal dancing together, but soon drifted into a version that involved gradual removal of their clothes – a dance that wouldn't be suitable for public viewing.

* * *

On Fireday, Jorac looked up his friends in the Constable service and had lunch with Cerom, Schrog, and Hox. To much amusement, he and Hox told funny stories about their time with the army and what they saw up north. After lunch Jorac spent some time exercising in the compound and chatting with the constables. But by mid-afternoon his impatience got the better of him, and he set off to visit Gleben. It wasn't exactly "late in the day" as Gleben had requested, but he couldn't stand it any longer.

When he got to the library, a friendly clerk helped him find Gleben, who was ensconced in a small private room with two older men. After the clerk left and the door was closed, Gleben greeted Jorac and introduced him to his companions, Scholar Sharfo and Scholar Hebalan. "We have some results for you," Gleben said, "but not as many as we'd like. Sharfo, would you tell him what you found?"

Sharfo was a gray-bearded man with a thin face and happy eyes; you could tell he spent most of his time smiling. "We still don't know if the language is from our neighbors to the East or to the West; there aren't enough examples of words that would convince us either way. But we've figured out most of the writing. It's in the simplest possible code – just good enough to stop someone from reading it over your shoulder, so to speak. Each letter always maps to the same one, so it was easy enough to figure out. We had to guess a bit on the numbers, though we think we have them right. What we're having trouble with is what it *means*. We think we have the translation right, but some words don't make sense, and certainly some of the text doesn't. Some of the words we don't recognize are probably people's names, but we can't be sure."

Hebalan read from the paper in front of him. "Here's a typical example. *'D 164. Rocky hill, poor chase. Ozifat still idiot.'* We aren't sure about that; we think it's the name of the rebel leader – it gets spelled a few different ways. Then the notes say the next line was in a different hand; it says, *'Sorry to hear that. Run away slowly. Try potty soon.'*"

Jorac walked over and looked at the rest of the translated page the man was reading from. He read the next few lines.

"Potty failed – all on foot. Will try tomorrow night."

"Do your best. I know it's hard."

"Success. Potty test worked well, Palamar also. 27 d. One squadmember hurt, 15 allies d. A very good night."

"Well done. Run away."

Jorac was chilled a bit when he realized he was reading about the night ambush that killed men – he'd seen the aftermath with his own eyes. And who, or what, was "palamar"? He read three more pages. They were in much the same vein, and seemed to be dispatches from the rebel's wizard back to – who?

Jorac looked at all the papers scattered across the desk. "Is it all like this? Short little dispatches?"

"Yes, mostly. Most are only a few words, but a few are longer."

"Do the longer ones say more? I mean, are they more useful, more important?"

The scholars exchanged glances, and Sharfo replied. "That's what we were trying to figure out. Here's what one says, *'You may think you're like the pigeon with the apple, but worry not. It's a difficult thing you do and you'll soon find yourself like the mouse with the mountain cat.'* And then the reply comes back, *'More like the eagle than the pigeon, I would hope.'''*

Gleben said, "And that's where we get the longest single entry, and it makes the least sense." He read:

> *"Ah, you have at last hit upon it properly. I don't see how we missed it before. The king fox, baying on a hilltop. And four eagles, not just one, and you playing the owl. I so look forward to laughing about this with you at a tavern, when we've won.*

And the reply is just, *'Ha! Perfect! I'll be there.'''* He shook his head. "None of this makes sense. It could be a code within a code, or else we're missing something."

Hebalan said, "I couldn't find any reference to a king fox in any of the zoology references. And the three animals together are rare, though it happens when there are a large number of mice about. But the mouse is mentioned with the mountain cat."

Sharfo added, "And pigeons rarely eat apples, it seems. We've consulted some bird experts about this passage – we didn't tell them why, of course – and they were puzzled too."

Jorac thought a moment. "I've seen mountain cats hunting mice – they do it quite well, but it's not much of a meal for them. You're right, it's puzzling. Is there anything else here that might bear on it?"

But most of the other pages were short passages, describing what Jorac recognized as the recent army campaign. When he tried putting the pages in order by the occasional numbers in the corners and what he knew of the campaign, he found the last entry was, *'Charg'd 22 P. All well. Tired.'* Unfortunately, that seemed to have been written a good week before the spoiled ambush on the hillside. He would have loved to find more about the days leading up to the ambush itself, but it just wasn't there.

"Did you make a list of the words – names, perhaps – that you didn't translate?"

Sharfo replied, "Not yet, but we certainly can. It shouldn't take very long."

Jorac spent another hour with them, going over the dispatches. He took the one finished set of translated pages, so he could give it to Pergimtor for immediate analysis, and the scholars said they would work on a second copy for the army's intelligence officers (though most of their analysts were probably still in the north).

Preparing to go, he thanked the three scholars, rather effusively, for their fine work, emphasizing the importance of their information for the Emperor's Constable Service, the Wizard Council, and the safety of Etrombia, and making sure they knew it was strictly confidential. He apologized for not being able to pay them in gold, but assured them he'd try his best to see they'd eventually get credit for their efforts.

They seemed pleased enough with that, and Sharfo and Hebalan bid him good afternoon and left. As Gleben also rose to go, Jorac said to him, "I think my next move should be to go talk to some army veteran, don't you? There are a few who are still here and not up north. I can ask them about possible wizard involvement the past few years. Maybe if I told them about what we found, they'd notice a pattern." He shook his head and said, almost to himself, "I don't know much about the part of the army that stays behind, but I guess I can find out if I ask around."

Gleben said, "I've met the man in charge. His name is Wakkar – he comes to the library sometimes, rare for an army man. I think he's a captain?"

"Excellent! I can ask for him. Suppose I leave the second set of translations with you to give to him? You can answer his questions better than I could anyway. Do you mind guarding a confidential set of documents again till he shows up?"

"Not a problem; send him to me. It will be interesting to get to know a real army man." Gleben did indeed have the soul of a scholar.

Jorac gathered up the original papers and Pergimtor's translation set and bundled them into his satchel. Doing that reminded him of the necklace he'd bought for Kimma, and had forgotten about until now. He said, "Say, did you find a small package, wrapped in light paper, in the satchel here?"

Gleben answered in a conspiratorial tone. "Yes, when I saw what it was, I had it delivered to your office. Didn't you get it?"

"Oh, thank you. I've been out of my office the past few days." He smiled ruefully. "You know about the Wizard Conclave? Well, the wizards would rather have five clerks in my office than one Constable this week. I'll go fetch it tomorrow. Thanks again."

Gleben's only reply was a broad wink.

Chapter 32 - A Wizardly Flu?

First thing the next morning Jorac visited the local army headquarters. It turned out to be in the base of the Emperor's palace itself, no doubt a remnant of an earlier time. Jorac introduced himself to a skinny, bored clerk at the front desk, and asked to see Captain Wakkar.

"Kellor, hmm. Constable, hmm. Wait, are you the observer, went out this year?"

Jorac nodded, and noticed he had the man's full attention now. The clerk rose quickly and went to the doorway behind him. He yelled, "Hey, Zreed! Duty calls! Take this guy to Colonel Wakkar!" The clerk turned back to look at Jorac, then turned back and yelled, "Hurry!"

Colonel Wakkar was a swarthy, beefy man, just starting to go gray at the temples. He rose from behind his desk and walked over to shake hands with Jorac, who could hear his peg leg thumping on the floor before he could see it. "Honorable Kellor, good to meet you. My friend Poznoy mentioned you in a letter he wrote. Have a seat."

Jorac thanked him and sat. "That'll save us some time, I imagine. You know I was sent out to look for an enemy wizard?"

"Yes, and I know you found him. The fire on that hillside. . . Poznoy is a dull writer, just facts, but he went on for half a page on that one. Must have been quite something."

Jorac would have liked to have seen it himself, but he just nodded knowingly. "Did you hear they captured some enemy papers, likely from the wizard?"

Wakkar looked at him with greater interest. "That I didn't know."

"We're keeping it very quiet of course. They were in code — a simple one, apparently. They seem to describe the campaign from the enemy wizard's point of view; short little dispatches, very cryptic sometimes. Have you ever heard of a 'king fox,' maybe with an eagle?"

Wakkar's blank look was enough for Jorac. "Here's why I'm asking. There was an odd, seemingly important passage that puzzled us." He closed his eyes and recited from memory:

> *"The king fox, baying on a hilltop. And four eagles, not just one, and you playing the owl. I so look forward to laughing about this with you at a tavern, when we've won."*

He shrugged. "Which might mean anything, but it seems strange – it's the only time they mention winning. The rest of the time all they talk about is delay or running away."

"Well, they're still doing it. The last I heard, the rebels regrouped, even without their leader, and they were still making the occasional attack around Tilville – even after we took the city without a fight. Extra-long campaign this year; they'll be lucky to miss the snows on their way back."

"I see. Well, I can't say I envy them the snow."

Wakkar shook his head. "Weather is better here, that's for sure. Before I forget, I should show you something." He opened a bottom drawer and pulled out a sheet of paper, and laid it flat on the desk in front of Jorac.

Jorac started reading. The introduction said, "By the authority of the Defender of the Realm, General of the Army of Vaggert and Etrombia, Count Danak Melsim. . ."

Before he got any farther, Wakkar said, "Now, don't let this worry you. I think we have it handled."

It wasn't until the third paragraph that Jorac understood the document: it was calling for his immediate arrest for nineteen counts of horse-thievery. Jorac looked up at him.

Wakkar smiled at Jorac. "The clerk wrote this on a separate sheet of paper. He didn't include it with the other orders." When Jorac still looked puzzled, he continued. "A single sheet of paper can get lost. That clerk is no fool; he doesn't want to embarrass his commanders, but he's heard the tales of that fiery hillside. Making it separate is his way of telling me this order should get, um, mislaid, for a time at least. When the army gets back, send me a note before coming here, just to check. But as of now, I've not seen this paper myself – I have shockingly sloppy clerks sometimes, poor sorters and filers, the lot of them."

Jorac smiled as the paper went back into the bottom drawer. Not everyone in the army was an idiot. "Thank you. If tomorrow you ask for Scholar Gleben at the library, he'll give you a copy of those wizard's papers."

"You think I should look at them?"

"I do – but keep it quiet until we can figure out why it's important. As a soldier, do you like it when the enemy does something, does it pretty well, and you can't figure out why the hell he did it?

Wakkar's pinched face and headshake was enough for Jorac. "Gleben's been told not to talk about it to anyone besides you. He'll be expecting you."

* * *

The next item on Jorac's agenda was to retrieve the silver necklace he'd bought for Kimma, so he headed for the Wizard's Tower. He prudently went in by the far side door, avoiding the probable crowds of Conclave-goers in the compound, but when he got to his office, he was surprised to find the door locked. He'd been given a key but never used it – in fact he almost never closed the door, deciding it was basically futile when surrounded by wizards. But he still carried the key on his belt, so he unlocked the door and let himself in.

Inside, sitting at his desk, was a weak-chinned, pimply-faced woman with scraggly red hair. Exquisite white wizard's robes hung on her scrawny frame, and she had obviously been crying.

She shrieked, "Close that door!" Jorac recognized the voice, and suddenly recognized the woman too.

As smoothly as he could, he said, "At once, Milady Darlora," and closed the door behind him.

"At least you recognized me, unlike Pergimtor. What are you doing here?"

"A small package was delivered while I was away. I need to pick it up."

She opened a drawer, and put the package with the necklace on the desk. "There you go. Now get out of here. I don't want anyone to see me like this."

Jorac didn't like the sight much either – Darlora was lucky she could change her looks – but he had to find out what was going on. He walked forward to take the package, and get a better look at her. "Your pardon, ma'am, but what has happened to you? As Wizard Constable, I need to know."

"I got sick. Now everyone will be blaming me for bringing this back to the Conclave." She sniffled loudly.

"I beg your pardon, but what are you talking about?"

"Dammit, look at me! It's – they're calling it Darlora's Tears. But dammit, I didn't do it! How could I know?" Her voice was tight, and tears did indeed start leaking from her eyes.

Jorac was at his most deferential, and tried to use his most kindly tone. "Know what, Esteemed Wizard?"

Between sobs, she explained. "That fucking cloud-cotton tree – it's not really a plant plague, it's an anti-magic... something, maybe a plague. So I started sneezing, and thought it was just a cold, and then I lost my power. And now it's spread to most of the Conclave. Everyone is snuffling and sneezing, so in a week or so they'll all lose their powers."

Jorac must have look shocked, because she continued, "Oh, don't look at me like that, they'll come back. Eventually. But it may take a *week*! Or even *more! Wahhh!*" She started sobbing again, while Jorac collected his thoughts.

"How could they blame you? It seems you're an unfortunate victim."

Darlora looked up in hope, nodding. "That's what I told Pergimtor! My whole mana-store, gone, like popping a soap bubble. I didn't have anything to do with it! Why did they name it after me!" Darlora started crying again, tears running down her face, which she wiped messily on her sleeve. Jorac felt the normal male impulse to comfort her, but stayed on the other side of the desk.

"Do you know how it started?"

"It was them! Two lower-level wizards. They found the cloud-cotton tree that caused all the worry, and didn't find the real cause. They caught it first, so they're really to blame. They tried to hide it at first – damn them! – so when Pergimtor sent me in to finish up the mess they made, they were probably laughing at me. I'll remember those two, that I will!"

"Yes ma'am." Jorac didn't think the two were at fault, exactly, but he wasn't going to get between Darlora and the unfortunate pair. "Do the effects come only from exposure to that tree or its seeds? Or are you saying the loss of magic is, well, contagious? At least to wizards?"

"Everyone is sneezing at the Conclave. So everyone will end up the same – like me!" She put her head down on the desk and started crying in earnest. Her response wasn't an answer at all; it wasn't as bad as talking to Wolburn, but the same self-centered attitude was in evidence. It must be endemic to wizards.

"Is there anything I can bring you? Food, or drink perhaps?"

Without raising her head, she waved him away. "Just go. Don't tell anyone."

Jorac said, "Yes, ma'am," and left the room quietly. He stopped to lock the door behind him.

* * *

Jorac needed to talk to Pergimtor, but when he stepped outside, he saw booths set up in the main courtyard and people wandering among them. Across the yard was a woman juggling fireballs, and near her was a dragon shaped from smoke. Nearby a barker was touting his potions, while another was shouting to the throng to step right up, the demonstration was about to begin. Jorac thought there was no point in searching in the courtyard; he'd be sneezing too hard to talk to Pergimtor even if he found him, so he ducked back inside.

By liberal use of his badge and a superior attitude, he managed to find the head wizard in a large ground-floor room, talking with some young men about an upcoming skit. He asked them to wait for a moment and walked over to speak with Jorac.

"High Wizard, the scholars have deciphered the enemy wizard's writings."

"Oh, yes?" Pergimtor was interested, but also distracted. His voice said that he too had the stuffy head Darlora had described.

"They're mostly daily dispatches back to someone else, another wizard, telling about the campaign. There are a few puzzling parts I'd like to get some help with."

"Well, after the Conclave we can find someone to help you." He glanced over to the men he'd left, who were looking back at him, waiting.

"I just talked to Darlora."

Pergimtor turned back to Jorac, with more attention. "She was distraught, yes?"

"Yes, to put it mildly."

Pergimtor shrugged philosophically. "She's a woman – very strong magically, but a certain type of woman at heart, vain about her looks. Since she's strong in her magic, it took some extra time for it to affect her. It looks like I'll be affected too, but I'm not worried. The two wizards who first lost their power reported it came back as strong as ever. This happens to apprentices sometimes, when they're learning to shape and shield their mana store – the bigger the store, the longer it takes the power to come back, but it always comes back. So I just have to adjust my tasks a bit. That's what we're working on now – we have to change the skit around, and shift a few of my responsibilities. A bother, that."

Jorac nodded, grateful that Pergimtor had a better attitude than Darlora. "Will it affect only those who were exposed to that tree? Or does it pass between people?"

"Oh, just the tree I think. And its seeds of course. A few more people came in contact with those, but we've locked the seeds away now. I can't see how something like that could become contagious."

"Can you tell somehow? With magic, I mean?"

Pergimtor was losing patience, and returned to his lecturing-a-schoolboy voice. "No, we leave anything affecting the nose alone. A wizard can help heal his own broken arm, for example, but many wizards have damaged their own powers just trying to cure a common cold. Every apprentice knows this. Now, I'm quite busy. Is there anything else?"

"No, sir. Thank you." Jorac made his way out through the near-deserted interior hallways, and didn't sneeze once.

* * *

By then it was mid-afternoon, and Jorac took his time walking home. Now he had several mysteries to deal with. Why did the enemy wizard want delay, delay? Were they deliberately keeping the army tied up? What were the animal references about, and did they mean something important to Etrombia? And the plant-plague was a new worry. He could tell Darlora was going to cause trouble when she got her powers back, and he might be expected do something – hopefully, something that didn't put him in her line of fire.

He changed out of his uniform, then went to Dorrie's house, where he found Dorrie and Kimma preparing dinner for the three of them.

While the women puttered in the kitchen, Jorac told them about his day. They smiled and teased him about the arrest warrant for horse-thievery. Then he told them what he'd found at the Wizard's Compound, from the apparently toxic cloud-cotton tree seeds, to a transformed (or un-transformed) Darlora, to Pergimtor calmly preparing to lose his powers for a time. They were more serious then.

Kimma asked, "So does this mean all the wizards are going to catch it?"

Jorac frowned. "That's what worries me, even though Pergimtor said he didn't see how it could be contagious. Dorrie, you were at the Conclave on opening day. Do you still have your magic powers?"

"I think so. Want me to try something?"

"Yes, please. Don't worry about me sneezing."

Dorrie made the rainbow lights appear from her fingertips. She'd had plenty of practice at it, and made a graceful gesture with her hands.

Jorac didn't sneeze. He just stood there, breathing normally.

The women looked at him in near-amazement. Dorrie said, "Why didn't that affect you? Do you have some sort of new shielding?"

He took a moment to answer. "I think I know what's happened. Lartie's read a lot of books, and he explained it to me. He says there are two things needed to become a wizard, and he thinks I have the rare one but not the common one: I can store the mana that makes a wizard, but not do anything with it. I got that cold after I sniffed the infected seeds Pergimtor showed me. So, right now I don't have a mana store, just like Darlora. Though I presume it'll come back."

Kimma said teasingly, "So you should gather those seeds and use them all the time."

"Perhaps. But if it *is* related to my head-cold, I'm not sure it's worth it – I was pretty uncomfortable there for a day or two." He shook his head. "What I'm afraid of is that it might be spreading from one person to another. Darlora told me everyone at the Conclave had a cold."

Dorrie said, "I was there again yesterday, and you're right. Everyone has a handkerchief out. I caught it a couple of days back, but it went away pretty quickly."

"And now you're okay? And you still have your magic?"

"So it seems. I heard this isn't the first Conclave where colds were passed around."

"Good. So apparently I was worried about nothing." He sighed. "Except the 'king fox' mystery." When he'd told them yesterday about the scholars' translations, the puzzling animal references hadn't rung a bell with them, either.

They sat down to eat dinner and went on to happier topics. Kimma's new dress was ready, and she'd be modeling it for them tonight after they ate.

Jorac drew the paper with the necklace in it from his pocket, and said "I hope this fits in with the dress."

Kimma squealed with delight when she opened it, and ran upstairs. Dinner was delayed until *after* the dress-modeling. The necklace would need to be shortened a little, but it would work very well. She looked wonderful in the dress, and Jorac wanted to ravish her then and there, but . . . *Propriety.*

* * *

The next morning, Jorac was awakened very early by a tapping on his bedside window. He rolled away from Kimma long enough to peak through the curtains, and saw Dorrie peering in, looking worried. She motioned to the door, and he nodded. He threw on a robe and let her in.

The first thing she said was, "I've lost my powers. When I woke up this morning, I felt something sort of pop."

Jorac had a sinking feeling. "Like pricking a soap bubble?"

"Yes, exactly. I thought you'd like to know."

"So, it *is* contagious." He concentrated. "Let's see. . . if the wizards stop controlling things, the weather may change – but it's usually nice this time of year anyway, so we may get by. But the fountains. . . that's the key. If they stop, people will probably panic. We've got to go to the Conclave and make sure they know that."

Kimma had gotten up when she heard them talking, and they shared a quick, worried breakfast. Kimma would go back to Dorrie's and postpone the only client appointment they had that morning, while Jorac and Dorrie would go and try to talk to the wizards.

At the Conclave, there was a new sign up, "Guild members only," and a squad of hired guardsmen at the gate. Jorac could see through the iron gates to inside the wizard's compound; the formerly festive atmosphere was somber now, with empty booths and small huddled groups of wizards in the courtyard. But he couldn't get in.

Jorac tried to charm, then bluster his way in, but even with his Wizard Constable badge he was firmly denied entry. The guards were checking guild badges and their owners against a written list; they apparently had very strict orders, and were following them.

Jorac went back to Dorrie and told her, "No dice. Sorry, but it's up to you to get in and make them understand somehow. Most of those people think – well, I don't know what they think, but they've never worked in the market, or walked through Swampside. We don't have near enough guards or constables to keep the lid on things if people decide the wizards are useless. Go talk to them. Give them the whole treatment, like you used to talk to folks in the market square. I'll go talk to Cerom."

* * *

Cerom had the day off, so Jorac went to find him at his house. His wife led Jorac to their dining room, where Cerom, looking relaxed and happy, was just finishing breakfast with his family. Instead of his usual neat look, he was wearing an old tunic and hadn't shaved. "Hi Jorac. What brings you here? Some disaster I suppose."

"I'm afraid so. Can we talk?" Cerom sighed, then led Jorac out to his tiny garden in back of his house.

"Cerom, I know you hate to be kept in the dark, and I don't blame you, but sometimes it can't be helped. This time you're in at the start, but I'm not sure you're going to thank me. . ." He went on to explain how it was quite likely that most of Etrombia's wizards were about to lose their power.

". . . And Dorrie's inside the compound right now, hopefully talking them into making sure the fountains keep working. Weather we can explain, or the occasional broken light or backed-up sewer, but not that. The fountains fail, people will worry, or worse."

Cerom scowled. "Worse, that's what. You know as well as I do we only keep a lid on this city with their help. No wizard power and we need twice as many constables, or ten times as many. Every bad character in town . . . well, I don't have to tell you. When will this hit us?"

Jorac said, "Well, it might not of course. I think the stronger the wizard, the longer it will take before their magic disappears, though the longer before it comes back. So if the weak ones recover before the strongest ones are affected, we might be okay."

"Assuming they spend their power on the city, not themselves."

"Right. We need to hope for that. But to answer your question, I'd guess anytime in the next week, plus or minus."

Cerom shook his head. "And the wizards are well known to be selfish bastards. Oh god, what a mess. The Harvest Ball is coming up this week, and we always have a bunch of drunken fools there, so we've already juggled our schedules around that."

Jorac said, "I had one idea I thought might help. We let the constables know, quietly, that the wizards are working some new people – greenies – into the fountain maintenance system. Then if something happens, that's a semi-plausible explanation, and at least everyone will be saying the same thing."

"That'll work, I guess." Cerom stared at the ground disgustedly. "Shit, there goes my day off."

"Sorry. Say, can I borrow Schrog for a day or so?"

"Not Hox?"

"I need someone who'll fit in, and I figure you can use Hox's size if you have trouble."

"Yeah, people get peaceful around him, somehow. Sure, give me a few minutes to get dressed and we'll go down to the guard office together."

* * *

At the office, Cerom went to speak to his bosses, while Jorac wrote a note for Lartie, asking him to come to the city, quickly but quietly. The boy might or might not be able to help, but he knew a great deal about wizards, and Jorac was looking for help from any quarter at this point.

A few minutes later, Schrog walked in to start his shift. Jorac saw he'd let his hair grow a bit, which made him look a little less rat-like. Jorac called him over.

Schrog smiled crookedly at him and asked, "How's Kimma?"

"She's happy. We're happy." Jorac didn't try to guard his face, and Schrog noticed.

"Eh, it be like dat. I figgered. Could do worse, da both of ya." That was as close as a blessing from her surrogate uncle as Jorac was likely to get, and he briefly grinned back at Schrog.

"Thanks. . . Hey, Schrog, there's a situation brewing. Sorry, I can't tell you much about it yet – Cerom's in talking to the brass now. But I need you to go fetch a boy – he's at a farm, about four hours away. Give this note to him. It's not a secret; if anyone asks what you're doing, you can go ahead and read it to them."

"Eh, I'm no scholar. What do ya want de kid for?"

Jorac suddenly realized Schrog probably couldn't read well, if at all, and was sorry he'd said it that way.

"Remember Hox and I told you about Lartie? The note says I've made some progress getting his inheritance squared away, and to come with you. He'll probably be happy to, but if he balks, persuade him. I think he might help us with our, uh, situation; he's pretty bright. He's one of those kids who grew up with just adults around, so he talks like a grown-up and he's read more books than most people – more than me, at least."

"Heh, more den me too, fer damsure. You clear dat with Cerom? 'Course you did. All right, lemme get somebody to tell the missus I'll be home late tonight. Her damn sister be dere, so I ain't missin' nothin', don' you worry."

"Bring the kid to Dorrie Velsop's house, okay? Here's some coin, get food for a couple of horses and yourself. If there aren't any Constable horses to spare today, let me know."

"Dat should be okay. But where exactly I be going?"

"It's on the road north, out of the West gate. . ."

Cerom came back from his meeting as Jorac was giving Schrog directions, and Cerom arranged for Schrog to get a pair of horses from the Constable stable and sent him on his way.

After he left, Cerom turned to Jorac. "Any other good news for me? Flood, fire, anything like that?"

"Not right now, but don't worry, you'll be the first to know."

* * *

When Jorac got back to Dorrie's, it was only mid-morning but already felt like a full day. No one was there, and he paced and stewed and thought about how the city was going to fare without the wizards' powers.

Soon Dorrie and Kimma arrived, bringing some of the meat-pies Jorac liked. Dorrie told him, "I talked to wizards till I was blue in the face, and I think I got them all to agree. They're scared and thinking like a group now – everyone is more equal when they don't have their powers."

"Did you see Pergimtor or the other council leaders? They'll probably make the decisions."

Dorrie flashed him a grin. "Unlike some people, I don't travel in those high circles. I've never met any of the council, let alone Pergimtor, so I don't know if any of them heard me or not."

Jorac shook his head resignedly. "Well, we had to try. But here's my thinking. Even if they wanted to, the wizards are going to have trouble doing much of anything, so we might as well count them out. Most of the army is in the field and won't be back for weeks. So it's up to us, the Constables mostly, and whoever else might help, to keep a lid on things."

Kimma said, "Like the chiefs in Swampside: You didn't see them very often, but you knew they were there, and just knowing kept folks in line. In a Swampside kind of way of course."

"Exactly. Cerom and I have been talking about what we can do if the fountains or wizard lights start acting up. He knows a few people, has a few ideas. I'm leaving that with him, since he's a Constable and I'm not anymore. My part is trying to figure out what else is going on."

Kimma looked at him sharply. "You mean you think the wizard plague might be part of a plot against Etrombia." Sometimes, he thought, it seemed as if she could almost read his mind.

"Right. And if there is a plot, the only plausible source of information we have about it is those captured papers. There's got to be something important about them, or else why did the rebels try so desperately to keep them away from us? If we could figure out what that something is. . ."

Fortunately he still had the set of translated papers he'd intended to give Pergimtor. They talked it over and decided the fastest way to get them analyzed was for a knowledgeable group to brain-storm the process. They discussed who would be both good at it and discreet, and whether the group could be gotten together as soon as tomorrow morning. Yes, they decided; they had all afternoon to send runners with messages.

Jorac made a list of invitees as they talked. "The three of us. Cerom – he knows the city inside out; he was born here. Lartie knows a lot about wizards – he's read more books that the rest of us combined; I sent Schrog for him this morning. Hox and Monrae were eye-witnesses to the recent skirmish with the enemy wizard. The scholar Gleben. Anybody else? I know, Colonel Wakkar; he's an army veteran."

Dorrie said, "You should get Veseen. He was there in the swamp, and has the wizard apprentice experience. He might help."

"Good idea." Jorac wrote Veseen on the list. "I don't think we need anyone from Swampside, do you? Hatlo and Hario don't seem to be the right type, and I don't really trust the rest of them much."

Kimma shuddered a little and said, "Me neither." Then she said, "But how about Schrog?"

"He's certainly smart enough, but I don't think he can read. He'd be totally miserable."

"Ah," she said with a nod, and Jorac continued, "I think we can meet at the University Library. There are some meeting-rooms there, and if Gleben needs to research anything we'll be near the books."

Kimma said, "You know, Miz Madouve met Gleben, but he wasn't at the party, so I haven't met him, not as myself."

Jorac leaned over and kissed her on her forehead. "Smart one. We'll introduce you."

Chapter 33 - A Council (of Sorts)

They spent the afternoon making the meeting arrangements and finding a place for Lartie to stay (fortunately, one of Dorrie's neighbors turned out to have a spare room they could rent). The rest of the time they spent talking and worrying.

Schrog and Lartie didn't arrive until rather late that night – a horse had thrown a shoe, and they'd stopped to have an evening meal on the way back. After Schrog left, Jorac introduced Lartie to Dorrie and Kimma; he was a most respectful lad. Jorac showed him to his room next door and gave him a quick rundown on his progress with his "inheritance" and the puzzle of the captured papers. Jorac told him to come to Dorrie's for breakfast, and then everyone went to their own rooms. Kimma didn't visit; it was the first night she and Jorac had spent apart since he came back, but both were too tired for night games anyway.

The next morning, Jorac started early, collecting people. He started with Kimma, Dorrie, and Lartie, then went to Constable headquarters and found Hox starting his shift. It took a formal order from Jorac to release him, since Cerom was off again, apparently on a make-up day from having worked the day before. Jorac sent Hox to collect Monrae, and then they all went to collect Cerom. He was more than a bit annoyed to see the six of them on his doorstep just after breakfast, but resigned himself to missing another day with his family, and the seven of them made their way to the library.

When Jorac had sent invitations to people the day before, Colonel Wakkar had sent back word that he couldn't make it but would be interested to hear the results of the meeting. Gleben and Veseen had agreed to come, and both were waiting when the group arrived at the front desk.

Jorac greeted Veseen warmly and thanked him for joining them on short notice, without much explanation. He noted that the scrawny adolescent he'd sent away last just before the big party in Swampside had grown noticeably in the months since.

Veseen was still slender, but he'd filled out a bit over the summer and now showed hints of becoming a rather good-looking young man. When Jorac found a minute alone with him to ask, Veseen said yes, he'd caught the wizard-plague but was recovering his power already.

As Jorac's note had requested, Gleben had arranged for the use of a private conference room, and he sent out for a pitcher of water and some cups before closing the doors.

* * *

Nine people sat around a large oval table in a library room. Jorac took a minute to introduce everyone (Kimma was introduced as "Wizard Velsop's ward, Kimathea Ravensclough"); then he got down to business.

"I want to thank everyone for coming here – not that I gave you much choice. Before we start, I must swear you all to secrecy. You've each proven you can keep your mouth shut, so I'm not worried about that, but I have to say it."

He waited until everyone around the room had signaled assent, then continued.

"Also before we start, I want to alert you to a situation at the Wizards Conclave. There's a contagious anti-magic plague going around that causes wizards to temporarily lose their power. We don't know how many will be affected or when, but we're afraid that essentially all the country's wizards are going to be hit within the next few days. If that happens, we can expect things we take for granted – fountains, wizard-lights on the streets, and so on – may stop working. I've requested the wizards to make the fountains their highest priority, but I don't know how much influence I have."

Gleben said, "So, what do you want us to do?"

"If anything happens to the fountains or wizard-lights, people will start to worry, or even panic. Cerom and I have talked about it, and he has some ideas for keeping order in the city. Our story is going to be that the wizards are having new trainees work on the city utilities, and people shouldn't worry;

minor glitches are expected. The wizard compound is locked up tight, so if we get the right people repeating that story, it should work."

Gleben said, "I'll be sure to mention that – we're often asked questions about the wizards, since they can be testy at times."

Hox and Jorac exchanged a knowing look, and Jorac went on. "Good; thank you. Now let's get to the reason I wanted us to get together." He took a deep breath. "I can't prove anything, but I'm worried. The wizards have been put out of commission at the same time the army is tied up with a long, drawn-out rebellion in the north. Maybe I'm over-reacting, but it seems like just too much coincidence. I'm hoping we can maybe gain some insight if we go over the facts together."

Jorac gestured at Hox. "Hox and I went north with the army this past Spring as observers. Our orders were to look for a wizard working with the rebels, and we found there was a powerful one. The rebels tried desperately to prevent it, but we managed to obtain some of his communication papers, and Scholar Gleben has helped to get them mostly translated. Some of what they say makes sense and some doesn't. We'll get to that soon.

"It also seems that the anti-magic plague erupted sometime this summer in a single rogue cloud-cotton tree and spread from there. Apparently, all our farm crops are magically enhanced to help ward off insects and produce better harvests – I didn't know that either, but I'm told it's common knowledge among the farmers in the 'inside' lands, the ones under weather control. This plague wasn't confined to plants and quickly spread to our wizards, who are conveniently all gathered in one place for their triennial Conclave. Infection with it causes them to lose power – technically, lose their store of mana. So they have to rebuild their. . . oh, container I suppose you'd call it, then fill it again. We think that should take at least a week or two; we aren't sure."

Cerom asked, "Are you suggesting the plant-plague was started deliberately?"

Jorac shrugged. "The only evidence we have so far is the single source and the convenient timing. But with the proven wizard activity in the north, I think it's something we ought to consider."

Gleben said, "Scholars are instructed to look for patterns, to understand root causes first, to better plan for the future. Can you start the story earlier, such as when we first met?"

Jorac thought he was angling for more information about the Wolburn sphere, but he understood curiosity as well as anyone, and Gleben had a point.

"Very well, let me start with this spring. Something happened in the swamp – we can't say what – that could have affected the stability of our Wizards Council, but as things turned out, it didn't. I can tell you that it was almost certainly an isolated incident with roots in the distant past, and not related to anything recent."

Cerom and Gleben both opened their mouths to speak, but Jorac continued, forcefully, "And now we'll move on."

He looked around the room. "What do we know about the wizard in the north? In the papers we captured he's communicating, via magic, with another wizard somewhere else – we don't know where. Mostly he's giving short reports and receiving instructions. Let's review those, to start." He took the translated papers from his satchel and handed them out.

"I believe what they're calling 'potty' was a type of magical fireball trap bound to a simple clay pot, triggered by proximity to horses. Hox, Monrae, and young Lartie will remember it well. See if you think it fits as well as I do."

That produced a flurry of talk and papers being passed around the table. Gleben had brought the working drafts and translation notes, and those were passed around too. With three or four conversations going at once, it started to get quite confusing, so Jorac called a halt and suggested that Lartie and Gleben to read the dispatches aloud like a script, with each speaking as a different character.

After the first reading, the group talked about the wizards and the campaign. In looking at the correspondence as a whole, they decided that the two wizards were likely childhood friends and possibly brothers, because of all the subtle references and private jokes, not all of which made sense.

Jorac and Hox, aided by Monrae and Lartie, provided details about the campaign from their viewpoint. They agreed that the wizards' tactics had seemingly been meant to run the army in circles and keep the rebels from fighting a decisive battle – and that they'd been pretty successful at it. In fact, as Jorac pointed out, they were still being successful at it. Everyone would have loved to see the dispatches from the remaining days of the campaign, but they had to settle for what they had.

After that discussion, they paused, and Gleben poured water for everyone who wanted it. While that was going on, Veseen idly looked at Gleben's list of names. He said, "Sweet Groniall with the silver ball, she plays in the kitchen, she plays in the hall."

Gleben looked up at him sharply. "Sweet Groniall, that's one of the names there. What did you just recite?"

"It was in one of the children's books my granny used to read to me. I remember the books were very old. She said they came from the time just after the Founding, so I never got to touch them myself."

Gleben thumbed through the translation. "Let's see what it says. . . Here it is; we were about to read this part out loud. It's from what we call the home wizard, not the army wizard:

'Sweet Groniall seems to be a miss.' And the reply is, *'An off chance anyway. Crazy. Added 18 farmers today.'*"

He added, "We should have put the page numbers and counts for each name we encountered, but we didn't really have time. But that's very interesting, the part about the silver ball." He stared at Jorac, expectantly.

Jorac wasn't about to explain about the Wolburn Sphere. He asked Veseen, "Did your stories ever mention a king fox?"

"Sure, that was one of my favorites. Want to hear it?"

This drew Gleben's full attention. He said, "Yes, please. Sit down, everyone, let's hear this. Go on."

Veseen was a little puzzled, but willing. "This was a picture book, a nice one with pretty colors in it. These books had two languages side by side, but I could only read the Etrombian. I don't think I have it all memorized, but I know most of it. . . Let's see, I'll remember it better if I try to say it like my granny did. . ."

He began reciting in a rather childish, over-dramatic, sing-song voice:

> Once there was born a fox who was much larger and stronger than all others. He lived on a hillside meadow, where he ate mice and rabbits and small stupid birds, just like other foxes. But unlike the other foxes, he wanted to be king. Now, everyone knew that only the largest mountain cat could be king, because he had the most strength, and he had the council of the owl, the wisest bird in the land.
>
> But the giant fox was determined that he would be king. He went to the rabbit warren and said, "I am King Fox. I am king of this hill." Now, the rabbits were very frightened, so they all agreed. He had eaten all the rabbits that he had been able to catch, and they thought that perhaps bowing down to this huge fox might make him seek other prey. They said, "Yes, King Fox. There are some fat mice over that way." And the fox went away to chase the mice, and left the rabbits alone this day.
>
> This fox was a very large fox indeed, larger than the largest wolf, so he went up to the wolf pack and said, "I am king of this hill. You will call me your king. I am King Fox." The wolves knew that the mountain cat was king of the hillside. Even if the cat only visited it now and then, the wolves did not gainsay his kingship. The wolves looked at the size of

*the fox, and talked among themselves, and left the
hillside without saying anything. They could find
another place to hunt, and fighting with this fox could
get someone hurt, for no good reason. But on their
way off the hillside, one of them sought out the owl and
said, "There is a fox on the hillside who says he is king.
If he is to be king, he will need your counsel."*

*The owl flew up to a small tree on the meadow and
talked to the fox. "Fox, why do you call yourself
king?"*

*"I am strongest, that is why. I have no fear of the
wolves, who have run away from me. I have no fear of
the mountain cat, for I am larger and fiercer than any
such."*

Veseen broke out of the recital, "I don't remember all of this
part. There was some more talk with the owl, a bit about a king
needing wise counsel, and the fox refusing. He says, '*I have no
need of you, owl. Your words I do not need, for I will do as I please on
my hillside.*' And there were some examples of how the fox was
bullying the other animals. Like, he made the heath-hen move
her nest, just so he could get a bit more shade. The next part, I
remember better." He started his recitation again:

*Finally, the owl had seen enough. He went to talk
to the eagle who flew high above the meadow. He said,
"Eagle, do you know of the one who calls himself the
King Fox?"*

*"Yes," said the eagle. The eagles never spoke
much.*

*"Life on the hillside is much worse since he started
calling himself king. Do you wish him stopped?"*

"Yes. How?"

*"Could you dive down from a great height, with a
rock in your talons, and hit him on the head?"*

*"Hit ground. Hurt." This was a long talk for an
eagle, three words.*

"Yes, indeed. Let me think. What if he were at the top of the hillside, where you could come in from the side?"

The eagle looked at the owl for a whole minute, without blinking, as eagles do. "Fox's head must be up." Five words, from an eagle! He was very interested indeed, to speak so much.

"I shall make it so. Tonight, as the sun is going down, will that be good with you?"

The eagle said, "Yes." And the eagle blinked, just once, to show that he was pleased.

That evening, the owl found the fox and landed near him — but not too near. He said to him, "All the animals on the hillside have decided that you cannot be king. We will call you Fat Fox, not King Fox."

This made the fox very angry of course, and he charged at the owl, who jumped into the air. He was almost not quick enough: the fox jumped up behind him and caught a bit of a tail feather in his jaw. But the owl got away."

Veseen interrupted himself. "The picture for this one was very funny. Or at least I thought so." He resumed:

The owl flew around and around the hill, to tire the fox. He stayed almost in reach of the fox, who jumped several times to try to catch him. Meanwhile, the owl was saying things like "Fat fox" and "Too slow!"

Finally, the owl flew up the hill, and the fox followed. When the owl reached the top of the hill, he tried to hover in place, so that the fox would stay still. It is very hard for an owl to fly in one place in the air, but he managed it for a time. He kept saying things like "The mountain cat is coming, fatty." The fox tried to jump at him a few more times, then just stood there yelling. He yelled, "I am King Fox! I am! I am Kiiiiiiiiing!"

And as the fox stood on the top of the hillside, holding up his head and baying about how big and strong he was, the eagle flew down with great speed and hit him between his eyes with the stone held in his claws. The fox was killed, and the meadow rejoiced.

Veseen stopped. "That was the end of the book. After I got a little older, though, my granny told me that when she was a young girl she'd heard that the real ending was that the fox was knocked unconscious, and all the animals that he'd been mean to came up and started biting him, even the ones who ate only plants. She thought it had been left out because it was very bloody and would frighten the children."

Gleben had found the "King Fox" passage in the papers, and read it aloud. *"The king fox, baying on a hilltop. And four eagles, not just one, and you playing the owl. I so look forward to laughing about this with you at a tavern, when we've won.* And the reply is, *Ha! Perfect! I'll be there."*

Jorac asked, "Veseen, do you know where that book is now?"

"No. . . You see, we'd only go visit my granny in the summer. She had a place in the hills, and it took us a day and a half to get there. She's dead now. The book might still be somewhere in that house, but I don't really know."

Gleben said, "The other language that was on the page – did it look like this?" He thumbed through his working papers and showed Veseen a page of some decoded but untranslated text.

"I can't say yes or say no. Sorry, but I just don't remember; I always skipped over that part. See, the books had Etrombian on the left pages, the other language on the right, and the pictures below, across both pages. So I just paid no attention to that part."

There was a long silence while everyone tried to match the story to the facts. When no one spoke, Jorac decided to try another tack. "Let's look through those papers again. Is there anything having to do with a tree, or a disease or anything?"

Another careful reading produced a possible passage: The home wizard said, *"Blort going out today. Avoid south farmlands."* To which the reply was, *"Heh, not likely."*

"That certainly isn't much to go on," Cerom said. "Can you tell when that message was sent?"

Gleben counted pages. "Assuming we have the sequence right, it was fairly early, perhaps two or three weeks from the beginning of our records, which we estimated was early spring."

They discussed whether they could determine the time from internal clues in the papers, and if so, whether it would do any good. Finally Dorrie summed it up: "We don't know if the tree was always bad and just started showing it this year, or if it got something like an infection or magic spell recently. And if this 'Blort' was the cause, we don't know how long it takes to affect the tree, so we have no way of proving anything one way or the other."

Cerom sighed in frustration, and so did everyone else.

They talked about other books Veseen remembered, and Gleben stepped out to ask someone to search for the same children's books in the library. Jorac knew that books that old would be very valuable indeed; it made him again wonder about Veseen's family.

Kimma said, "Scholar Gleben, I can see you're thinking about something. Have *you* ever heard of books like that?"

"Not for a long time. You see, part of the treaty at the Founding, 233 years ago this past spring, was that the settlers from Zargrona pledged to follow the Etrombian king, King Wafeloc, and take up the Etrombian language. Basically, they agreed to quit writing in Zargronian and translate all their books into Etrombian, which is a related language but easier to read and write. At that time such a change wasn't as hard as it would be now, because few people were literate and books were rare. Apparently everyone made a conscious effort to make the switch, but we still have a few surviving books in early Zargronian, and a few dual-language books written in both languages. They're merely curiosities; these days the only people who learn Zargronian from books are traders and the occasional scholar."

Kimma asked him, "So, do you believe the book Veseen remembers from his childhood was a one of those early dual-language ones? And if so, is that a clue to the enemy wizards' nationality?"

"An interesting question. Speculatively, I would suggest that the second language in Veseen's book was Zargronian – we know of books like that, and I've never heard of them for other languages. But just because someone repeats a story told in an antique children's book written in Zargronian, it's a large leap to assume that indicates he's from Zargrona. Many folk tales are common to our whole language cluster; they appear in Zargrona, Etrombia, and Parlund as well."

Kimma sighed. "In other words, that's no help either, and we still don't know."

They went back and looked through the list of names again. Jorac asked if anyone recognized "Palamar."

After a few moments of silence, Lartie spoke up. "Well, in my uncle's books, there was a mention of a wizard spell called 'Balamar' that aided vision at night." He was getting much better at playing the precocious young lad, and giving people a believable source for his assertions.

"Ah," Jorac said, "I'll bet that's it. Seeing in the dark was part of what first made the scouts suspicious that there was a wizard involved, and got me sent out there. Let's get some lunch, shall we? Gleben, what are our options? We can find a private place, or bring some food here."

"The library generally doesn't allow any food in the rooms, just water, but I daresay they'd make an exception for you."

* * *

The discussions over lunch and early afternoon produced no further breakthroughs. There were no children's books in the library matching Veseen's description, and anyway they didn't expect to gain much even if some were found. They found no more useful clues in the papers – ones that made any sense, at least.

Gleben summed up their findings. "So, we think there's been a squad of outlanders in the north, fomenting rebellion. From what Jorac remembers of army tales, they've been there at least three or four years. They have a wizard with them, this year at least. The wizard is communicating with someone, likely someone he knows well, who constantly advises delay. Their messages are consistent with an attempt to keep the Etrombian army in the north, but their purpose for doing so isn't apparent. Our only hint, a remote one, is the tale of King Fox, which seems to be important, and thanks to the young gentleman, we know something about its origins. But, unfortunately, not what it means in this context, where it's clearly a metaphor. It might be a hint about next year's rebellion, or an inside joke we can't guess at all. It might be a comment on an internal matter in any of several foreign states. And though the wizards themselves are probably from Zargrona or Parlund, they might be working for another foreign state; we only have two men writing."

They sat there, frustrated. Dorrie said, "Not much we can do, then. We should ask around about King Fox, I guess. Gleben and his folks will do that better than the rest of us, but maybe an old granny knows something that didn't make it into the books."

When no one else had any further ideas, Jorac thanked them all and the meeting broke up.

As Cerom was leaving, Jorac pulled him aside and said, "Tell Schrog all this, okay? He's canny, and can keep his mouth shut."

"Alright, but no one else, right?"

"Exactly. I didn't want to put him on the spot with all the reading we're doing here. I don't think he can read."

Cerom smiled. "No he can't, and that was kindly done. I'll fill him in."

* * *

Kimma came back to Jorac's house that night. He'd been tired at dinner and hadn't felt like making conversation, but he was happy to see her alone again, and they talked awhile.

She kissed him and said, "I can see you're unhappy. It was a pretty frustrating meeting, wasn't it?"

He shook his head in disgust. "I wasted eight people's time for nearly a whole day, and we didn't accomplish one damned thing!"

"Well, I admit there weren't any big breakthroughs. But we did find out about King Fox."

"That was interesting, but I don't see how it actually helps with anything. We still don't have the slightest clue about who those two wizards are working for, or what they're trying to do. But there's something there, I feel it in my bones."

"So do I. There's something going on, and if it's all one big conspiracy it's pretty elaborate. Don't worry, nobody thinks you're crazy. We just don't have enough information yet, so we have to keep looking. Maybe you should talk to the army man again?"

He thought about it. "Yeah, maybe I should. What I'm afraid of is we won't figure it out until it's too late."

"Yes. . . we'll keep working on it, but . . . well, it's not too late for some things." Kimma smiled at him, a secret, enticing smile.

Jorac shook his head to break his mood, and smiled at Kimma. "When you're right, you're right, smart one." He bent down and kissed her, and said, "Did I ever tell you how much I like a smart girl?"

Chapter 34 - Worry and Dancing

The next morning, Jorac couldn't get into the Wizard's Tower area at all; the doors seemed to be locked tight and many were guarded. No one already inside was getting out, and even Dorrie with her guild badge couldn't get in. Dorrie also reported that Veseen had been hustled inside as soon as he returned yesterday, and she overheard something about a "special project" for the apprentices. If it meant keeping a lid on the city, Jorac didn't care who was drafted to help.

But he was still concerned that Pergimtor hadn't seen the papers Gleben had translated. Suppose his group had missed something important in them? He walked all the way around the Wizard's Compound, and finally found an unguarded entrance, a back door in the clerk's area. From there he made his way to his office through some pass-through closets and some little-used back hallways. This time his office was unlocked but empty. He wrote a short note: "Enemy wizards' papers decoded but still puzzling. Situation very worrying. See me for details, please, as soon as you can!" He signed and sealed it, and addressed it to Pergimtor. Through the doorway outside his office, he could see the message bin he used to send notes to Pergimtor, in an area patrolled by an occasional wandering guard. He took off his boots and waited until the guard was out of sight, then quietly dashed over and dropped the message in the bin. He wasn't really surprised when nothing happened and it just sat there.

He moved quickly back to his office, put his boots back on, and wondered what to do next. He could confront the guard, or slip out and wander the halls in search of Pergimtor, or go up the 156 steps and hope he found a cooperative wizard up there. He didn't like any of those choices. In the end, he left just as he came, with no progress, unless you counted progressive frustration.

Out of sorts and uncomfortable, he walked to the nearest public fountain and strolled casually by. It appeared to be running clear and clean as normal, so he turned and went back home, still dissatisfied.

That evening he went with Kimma to his final dancing lesson – the Harvest Ball was only three days away now. He enjoyed seeing her in her "practice" dress, and tried to remember the steps, but he was distracted. He'd learned the Kalzie well enough, but the more intricate dances were beyond him today. He kept looking up at the sky, trying to decide if the weather was changing unexpectedly. And of course looking at Kimma was distracting all by itself. . .

* * *

The next two days nearly drove Jorac crazy. Kimma and Dorrie continued to work Dorrie's trade, meaning Kimma could only see him at mealtimes, and her nightly visits ended too early in the morning to suit him. Cerom and his people were busy and stressed, and didn't welcome chitchat. Lartie was waiting for his accounts to be settled but at least had plenty of books to read; he'd struck up a friendship with Gleben. Seeing Lartie happily lost in a book, Jorac borrowed an action story and tried reading it, but found himself too distracted to get more than a few pages in.

He visited the Wizard's Compound, but it was still locked up and well guarded. Apparently he wasn't the only one being turned away, since the guard out front had been coached to put a good face on it. "Wizard party, you understand. Don't want the likes of you and me getting in the way, but they're just having their fun. Only happens every three years; they'll be done in a few days."

Jorac smiled a false smile and nodded, then walked down to the market and wandered among the stalls – it all seemed normal – and looked at the fountain nearby – also normal. The talk was about the autumn trading ships that were expected to arrive, and the quality of the goods, not about anything having to do with magic, or the fountains, or the weather. In other words, nothing out of the ordinary was happening.

Still, Jorac was increasingly uneasy, for reasons he couldn't put into words. Kimma shared his worry, but neither of them could think of anything useful to do about it, so they put it aside when they were together. They tried to concentrate on things they could do something about, like getting ready for Kimma's entrance to society in a few days.

* * *

Finally, the morning of the Harvest Ball came. The fountains were still flowing clean and cold, and the weather was still pleasant – this time of year it didn't need much moderating, and Jorac wasn't sure if it was still under wizard control or not. He tried one more time and still couldn't get into his office. The whole Wizard's Compound area was locked tight, including the back way he'd found earlier; not that he was surprised.

He stopped off at Dorrie's to make sure things were still going as planned. Dorrie had hired a carriage for Kimma's grand entrance, and it would take the two women to the ball. Rather than leave Lartie home alone the whole day, they'd agreed he could tag along; there was a well-known scholarly book shop not far from the ball he said he'd been wanting to visit. He'd even agreed to dress like a young noble for the occasion.

Jorac briefly saw Kimma – she looked smashing in her new dress, and her hair had some extra shine to it. He couldn't really concentrate too well when she was in the room, so he left and went home to get dressed in his newest full-dress uniform, just delivered the day before. It was a little tighter in the seat than he liked, and the cloth was a bit thinner than he was used to, but he'd been assured that it looked good on him. He buckled on both his swords, in his fanciest scabbards, and set off. It was still several hours before the festivities started, but he couldn't sit still.

The Harvest Ball was always held at the Royal Park on Fish Island, a narrow spit of land just north of the high Wizard Bridge. The whole island was only about four blocks long, but was served by two narrow, low bridges from the nearby east bank, where there was a small commercial square. The island had no permanent structures, unless one counted the small wizard fountain on the north end and the ornamental arch at the stone bridge on the south end welcoming visitors to the Royal Park. When not in use for events like the Harvest Ball, the island was home to a herd of goats who kept its vegetation from running rampant.

Today, Jorac saw that the island's trees and bushes had been trimmed, and the vagrants who illegally camped there had been rousted. The whole center of the park had been roped off and a temporary guard post set up at the entrance. Two huge canopies had been erected in the middle, and wagonloads of planks and empty barrels were being assembled into the long tables that were the hallmark of the day. The young men of good breeding would sit at one long table, and the women at another, while the area between them would be used by servants bringing food and drink to everyone. For the first few hours, the ladies and gentlemen could only look at each other; after the luncheon, the formal dances would begin. The drinking and dancing would go long into the night, with an increasing emphasis on drinking as the night wore on. The whole festival was supposed to have a rustic feel, and from what Jorac had seen of it as a constable, it was missing only the barnyard smells and off-key musicians to be a match for the harvest festivals he remembered as a child.

But today he couldn't just sit back and enjoy himself, for several reasons. The first was Kimma, who would certainly be here, and expect him to be at his best. The wizard problem was another – there was a fountain right here in the park, and a number of wizard lights above it. If anything happened to either of them, people would immediately notice, and the evening would be difficult at best and riotous at worst. And the last was the event itself – light socializing with young nobles was *not* his favorite pastime.

The first person he met when he crossed the bridge was Cerom, who was wandering around, checking on the constable stations around the periphery. They walked together toward the entrance to the roped-off center area.

Cerom said, "Anything new on that King Fox of yours?"

Jorac shook his head. "Gleben hasn't reported anything, and I'm out of ideas too. I guess we'll have to wait for the wizards to get out of their conclave and pay attention, or for the army to get back."

"I'm at a loss myself. Let's hope it doesn't matter." Then he smiled and said, "But hey, today is supposed to be a fun day, if you're not on duty at least. I'm sure that lady of yours will be here – even with your chaperone, she seems worth it."

"I think so. She had me go to dance lesson, even."

Cerom grinned at him. "Dance lessons? In pretty deep, are you?"

Jorac shrugged helplessly and grinned despite himself. He was, and he knew it.

When they reached the entrance to the roped-off area, a guard stopped them. "Your pardon, sir, but swords aren't allowed in, not for anyone. There'll be a fellow here later, set up to keep them safe for you, but he's not here yet."

Cerom said to Jorac, "He's right, you know. Too many young drunken fools by the evening. Even if you're sober, they could grab your sword."

"Are you going to be on duty near the park?"

"All day, I'm afraid. Sure, I'll carry them for you till he shows up. I'll look good wearing those fancy scabbards."

Jorac unbuckled his belt handed them to Cerom, and said quietly, "Don't you have something a little more potent than that club? Just in case, you know, something happens?"

Cerom whispered back, "Don't worry, I've got a couple of stout fellows with heavy sticks stashed nearby. And Hox will get that duty later." In his regular voice, he said, "No, I don't mind carrying them; they're lighter than they look. You have fun today."

Once inside the central area, Jorac scouted around and got a seat at the corner of the bar near the entrance, where he could sit and view the whole area as the festival-goers began arriving. It was mostly as Dorrie told him to expect: the youngest boys and girls, basically older children, arrived first and were seated at the far end of the rows of tables. Some teenaged boys and girls arrived next, all trying to look very grown up; the young ladies succeeded, the boys not as well.

In a while Cerom came over to him with a numbered piece of paper. "Here you go, Jorac – check number one. The man over there has your swords, and you can pick them up as you leave."

"Thanks. Quiet so far?"

"Yep. No trouble until sundown, usually. Then we see all sorts of stuff – mostly youngsters who drank too much, but some pickpockets and the like as well. Having fun?"

"So far, pretty dull."

"It'll pick up when the ladies arrive, never you fear."

* * *

Jorac's side of the park started to fill up with more men, including ones in their twenties and thirties. They were fancily dressed, but they weren't really there to display their own costumes; they wanted to watch the ladies arrive – that was one of the highlights of the day.

Dorrie had explained that Kimma needed to arrive at the right time – not so early as to seem anxious, yet not so late as to assume she'd be accepted, or compete with those who thought themselves in the top echelon of society. Her good looks alone could threaten the young ladies prone to jealousy, and she didn't want to make any enemies by accident. Tonight she'd be playing the country cousin, with her dress intentionally a year or two out of fashion. She'd be polite, humble, and nice to everyone.

Up to now, people had left their carriages on the mainland and walked in across the two short bridges, but now a few carriages started lining up near the south bridge, preparing to drive across. These would be the ladies. Jorac watched as the men crowded to his left, over near the entrance, to watch them arrive. Jorac had picked his place carefully and didn't have to do more than turn to see them. The first carriage stopped and a pretty young girl in a dazzling, shimmering silver dress emerged. Jorac thought she was about fifteen years old, and he heard one of the men next to him say, "That's Nisbot's daughter, growing up nicely. In a year or two she'll be quite something." The girl went to the ladies' side and was met by some older women that Jorac took to be her family, as her carriage left via the other bridge.

Another one of the early arrivals brought an appreciative catcall from one of the boys behind Jorac, which brought a liveried guard over. "Young sirs, if you cannot behave as gentlemen, this isn't the occasion for you. Behave yourselves, make the ladies at ease, if you please." Thereafter, there were just murmurs and quiet talk from the men's side.

After another eight or ten carriages had let out beautifully dressed young ladies in ones or twos, Jorac could see the fancy carriage that Dorrie had rented for Kimma driving onto the island. His pulse quickened, as much anticipating the men's reaction as looking forward to seeing her himself. Most of the ladies who'd arrived so far were known to this group, and identifying them was part of their fun. They'd never seen Kimma before, and he wasn't sure how they were going to react.

Finally she stepped out of the carriage. Her dress was a soft pumpkin color, made full (but not too full) by petticoats underneath. It wasn't as ornamented as some dresses Jorac had just seen, but it still had a great deal of lace and bead-work – just the right amount, according to Dorrie. And he could see the small silver butterfly at her neck, which made him smile. She looked absolutely, stunningly gorgeous.

"Wow!" said one in a low voice.

Jorac heard, "Who is she?" and "Never seen her before – and I'd remember" from the crowd. One of the older men said, "I'd take *her* to the library," which struck Jorac as inane, but it brought a laugh from another man next to him. "A rare book indeed. I bet her dance card fills up right quickly. I'm heading straight there, myself."

Jorac felt a completely unreasonable urge to either hit the man or smugly tell him who she was going to be sleeping with that night. Of course Kimma would kill him if he did anything of the sort, and anyway he was proud of her too. He watched as she found Dorrie at a table near the center – how had he not seen Dorrie arrive? – and sit down gracefully. *So far so good. Kimma and Dorrie are actually society ladies, starting tonight.*

With Kimma's arrival out of the way, Jorac lost some of his interest in the rest of the proceedings. As the ladies got older and the dresses got fancier, he found himself surveying the crowd instead. He was surprised to see Skowers among the men watching the ladies arrive, but then decided he should have expected it. Pretty young ladies would act like nectar to a bee for Skowers, and Jorac decided that was an apt metaphor for a man who made money smuggling honey past the tax collectors.

After a while, he began to get restless. Sitting was all right, but a little claustrophobic. He got up and found a standing place near the bar. It was the one spot where he could see most of the crowd but not look too out of place.

He saw Zarl and Parf Leganwei come into the ball area, putting their sword-check tickets into their pockets. He was glad they didn't watch Kimma arrive – it was bad enough listening to strangers talk about her; he didn't need to hear it from these two. Still, at least they were people he knew, so he caught their eye and waved them over.

"Hi guys – let me buy you a drink."

Parf accepted immediately, while Zarl was suspicious. "All right, sure. But why?"

Jorac ordered three cups of punch, and turned to the Leganwei brothers. "No reason. I just wanted to see how you guys are doing. I imagine you've been bored; I only talked to your father once, but he seemed like the type to do what he said he would."

Zarl said bitterly, "He's stubborn all right. This is the first time I've been out of the house in *months*. I should be mad at you."

Jorac paid for the punch, and handed it to them. "Here you go. Me, I just told the truth. Saved you from bad news with that laundry lady. It wouldn't do to have that talked about."

Parf nodded, and said, "We thank you for that. Right, Zarl?"

Zarl said nothing, and buried his nose in the cup.

Jorac said, "Don't worry about it – I won't be telling any stories. And you won't hear any stories about me misusing a sword when I was your age either, but that's because my family lives way over by the mountains." Jorac was never a bully as a teenager, but he did manage to cut one of his mothers dresses to tatters when it was on the clothesline. "Let's just say you aren't the first person to make a fool of himself, okay?"

Zarl looked down at the ground for a long moment, then up at Jorac with a look of acceptance. "Okay. I'll buy the next round of drinks, and we'll be square."

Jorac nodded, and gave him a crooked smile. "Good enough." He wondered how "reforming rich young louts" got into his job description, but mentally shrugged. It would never hurt to have a family as well-placed as the Leganwei clan on his side.

* * *

A gong sounded, and in the silence that followed, a liveried guard with a resonant voice bellowed, "Ladies and gentlemen, please take your places. Luncheon is served."

Jorac hurried over to the middle, where Kimma would be sitting. He tried to get a table opposite her, but was too slow – other men jostled for the opportunity, and he had to sit two tables away. She still saw him, and they exchanged brief smiling nods – their *acquaintance* was not a secret.

The lunch itself was fairly dull, and the food was plain – fowl of some sort in a sauce, fine bread, some leafy vegetables. Jorac noticed that everyone ate quickly, encouraged by someone who said to his neighbor (but loudly, so everyone could hear), "Eat up, the quicker we finish, the quicker the dancing starts." In fairly short order the diners finished and got up, the servants came down the center aisle and cleared away the plates, the tables were moved to the edges of the roped-off area, and the band started tuning their instruments.

A few of the liveried guards stood in the now-vacant area in the middle, watching as the tables were efficiently dismantled and moved away. Soon the gong sounded again, and the resonant-voiced guard raised his arms and bellowed, "Ladies and gentlemen, may the joys of the bountiful harvest bring blessings on us now and for years to come. The dancing may now commence." Jorac was standing very near the guard and heard him continue under his breath, "And may the gods watch over fools and drunkards tonight."

Jorac immediately headed straight for Kimma, where he found himself in a crowd around her seat. He pushed a bit to get near the front, and to stop trouble had to give his best glower to the lanky older teenager who objected to it. He had to turn sideways, but edged to within sight of her. The crowd maintained an unspoken distance of about three feet all around her, but beyond that radius it was packed tightly.

Kimma was smiling sweetly, softly at the assembled group, and writing a name on her dance card as the lucky man she'd agreed to dance with was doing the same. "It's 'Ravensclough – c-l-o-u-g-h.' Thank you, sir, I look forward to it." The man, who was in front of Jorac, pushed his way out of the crowd smiling broadly, and Jorac took his place.

Kimma picked another man for the next dance, her fourth one, and then looked around again, finally making eye contact with Jorac. This was his cue.

"Mistress Ravensclough, might I have the pleasure of your next available dance?"

"Let me see – the fifth dance is the Kalzie. Do you know that one?"

Jorac smiled – he hoped it wasn't too big a smile. "It's my favorite."

"Very well then, Honorable Kellor, I'll put you down for that one." She carefully wrote his name in the fifth spot in her dance card, then firmly closed it and stood up. Smiling graciously, she said, "I'm afraid I'll need to wait a bit before accepting any more invitations. It's bad luck to fill up your card too soon – ask me later, if you will."

The pack split up and the men sped away, many hurrying to other crowds near other seated ladies nearer the entrance – those were the later-arriving, fancier ones. Jorac stood back a few paces and watched as Kimma consulted her card and leaned in to talk to Dorrie. Soon the first piece of music started, a few seconds of introduction followed by a pause. The swift-footed young man who had the first dance showed up to escort Kimma to the dancing area.

Jorac nodded to Dorrie and walked over to chat with her a moment. He said softly, "Skowers is here. Make her skip some dances so she doesn't get too tired, okay?"

Dorrie said, just as softly, "I know. Move along," then said to someone behind him, "Oh, hello, Countess." Jorac did as he was told, and moved back to the men's side of the dance floor as the dances were beginning.

He watched the first dance from the sidelines – it was a simple affair, a turn and a dip one way, then the same thing the other way. Kimma looked acceptable doing it; certainly she didn't make any blunders, and the look of concentration on her face was shared by other dancers as well – everyone wanted to do well on the first dance.

The second dance was a line affair where the ladies stayed in place and the men went down the line, bobbing back and forth to each lady in turn. Jorac dutifully joined in this one, and saw that Kimma and the other ladies were relaxing a bit; this dance was easy on them, more work for the men.

Afterward, feeling rather virtuous, he went back to the bar and had some more of the weak punch. He stood by the bar and watched the next couple of dances – there was a short break between each one to allow the ladies to return to their seats and get new partners. Kimma sat out the third, danced the fourth, and then the Kalzie came.

Jorac would always remember that dance. Kimma was beautiful; her hands were soft and her face was full of love. But soon it ended, and they were brought back to reality. They had to stop holding hands when the music stopped, though they might have lingered just a little. Afterward he got her to write his name on her card for a later dance, then regretfully escorted her back to her seat.

In an unwary moment Jorac had promised Dorrie he'd dance with other girls, so he thought he'd get it over with, and asked two other young ladies from the back row to dance with him. Both were forlorn-looking and rather plain, and accepted immediately. It went well enough with the first one, but not with the second; the dance with her proved to be an energetic one that required quick, fancy footwork. He made a hash of it at first, but remembered some old toe-behind-ankle sword-work drills that he could adapt to the rhythm, which sort of worked but was no doubt totally unorthodox. At the finish, he bowed low to her, and was happy to see a thin young man, doubtless better schooled in dance, come to ask her for the next fast dance. She was a good dancer and deserved a better dance-partner than he was.

After that, he went back to lounging with the drinkers, near one of the makeshift tables that were now serving as both bench and bar. His second dance with Kimma was coming up – it wasn't as simple as the Kalzie, but it had only one bit of tricky steps. And he'd get to hold her in his arms a bit in that dance.

That part would be fun, as long as his imperfect mastery of the tricky steps didn't lead him to step on her feet. He was beginning to think he might make it through the Ball, and he'd pushed away the vague sense of foreboding – for now at least.

Chapter 35 - Unwelcome Visitors

Jorac had just come back from the jakes – the punch was weak but he'd been drinking a lot of it – when he saw Cerom coming toward him with a worried look on his face. Behind him was Schrog; Jorac was surprised to see either of them in here with the young nobles.

As they approached, Schrog said, "I was talking to Cerom, and I had dis idear. . ." His voice trailed off, and he looked around to see who was listening.

Jorac stepped closer to him, and Schrog continued, more quietly.

"He told me about dat King Fox and such. I was wonderin'. . . maybe . . . well, dem trading ships from Parlund, dey carry dat eagle flag."

Cerom nodded and said, "They do. They come every fall, and they're big – probably the biggest ship that can sail up the river. It's usually just one ship a year, loaded with gems and timbers and honey, and it leaves with potions and cloth and probably lots of other things. For all that they outlaw magic there in Parlund, they sure like our potions."

"Only, I heard, dis year we gots four of dem, coming up de river late dis afternoon. My ma, she knows a guy who gets word from de river watchers. She tol' me, dey bring in dem green stones de ladies use for rings, and if dey be bringing in *four* ships, de price is gonna drop. So she was gonna sell hers now – she got a few in a deal."

Jorac stared at them and his stomach fell to his feet. "No army. No wizard power. What could four big ships do to Vaggert if they're full of soldiers and catch us by surprise?"

Cerom said, "So you think this is planned? Pull the defenses away from the city, and strike for the head, meaning the Emperor?"

Jorac looked at the two of them. "Does it fit?"

He saw they both had sour, worried looks. Jorac thought his face probably looked like that too.

"Dat's why we came."

Cerom said, "We wanted to see what you think – same as us. The boat-watchers just sent the word in; they'll be near Swampside in an hour, maybe a little more. The wind is perfect for the trading ships, like most afternoons, so we guess they'll be here in the city in a couple of hours. I've started rounding up the Constables, moving them to the west side of the bridge. If nothing happens, they'll still be fairly close to the drunks we'll find here tonight. . ."

Jorac looked at him. "But you think it will happen – well, me too." He turned to Schrog. "Is there any way of rounding up the Swampside toughs?"

"Not to fight on de same side, 'lessen you pays dem first. Can't be done in an hour."

Cerom asked him, "Any way of stopping a ship?" Something in his voice said he was expecting a positive answer.

Schrog sighed. "Well, it don't come from me, or nobody I know, right? You know dere's dat bend in de river, right by Swampside? Tricky to navigate, gots to make a couple of turns, quick-like? Everybody knows, you try it at night, chances are you be wreckin' your boat. Natcherly, da Swampies love a good boat wreck. Lots of coin to be made from a wreck." He laughed a little, as if remembering.

"So let's say – now, I'm just makin' sump'n up, like, daydreamin' – let's say dere's a small boat out dere, painted dark an' covered in gray canvas, real hard to see at night. And dere's a couple of guys in de boat, wit' a couple of strong, sharp metal hooks tied together wit' some good strong rope. Suppose dese guys gets real close to one of dem big boats, and dey waits till it's makin' a turn, right? And when de rudder's turned sharp, dey hook de rudder, and dey hook de side of de boat wit' de 'udder hook, what do you t'ink de boat might do?"

Jorac said, "Keep turning when it needed to go straight, and probably crash right into the riverbank near Swampside." Once again, he mentally saluted Swampie resourcefulness. "But these ships aren't coming in at night."

"Yeah, it would only work de once't if someone ever tried it in de daytime. But nobody been trying to run de river at night in a few years, so maybe, if it ain't gonna work no more anyways, maybe dey get persuaded to try de hooks in de daytime. Dat is, if dey figgers dey kin get away wit' it, not get in trouble I mean. Or get asked too many questions about how dey knowed it worked, neither."

Jorac nodded decisively. "In a case of national emergency like this, I'm sure that could be arranged." He looked around. Skowers had to be here somewhere – unless he'd already found a lady to sneak off with. Jorac scanned the crowd anxiously, and finally saw his quarry on the far side of the area, getting ready for a dance. "There. Schrog, please go get Skowers and bring him here – apologize a lot, okay? No wait, there are too many people here; let's gather over on the mainland. There's a scholar's book shop there by the bridge; we left Lartie there this morning, and I think he needs to hear this too. Let's meet there."

While Schrog set off, Jorac said to Cerom, "Strike for the head, right? So they'll land at the Westside docks south of the bridge, so they can head straight uphill to the palace."

"That's what I thought. There's no reason for them to land at Southgate; that's on the wrong side of the river. The Old Bridge wharf there" – he pointed south – "will only take one ship, and it's on the wrong side too. They'd have to cross the high bridge if they landed there. So we'll meet them at the Westside docks. I'm trying to get all our swords and archers ready."

"If they're just traders, no need to upset them."

"If they're just traders, they won't even see us. We'll be hidden away. But if they're raiders, we'll give them a bit of a surprise."

"I hope so. Or really, I hope not."

"Me too. Gotta go."

Jorac walked back to the entrance, but the guard wouldn't let him into the ladies-only area away from the dance floor until he showed his badge. "Business, I'm afraid," he told the guard.

As he looked for Dorrie, he also scanned the dance floor for Kimma but didn't see her – this dance was a whirling sort that made it hard to keep track of anyone. Dorrie was watching the dancers from a comfortable chair, in a row with the other "aunties." She had her head together with the lady next to her, talking quietly.

Jorac bowed. "Your pardon, Madame Velosp, but I must speak with you urgently."

"Wizard Constable – does the empire need my help again?" The lady beside Dorrie raised her eyebrows.

"I fear so. If you will excuse me, Milady."

When they were alone, Jorac said, "Cerom told Schrog about King Fox and the eagles. Schrog just heard there are four big ships headed here from Parlund. They fly an eagle flag, and usually there's only one a year. This time there are four, with no explanation. They don't get along with us, and anyway, this all makes sense. The army's gone, the wizards are out of commission. The silver ball didn't work, but they had other plans – and here they are. So, what do you think?"

Dorrie's face had the same sick look that she'd seen on Cerom and Schrog. She looked around the dance. "What can we do about it? I can talk to some market guards, if you think that will help."

"Let's meet over on the mainland, at that book shop where we left Lartie. See if you can find Kimma."

Jorac hurried across the low stone bridge to the mainland and into the book shop. In the dusty, shelf-lined front room were an elderly clerk and Lartie, who was sitting cross-legged on the floor, reading a fat tome in his lap. He looked up in surprise when Jorac burst in and asked him to come outside with him at once.

They stood in front of the shop while Jorac grimly explained what was happening. "Those papers said they'll strike for the head, meaning they'll land at Westmire and head straight for the palace. Cerom's organizing a defense to meet them there at the west-side docks, and I'm trying to see what else we can do. I've told some people to meet me here."

Lartie stared at him with big eyes. "Obviously, one thing we need to do is get word to the wizards. They may not have much power at the moment, but at least they have knowledge."

"Right!" said Dorrie, who'd come up behind him. To Jorac she said, "Kimma was still dancing, so I came by myself. I'll go back for her after the next dance."

"Dorrie, you keep Kimma safe. When you've brought her, I'd like the two of you to head over to the Tower and let the wizards know. Think you can get the message to them?"

Dorrie shook her head. "I doubt it. The compound gate was locked up as tight as ever when we came by earlier. I'm willing to try, but unless we can at least find a guard or someone to talk to, I can't think of any way we can communicate with them. . ." She stood there frowning.

Jorac tried to think of other answers. After a moment, he said to Lartie, "Did your uncle ever tell you about the Wizard's Compound? I think you told me he apprenticed there. Do you remember any stories about sneaky ways to get in, for instance?"

Lartie looked worried, and hesitated. When Jorac and Dorrie looked at him expectantly, he sighed. "There was a story or two. He mentioned some crawl-ways in the attics, places a boy could slip through. I think I remember what he said."

Jorac said, "We need the wizards to stop the wind if they can – it's bringing the ships up the river. If we can slow them down, maybe we'll have a chance."

Lartie looked a little scared, but then drew himself up bravely. "I'll get in there, one way or another. I think I know how. But you two had better write a note for me, so they don't think I'm a mere thief, or insane."

Just then, Skowers arrived with Schrog. Jorac quickly explained what he thought was happening, and said, "Can you two figure out how to stop one of those ships?"

Skowers was red-faced; he'd definitely been drinking. "It seems rather thin, if you ask me. I don't know anything about that, I'm afraid."

"Dat ain't a problem." Schrog's tone wasn't friendly. "I knows who to talk to. You just gots to get me dere."

"I'm sorry, constable, I can't possibly consent to joining your conspiracy on your say-so. I've got to get back to the ball, actually."

Schrog said, "I wonder if dat lady you was talkin' to knows where you be born?"

Skowers turned and glowered at Schrog. If looks could kill, Schrog would have been a puddled mass of rotting flesh.

Schrog just stared back at the taller man. "I ain't saying nothin' to nobody. Not my style. But I needs to go talk to some folks, ones dat you know, right now. Dat's all."

Jorac added, "Maybe you can make some excuses to your lady friend, and come back quickly?"

Skowers turned to look at Jorac, and back at Schrog. "I'll be right back. Damn you." He turned and went back toward the island.

Schrog said, "Some paper be helping. Dat way dey knows you ain't tryin' to catch 'em out. Maybe you kin write some kinda permission or such."

Jorac and Dorrie went to a nearby note-stand that sold fancy paper and pens, to enable love-notes to be written and passed at the dance. He bought an expensive piece of paper and wrote a brief note for Lartie, telling Pergimtor of probable invaders and pleading that they stop the winds on the river if at all possible; he and Dorrie signed it.

They carried the note back to Lartie, waving it in the air to dry the ink. Dorrie offered to hire a carriage and take him to the Wizard's Compound, which would save time. But, she explained, Kimma would have to go with her because a proper young lady couldn't be left alone at a public dance. Jorac didn't like the idea of Kimma being out of his sight, but reluctantly agreed. Lartie said he'd be in the book shop when they were ready, and went back inside.

Soon Skowers was back, stomping toward the group. "All right, let's go," he said to Schrog. "I have a horse, but he can't carry double. You'll have to walk."

"Wait a second," Jorac said. "I need to write out something for you – be right back." He went to the note-stand and paid for another note – the clerk there raised an eyebrow but said nothing. Jorac selected the largest sheet of perfumed paper and wrote on it in large letters:

"Citizens of Vaggert: Please assist Constable Schrog in determining if the ships carrying the eagle flag are legitimate traders, or (as we fear) invaders. If they prove to be invaders, please do your utmost to stop them, by any possible means. Such methods are entirely up to your imagination, and I will personally and professionally guarantee you will not be prosecuted for this action." Jorac signed it with his full title as Wizard Constable, City of Vaggert, Empire of Etrombia.

He took it back to the group and read it aloud to them. Skowers said, "You know this could put you in jail? In fact, it'll probably do just that."

Jorac shook his head. "Schrog can handle it. If they're traders, we just wave to them. But let me ask you, have you had any dealings with people from Parlund?"

"They're . . ." He looked at Dorrie, demure in her ladylike finery. "I've heard they tend to be somewhat arrogant. As if dealing with us makes them somehow unclean. Rather irritating."

Schrog just looked at Skowers with a raised eyebrow.

Dorrie looked at them wisely and said, "Sorry, I think the latest dance should be over by now – I need to go get Kimma." She winked at Jorac as she left.

Once she was out of sight, Skowers let loose. "Oh, hell yes! They're assholes, every one of them, and they act like they're holding their nose every time they talk to us. I tried to buy some honey off one of their inbound boats at a place deep in the swamp one time, and they wouldn't take silver or gold – only good copper, lots of it. And their trader called us animals and idiots when he thought we couldn't hear – we had a guy who could speak some of their tongue. So don't think I have any love for them. I just don't think they'd do it. It's suicide."

"I hope you're right. If you are, the only thing we've lost is a little time. But the army is late coming back from the rebellion in the north."

"There are wizards right over there. Four boats would be simple – easy to see if they had soldiers, easy to sink."

Jorac and Schrog looked at each other, and then at Skowers.

A dawning realization showed on Skowers face, along with a bit of worry. "There's something you aren't telling me."

Jorac said, "Yes."

Skowers looked at Jorac and started to speak, but Jorac interrupted him by pointedly handing him the note he'd just written. "Schrog says those ships will be at Swampside in less than an hour."

Skowers gave Jorac a searching look, then turned to Schrog. "My horse can carry double for a little while; let's go. I know where we can get some faster ones."

* * *

"I'm not leaving."

Jorac said, "But Kimma – "

"No. Oh, I'll go with Dorrie to take Lartie to the wizard's compound, but I'm coming back. That's final."

"Dorrie. . ." Jorac turned to her, pleading.

Dorrie shook her head as well. "I'm coming back too. It may be nothing, as you say. It won't do for us to skip out of the dance early – people will start to talk. Now you go back over there. Maybe you can pass the word to some like those young Leganwei boys that they should pick up their swords and leave early."

Jorac looked at the two women and raised his hands in surrender. "Okay. If it happens, help keep everyone calm, okay? You two have level heads at least."

Kimma said, "If you're right about the invasion, that island is easy to defend. We can pull up the boards on the north bridge, and that just leaves the stone bridge. Those people would be safer there than trying to get back home. They mostly live up around the palace, right?"

Jorac nodded. Kimma continued to surprise him. She'd reasoned that like an army veteran, which was what he was supposed to be. He'd better start thinking like it.

"Alright, I give up. Kimma, love, stay safe, okay? Now go; I'll go talk to Zarl and his friends."

He gave her hand a final squeeze, and they parted. He was worried, but shut that out of his mind – he had work to do.

Chapter 36 - Unwelcoming the Visitors

Jorac found a slightly drunk Zarl and Parf, and explained that their swords might be needed. At first they thought he was joking and laughed him off. Only when he repeated his request for armed help, in a conspiratorial voice, in front of some of Zarl's friends, did they take it seriously.

In his best stage whisper, he told the Leganwei brothers, "I'll let you know when the ships are nearby. Remember – if they come, they'll have armor and heavy swords. Just dance around, slow them down a little. No one get fancy; don't be a brave, dead idiot. And above all else, keep it quiet. If the ladies hear about it, they'll run home and be right where the invaders are. Just find a few people you trust, and sort of drift that way slowly."

The two boys nodded seriously, and were looking around the dance floor when Jorac walked away.

A dozen more semi-trained swords couldn't hurt, and if I'm wrong, they haven't lost much except some drinking time. He looked around to see if there might be some other source of manpower.

He had to gamble on starting rumors, but with the help of his badge he gathered the liveried guards together and told them there might be unspecified trouble tonight. If there was, they were to pull up the north bridge's timbers and barricade the south one. They exchanged a look – they obviously thought Jorac was at least simple-headed, if not drunk or deranged.

One of them patiently explained, "Sir, those are our orders anyway, if there's any trouble on the mainland. Most of the young heirs and such are here tonight; they need to stay safe." *I can see what they really want to tell me is to lay off the punch*, Jorac thought sourly.

He just thanked them for their time, and went away to worry some more. He thought of who was available to defend the city – constables, the rump of the army, private guards, a few normal citizens. Plus the wizards, if any had been isolated from the plague or had recovered – and if Lartie had managed to get word to them there was even a problem. He couldn't think of anything else to do, so he walked up on the high Wizard Bridge where he could see when Dorrie and Kimma's carriage came back. He stood there and stared downriver, where he saw nothing unusual, and tried to quiet his mind.

* * *

An hour later, as afternoon started to give way to evening, Jorac again stood on the high bridge and counted the ships as they came around the final bend in the river. They were large and boxy, as Schrog had described, and looked identical, even to the color and layout of the sails. Jorac was no sailor, but something about the sameness of the ships spoke of a common command. He counted one, two, three, but there was no fourth ship. He didn't know whether to be relieved or worried about that. Was the initial report wrong? Or was one of them stuck in the mud at Swampside?

The wind seemed to be gradually dying out, which Jorac hoped meant Lartie had been successful. Or it could mean the fountains were about to die out too, in which case there'd be an even larger set of problems to worry about. He peered north across the bridge. He couldn't quite see the fountain on the nearby island, but the fact that no one was suddenly pointing at it cheered him a little.

As the wind died, the ships lost their way. The sails that had been puffed out at an angle to the river started to flap, then sagged down and hung loosely. When the ships started to drift in the river, Jorac saw to his surprise that they also carried oars. Six huge oars sprouted from each side of the first ship, then the others, and soon all three were rowing up the river. He could see on deck that there were four or five men per oar. With oars that large, the strokes were necessarily slow, but they were making steady progress against the outflow of the river.

A realization dawned on Jorac. A trading ship that size wouldn't have the crewmen to handle that many oars! They had over fifty people per ship just rowing. He made a quick estimate of their speed – he guessed he had about twenty minutes before they arrived – and ran back down the ramp toward the dance.

He stopped at the sword-check booth, where he had to rouse the dozing attendant. A quick look at the collected weapons showed perhaps thirty swords – he was hoping for more. "Here's my check – get my swords ready now – two of them. I'll be right back." He ran inside to the dance. He didn't see Dorrie or Kimma, but he quickly found Zarl and Parf.

"They're coming. Three ships, and they're *not* just traders. They have oversize oars, and they must have fifty people per ship just pulling those. No telling how many more. Grab your swords, get your friends. Get up on the high bridge there and sneak across to the west side – you'll have to crouch low so they don't see you. And hurry."

The young men looked impressed as they left to gather their friends. As Jorac scurried back to the bridge, he hoped he wasn't sending them to their doom.

From his vantage point on the bridge, Jorac was impressed that, even when propelled by muscle power, the Parlundian ships stayed in line; they clearly knew what they were doing. There was nothing he could do yet; he didn't know whether to go across the bridge and help with the upcoming fight, or go back and try to find Kimma and Dorrie and. . . do what? So he waited, and worried.

Finally the big ships approached the bridge where Jorac was standing. He watched as the first one came near his side of the river, then made a sweeping turn toward the small cluster of docks on the Westmire side. There were just two docks large enough for ships this size; one was the remnant of the old King's Bridge, now converted to a dock, and the other was New Dock, just to the south of it and almost as large. Interestingly, neither dock had a ship on either side of it right now – he wondered if that was a coincidence.

He heard a shouted order from the first ship and watched as the pace of its oars changed and it made a wide turn and headed toward the south dock. While the second ship was starting its turn, the first one backed its oars and slowed down. At the last moment, the huge oars on the dock side were pulled in and a man swung off the front on a rope and tied the ship to the mooring post on the dock. It was a tidy bit of seamanship, obviously well practiced.

The second ship had turned and was heading for the second dock as the third ship started its turn. Jorac briefly stepped across to the north side of the bridge and looked over at the island, where he could see the dance was continuing. He supposed it was for the best that most of them didn't know what was coming; if there was an attack he hoped Dorrie and Kimma could help organize a defense and keep them from panic. He shook his head and came back to watch the ships in the river. The rowers were really quite skilled.

As the second ship made its run to the dock, there was a lot of milling around on the deck of the first ship. Jorac peered at them but couldn't tell just what was happening there. When he glanced back at the third ship, he saw it wasn't turning! Instead it was headed north toward the big, rickety old dock sticking out from the silted-up riverbank just south of Jorac's perch. Big ships couldn't pull alongside that dock anymore; these days it was mostly used for pleasure craft and a few barges with loads too big for the bridge. But a big ship *could* pull up to it across its end. . .

Jorac had a flash of understanding. The "head" the eagles were heading for was both the emperor on the west *and* the wizards on the east! And he'd arranged for the west side of the river to have all the defenses, and the east side bare. At full speed, he ran east down the stone ramp of the bridge and turned south toward the old dock.

He arrived just as the Parlundian ship was pulling up. There was a row of four flimsy wooden sheds across the west, river-facing end of the dock; he'd been here before and knew they were filled with equipment like ropes, fenders, and fending-off poles. He ran out to the northwest corner of the dock, beyond the last shed, just in time to see a sailor swing off the ship on a thick rope and start to wrap it around the dock's corner post. When he heard Jorac running toward him, he pulled out a huge knife and slashed with it. He was dark-skinned and wiry and had a feral look on his face.

Jorac skidded to a quick stop and drew both his swords. The sailor dropped into a low crouch and made a few sweeping feints. He danced a little from sided to side, then sprang up at Jorac, leading with his knife. He didn't get far; Jorac cut him down quickly. It had been some years since Jorac had been in a real sword fight, but his body and brain remembered what was needed. He saw the blood leaking from the man, but it didn't bother him right now. He started cutting at the fat docking rope, and then a noise from the ship alerted him.

He glanced up and saw several men on deck, leaning over the sides, aiming bows at him – an arrow whizzed by his neck even as he looked. As quickly as he could, he jumped back behind the nearest shed. A crossbow bolt came through the back and some splinters hit him – the archers couldn't see him, but they could estimate his position. The front of the ship drifted away from the dock a little, and he was glad to see the mostly-cut docking rope break and slip into the water.

When he looked down toward the south corner, he saw the ship's stern was sticking out far past the dock; its middle was just past the row of sheds. In the narrow space between the last shed and the water, a man was hooking a gangplank to a gap in the dock planking with two heavy metal hooks. Jorac ran forward and simply kicked the man into the water. As he dodged back behind the nearby shed, a crossbow bolt whistled by his ear so close it stung a little. He peeked around the shed and saw a soldier in leather armor coming down the gangplank. As soon as the soldier stepped onto the dock, Jorac stepped out from behind the shed and struck him with a vicious blow to the neck. The soldier staggered a few steps toward shore and fell heavily, and Jorac jumped back behind the shed again. He heard a few arrows hit the shed and bounce around inside, but nothing came through to hit him.

Another soldier came down the gangplank, running this time; Jorac could hear him coming. He stayed behind the shed, ducked low, and timed his hard swing at knee level just right. His sword went right through the leg, and the man screamed as he fell to the deck, fountaining blood from his leg. He squirmed around as his life's blood drained onto the dock – Jorac knew the blood could make his footwork uncertain if he wasn't careful. He peeked at the ship and saw the gangplank was empty, so he leaned his swords against the shed wall, grabbed a long oar, and pushed the dying man into the water. He hadn't shifted into a Berserker trance, but there was his *home* on shore he needed to protect, and he'd do it as best he could, whatever it took. Moving quietly, he picked up his swords again, found a knothole in the shed where he could watch the gangplank, and waited.

A large man in heavy armor came clanking down the gangplank carrying a halberd; chain mail hung from his heavy metal hat, and strong plate covered his torso and legs. He stopped several feet from the dock and used his halberd to bash in the south side of the shed, so Jorac couldn't surprise any more attackers that way. Jorac had seen it coming and moved back just far enough; when the man stepped on the dock and thrust the halberd at him, Jorac backed up further to encourage him to attack. At the next thrust, Jorac hit the long weapon with his right-hand sword to push it out of the way and side-stepped closer to the man. With his left-hand sword, he made a single rapid, thrust up under the man's chin. It was enough; he fell at the edge of the dock, and the weight of the armor on his chest and shoulders drew him off and into the water.

Jorac moved back near the gangplank and waited. There was a small rowboat standing on its end in the remains of the half-demolished shed, so he stood behind that to ward off any crossbow bolts as he waited. He wasn't tired or thirsty or anything, just focused. No one would be getting off that ship alive, as long as he could stop it.

He heard talking on the ship, but he couldn't understand any of it, so he paid it no mind. Soon one more lightly armored man almost danced down the gangplank; like Jorac he carried two swords. Unlike Jorac, he hadn't been practicing with the best fighters in Etrombia for weeks on end. Between the uncertain footing on the dock and the need to stay behind the sheds, it took Jorac almost a minute to kill him with a double-lunge move that Taj had taught him. The man fell face first between two sheds after Jorac put a sword six inches into the middle of his chest.

The arrows from the ship had stopped as the two fought, so Jorac quickly moved back to behind the rowboat before the archers had a chance to find him. He took stock – he'd collected a cut on the back of his right arm that barely broke the skin, and a deeper cut on his left bicep, but nothing that slowed him down. He was in full Berserker mode by now, and yelled up at the ship, "That the best you got?"

From the ship, he was surprised to hear an answer in accented Etrombian. "Hoo, you good. We come down."

Two tall, strong-looking men came down the gangplank; each had a large hammer in each hand. They were young but balding, with beefy blacksmith shoulders, and they looked almost alike except that one wore a blackish sleeveless shirt and the other a dull green one. When they got near the end of the gangplank, they turned sideways and started swinging the hammers in a weaving pattern, almost hitting each other's arms, and almost hitting their own. They kept much closer together than fighting men normally would, but they seemed to know the pattern well and never interfered with each other.

At the bottom of the gangplank they turned sideways at the same time, and first one, then the other stepped onto the dock. Jorac could find no opening to attack them. The hammers were long-handled, heavy blacksmith hammers but the two – brothers perhaps, or at least kinfolk – swung them as if they were light sticks. Each swung the inside one in front of the other, overlapping their swift stokes, providing defense and attack at the same time. Any one person wouldn't stand much chance with them.

The two stepped forward as one, and the black-shirted man spoke. "Hoo, you good. Kralak, he think he take you quick, but you take him quick." His strokes didn't falter as he talked, not in the slightest – many men could talk or fight, but not many did both at once.

The green-shirted man said, "You take Ulox too. But now you die. Djouk and P'louk, we kill you before we kill wizards. You tell Gods our names," and the two took another synchronized step forward.

Black-shirt said, "Gods hear our names before. Many times."

With the swift windmilling action of their arms, either one would have been a test, but together there was absolutely no opening for Jorac to exploit. Helplessly, he retreated a step, then another. The one time he got close enough to test the pair, a sword was nearly struck from his hand, and he took another step back. The hammer heads were as big as his fist, or a little bigger, and moving very fast. The steps the pair took toward him were slow and small, which kept their legs from being exposed, but they kept coming.

Jorac slowly backed away from them, up the row of sheds. Mindful of the archers on the deck, he moved quickly across the gaps between sheds, but a crossbow bolt came through a shed wall and struck him a grazing blow in the thigh. It had been slowed some by the shed, but it *hurt*. Jorac normally didn't notice pain in a fight, but this time he did. Swords still in his hands, he rubbed his side, pretending to be more hurt than he was, to try to get the hammer wielders to break their weaving pattern. It didn't work; they just stepped forward one more small step, never changing the pattern or its cadence.

As Jorac retreated, he considered his few options. He didn't dare turn his back on them; about the best thing he could think of was to dive off the dock and hope for the best – perhaps he could throw his swords at the two as he went. He knew he wouldn't have time to drop the swords and draw his dagger, and he'd make an easy target in the water, but it was better than being crushed by a hammer here on the dock. And he'd better make up his mind soon – he wouldn't be behind the shelter of the sheds much longer.

The relentless hammers kept inching toward him, and soon he was beside the last shed, out of options and just seconds away from a desperation dive into the water. But suddenly, green-shirt on the left yelled "Ow!" and his ear and cheek spouted blood; he stepped back a bit behind the other man. Black-shirt on the right took a slight step forward and expanded his swings a little while his wounded companion put his hand to his head. Jorac had no time to question; he just looked for an opening, thought he saw one, and was getting ready to attack when green-shirt grinned and said, "I not hurt, just hurt ear." He stepped forward and they went back into their pattern, and Jorac had to back away again.

After the pair had moved another step forward, the wounded man's jaw suddenly exploded in a big splash of blood and he made a wordless bleat, almost like a butchered sheep. Falling backwards, he released his outside hammer, which – perhaps by design – came right at Jorac's chest, flying in hard.

Jorac managed to twist enough to take the hammer on his shoulder, which probably saved his life. It still struck a crushing blow, and he was slammed back by the force of it. His left arm went numb and he dropped his sword point, then dropped the sword altogether. He still had another sword but he was hurt.

Black-shirt looked down and saw his companion lying there in a broken heap. He whimpered a little, and then with wild fury on his face, sped up his attack. His hammers were a blur now, almost whistling in the air.

"You kill Djouk. You kill my brother. Now you die. Now!" He took a longer step forward, and Jorac again had to retreat. He could see an opening now if he had two swords; he had to block one hammer and come in just behind the other one, but he couldn't do it that way with only one good arm. He took another step back and feinted with his sword at his opponent's eyes, which for the first time made the man step backwards, and gained him some ground. That was a move P'louk's brother would have blocked before, but it still wasn't quite an opening – the hammers were moving fast enough that completing the thrust would have gotten Jorac's sword knocked from his hand.

P'louk moved forward again, and Jorac moved back, ever closer to the edge. Trying to swim for it would probably be futile at this point – with one bad arm and a wounded leg he'd be lucky not to drown. And dammit, he wasn't going to run away. He couldn't remember exactly what, but he was protecting something there on the mainland, something that he would NOT give up. So he took a step back – his last step before he moved beyond the safety the sheds – and when the hammer-wielder took another step toward him, Jorac jumped up and forward. He tipped his sword back with his wrist as he jumped, then snapped it forward, just after one hammer went by and just before another came past, and split P'louk's face open. A hammer came down on his side and back just as he managed to make a last effort and push the point of the sword forward, into P'louk's brain. The large man fell nervelessly, taking Jorac with him, and they hit the dock hard. A hammer came down on Jorac's head – not hard enough to break the skin, but hard enough to make him gray out and see stars.

He blinked his eyes a few times, and finally his sight returned. He tried to get up several times before finally succeeding – it wasn't easy with a damaged arm and leg. He managed to pick up a sword and just stood there for a few seconds. He vaguely knew it wasn't safe here, so he dimly struggled across the dock to the one place he knew was safe, behind the rowboat near the gangplank. He waved his sword over his head and yelled hoarsely, "That the best you got?"

This time there was no response from the ship.

More quietly, he said, "Thought so. Now go away." He wasn't thinking very clearly, but he knew the people on the ship annoyed him, and they should just leave.

* * *

He didn't know how long he'd been there. He leaned against the rowboat, watching blood slowly drip down his injured arm and puddle at his feet. And then he watched a giant man half-drag, half-carry a large sheet of metal across the dock toward him. He wasn't worried; he knew that giant, and knew he was a friend, even if he couldn't remember his name right now. A few arrows and crossbow bolts pinged off the metal plate – it was a big curved copper piece meant for the bottom of a ship. Looking more closely, Jorac could see there were a couple of people behind the giant. Either that, or Hox – yes, that was his name – had sprouted two more sets of legs. The thought made him grin stupidly.

Hox reached him and said, "Why are you smiling like that? Happy to be alive?"

"I thought you had six legs. It was funny."

Hox turned to the men behind him. "Get him out of here. Keep close behind me, don't expose yourself."

Jorac said, "Yes, don't expose yourself. Propriety, always propriety." He started laughing a bit, but that hurt his ribs too much, so he just grinned.

One of the men said, "Can you walk?"

Jorac looked down at his leg, and said, "I don't think so, my leg got hurt. And my arm doesn't work at all. But you should see the other guy." Jorac grinned and almost started laughing again.

The other man said, "We did – all of them. Can you lay on this tarp? We can carry you out of here, if Hox can keep between us and the ship."

Hox said, "I can do that. He's losing blood, better hurry."

They carried Jorac off the dock, shielded behind the copper plate. Jorac lay there in the tarp and watched the puffy white clouds in the early evening sky – that was all he could see, and they were nice. It was a pretty, blue-colored sky today too, this time of day it was always a nice color. He wondered why he didn't notice that more often. He said, "Nice clouds up there today."

Hox's voice was worried; he said, "Let's hurry. Keep up now."

They went a little faster off the dock and up the street, then turned a corner and set him down on the ground near a carriage. There stood the most beautiful girl in the world, with a crossbow in her hands. A double crossbow, he remembered – it looked like she was loading it. She dropped it and knelt down over him with a desperately worried look on her face.

He couldn't have that – he didn't want her to worry. He smiled up at her and said, "Marry me." Her surprised look was the last thing he remembered.

Chapter 37 - Jorac Has a Headache

When Jorac woke it was only a few hours later, but much had changed. Now he felt every pain in his abused body – he had a splitting headache, there were several cuts on his arms, a superficial but painful wound on his leg, and every breath hurt his ribs and shoulder.

But his brain worked better – he wasn't in that giddy, half-confused state that Hox found him in. He could see he was inside somewhere, in a room he didn't recognize, lying partly upright on a bed. There was lantern-light and he could hear someone nearby; he turned his head and saw Dorrie there, watching him. He said, "Water, please?"

Dorrie reached for a cup with a straw and let him drink. When he was finished she said, "How do you feel?"

"Like shit. What happened to those ships?"

"Over on the west side, a couple of hundred men got off and made a rush for the palace, but the constables and soldiers and such stopped them, so they just turned around and retreated back on their ships and pulled out. On this side, they never even got off the ship. Pretty soon all three ships turned around and went back out together."

Jorac started to say, "Did they. . ." but there was a noise outside the door and a woman's voice quietly said, "Dorrie?"

Dorrie called, "Come on in. He's awake."

The door opened and Kimma came in. She dropped some things she was carrying and rushed over to his bedside. He smiled up at her.

She smiled back at him with a radiant smile. "Oh, I'm glad to see you awake so soon. That's a good sign." She reached out and tentatively touched his arm. "Where do you hurt?"

"All over. My shoulder is the worst, I think."

"We have a healer coming – a licensed one, I mean. Sorry I wasn't here when you woke up; I figured you'd be out longer. I was helping out on the other side of the river."

Jorac could hear the wink in Dorrie's voice when she said, "My young ward here learned a bit about healing from her old granny. So she was helping out with the wounded – fewer of those than you might think, thanks to you. But she made me promise to sit right here with you."

Jorac took another drink of water, and said to Kimma, "You did right. And thank you for saving my life, my love."

Kimma took a deep breath, as if mastering some strong emotion. "I thought I'd lost you," she said hoarsely.

Jorac reached across his body with his good hand and took hers. "I guess I was worried about them getting to you. Maybe I get a little crazy when I fight."

Dorrie said, "Maybe? The whole Harvest Ball saw that fight. Half of them went up on the bridge to watch. And at the end, you got up and challenged the whole ship, *again*. They'll be talking about that for ages."

"Well . . . one of those hammers kind of hit me on the head, at the end."

Dorrie continued, "And Hox said you thought he had six legs?"

"Two men were behind him, and he's so big all I could see were their legs."

Kimma said, "And do you remember saying the clouds were nice?"

"Well, they were. You notice things like that when you're being carried in a tarp and that's all you can see."

Kimma said, "And. . ."

"I meant everything I said today, my dear. Dorrie, I asked Kimma to marry me, but I didn't hear her answer. I think I passed out."

Kimma squeezed his hand and he said "Ow, my hand, gently please."

She backed off the pressure but kept holding his hand. Her face was scrunched up with emotion, and she didn't answer right away. Finally she took a deep breath and said, "I've thought about it – a lot – and I've talked it over with Dorrie, too. There's nothing in this world I'd rather be than your life companion."

Jorac could see her face contort again with emotion, but she took another deep breath and continued. "But I'm not the type to be a good wife. I'd be miserable if I was chained to a stove, or a nursery, and I just can't do that. If you married me, you wouldn't get a real wife, all you'd get is plain little Kimma, the whore's daughter who likes to play at being someone else."

"But Kimma... The stuff you're worrying about, it's just little details. Not important." he said flatly. "I want Kimma, no matter where she came from. That's the one I want for my life's companion. You."

Suddenly he felt overwhelming emotion filling his lungs and making it hard to breathe. His voice sounded funny to him, and he could hear his pulse in his ears. Maybe it was the wounds he'd received, or maybe just laying his feelings bare that did it. "And she's not plain at all."

Kimma's face was lit with a wide smile of joy and relief, plus a few tears straggling down her flushed cheeks. He glanced at Dorrie; her eyes were brimming too.

Jorac turned to Dorrie – that was a mistake; it made his head hurt worse. "Dorrie, we'll need your help and your good sense selecting a governess. And before then, a cook."

He turned to his eyes Kimma. "Hox will tell you I can't cook either – and I think we can afford both, don't you?"

Kimma smiled a happy smile, leaned down and very carefully kissed him.

"Yes my love, I will marry you."

Jorac smiled back – at least that didn't hurt. "You just have to promise me one thing."

"What's that?"

"You won't ever forget your crossbow."

He got to hear Kimma's laugh again. He still liked it.

* * *

Jorac stayed in the tiny house near the docks for the next three days. A variety of healers came to see him, changing bandages, examining the stitches in his leg with approval, and tut-tutting about his shoulder. None of them could do much; none were wizards, and even if wizard healers had been available, Jorac wouldn't have let one work on him because of the chance of sneezing – even the simplest of movements hurt.

After much consultation and some painful range-of-motion tests, the healers decided nothing in his shoulder was broken, but it was so thoroughly bruised that it had swollen into near immobility, and would be long in healing. He had at least two cracked ribs and various cuts, scrapes, and painful bruises over his whole body. He made the mistake of looking at his torso once when the bedding was being changed: the red, yellow, and purple coloration of his skin was amazing – but it would have been a good deal more interesting if it had been on someone else.

The owner of the house had moved out to let Jorac stay, since there was only room for one bed. Kimma, Hox, or Monrae stayed on guard to keep out unwanted visitors; lots of people – it seemed like hundreds – wanted to see or talk to Jorac. Sometimes, Hox's improving Schrog-like growl had to be used to scare away the most persistent of them. The one person Hox allowed in was Brozadam , who came the day after the fight, just after a healer who'd fed Jorac some pain medicine had left.

"Jorac, I hear you fight good. You hurt but they not know, so you wave sword, challenge them. They scared, not fight. I teach that, next year."

He turned to Kimma and said, "You be Kimma. Call me Brownie, yes? Jorac ask me bring you letter, now I see why – you shoot crossbow good. I can see it?"

Jorac lifted the double crossbow from the far side of the bed and handed it to Kimma, who passed it to Brozadam . Kimma was making him keep it by his bedside this week – he had no enemies he knew about, but there were surely agents of Parlund who wished him ill, and he couldn't whip a baby bunny right now.

Brozadam turned it over in his hands. "Weak power, yes, but two shots, good, very good. You practice, practice, yes? Keep Jorac safe." His wide grin lit up the room. "He fool like me. Need help stay safe. Jorac, you visit me when heal, yes?"

Jorac smiled and nodded at him as he put away the crossbow.

"I go now or Hox push me out. You rest."

Kimma said, "Yes, you rest now."

Jorac said, "I will, thanks," and was asleep almost instantly.

* * *

The vile concoctions Jorac was given every few hours helped the pain only a bit; they mostly made him logy and gave him weird dreams. He'd even dreamed that Lartie was actually an old man, a wizard who'd found a way to make himself young. That dream he remembered, and in a lucid moment, decided it might be his subconscious speaking the truth to him. But when he thought it over, he concluded it didn't matter much – young or old, Lartie had proved his loyalty to Etrombia. The boy's story could be investigated if there was ever a need, but for now he was just going to leave it alone.

On the third morning, he refused anything but some soup and bread, and for the first time in days, paid attention to his surroundings.

He heard people asking about him – his fight had been seen from the island or the bridge by all the young nobility in the city; as a result, he was suddenly famous and wildly popular. The owner of the tiny house was planning on charging admission after he had left, and he even heard a bard trying out a new song about him, asking his guardians for personal details. Luckily, Hox and Monrae were closemouthed about him, and Kimma was downright secretive, which was just the way Jorac liked it – some of the questions went well past politeness.

About herself, Kimma was a bit more forthcoming. Several times, Jorac heard her say, "Well, in the countryside, every well-educated young lady is taught to dress a wound, and to use a crossbow; you never know when such a skill may come in handy."

No one dared disagree – not after they'd seen her use both those skills. But she said these words in such a cheerful, open manner that her audience's response was more awe than fright. She no longer had to worry about not getting noticed, or not being accepted as a Noble Lady – she only needed to worry about finding time to attend all the gatherings she'd been invited to. Jorac would doubtless have to attend some of them too, but not yet, for which he was properly grateful.

* * *

On the fourth day, Jorac was judged well enough to endure the wagon ride home. Kimma had so far managed to keep the location of his house secret, and Hox went along to see that they weren't followed, so when they got there Jorac at last got a full night's sleep. He also got to hold Kimma by his side, albeit quite gingerly. It helped, somehow.

He spent the next few days impatiently trying to follow the healers' orders, finally graduating to some light stretching that wouldn't pull his wounds. He wasn't a cheerful patient but he tried to be a dutiful one, partly because he was always under Kimma's eye. When she was thinking like a healer she was no-nonsense and downright bossy – but even the bossy Kimma made him just smile sometimes, to her exasperation. Still, he was more glad than sorry when she gradually started working with Dorrie again, leaving him alone part of the time.

A week after he got home, he was surprised to see Pergimtor at his door, with Dorrie and Kimma behind him.

"Thank you, Madame, young lady, for your part in this. It is much appreciated," Pergimtor was saying. "I regret that I must ask you for some privacy now."

Dorrie said, "Certainly, High Wizard." Kimma added, "I'll return in an hour with the healer." And then they departed, leaving Pergimtor alone with Jorac.

Jorac greeted him and waved him into the little front room, saying, "Have a seat?"

Pergimtor looked around and sat on the loveseat, while Jorac gingerly lowered himself into an armchair. Everyone had told him his recovery was doing very well, considering where he started, but he was still quite sore sometimes.

Pergimtor leaned back comfortably and took in the house. "Nice little place you've got here. A good place to rest and recover." He smiled in his dry way. "Madame Velosp tells me the healers are quite hopeful that you'll make a full recovery – a natural one, without any magical intervention. That's always the best. Especially in your case, I should think."

"Yes, sir. It would really hurt if I was sneezing all the time."

Pergimtor nodded. "Well, I'm glad to see you doing so well. I read your report. Actually, all of them. I think we have you to thank for essentially saving the realm."

"Thank you, sir, but it wasn't me, at least not just me alone." Accepting praise always made Jorac uncomfortable. "Hox's wife came up with the way to set off the horse trap. And Constable Schrog figured out the clue about the four eagles in time to make some plans to beat them."

"Yes, but you're the one who got it done. We found someone who could talk to that man you kicked into the water. If they'd gotten off that ship, they were going to head straight for the Wizard's Compound, and I don't think we could have stopped them. They had a hundred soldiers on each ship, and all we had was weak wizards and apprentices – and they had their hands full just keeping the fountains going."

Jorac had heard stories from the other side of the river, too. There, Cerom's constables and a handful of civilians like Zarl and Parf had slowed the invaders down enough to let the palace guard and few army troops organize a solid defense near the base of the palace walls. Pergimtor, being a wizard, hadn't mentioned that part of the fight.

"The Wizards Council has decided to bestow upon you a life annuity of a hundred gold a year, as an expression of our appreciation. And yes, we heard about your upcoming marriage. It will devolve to your spouse if she outlives you."

Jorac blinked at him in astonishment. "Thank you, sir. I hardly know what to say. That's very handsome of you and the council." The last time Pergimtor had said something like this, he'd immediately sent Jorac off with the army; he hoped nothing like that would be forthcoming this time.

"And we're naming the elevator we're installing in the tower after you. Do you know how many stairs we have there?"

Politely, Jorac said, "One hundred and fifty-six, sir."

Pergimtor stared hard at him, then nodded. "That's right. It will be water powered, so it won't need a spell to make it work. When I called a council meeting a few weeks back, I wasn't sure some of the old fellows would make it up the stairs."

Jorac didn't want to say anything about the wizard council or the stairs, so he just nodded, but he had to fight back a grin.

"I suppose you'd like to know what happened while we were locked up in there. Well, it wasn't so desperate as you probably imagined, but still a bit strenuous. We had the upper classes of apprentices running the wizard lights at one point, but we were able to isolate a few late-arriving full wizards, and they managed to keep the fountains and sewers working properly. The weather spell will need some extra attention this year, but that's usually cast weeks or months in advance, so that will work out too."

"I'll admit I was a little concerned. If the fountains stopped, the populace would – worry."

"From what your Madame Velosp said, it would have been more than just worry, more like riot. But that's all in the past now."

Jorac nodded – it didn't hurt if he did it slowly. "I'm just glad you were able to stop the winds on the river when you did. That gave us the extra time we needed to get the defenses set near the palace."

"Yes, that was me. It took a bit of extra power, but I was recovering by then. I'd been exposed to it quite early, so I recovered earlier too."

"Thank you. It really helped. Tell me, did you ever find out what happened to that cloud-cotton tree that started the plague?"

"It's dead – it was dying anyway, but we burned it as a precaution. The farmers there remember a wagon parked by that tree for a day or two in early spring, but not much more. A young boy thinks he heard another language from the wagon, but it might have just been words he didn't understand."

"So, some sort of spell was cast on the tree?"

"Quite likely – a very complicated one at that. There were several layers – they had to leave the cotton part alone but reprogram the seeds to release some sort of contagious agent that both interfered with our mana collection and efficiently spread itself around. It was quite a complicated construction, and one aimed directly at wizards. Luckily it seems to only affect you once, then you develop resistance or immunity. We're more than a bit unhappy about it, believe me, and we're already looking for whoever did it."

"I was wondering about that. You know, it affected me too? I didn't sneeze around magic for a few days." Jorac refrained from mentioning how nice it was.

"That's interesting. When you've fully recovered, we should test your allergy again. Oh, and I wanted to ask you, how did that young boy get into the compound?"

"A relative told him some stories about his wizard apprenticeship, about sneaking in to where you weren't supposed to be. There are some attic passages that only a child can use."

"Yes, well he was most persuasive, and you could tell he was smart. I'm always looking for bright young lads like that to help out in the offices. Even if they don't turn out to have wizard power, it gets them a leg up in the world. Where can I find him?"

Jorac had foreseen something like this, and had gotten Schrog to quietly take Lartie back to the little farm. The boy had turned up at Dorrie's looking bedraggled the morning after the fight, and Kimma and Dorrie said they'd praised him to the skies for not only slipping right into the midst of the Wizard Council, but convincing them of the need for immediate action. Before leaving, Lartie had insisted on visiting Gleben for some books, but had gone willingly enough.

"No. You can't find him. And you shouldn't try."

"What?!" Pergimtor was certainly not used to being thwarted. And never in the flat, no-nonsense tone Jorac had used.

"Remember the charter that hangs on my office wall? It says I'm responsible for protecting the realm. I'm doing that. Leave the boy alone – don't ask about him, don't look for him."

Pergimtor stared hard at him.

Jorac was surprised at himself; a year ago he'd never have talked like that to the head wizard. "I'm sorry, sir, but you have no idea what harm you could cause if you find him."

Pergimtor said, "Ah, a noble lad, perhaps? Slumming, in a place where he shouldn't be? Then how did you meet him?"

Jorac stared back at Pergimtor. Then he let his expression break a little – if Pergimtor wanted to make this wrong guess, it was safer for everyone. "I really couldn't say. My job does take me all over the city, and the countryside, too."

Pergimtor nodded, perhaps a bit reluctantly. "Very well, this secret will remain yours. I don't say this very often, but I'll trust you. You've proven your loyalty and good sense."

Pergimtor's expression changed to one of mild puzzlement, and he produced a piece of paper. "Now there's just one more little item. We know one of the invading ships was wrecked in Swampside, thanks to your note. I've heard that some shipowners are very unhappy now that they've learned some of the old wrecks in that area were not entirely accidents, but that's for someone else to worry about. What I'm wondering about is what this bill is for. It's for ten gold pieces from someone named Madame Revar. She says it's for 'services related to aiding and abetting the detainment and capture of enemy invading soldiers.' Her grammar and spelling are both awful."

It was all Jorac could do not to laugh – that would have hurt his ribs – but he smiled a wide smile. "I think you should pay it. If you don't, I will. You know the captives we took in that fight? I heard we captured the man I kicked into the water on this side of the river, and two injured ones on the west side, but somehow we got forty, hale and healthy, down in Swampside. Lots of the soldiers off that wrecked ship got on the undamaged ships when they were going back out downriver, but far from all of them. From that bill, I can tell the reason we captured so many. It's hard to run for a ship when your boots are off and your pants are down around your knees."

It was the first time Jorac had ever heard Pergimtor laugh out loud. "Oh, ho ho! The loyal pimps of Swampside, to the defense of the realm! Oh, I like that. I can't wait to tell that one in the council. I'll tell it to the emperor too; he'll get a kick out of it." He waved the piece of paper. "Maybe I'll give her a bonus."

Jorac was faintly alarmed. "I wouldn't want to encourage her, sir. If my guess is right, those missing boots were probably stolen while the men were, um, otherwise occupied."

"Well, perhaps you're right. Anyway, good job all around. You'll need to look for an assistant, I think. What you've turned this job into is too big for one man."

"And a clerk, sir, to handle the reports." If there was one thing Jorac was tired of, it was writing reports.

Pergimtor considered, and nodded. "Very well, a clerk too. Now I must go. I'll expect you back in your office in a few months, but don't push yourself too hard. You are a pushy one, aren't you, even to yourself?"

"I hope not, sir."

"Oh, you don't mind pushing people around, but you're not a bully. You just like to get things done. We picked the right man – your allergy was just a bonus."

And with that, Pergimtor departed, leaving Jorac wondering anew who'd said what about him to get him picked as Wizard Constable.

Chapter 38 - A Man in a Bathrobe

The emperor turned out to be a short, balding, middle-aged man, tending a bit toward plumpness.

"What am I going to do with you?" he said affably. Emperor Benneso the Third had a pleasant bass voice that didn't really match his looks.

"Your Majesty?"

This certainly wasn't what Jorac had expected when he was called to appear at the emperor's palace six weeks after the fight. He was stripped of his swords and escorted to the emperor's bedroom, where Emperor Benneso the Third, Defender of Etrombia, King of each of the seven provinces that made up the empire, was lounging in what looked like a ratty bathrobe. Pergimtor had said the emperor was a "cheerful, earthy sort," but Jorac had no idea he was *this* informal. The way he acted, he'd have been happy in any working-class tavern in town.

"Oh, call me Bennie. Everyone else does, behind my back at least, and I don't mind. Grab a chair – that yellow one there is comfortable. You want some tea?" He poured tea from a dainty teapot into a thick-walled mug. The emperor had dismissed the servants, but Jorac was sure there were guards observing from behind the curtains in the doorways.

Jorac sat carefully, and said "No, sir, Bennie, thank you."

The emperor sat and looked at him as if awaiting a further response, so Jorac said, "If you don't mind, sir, what I'd like to know is what you found out about the invasion. I can guess some of it, but I hope you've learned more."

"They came from Parlund, sure enough. The soldiers we captured had been assured the army was tied up in the north and the wizards weren't going to be a threat. They were supposed to kill all the wizards, take over the palace, and then – who knows? One fellow thought they had some way of sending an immediate signal back to Parlund when they succeeded."

"A magical signal, from those that say they hate magic?"

The emperor paused to drink some tea. "Perhaps. These soldiers didn't know much, and their leaders all escaped."

"A coordinated attack like that has got to have a fairly high-level sponsor, doesn't it, if they had the resources to tie up the army and sideline all the wizards? Was the Parlundian government at the center of it? They have a king who doesn't like us because of our wizards, or so I heard."

The emperor shrugged. "These were all hired soldiers – guards, mercenaries, and the like. They were recruited in seaside towns a year ago, and trained together, but none of them were in the Parlund army. And of course they didn't know who set the whole thing up."

"I think they call that 'deniability,' when everyone can point the finger somewhere else."

The emperor grinned at him. "Right. I see you may have the makings of a politician in you." Then he shook his head ruefully. "But anyway, that's all we know about the attackers so far. We're still trying to figure out just what to do about them – we'll be talking about it in council today. But right now, what are we going to do with *you*?"

"Sir?" Jorac had no idea what he was driving at.

"Lets see. Pergimtor tells me you did something noteworthy – but he won't say just what – almost a year ago. At my birthday bash I tried to ask my nephew about it – I think you call him Veseen now – and he wouldn't say anything either. Says he swore an oath, and it's for my own good."

Veseen was related to Emperor Benneso? And Jorac had run him all over Swampside, even into the swamp itself, and almost gotten him killed fighting a crazy wizard? His mind reeled.

The emperor was still speaking. "... and then you stole Melsim's fancy horse, but it seems you found something useful to do with it – like saving the army. I told him to stuff that warrant for horse theft up his noble bum. And then six weeks ago, you held off one of those invading ships by yourself."

"I had help. Lots of help."

"The soldiers from the two ships that landed at the docks killed twenty men before they were driven back, and I hear it was your warning that kept it from being worse."

"Constable Schrog figured it out first. And Scholars Sharfo, Hebalan and Gleben were the ones who puzzled out the code that got us started – I promised I'd try to get them public credit for that if I could."

The emperor glanced at a closed curtain in a doorway and said, "I'll make a note of that." Then he turned back to Jorac. "And then you arranged for one of their ships to be wrecked in Swampside? That likely made the difference."

"I just wrote a note."

"And got that note to the right people. It was your warning that saved the palace, too. I got that from the Leganwei boy himself."

"Chief Constable Cerom gave the warning, and set up the defenses."

"Yes, I've heard their stories. Well, here's one you can't deflect the credit on. You killed eight men all by yourself there on the docks, and stopped that ship cold."

Jorac said weakly, "Six, sir."

"What?"

"Six, your majesty. One was shot with a crossbow, and one I just kicked into the water."

"And then you challenged the rest of the ship to a fight, and none of them would?"

"I'm not sure they understood me."

"Well, those two with the hammers did. As for the rest, we won't be able to ask them, since they got away, but the people up on the bridge could hear you, and that's what they said happened. Do you say you didn't challenge the whole ship?"

"Well, no, sir. Your majesty, I mean."

"Bennie."

"Well, no, Bennie. I'd just had a hammer dropped on my head, mind you. But I did it."

"Right. As I said, what am I going to do with you? You seem better now – are you healing well?"

"Yes sir, thank you, I think I'm going to be fine. Some of the General's Guard are helping me with my exercises."

"Speaking of my General – he'll obviously have to go. Do you want Melsim's job?"

Jorac shuddered a bit. "No, sir. Colonel Wakkar might be suitable, despite his missing foot. Or you might give the General's Guard a little more say in who's selected, but please not me. I'm not the administrator it would take for that job, nor the politician."

"You must want – put it this way, there must be something I can do for you."

Jorac knew there would never be a better time to ask. "Well, Bennie, I'd like you to come to my wedding. I'm marrying Kimathea Ravensclough in the spring."

The emperor leaned back and beamed at him. "Well, I'd love to. I'll need to do it incognito, of course, so I can have some fun. Who's the lady?

"The one who saved my life with a couple of well-placed shots from her crossbow."

"Ah, that one – I heard about her too. A beauty from the provinces, isn't she?"

"Yes, the family produces mostly women, and with her father recently passed on, I'm not sure there are any more Ravenscloughs left – after her, I mean."

That was the story that they'd told everyone, and it seemed to pass muster. Up until now, that is. The emperor stared at Jorac for a few seconds, then got up from his chair and came over beside Jorac. In a quiet whisper, he said, "I know all the noble families – I have to." Then he winked at Jorac, and went back to his seat.

The emperor settled comfortably into his chair. "Ah yes, I inquired about her just after the fight. I found someone who knew her mother; he spoke highly of her. It's a pity to see a noble family like the Ravenscloughs dwindle away when it doesn't produce enough male heirs, but sometimes it happens. I'll see that their arms are added to your family's shield, hmm?"

Jorac sat there ashen-faced, then nodded. "I'm not sure my family has an official shield, your majesty. My father is a baronet, Sir Widdel Kellor, but he's basically just a sheep farmer, and proud of it."

"Well, I'll have my heralds look into getting you some. Are you firstborn?"

"Sir? Uh, no your m-- Bennie, I have two older brothers."

"Can't just make your father an Earl, then. I guess it'll have to be you. Don't give me that look, you know I have to do something or I'll never hear the end of it. You'll get a tiny castle in the far north, and a few dozen gold the first few years for upkeep, and some uppity servants and surly tenant farmers to worry about. After that, you'll have my high taxes and those cold stone rooms to bother you. Serve you right for giving me this mess to deal with – now I have to figure out what to do with our esteemed neighbors to the southwest in some way that doesn't bankrupt us, or let them invade."

Jorac was rarely speechless, but now he gulped, and said something like "Umgrd". It wasn't quite a word, but better than sitting there with his jaw hanging open.

"All right, you'll be Jorac Kellor, Earl of Veldry. Don't get excited yet; the paperwork will take months, and has to go through the council. But send your wedding invitation to Viscount Benner here at the palace, and we'll go – me and the missus. Have plenty of good dark ale, she likes that, and a decent string band, and we'll make a night of it."

Regrouping, Jorac found his voice. "Your majesty, thank you. My bride will be quite overwhelmed. As am I."

"You deserve it, boy. Good and bad, you deserve it all."

The End

Tom Van Natta lives in Princeton, NJ, with his lovely wife and several michevious cats. (Any remaining typographical errors are entirely the fault of the cats, who make shockingly poor typists.)

This is his first full-length novel.

www.ingramcontent.com/pod-product-compliance
Lightning Source LLC
Chambersburg PA
CBHW051434260626
47162CB00001B/87